What the critics are saying...

೫

5 Angels RECOMMENDED READ "Keeper of the Spirit is the beginning of an amazing saga. The emotional depth that **Ms. Storm** was able to portray in this book is simply awesome...this was one of the best books that I have read. **Ms. Storm** made me laugh, cry, and hate in this book. I look forward to reading the rest of this series and I know that I will revisit these families again and again." ~ *Fallen Angels Reviews*

4 1/2 Stars from Romance Junkies!! "KEEPER OF THE SPIRIT is an amazing tale that will leave the reader marveling at the wonders of the human spirit and the inner strength one must find to endure a tragedy. Full of fascinating characters, interesting historical ideals, and tales within the story that had me spellbound while I read." ~ *Romance Junkies Reviews*

5 CUPS "From the very first page, Ms. Storm captured my interest. This book is a heart-wrenching page turner that pulls at your emotions...suspenseful writing that keeps you on the edge of your seat. The secondary characters resonated in this book as well, and I was very happy to see that this is first book in her new Keeper Series." ~ *Coffee Time Romance*

"KEEPER OF THE SPIRIT is an entertaining romance with engaging characters. All of the secondary characters enhance the story. It is well written with good dialogue. A touching story and an engaging romance, KEEPER OF THE SPIRIT is an excellent choice for your winter reading enjoyment." ~ *Romance Reviews Today*

5 *Angels* and a RECOMMENDED READ "It has been quite some time since a story left me in awe. I was left unable to pinpoint one moment of this story that made it great: the entire story moved me in a way no other book has in quite some time. Ruby Storm should be applauded for her outstanding job. I can only imagine the next two installments in this trilogy will be nothing short of amazing like this story." ~ *Fallen Angels Reviews*

"This book has all the ingredients for a non-stop page-turning read: passion, romance and action. The author has written a wonderful book which shows the triumph of the human spirit." ~ *Loves Romances Reviews*

Ruby Storm

Keeper of the Spirit

Cerridwen Press

A Cerridwen Press Publication

www.cerridwenpress.com

Keeper of the Spirit

ISBN #1419954377
ALL RIGHTS RESERVED.
Keeper of the Spirit Copyright© 2005 Ruby Storm
Edited by Pamela Campbell
Cover art by Syneca

Electronic book Publication September 2005
Trade Paperback Publication March 2006

With the exception of quotes used in reviews, this book may not be reproduced or used in whole or in part by any means existing without written permission from the publisher, Ellora's Cave Publishing, Inc., 1056 Home Avenue, Akron, OH 44310-3502.

This book is a work of fiction and any resemblance to persons, living or dead, or places, events or locales is purely coincidental. The characters are productions of the authors' imagination and used fictitiously.

Cerridwen Press is an imprint of Ellora's Cave Publishing, Inc.®

Also by Author

&

Books 1 & 2 of the Keeper Trilogy released on digital e-books through Cerridwen Press.

www.cerridwenpress.com

Keeper of the Heart

Keeper of the Dream

If you are interested in a spicier read and are over 18, check out Ruby's erotic romances at Ellora's Cave Publishing **(www.ellorascave.com).**

Cracked: Prelude to Passion

Diamond Studs *(anthology)*

Lucy's Double Diamonds

Payton's Passion

Perfect Betrayal

Twilight Kisses

Virgin Queen

Keeper of the Spirit

ა

Prologue
New York City
August 20, 1869

☙

A petite red-haired girl crept silently down the brick path, glancing warily in one direction, and then the other. Crouching at the end of a stone hedge, she hardly dared to breathe. Where was he?

The muffled crack of a twig snapping nearby was enough to make her spring for the leaf-covered path and run like the devil himself pursued her. An instant later, something hard slammed into her shins, catapulting her small body headfirst into a rosebush.

Eleven-year-old Emma Sanders crawled out of the bush and yanked her petticoat free of a prickly branch that held her prisoner. Rolling onto her backside, she swiped at the first tears that welled in the corners of her eyes and gritted her teeth with determination to stifle the flow. Emma wouldn't give the wickedly laughing boy the satisfaction of seeing her cry.

Another younger boy rounded the hedge a moment later. Concern wrinkled his brow when he saw his friend mopping blood from her bruised knee.

"What happened, Emma? I heard you cry out."

She bit a trembling lip to hold back forbidden tears and glared up at the elder of the two boys through venomous eyes. "Your nasty brother tripped me on purpose, Jacob, and I fell into the rosebush!"

Samuel Fontaine shook his blond head. "That's the game, isn't it? I'm it, and I caught you fair and square."

"You did not!" she shot back. "You hit me on the leg with a stick, and that's not fair." Her watery gaze moved to inspect her swelling shin, which changed color before her eyes.

"You never play fair, Samuel." Jacob agreed. "There was no need to hit her." He helped Emma to her feet and brushed the grass and dirt from her dress. "Come on, Em, I think maybe we should get those scratches cleaned up."

A caustic snort left Samuel's throat. "Go ahead, you babies. It's just like the two of you to make such an issue out of nothing. It's a stupid game anyway."

He watched Jacob take Emma's arm and lead her toward the kitchen door of the house she'd grown up in. Once again, he was the outsider.

The two of them made him sick. Jacob was always ready to protect the little witch. His younger brother continually included her in their games and outings. Emma was too prim and proper for his liking. He shook his head in disgust, stomped off as the other two entered the house, then paused when he suddenly remembered the litter of kittens he'd discovered in the stables the day before. His pace quickened along with the malicious smile that touched his lips as he mentally devised new ways to torture the babies and their mama.

Chapter One
൮

Raven-haired Tyler Wilkins stood at the window of his hotel room, observing a lamplighter move from post to post across a wooden sidewalk below. Once again, his bloodshot green eyes took in the litter and overall filth that covered the streets. What he'd seen so far of New York City only assured his tired mind that he couldn't wait to return to his home in Minnesota. He missed the fresh air and wide-open spaces already, even though he'd left the grueling long days of his family-owned logging business behind.

Flexing his broad shoulders to relieve the ache in the back of his neck, he reached up to rub the offending spot with a heavy sigh. A moment later, his fingers threaded their way through his dark hair to where its thickness lay against his collar as he retraced his steps to the bed and began to unpack the month's worth of clothes that lay in an open valise.

Tyler pulled open the top drawer of the cherrywood bureau and neatly stacked the starched and pressed shirts. A fleeting smile curved his mouth when he thought of Mamie, the old Negro housekeeper back home. She'd been so excited about his trip and had stuffed just about everything he owned into the suitcase, from riding clothes to formal dinner jackets...

"You all jes never know, Tyla," she stated on the morning of his departure for New York. "My mammy allus said 'be ready for anythin', Mamie, allus be ready for anythin', cuz you jes never know what be 'round the corner." She moved between the bureau and the bed, where his bag lay open on the coverlet. "And you, boy," she reprimanded, "ain't been round no corners or done anythin' or gone nowheres 'ceptin that darn sawmill of yours nigh on two years now. Goodness! 'Bout time you be vacation-bound and be doin' some relaxin'. Yessiree!"

"It's not a vacation, Mamie," he replied absently. "I'm going for a business meeting with Mr. Sanders of New York."

The old Negress placed another shirt in the bag and turned to the bureau. Tyler lifted it back out again when she wasn't looking and dropped it on the bed.

"Business, business," she mumbled on. "Is that all you be thinkin' about?" She shook her head and smacked her lips, then had the audacity to walk up to him and shake a finger beneath his nose. She deftly returned the shirt to its place inside the bag. "You leave that shirt where I put it!" Her scolding words suddenly softened when she spied the uncertainty in his eyes. "Listen here, boy. There ain't being a thing for you to worry 'bout back here when you are gone. Trevor knows how to handle anythin' comes up at that darn sawmill and me and your sister Carrie can handle Miss Janie jes fine. You need some time away from this here place. It's been too long a-comin' since you did anythin'."

"I know, Mamie." Tyler closed his eyes and fought for the strength to continue. "It's just that this is the first time I've left Janie alone since…"

The words trailed off in mid-sentence. His jaw hardened. Tyler spun on his heel, crossed to the fireplace and stared into the dying embers as the previous years and the pain he now clutched close to his heart returned to haunt him.

Two years had passed since his beautiful wife, Sara, was killed when she jumped in front of a runaway carriage to save their five-year-old daughter, Janie. Witnesses said Janie darted out into the street and Sara, who was a step behind her, grabbed the little girl by the arm and tossed her aside just as the careening carriage bore down on them.

Sara never had a chance.

Since that day, Janie had retreated into a silent world. Tyler had taken her to the best doctors and psychiatrists in the state, but none of them could coax the return of the girl's sweet, innocent voice or her former happy self. The only prognosis was time and patience. She would speak again when she was ready, but her father was beginning to give up hope. He'd tried everything—and nothing had worked.

Tyler hadn't left his daughter for more than one night since the accident, and leaving her now tore at his heart. He shook his head in silent rebuke wondering for the hundredth time why he'd let his brothers talk him into this insane idea of going to New York.

Mamie reached out a warm hand, placed it over Tyler's where it rested on the fireplace mantel and gave his fingers a heartfelt squeeze. "What's done, is done, boy," she spoke softly. "Now ain't the time to be livin' in the past. Go to that New York and be enjoyin' yoursef. It be time for you to start livin' for yourself, and not jes for Janie. That daughter of yours is surrounded by people who be a-lovin' her like crazy. She be jes' fine. You have to believe that."

Tyler turned to peer down into the craggy brown face of the woman who'd raised him from a lively young boy of nine, when his own mother had died giving birth to his baby sister, Carrie. His brothers, Trevor and Cole, were only seven and four at the time.

A part of his father left with her that night. Tyler remembered all too well Thomas Wilkins' retreat from society, and the ever-present sadness and loss he wore like a cloak for the remainder of his years. Until the day his father passed away, probably of a broken heart, the elder Wilkins worked like a man possessed to establish himself as one of the richest timber barons in Minnesota. By the state's first anniversary in 1859, his efforts had created a logging dynasty for his sons. The hours spent at the mill though, robbed his children of the love and comfort they craved from him after losing their mother.

Tyler studied Mamie and reflected on how the old Negro woman had always been the closest thing to a mother as he and his siblings grew to adulthood. Even after all those years, he could still remember the feeling of her soft, rounded shoulders and comforting arms whenever he needed it. Her devotion was like an anchor for all of them.

Tyler had tried desperately to follow Mamie's lead during the last two horrible and lonely years. He continually strove to stay accessible for his daughter, always ready with a loving smile and secure arms for her to cling to even when his own grief became overwhelming. Never did he want Janie to go through the pain he and his brothers had—the pain of losing both parents, when only one had died.

Now, years later, except for a multitude of wrinkles on her face, curly dark hair gone white, and a slower step, Mamie was still there for all of them. He collected her into the circle of his arms with a loving squeeze. He sighed against the stiff gray curls. "What would I do without you and your many, and I emphasize *many*, words of wisdom?"

The mood lightened as she playfully slapped him on the arm. "Oh, go on with you now, boy!" She stepped back, hands resting comfortably on wide hips. "Don't you be sweet-talkin' me. You have a good time in New York. Mamie'll take care of everythin' while you's away."

"I know you will," he replied. "You always do…"

A shrill whistle from the street below brought Tyler out of his reverie. He hadn't even realized he was standing at the window again. Thoughts and emotions tumbled over one another in his mind. Could he do what Mamie suggested? Could he simply allow himself to enjoy the sights of New York and take this time to reflect on what he needed to do to get on with his life?

He shook his head. It was so hard. He would turn thirty this summer. He was a man with extreme responsibilities for a hurting daughter and a thriving business, yet he felt at loose ends. The numb state of limbo that he'd existed in had taken its toll emotionally. Since Sara's accident there had been no excitement, no genuine happiness. His main objective had been to keep his emotions at bay until he retired at night to his own private hell where no one could witness his suffering.

A sad smile curved his lips as he realized the extent of his siblings' support and love during the worst time of his life. The smile turned into a frown though, with the sudden awareness of the hell they must have gone through themselves upon Sara's death. They had put aside their own pain to take care of him. Shame seared Tyler to the very core. He hadn't even tried to restore his life. He'd simply existed.

Sorrowful eyes gazed out into the darkness of the night. An image of Sara floated into his mind. The pain of loss knifed through him again, as deep as the day of her death.

Her death still didn't seem real most days. Every so often when he sat on the porch back home with Janie, Tyler still half expected to hear Sara call out to them that dinner was ready. Other times, he'd hear her seductive voice in the shadows of their bedroom, urging him to hurry beneath the covers.

He leaned his forehead against the coolness of the windowpane and closed his eyes, envisioning her ready smile, the long blonde tresses that curled coyly about her shoulders and the complete trust and contentment in her eyes when she gazed at him. He could almost smell the fragrant scent of the perfume that clung to her silky skin, almost feel her body pressed against his when they were making love.

He squeezed his eyelids shut and balled tight fists against the windowpane. His forehead lolled against the glass. He wanted to laugh again. He wanted to *live* again. The familiar ache filled his chest, then grew stronger. His agonized whisper in the darkening room became a desperate plea.

"What should I do? Please...you've got to help me. I keep stumbling without you at my side."

His body sagged against the window as if it awaited an answer. The minutes passed until another image of Sara's sweet smile and a quiet understanding crept into his heart. She would always be with him through Janie. And what had he done? He'd handed his daughter an unjust world by not living life to its fullest. It was his duty, as a father, to make life as meaningful as possible for his only child.

Tyler's weary eyes fluttered open, and the wetness on his cheeks surprised him. Exhausted and emotionally drained, he wiped the tears from his face with the back of a shaky hand, then moved to the bed and tossed the valise onto the floor. Sinking onto the rose-colored quilt, he stretched out and stared at the crystal chandelier that hung from the ceiling. Jumbled thoughts slowed in his mind.

So many separate pieces, he mused silently. *But when you put all the pieces together, they create a whole. My life needs to be like that. It's time to put all the pieces back together again — time to make a whole.*

He closed his eyes. As the remaining tears dried on his face, Tyler Wilkins slept soundly for the first time in two years.

Chapter Two

Dust and gravel billowed around the horse's hooves as it skidded to a halt in the stable yard. Emma's cheeks flushed pink from the cool morning air, setting off her green eyes, which sparkled with humor. Vaulting from the saddle, she watched Jacob round the bend, urging his horse to a breakneck speed until he reined the animal to a dancing halt before the stable.

He shook an amicable fist. "One of these days you're going to break your neck riding like that!"

She tossed her head, laughed up at him and rested one hand on a slim hip. "Oh, come on, Jacob! I know exactly what I'm doing! Just admit it—I'll always be the better rider."

She reached to gently stroke her horse's sweat-slicked neck again and casually watched as he struggled against his mount for control. Finally, Jacob won out and the strong-willed animal calmed. A happy sigh escaped her full lips. "I love this horse. Bonne runs like the wind!"

"I can't imagine what your father was thinking when he purchased that beast for you," Jacob returned. "Even if you do handle a horse better than most men."

Emma cocked a slim eyebrow at his comment and continued to gently stroke the white Arabian she'd been gifted with on her twenty-second birthday just six weeks earlier. Horses had been her passion from the time she was a little girl.

"Do you want to join me in the house for lunch?"

"You know I can't, Em. Samuel's arriving home today."

The sparkle in her eyes immediately dimmed. Emma shuffled her feet in the dirt. Jacob's brother was returning after six long years of schooling at Howard College in Washington, D.C.

"I suppose our rides together are going to be cut short now." Emma struggled for nonchalance.

Jacob had expected this conversation. "There's no reason why the three of us can't spend some time together. I want both you and I to get to know him again." Jacob watched her eyes darken dangerously and vowed to do whatever it took to end the friction between his brother and his best friend.

Emma loosened the cinch on Bonne's saddle with agitated hands. "I'm sorry, but you go right ahead. I, on the other hand, can't quite forget all the years of abuse."

He slid from his horse, placed his hand upon her shoulder and searched her familiar green eyes. "You are my best friend in the world, Emma. I would love to see you and my brother get along. Don't be such a ninny! People change—you know that. We've got the entire summer ahead of us, and I would like to include Samuel."

He could see by the set of her jaw that she wasn't about to change her mind—at least not right away. It was a look he knew well, due to their many years of friendship. "I promise to see you as much as I can. With Samuel arriving home though, I'll be busy with him and my father down at the mill. But, first chance, we'll go riding or sailing or whatever you want to do." A wry smile curved his lips. "You know, Em, it's about time the three of us grew up."

She kept her eyes downcast and contemplated his words. She and Samuel had been at odds her entire life. He'd always been jealous of his little brother's affection for her, and Jacob couldn't see it. Emma, however, saw it all too clearly.

Her shoulders sagged with a deep sigh that voiced her confusion. The summer stretched out before her, and now the time spent with Jacob would be limited, at best. She clamped her lips shut and busied herself with the mare.

Jacob continued with maintained patience. It was his turn to release a small sigh. He was getting nowhere with her. "Please, rethink the past. We're adults now. Things will be different."

He gave her stiff body a hug of goodbye, then gathered up his horse's trailing reins and swung back into the saddle. Glancing down, he tried once more to placate her, this time with a little humor. It worked—usually.

"Now, be a good little girl and say farewell. Tell me how you'll be anxiously awaiting the return of my brother and me." He fought the grin that threatened to undo his stern, controlled expression.

No matter how she tried, Emma couldn't remain upset with him for very long. A tiny smile tugged at the corners of her mouth. He'd always managed to cajole her out of a peevish mood. She loved him as childhood friends do and could not resist his teasing manner.

"Oh, go on with you, Jacob." She shook a slender finger at him, her jaw stiff in feigned sternness. "Just make sure you don't forget about me this summer."

He laughed with relief. Blowing a kiss in her direction, he reined his horse toward the road and kicked the animal into a gallop.

She watched him until he disappeared around a bend, then turned just as Jim, the hired stable boy, exited the barn. His freckled sixteen-year-old face beamed.

"How was your ride, Miss?"

"Exhilarating. Bonne flies like the wind and handles wonderfully." She flashed him a grin. "Do you have time to cool her down?"

"Yup, no problem. I'll take care of everything."

She turned and strolled toward the house. Her eyes drifted to the empty lane and wondered what the summer would hold with Samuel back in their midst.

* * * * *

Emma entered the dining room the following morning to find her father already enjoying his breakfast. The elderly gentleman met his daughter's "good morning" with a grin and laid the morning newspaper beside his plate, amazed once more how much she resembled his late wife with her rich auburn hair and green eyes that sparkled like shining emeralds. Emma wasn't as tall as Margaret had been, however, and took more after his side of the family. He was only five feet, eight inches tall and, though he used to look his late wife squarely in the eye, Emma came up only to the top of his chin.

Edward admired his daughter's passion for life, her generous nature and the level of intelligence she possessed—a quality that he'd insisted she develop at an early age. He even loved Emma's stubborn nature when it came to her insistence that she would never marry. She was determined to learn his shipping business from the ground up and would eventually take over its stewardship whenever the day came that her father decided to retire.

He used to think she would someday find someone and fall madly in love. All her girlish ideas of running the company would then slip away as she settled into a serious relationship. Lately, he wasn't so sure. Emma was at the shipyard office every day—and seldom accepted invitations from her various suitors.

Edward hoped that her feelings concerning wedded bliss hadn't resulted from years of watching her parents struggle to make their marriage work. They'd each loved the other in their own way, but theirs was an arranged marriage and, although both he and Margaret had hoped to find passionate love, it had never happened. Instead, they became contented partners in life.

After Emma was born, Margaret Sanders never quite recuperated and he'd felt he shouldn't force his husbandly rights on the sickly woman. So, instead, they spent their married years trying to do right by their daughter. How they'd created such a perfect creature was beyond him.

"Well, my dear, you're looking especially ravishing today."

Emma pirouetted before him, spun to a halt and promptly planted a loud, smacking kiss on his cheek.

"Thank you, Papa!" Her responding smile deepened, and so did the matching set of dimples in her cheeks. She stepped back and held out her hands. "How do you like my new riding outfit? This style is all the latest rage."

"Latest rage for what?" Edward's brow dipped in disapproval. "You know you should be riding sidesaddle like all the other genteel ladies of society and not racing astride like some hooligan being chased by the police—with a pair of pants on no less!"

Emma's laughter tinkled across the room as she seated herself at the table. "Oh, Papa, these aren't pants. It's a split skirt for easier riding." She leaned forward with her elbows on the table and affected a sweet, angelic look. "Would you rather I rode through Central Park with my petticoats wrapped up around my waist just so I could ride the way I want to ride?"

Edward nearly snorted his morning coffee through his nose at the suggestion. "Good God, Emma, you are incorrigible!" He sipped at his coffee a bit more carefully. "Since you're probably fishing for a compliment, I'll bite. Your new outfit matches your eyes perfectly."

"I love you, Papa. Thank you for being so good to me."

"Yes, well, one of these days I'm going to marry you off and you can be some other poor oaf's problem." Edward pointed a finger in the air, never at a loss to bring up her unwed status. "And I'm going to make sure he's the kind of man who can't be swayed by your sweet-talking ways like I am on a daily basis."

Her laughter filled the air as she began to eat.

"I forgot to tell you I'm meeting with a gentleman from Minnesota today." Edward said as he finished the last of his breakfast. "I met his father once, years ago when he was just getting into the logging business out there. The man and his brothers are now running the operation and are searching for someone to ship his lumber to England." He nodded his head in approval and continued. "Quite smart of the young fellow. There's an untapped market in Europe and not many companies from America are willing to risk overseas shipping, what with all the pirating going on. If he does it right though, and I can talk him into the expense of sailing at least four ships together, I think he'll do quite well."

"Isn't that taking quite a risk?" Emma questioned. "Look at what he could lose if all four ships encounter bad seas and are lost."

"Look at what he could lose if one ship goes alone and is pirated," Edward replied. "With today's market being the way it is, I would... Are you listening to me?"

"Most definitely."

"Doesn't seem like it."

Emma waved her hand in his direction. "I was just thinking about your meeting and wondering how serious this Minnesotan really is. His father was probably the key factor in this logging business of his, and he's just riding along on 'Daddy's' laurels. He's got so much of 'Daddy's' money that he's bored and has to figure out a new way to spend it."

"Shame on you, Emma, for judging someone before you've even met him. That's not like you at all. My correspondence with this gentleman shows him to be a smart businessman with a lot of potential to further his wealth."

Emma raised her hands in quiet deference. "Okay, okay. It's just that I don't think much of today's society of *men*. Most of them my age are too soft and too busy spending their fathers' money to ever be serious businessmen. You have to admit it's something we see all the time." Leaning forward again, she proceeded to try and explain her feelings on the subject that continually rose between them. "That's why I want to learn your business from the ground up. I want to run it the way you do—with a firm hand, but with fairness and with the idea that there's always room for expansion. I'm afraid you'll sell it to someone who won't take care of it properly. Just because I'm a woman shouldn't affect this matter at all."

"Your gender has nothing to do with it, Emma. I'd just like you to find someone to share the company with. Running a shipping business is a daunting task."

Emma hid a smile. Her father's wish for her to be married was something he consistently alluded to, but she didn't have the time this morning for even a good-natured argument and decided to change the subject. "I'm going riding with Jacob. It'll probably be the last time for quite awhile. In fact, I can't believe he actually found time for me today."

"Why is that? I know how much you enjoy his company. Do you think—"

"Papa...Jacob is only my friend and nothing more. He's been busy with Samuel now that the prodigal son has returned home." She sighed and rolled her eyes.

Edward nodded. "Samuel's father did tell me that he was coming home for good. He mentioned how happy he was about it."

Emma casually buttered her toast. "I can't stomach Samuel. I can't say as I've missed him at all in the last six years. He's such a bully. But, you know Jacob. There isn't a mean bone in his body, and he feels he can't say 'no' to his brother after he was gone for so long." Her lips pursed as she thought further on the subject. "Well, Jacob can just spend time with him if he wants to, but he can do it without me. I've been pushed around by Samuel enough in my lifetime."

"I know what he was like, Emma. But at least give him the benefit of the doubt. He's an adult now and six years is a long time. You're usually so fair-minded, no matter who it is we're discussing. That's twice now this morning that I've listened to you shred someone's reputation without even knowing the true person—or at least waiting to see if six years could make a difference."

"I'm sorry." Emma's response was conciliatory. "I guess I'm being selfish because I'm going to have to share Jacob this summer. He's my best friend, and I'm going to miss him."

"Well, honey, I'm going to give you the opportunity to make a more sound judgment of both men. On Saturday night, I'm holding a reception at the St. Nicholas in honor of Mr. Wilkins. John and Miriam Fontaine will be among our guests since they are suppliers of iron for the shipyard. Both Jacob and Samuel have been invited to the festivities."

Emma decided her father was right. She would let her feelings ride about both men in question—until she had reason to do otherwise. She couldn't resist one last comment, however. Her cheeks dimpled. Bright green eyes lit with mischief as she contemplated a wager with her father.

"Let's make a deal, Papa. I'll wager your Minnesota friend is a pansy. I'll also wager that Samuel Fontaine is just as crude as he always was and we'll both find out Saturday night."

Edward rolled his eyes. "Like I said," he replied with suppressed laughter shaking his shoulders. "You are incorrigible." He stood and reached for his coat, where it was slung over the back of an empty chair. "And, by the way—you're on."

Chapter Three

Tyler stumbled from the hotel bed, shirttails askew, hair tousled and bloodshot eyes still blanketed with sleep. Staggering to the door, he fumbled with the lock and finally pried the blasted thing open.

"Can I help you?" Tyler squinted through bleary eyes.

A bellhop stared back at him with distaste written all over his tight-lipped, scrawny face, the expression making it obvious the young man was used to a higher class of patrons in the hotel. Tyler blinked. He must look like he'd spent the night whoring and drinking.

"This arrived at the front desk a little while ago for you...ah...sir." He cleared his throat and, with a quick glance up and down, handed Tyler a sealed envelope. He pulled his hand back quickly, assuring that he didn't make physical contact with the disheveled man in the doorway.

Tyler quelled the sudden urge to punch the ill-mannered bellhop in the mouth.

The hotel employee ignored the other man's glare, however, and continued to stand stiff and expectant in the doorway. He let out a haughty sniff and raised his chin higher to peer through spotlessly clean spectacles.

Tyler shook the remaining cobwebs from his head. It finally dawned on him that the man waited for a gratuity. *Like hell, you arrogant little bastard*, he answered the other man's tolerant expression silently, then promptly slammed the door in his face. Returning to the bed, he tossed the envelope onto the rumpled quilt and headed for a porcelain pitcher. Pouring cool water into a matching bowl, he cupped his hands and splashed his unshaven face. Proof of his instant enjoyment came as an audible sigh. Feeling slightly more awake, he grudgingly moved to sit on the bed, reached for the envelope and tore open the flap.

The note was from Mr. Edward Sanders, welcoming him to New York. It stated that Sanders "hoped his journey had been quick and uneventful."

Tyler snorted. *Uneventful – yes; quick – no.* He could still feel the vibration of the bouncing train.

The letter continued with an invitation to lunch at one o'clock that very day. It seemed Mr. Sanders wanted to meet him before sitting with the entire Board of Directors at five o'clock that evening. That way, Tyler would find at least one familiar face at the meeting tonight. Sanders also wanted to first discuss shipping plans privately, so as to be more informed of the extent of Tyler's commitment.

"That crafty old dog," he muttered. "Can't wait to see how much money he's going to make."

Turning his attention back to the paper, he read that Sanders would send a private coach to retrieve him in front of the hotel at twelve-thirty. It said nothing in the missive about where to send a refusal.

His wide shoulders drooped with a tired sigh. He got up to ring the maid for some bath water.

* * * * *

Tyler stepped from the carriage at the front gate of Edward Sanders' home. Not a single twig or dried leaf littered the flawlessly groomed lawn. The house, too, was anything but modest. Whitewashed walls boasted red brick around the outer foyer and windows, and a third story towered above the other equally lavish homes that lined the street.

Pushing the gate open, he crossed the sidewalk and stepped onto the porch. Before he could raise his hand to use the knocker, the door swung open.

A neatly outfitted maid smiled up at him with a big toothy grin. "Welcome, Mr. Wilkins. Mr. Sanders has been expecting you.

If you'll follow me, sir, I'll show you to the library where he's waiting."

Tyler couldn't help but glance at his surroundings as he stepped into the cool foyer. The interior of the home was beautiful, but not ostentatious. Following the maid down the hall, they entered a beautifully furnished library through huge mahogany doors. A man in his late fifties stood from behind a massive oak desk and stretched out a hand. His genuine, friendly smile immediately put Tyler at ease.

"Ah, Mr. Wilkins. I'm Edward Sanders. It's so nice to finally meet you face-to-face."

"Hello, Mr. Sanders," Tyler replied as he accepted the warm handshake. "It's nice to finally meet you, too."

"Edward, call me Edward. I'm not one for formality." His sweeping arm indicated the two high-backed chairs that sat before the desk. "Sit down, please." His gaze then shifted to the maid, who stood gawking at his guest. Edward chuckled and gained her attention. "Angie, would you please get some coffee for Mr. Wilkins and myself?"

She bobbed her head in eager agreement.

"Thank you. I think we'll be eating informally here in the library. Would you arrange things for me?"

Tyler seated himself and waited patiently for his host to finish speaking and for the maid to leave the room. "Excuse me, Edward, but, please, call me Tyler. I'm not much for standing on formality either."

Edward's responding grin showed his immediate pleasure as he settled himself in the chair across from Tyler. Their conversation swiftly took them through the next two hours. By afternoon's end, they'd developed a tenuous friendship born out of mutual respect and camaraderie.

* * * * *

Tyler settled back in his chair, confident in the fact that a business arrangement would be made before he left for Minnesota. He found himself actually looking forward to the next four weeks and was more than a little surprised to realize that he was excited about something again. It felt good.

"So, Tyler…enough business for awhile. Tell me what northern Minnesota is like. Have you noticed any resemblance to New York's woodlands?"

Edward smiled inwardly as Tyler answered the inquiry. The man seated across from him was self-assured, articulate and intelligent. He was no *pansy*, as Emma had called him earlier, riding on his father's laurels. It was quite evident that the man had worked hard to get where he was. He exuded a natural penchant for business.

Emma, he mused, *you just lost one of your wagers.*

Judging by the tittering going on out in the hall, Edward also concluded that Tyler Wilkins exuded a masculine eminence that certainly hadn't been missed by his maid or the cleaning girl. There was something else about him though, something Edward couldn't quite put a finger on. There was a sadness that lingered just below the surface.

Edward took another sip of his coffee. "Well, Tyler, all I can say is that it appears your father built quite an empire out west."

"Yes, sir," Tyler replied confidently. "He was well respected in the business community. My father sincerely believed that the area's natural resources would make it a great state someday. I was only eight years old when Minnesota was admitted to the Union. I can still remember his pride. My father deserved the accolades that were written about him."

"And you've managed to build upon his original foundation. One of the reasons I contacted Northern Pines Lumbering was because of its major growth over the last ten years. You and your brothers have done a fine job."

Tyler shrugged. "My father taught us that hard work will eventually be rewarded if one sticks with it long enough."

A grin touched Edward's lips. Tyler's ego would not be inflated by compliments. He liked this young man more and more as the afternoon passed. Reaching for a small box on the desk, he offered his guest one of the sweet-smelling cigars inside. "We've got some distance problems to work out."

Tyler's reply was instant. "With the prices of virgin oak, white pine and tamarack being what they are, we would get a jump on the European market. My brother has the distance problem worked out neatly. I'm sure your Board of Directors will have no problem understanding how lucrative this partnership will actually be."

A slow smile crept across Edward's features when Tyler rose from the chair and moved to the open window, allowing the pungent smoke from his cigar to drift from the room. He wanted to be around when Emma met this man—and he wanted to bask in the astonished expression on her face.

He didn't have long to wait. The front door slammed and short, staccato steps neared the open door of the library.

"Papa?" a feminine voice inquired. "Papa?"

"I'm in the library, Emma!" her father answered. A second later, she burst through the door before he could rise from his chair to greet her.

"There you are! I had *such* a wonderful day today! I met up with Jacob's cousin, Marion. You remember her." Emma barely paused between sentences as she crossed the length of the room, then stood on tiptoe to press a kiss to his cheek as he rounded the desk.

"She's the one from Boston. Remember? Well, she's in town to celebrate her engagement to a local man. Can you believe that? A man in *New York City*. Isn't that wonderful? Anyway, she invited me along to help her shop for a trousseau, and so away we went. We had lunch at one of the posh restaurants downtown and spent money like it was water!" Her hand fluttered across her chest as she continued. "Oh, I met her fiancé, too. He's quite handsome. Marion is absolutely ecstatic." Without taking a breath, she rambled on while pulling at the ends of her gloved fingers, sliding the costly leather from her hands. "Then we went riding in Central Park. The entire time, we talked about Samuel. Do you know she's been doing her best to dodge him? She doesn't care one bit for him, either." She tossed the gloves carelessly onto the shiny surface of her father's desk. "So, I'm quite sure that I won the wager. You know, the one from this morning? And, I bet I'll be right about our other wager, too." She crossed her arms in a pose meant to prove the point just a tad more and leaned a slim hip on the edge of the desk. "So, tell me, how was the 'boy' from the backwoods of Minnesota? Was he a pansy, like I expected him to be? Come on, confess, Papa. Was I right? Is he still trying to figure out how to use the indoor toilet at the hotel? Does he even know we *have* indoor toilets in New York?" Her shoulders shook with glee upon coming up with such an ingenious assumption.

Edward cleared his throat uncomfortably. It was then that Emma noticed the pained expression on his face.

"Are you feeling ill, Papa? You look sick."

Edward's eyes darted to the corner of the room, and then back to her. "Uh...Emma, I would like you to meet someone. Mr. Tyler Wilkins."

She turned slowly and, for the first time, realized that there was someone else in the room.

Tyler's first impression of Miss Emma Sanders changed from that of a petite, whirling tornado dressed in green to that of a spoiled brat in a matter of seconds. Granted, she had a mop of the most beautiful auburn hair he'd ever seen, and her riding habit clung alluringly to rounded, lush curves. She was obviously doted on by her father and accustomed to getting her own way. She rode about town on an expensive horse, spent money like it was "water" and giggled at anything that walked by in a pair of pants. She was a prima donna to the core, who saw herself as better than anyone else, especially if that *anyone else* was from Minnesota.

"Oh, I'm sorry, Papa. I didn't realize you had company." She turned toward Tyler with a sheepish smile. "Mr. Wilkins? I'm Emma Sanders. I'm sorry about blabbering on like that."

Tyler stepped out of the late afternoon shadows. A jolt of strange excitement coursed through Emma's body when she stared up at his rugged, finely hewn features. The raw, male aura he exuded claimed her fast-dwindling composure, and she swallowed in an attempt to regain it. The effort proved useless, however, when he stopped only inches from her and reached for her hand. Slowly lifting it higher, he tilted his head. Never taking his gaze from hers, he lightly kissed the back of her palm.

"I'm pleased to meet you, Miss Emma Sanders."

His green eyes—so like her own—mesmerized her frazzled brain. Emma snatched her hand away and hid it behind her back to hide its trembling. Clearing her throat, she struggled to make her voice sound normal.

"Are you from the area, Mr. Wilkins?" The words came out in something that closely resembled a squeak as Emma fought to pull her gaze from the dark wavy hair resting on the collar of his jacket.

Edward caught the devilish glint in Tyler's eyes. Once he realized his guest wasn't nearly as offended as he should be, he began to enjoy the little show that unfolded before him.

"No, I'm sorry to say I'm not from your fair city. Since you seem to hold New Yorkers in such high esteem, I wish I could be among them." Tyler took a step back and lowered his gaze to hers. "No, Miss Emma Sanders, I'm sorry to say I'm just in town on business." He paused for effect. "In town...from Minnesota."

If ever Emma had wanted anything in her life, it was that right at that very moment, a huge black hole would open beneath her feet and swallow her up. Instantly, her cheeks flamed with embarrassment.

"Mr. Wilkins, I'm terribly sorry. You see...this morning, my father and I...I mean...just me, well...my father had nothing to say about you except good things. Please don't think he was a partner to my thinking." She inhaled deeply in an attempt to seek some sort of composure.

He stood before her—so calm, so smug—waiting for an apology. Emma clamped her mouth shut when she realized the oaf actually took pleasure in her discomfort.

"Excuse me, Mr. Wilkins. I should never have interrupted your business meeting with my father. I'll leave the two of you alone now." She spun and exited the room in such haste that only a trace of perfume lingered.

Tyler winced when the door slammed and turned to his host. "I apologize for that, Edward. It wasn't very nice of me to purposely embarrass your daughter. It's just that I've never been called a *backwoods pansy* before and reacted without thinking."

Edward waved off his concern and burst out laughing. "No, no Tyler! It's I who should apologize for my daughter's behavior. I'm sorry to laugh, but that was the best dressing-down I've seen in ages. Touché, my man." He picked up the papers lying before him on the desk and chuckled aloud once more. "Now that you have had a chance to meet my beautiful, demented daughter, I think we should leave for our meeting with the Board."

Tyler followed the other man from the room with a shake of his head as he silently contemplated whether or not he should be angry with the little redheaded brat.

Chapter Four

Tyler sank onto the hotel bed. Even though he was exhausted, excitement soared through his blood. The meeting with Edward's Board members went well. He'd been in complete control as Edward's associates fired one question after another at him. Before the evening was out, he had the entire group of men eating out of his hand with the powers of persuasion he'd carefully used during the meeting.

It had been a long time since he'd actually done something invigorating. His normal day consisted of rising from a troubled slumber to survive the following hours, only to get up the next morning and do the same thing.

He truly liked and respected Edward Sanders and hoped to strengthen the budding friendship between them. Throughout the entire evening though, and even during the late supper he and Edward partook of, he'd purposely kept the Emma Sanders episode at bay. Every time her father mentioned her name, he experienced a tightening in his gut—a sensation that he'd purposely tucked away in the corner of his mind to be pondered later in the quiet of his room.

Now, lying on the bed and staring up into the half shadows, he envisioned her thick auburn hair, petite body and those dark-lashed, green eyes so much like his own.

What was it about Emma that kept her constant image in his mind? It had to be her sheer loveliness. Tyler was positive he'd never encountered anyone as exquisite as she, or as tiny and delicate. Even Sara, whom he'd always thought to be beautiful, had not possessed such perfect physical features.

That beauty, though, didn't parallel Emma's true nature. How could a man as courteous, hard-working and honest as Edward Sanders have such a callous and narrow-minded daughter?

Reflecting further, Tyler decided that loyalty and pride in his home had been offended, not himself personally. Where he lived, police whistles didn't blow constantly throughout the evenings. His home state of Minnesota wasn't a wasteland filled with illiterates, as she inferred. Opera houses could be found in the bigger cities, along with a fair amount of culture. Families worked hard to carve out lives for themselves in a sometimes cruel environment. It was a land of raw beauty twenty-four hours a day, a place he was proud to call home. He shouldn't feel like he'd have to prove anything to her.

His eyes clamped shut as the tendrils of shame enclosed his heart in a steely grip. Emma Sanders had flit around the corners of his mind all evening, when he should have been thinking of Janie and how the little girl was handling his desertion.

He missed his daughter terribly. He missed the feel of her tiny body cuddled in his lap on a cold winter night. He missed the special smell that was just Janie, and he missed the feel of her tiny hand in his when they walked to the stable to see the animals. He even missed the quiet solitude that now surrounded her. She may be only a small child, but Janie was his lifeline. She was the reason he went on day after lonely day.

The mere thought of his daughter brought tears to Tyler's eyes. He squeezed his lids to keep them at bay.

Rolling onto his side with an agitated groan, he stared at the floral print on the wall. *Strange,* he thought as his eyes fluttered shut. *They're almost the same color as Emma Sanders' hair.*

His eyes flew open again. Muttering a curse beneath his breath, he flung himself onto his other hip and promptly and resolutely forced Emma Sanders from his thoughts.

Goodnight, Sara. Janie, I wish I was home to kiss you goodnight...

As he drifted off though, images of thick auburn hair and sultry green eyes floated through his mind.

* * * * *

Emma tossed from side to side in the large, canopied bed as the day's events raced through her mind. She couldn't get Mr. Tyler Wilkins out of her head. Every time she thought of him, her cheeks flamed anew. Her embarrassment was tempered only by the fact that she'd found him to be as arrogant as they come.

She groaned with the realization that she'd be forced to see him again Saturday night at the reception. Short of drowning, there was nothing she could do to get out of going.

Emma willed herself to lie rigid beneath the coverlet and concentrated on falling asleep. Once she let go of her embarrassment, however, her curious mind wandered again. She found herself speculating on how the excruciatingly tall Tyler Wilkins would look when decked out in his finest for the formal affair. His black hair would frame his face. A starched white collar would set off his suntanned face...

And those eyes... It was sinful that a man should possess such lashes as his—long, dark, thick lashes that fringed startlingly green eyes.

Her mind's eye traveled along broad shoulders next. There would be a black dinner jacket stretched tightly across their width, and long, lean legs—

She bolted upright in the bed.

"Stop it!" she hissed. What was the matter with her? Tyler Wilkins probably couldn't participate in a decent conversation with polite society. He'd already proven that he wasn't a gentleman by provoking her the way he had in front of her father. No real gentleman would purposely embarrass someone in such a manner.

Emma smacked her pillow with a closed fist, and then plopped back into its soft center.

She would simply ignore him through the entire reception. If he had a shred of decency, he'd leave her alone and pretend the embarrassing meeting between the two had never happened.

She would also do her best to avoid running into him for the rest of the week by staying away from the shipyard office and make herself scarce during any meetings they might have at the home.

"And wait until I get a chance to talk to you, Papa..." she fumed angrily as she adjusted the pillow again. He could've easily warned her there was someone else in the room.

Emma rolled onto her back and squeezed her puffy eyelids shut, determined to fall asleep. Somewhere in the recesses of her mind though, she pictured dark wavy hair and flashing green eyes that had mocked her as he kissed her hand.

* * * * *

Edward rose from the breakfast table the following morning, prepared to leave for the office, but paused when Emma flounced haughtily into the dining room. She threw a swift glare in his direction, then ignored him as she moved to the buffet to fill her own breakfast plate. The serving spoon clattered loudly against the ceramic surface each time she scooped a portion onto the dish.

Edward raised an inquisitive eyebrow at the sight of her pale face and puffy eyes. "My…you look rather tired and out of sorts this morning."

Emma turned on a slippered heel and walked stiffly to her seat, then set her plate down on the table with enough force to rattle the water glass sitting beside it.

"Thank you, Father, for the wonderful compliment. I shall carry it with me the entire day." The words were spoken in conjunction with another pointed glare.

"Oh, excuse me," he replied, "I didn't realize you were in a mood this morning." Edward sipped at his coffee indifferently as he resumed his seat. Finally, her silence and his curiosity got the best of him. "Okay kitten, let's start over. What's the matter?"

She pushed the food around on her plate with a silver fork. "I didn't sleep well last night."

"What kept you awake? Anything you need to talk about before I leave?"

"It's nothing. Well…yes it is." She laid the fork aside and glanced up. "I'm a little perturbed with your behavior yesterday, and more than a little embarrassed about my meeting with Mr. Wilkins." Rising scorn etched her face. "It was as if the two of you enjoyed my discomfort."

Edward's mouth opened, but she halted his words with a lifted palm.

"And even if I *shouldn't* have said the things I did, I thought it was rather ungallant of Mr. Wilkins to back me into a corner the way he did—and rather rude of you to let him. I think he's arrogant and could use some lessons in gentility."

"What do you mean? I'm rather impressed with him."

"Well, I'm not!" Emma pursed her lips and tore her angry gaze away from her father, then picked up her fork again to stab at the contents of her plate. "Fine. Just don't expect me to play hostess to him on Saturday night. I refuse to give him the time of day."

Edward rolled his eyes heavenward and sighed. "I'm sorry, honey. You never gave me a chance to warn you about his presence. You were rattling on so about your day that I didn't want to interrupt you. Then the next thing I knew, you had insulted him. Don't be angry with me. I'm sorry you were embarrassed."

Her stern feathers softened guiltily when she realized that her own words of yesterday afternoon couldn't be ignored. "You're lucky I can't stay annoyed with you."

Edward opened his mouth to speak again, but Emma charged on, wanting the last word.

"And even though I feel terrible, I still think I won the wager. Mr. Wilkins' actions proved him to be a backwoods oaf. Hopefully, we won't meet up again, so be forewarned. I plan to keep my distance next Saturday evening."

Edward rose and headed out of the room, but hesitated a moment beneath the arched doorway. A mischievous grin lifted the corner of his mouth. "We're having guests for dinner tonight. I left a note for Angie as to how many people will be attending. Would you please check the guest list for me and set up the seating arrangements? Angie has all the other details."

"Of course I will, Papa. Don't I always?"

When she glanced up, her genuine smile touched Edward's heart, yet he wondered how long it would last.

"Now, before you leave, is there anything else you can think of that you would like me to do? Maybe this will be the one time you won't have to send a messenger with a last minute request." Her usual teasing banter was back.

"Oh, yes, there's one more thing," he replied over his shoulder as one more step took him into the outer hall. "Make sure you seat Mr. Wilkins next to me. I want him to feel as comfortable as possible tonight."

With that plucky statement out of his mouth, Edward hurried for the front door.

* * * * *

Tyler entered the foyer of the Sanders home later that evening to the sound of boisterous voices filtering out from the library. Angie took the coat from his arms and made to lead him to the other guests.

"No need, ma'am. I can find my own way."

She grinned up at him, bobbed a small curtsey and continued in the other direction with a dreamy look thrown over her shoulder and a toothy smile plastered across her face.

He continued toward the library door, but a movement from the stairs to his right drew his attention. He paused to glance upward and saw a vision in gold gliding down the flight of steps.

The sight of Emma Sanders' small, yet shapely form snatched his breath away. Her long, flowing gown dropped from slim, satiny shoulders, collecting in a vee across the tops of her creamy white breasts. The sight was enough to send a jolt straight through his stomach. The evening dress draped her slim hips, and then flared slightly to the tips of her gold slippers, which peeked from beneath the silken threads.

Emma saw Tyler at exactly the same moment that he saw her. She hesitated for a split second at the top of the staircase, inhaled deeply to regain her composure, and continued down.

Papa, you are a dead man...

She forced a smile to her lips when she reached the bottom of the steps. "Hello, Mr. Wilkins." Heat flushed her cheeks. She struggled valiantly to stop it, but to no avail.

She took another deep breath. "It seems my father has decided to be the *host extraordinaire* while you are visiting New York. I hope he isn't taking up too much of your time?"

"On the contrary, Miss Sanders. I'm a lamb lost in this city of wolves and appreciate the friendship he's extended to me. Please, call me Tyler. Since your father has decided to be my mentor, I can't see the need for us to stand on formality."

Emma stared hopelessly into his smoldering green eyes. *Damn, but he's handsome!*

Thankfully, it appeared that he'd decided to ignore the humiliating events of their first meeting. Mentally shaking her head to clear it, she searched for something to say. "Ah...if that's the way it's to be, then you may call me Emma. Miss Sanders makes me sound like a little schoolgirl."

His eyes sparkled when a devilish smile appeared. "Ah, Emma, a schoolgirl you most definitely are not."

Her immediate discomfiture turned quickly to anger. How dare he talk to her in such a manner?

She straightened her shoulders, failing to realize that the movement made her breasts stand out even more impudently, and spun away. It took three steps toward the library door before remembering her manners. She stopped and cast a quick, if withering glance over a creamy white shoulder.

"If you'll follow me, *Mr.* Wilkins, I'll show you to my father."

A smile played at the corners of Tyler's mouth. "Of course, I'd follow you anywhere."

Emma gritted her teeth and stomped to the library entrance without looking back. *To hell with him! He can follow me or stay behind! I couldn't care less if he winds up in the cellar!*

Tyler shook his head and wondered what the hell had gotten into him. Only two days ago, he would never have dreamed of talking to a business associate's daughter as he just had.

Behave! he told himself sternly. But, forced to watch her perfectly shaped derriere draped in gold and leading the way, he knew it would be a difficult task.

*****

Emma spent the next hour trying to ignore Tyler, but finally gave in to her own curiosity. Secretly, she watched him from across the library as he visited with various Board members. She was angry with him, true, but even so, was inexplicably drawn to him.

He swirled amber liquor in his glass ever so slowly, and then tossed his head back to laugh at something one of the men said to him. A head taller than any other man in the room, he was a commanding presence.

Lost lamb, my eye! she spouted silently. The men had kept him in constant conversation from the moment he'd entered the room. And, for the last hour, Emma watched through seething eyes as the women whispered from behind delicate fans and ogled the guest of honor from every corner.

Feeling a headache start behind her eyes, she wondered how she was going to make the evening with all the contradictory emotions that coursed through her body. Thank goodness she'd had the presence of mind to seat him at the other end of the table for dinner.

*****

Across the room, Tyler found it difficult to concentrate on the flow of conversation around him. His gaze continually searched for Emma over the rim of his glass.

She's avoiding me.

That was fine though. It gave him a chance to secretly study the woman who'd made his stomach roil from the moment he'd spotted her on the steps.

She now visited with one of the elderly women attending the party. Though she appeared interested in the conversation, the constant—if discreet—fingers to temple motion indicated a headache.

Thick auburn hair, piled high atop her head, shone in the bright gaslights that adorned the elegant library. When she moved, the golden gown shimmered and seemed to flow like rippling water from her white shoulders. Her face was deliciously flushed. Whether from the champagne or the heat of the pressed bodies in the room, he couldn't tell. One thing though, he did know for sure. The overall effect was divine.

His attention swung back to the man who whispered a risqué story to him. He threw back his head and laughed, then admitted to himself how much he was enjoying the evening. Lately, the only pleasure he derived from the sometimes endless days, came when he held his young daughter in his arms until she fell asleep. Reestablishing himself as a member of the business community was a heady emotion. He'd existed in his own little world for so long that he hadn't realized how much he'd actually missed.

The sound of a spoon clinking against a glass gained the attention of the small gathering. Immediately, the guests hushed to hear Edward's words.

"I just have to say how happy I am to be forging this new partnership with Mr. Wilkins. It's been two very interesting days. His enthusiasm is contagious, and I'm looking forward to the next four weeks."

"I couldn't agree more with you, Mr. Sanders," Tyler acknowledged. "We've definitely got our work cut out for us."

Edward set the glass down, clasped his hands behind his back and let his gaze encompass the entire group. "I hope you'll all be able to attend Saturday night's reception. We've got quite a gala planned with many more guests from around the city. That said," he continued, "I've just been informed that dinner is to be served. If my beautiful daughter would be so kind as to let my guest from Minnesota escort her to the dining room, we can all retire there for our evening meal."

Emma longed to stomp on her father's foot, but he wasn't close enough. The crowd slowly parted before her. She had no choice but to ignore her pounding head and force a wan smile to her mouth.

Tyler moved across the room to offer his arm. "Would you do me the honor, Miss Sanders?" He waited patiently as she graciously accepted his arm.

They proceeded to the dining room without a word. Tyler pulled out a high-backed chair and seated her in a very gentlemanly fashion.

Emma's good manners mandated that she thank him.

"Thank you, Mr. Wilkins. Enjoy your meal." She refused to look up.

"You're welcome, Miss Sanders. I'm sure I will." With a nod of his head, he continued on to his seat at the opposite end of the table near Edward.

* * * * *

The dinner lasted for two hours. Not once during the entire meal did Emma feel Tyler's gaze upon her. He sat an eternity away, by her own choosing, with her father on one side of him and an elderly matron on the other. He laughed and chatted the evening away—and totally ignored his hostess.

Emma fumed at the other end of the table and failed miserably to keep her cleavage covered as best she could with a wine glass. The older gentleman who sat beside her had imbibed a little too much brandy during the evening and now openly ogled her chest. Again, the old letch's knee bumped up against hers. She swore silently, knowing that if she moved any closer to the edge of her chair, she would be on the floor at any moment.

Her headache raged. She did her best not to snap at the lecherous old goat. Just when she felt she couldn't take anymore, her father stood to invite the gentlemen back to the library for a nightcap and a cigar.

Emma leapt up. "Ladies, why don't we retire to the parlor while the men end the evening with a drink." The invitation was issued through clenched teeth.

The women settled themselves in the parlor a few minutes later, amid sincere thanks for a delicious meal. The elderly matron, who'd sat beside Tyler during dinner, clapped to gain the women's attention.

"Ladies! I know how you all must be so jealous of me! My, what a handsome fellow that Mr. Wilkins is. I haven't enjoyed a dinner companion such as the likes of him for some time. My goodness, if I were twenty years younger... Ohhh!" She waved a delicate fan in front of her face and rolled her eyes heavenward. The other women tittered along with her, which only increased the excitement concerning the handsome dark stranger who had suddenly graced their presence.

Emma listened with an exasperated press of the lips as they expounded on the glorious traits of one Mr. Tyler Wilkins for the rest of the evening.

* * * * *

The night finally ended and the last of the guests took their leave. Emma closed the front door, heaved a tired sigh, then turned to lean back against the burnished wood. Her eyes closed against threatening tears. Another heavy sigh escaped into the quietness. It had been an awful evening. The muscles in her neck ached and her head pounded ferociously.

One more comment from those old biddies about the wonderful Mr. Wilkins, and I would've thrown up right in front of them...

She pushed herself away from the door, kicked off her slippers and immediately followed with a sigh of sheer pleasure with the feel of cool tile beneath her feet. Bending to gather up the slippers, she first wiggled her toes, then straightened and shuffled toward the bottom of the staircase.

"You look as if you might not make it up the stairs."

Her heart jumped erratically at the sound of his voice. Tyler stepped from the hallway, his evening coat casually draped over a forearm and looking as fresh as if he'd just awakened.

Emma's face flamed with illogical rising anger. She had foolishly thought she'd escaped his presence by hiding with the other women. He was the last person she wanted to encounter. Tyler hadn't given her the time of day since the sumptuous meal began, and had rudely ignored her when the men left for their cigars.

And those women thought he was such a gentleman. Gentleman? Humph! I'll be damned if I'll sit and chitchat with him now.

She continued toward the staircase in a nonchalant manner. "Oh, it's you. I thought you'd have left by now," she tossed out a caustic remark in his direction.

"I waited so I could thank your father in private for the nice evening." He glanced down at her as she passed him on her way to the steps.

"Well, I'm sure he was impressed with your thoughtfulness," Emma returned, refusing to even look over a shoulder as she muttered the words. She started up the staircase, but couldn't resist one parting shot. "Good night, *Mr.* Wilkins. Don't let the door hit you in the backside on your way out."

You little snip, he ground out silently.

He eyed her svelte body as she sauntered up to the second floor, then reached for the front door. He turned back and threw one final comment in her direction.

"Oh, never fear, I'll watch so it doesn't, *Miss* Sanders. By the way, you should be more careful about whom you bend over in front of. I saw almost as much of your bosom as that lustful old man who sat beside you at dinner tonight."

He yanked the door closed behind him. As the brass lock clicked into place, one of Emma's slippers bounced off the wooden surface and landed on the cool tile.

Chapter Five

༄

Tyler stood before the mirror in his hotel room, adjusting his necktie as he contemplated the coming evening. It was Saturday—the night of Edward's reception.

It had been a long week. The negotiations with Edward's Board members had been grueling, to say the least. And, when the daily meetings ended, someone in the group inevitably insisted that he dine with them. The meal always led to a late evening, something he wasn't accustomed to.

A wave of homesickness hit him abruptly. If he were at the ranch right now, he'd be tucking Janie in and saying her prayers for her. Life in New York was so unlike what he was used to back home.

An image of the family sawmill flashed in his mind, forcing him to acknowledge the fact that he missed the smell of a newly cut tree and the sound of his crew laughing as they discussed the day's work. Just about now, they were headed home for a hot meal and a well-deserved night's sleep. He also missed his brothers' companionship and gathering around the table at the end of the day to enjoy a simple but hearty dinner while they made plans for the next day's work. This was also the time when his thoughts would turn to Sara because once more, he had to enter his empty bedroom—

He fought the lump that formed in his throat. Missing his dead wife was a horrible sickness. Somehow, he felt closer to Sara when he visited the family cemetery. Granted, if anyone ever heard him talking to a stone and a mound of dirt, that person would think he'd lost his mind. But sitting in the grass beside her final resting place was the only way he could find comfort, and he refused to give up that cherished bond.

"I'll be back, Sara," he stated firmly to the man in the mirror. "In three more weeks, I can come home."

He lifted his black dinner jacket from the back of a nearby chair. Stuffing his muscular arms into the long sleeves, he reached for the door handle.

He paused though to glance around the room, not quite sure what he sought. His tired eyes settled on the chandelier. He stared at the numerous bits of shimmering crystal.

Pieces, he thought. *Pieces create a whole. Sara, I've got to keep trying.*

* * * * *

Emma sat before a gilded mirror and patted the finishing touches to the soft, auburn curls that framed her face. She reached for a pair of emerald earrings and clipped them to her tiny lobes. Next came a matching necklace that had belonged to her mother. Fastening the clasp, she gently straightened the chain so the beautifully set emerald lay against the rise of her cleavage.

A quick glance at the clock told her that Jacob would soon be knocking at the front door. During one of their now rare rides earlier that afternoon, he'd asked to escort her to the reception, and Emma had agreed. Her mind shifted to their conversation as they had leisurely walked their mounts through Central Park…

Emma had teased Jacob mercilessly about being quiet and secretive.

Finally, he turned in the saddle. "I've got something to tell you." He took a deep breath, then charged on. "I'm leaving in two days."

"And where might you be going?" she asked in a light, bantering voice that displayed her immediate lack of concern.

Jacob stared off into the distance and chose his words carefully. "You know that I've never really had a genuine interest in the mill. My father has made it clear that he wants both Samuel and me to take over its operation someday, but Samuel is the one who always talked about becoming the working manager. Now that he's back, I feel I can finally pursue my own dreams. He's been by my father's side since he returned and is doing a good job."

Emma snorted in an unladylike manner with his last words.

"It's true!" Jacob bristled. "Tonight when you see him, you'll know what I mean. He's visiting the operation daily. Mother is so happy with the change in him. He's been considerate, kind and genuinely happy to be back in the bosom of our family."

"Are we talking about the same person here? Samuel was one of the biggest bullies I've ever come across," Emma stated incredulously. "Don't you remember how he treated us?"

"We were children when he left. I know at times he could be nasty. I often despaired that he would never change, but he's not like that anymore. You'll see tonight. In fact, I think you will be quite surprised." His eyes begged for her to give his brother the benefit of the doubt. "Please, for my sake, try to get along with him and see him as the adult he is now, not the child that he was."

Emma shook her head. "I don't know if I can." She remembered all too well the times Samuel had purposely tormented her when they were children—things that Jacob didn't know about. Even as a child, Jacob looked for the good in everyone—including his malicious brother—and always held out hope that someday Samuel and Emma would mend fences. Apparently, he thought now was the time.

Emma didn't. She refused to put forth the effort to "mend fences" where Samuel Fontaine was concerned. She'd suffered the consequences of his cruel streak from the time she was very young and found it hard to believe that someone could simply change their personality—even in six years' time. She'd been fortunate enough not to run into Samuel since his return. Tonight, however, she would have to see the elder Fontaine brother again, and she wasn't looking forward to it.

"Just give him a chance...for me," Jacob interrupted her thoughts.

"Oh, all right!" She gave in as she grasped for some avenue to change the subject. "I know if I don't agree, you'll hound me the rest of the day. Besides, right now I want to know where it is that you're going."

Jacob inhaled deeply. "I'm leaving for Africa."

Emma's eyes widened in disbelief. "Africa? What on Earth are you going there for?"

"Em, I'm so excited. I'm going to work at a mission and teach the local children Christianity. I'll also help treat their medical problems. We're even going to start a school! I've already discussed it with my parents. At first, they were upset, but Samuel helped me talk them into it. He'll be here to learn the business and, eventually, my father will hand over the reins to him. I, on the other hand, am finally free to do as I want." He reached out to squeeze her hand, his eyes sparkling with enthusiasm.

Emma searched the face of her dearest friend in the world and wondered what her days would be like without him. She'd depended upon his companionship her entire life. She'd told him her deepest secrets and her wildest dreams. She had always been so sure that their lives would be entwined forever.

Instant tears welled in her eyes at the thought of his imminent departure. "Are you quite sure about this, Jacob? Isn't it rather sudden?"

"I've been thinking about this for the past two years," he replied. "Please understand, Em. Now that Samuel's home, it's finally my turn to do what I want with my life."

"But you've never said anything about this." Her gaze lowered as her hand again found the pommel on the saddle. "I guess I thought you and I would be working together as business partners until we were old and gray. Friends forever." A sad sigh escaped her parted lips. "It's quite a lot to take in all at once."

It was Emma's turn to stare into the distance. The only sound for a long moment was the creak of the saddle as it moved with the smooth rhythm of the horse beneath her. She swallowed the lump in her throat and finally met his eyes. "I guess that was rather selfish of me, wasn't it? I'll miss you with all my heart, but your happiness comes first. Promise you'll write long letters full of your days in Africa."

Jacob grinned, reined his horse closer and reached out his hand. She grasped his fingers and gave them a quick squeeze while blinking the tears from her eyes.

"I promise to write every day." He brought her tiny hand to his mouth and gently kissed her knuckles. "We will always be friends, Em—forever."

She blinked against a new rush of tears as she pushed herself up from the settee, picked up her evening shawl and crossed to the door.

What will life be like after he's gone? she wondered again as she left the room, then her shoulders squared. *Well, at least he'll still be here to get me through tonight.*

The evening loomed before her like a thunderstorm on the horizon. Not only must she contend with Jacob's insistence that she change her mind about his recalcitrant brother, but she would also have to see Tyler Wilkins again. She'd managed quite adeptly to avoid being anywhere near him in the past week, but her reprieve would end tonight.

Try as she might, she couldn't sort out her feelings toward the arrogant Minnesotan. One minute he was the handsomest man on Earth, and the next she was ready to scratch his rugged face bloody. Granted, they'd been together only a few times, but each of those times he'd gone out of his way to goad her. Consequently, she ended up either blubbering like an idiot in his presence, or acting like a shrew.

Emma caught her reflection in the gilded full-length mirror at the top of the stairs and paused for a moment. The gown was the same shade as her eyes. She'd chosen it very carefully and, though she would never admit it aloud, she'd thought of Tyler Wilkins when she'd purchased it. The dress exposed more cleavage than she was accustomed to, but something had made her throw caution to the wind. She wanted to look like a woman tonight.

For him?

Emma shook her head.

It's official. I'm losing my mind.

Tyler Wilkins *and* Samuel Fontaine were the last two men on Earth she wanted to impress.

Lifting her chin with new resolve, she descended the steps to greet her father and Jacob. Her chin drooped again, however, when she overheard snatches of their conversation. They were talking about Jacob's imminent departure.

* * * * *

The ornate ballroom was aglow with warm candlelight. The ten-piece orchestra already provided soft music and most of the guests were in attendance. Emma's eyes roamed the crowd, searching for a familiar—yet decidedly disturbing—face. She didn't see Tyler Wilkins anywhere in the close press of people.

"Are you okay?" Jacob asked from where he stood beside her. "You seem…tense."

"I'm fine," she said as she smiled up. "I'm just anxious about the evening being a success."

Her heart jumped a moment later when Jacob's parents called out a greeting. A tall man in his mid-twenties stood with them. His blond hair was neatly combed to the side and a groomed mustache curled over his top lip. He stared quite openly at her.

"Samuel Fontaine," she muttered. An initial stab of fear pricked Emma's chest as she stared at him, then took a deep breath and forced it aside. She clung to the fact that, even though Jacob was rather naive when it came to his brother, six years had gone by since she'd last seen Samuel. Hopefully, the younger Fontaine brother would be right in the new assessment of his sibling.

The two groups met in the middle of the room. Emma peeked up at Jacob, read the plea in his eyes and forced a smile to her face for his benefit.

"Well," Samuel spouted enthusiastically. "Could this be little Emma, all grown up?"

Her eyes darted to Jacob again, and then to his parents, but it appeared that she was the only one in the small group to notice when Samuel's eyes discreetly surveyed her petite form from head to toe.

"Did you think I would stay the small child all these years, Samuel?" Her reply was tinged with bravado.

"I can certainly see that you didn't," he answered in a voice that deepened with appreciation.

The small group failed to notice the barbs that were already being thrown. They saw the meeting as a simple reunion of two childhood friends who had not seen each other for many years. Emma's brittle smile mirrored the one plastered on Samuel's lips. Tangible hatred leapt from one to the other.

Mrs. Fontaine rested her gaze on Emma. "You look lovely this evening, my dear."

"Thank you, Mrs. Fontaine. That's nice of you to say." Emma did her best to ignore Samuel's leering stare as Miriam Fontaine slipped an arm through her eldest son's.

"Samuel's father and I are so happy to have him home. I have to admit it's been hard to share him since he arrived from college. That's why you haven't seen him about the city. But I'm sure, Emma, that I can manage to give him up for a short while tonight so the two of you can catch up." She looked up at her son with motherly love as Samuel patted her hand gently.

"It would be delightful to talk with you later, Emma," Samuel's voice dripped with sweetness. "I hope you'll save a dance or two for me."

Emma cringed inwardly.

The glowing promise in Samuel's eyes made his thoughts only too clear.

"If you can't get on her dance card, Samuel," Jacob chimed in, "I promise to give up all my dances—except one."

Emma's strained smile prevented a response, however. Her heart jumped again when Samuel reached for her hand and lightly pressed a kiss on the back of it.

"I'll eagerly await my turn, Emma."

The bile rose in her throat. She had all she could do to avoid making a scene by snatching her fingers away when he surreptitiously flicked his tongue over her silky skin.

"If you will excuse me," she managed as she slowly withdrew her hand from his, "there are still some things that I need to attend to."

Emma practically flew past the tables stacked with special delights. She slowed her flight, chatted with people along the way and displayed an unperturbed look of calm that belied her unsettled state and racing mind.

Samuel was still trouble and she was the only one who realized it.

* * * * *

Tyler watched Emma closely from across the room. Witnessing what looked to be a reunion of sorts, he stiffened imperceptibly when he observed the blond man take in Emma's womanly curves rather coarsely. It mattered little that he'd done the same thing himself when she'd first entered the room on her escort's arm. What disturbed him most though, was how she just continued to smile at the ingrate.

She let the stranger grasp her hand after a few words. Pleasantries were exchanged. The blond man then kissed the back of her hand and made no effort to hide the fact that he stared right down the front of her gown—and again, Emma just continued to smile.

Christ, is she encouraging such behavior? Maybe Miss Emma Sanders of New York isn't the nubile little virgin I thought her to be. Hell, she's just a damn good actress!

The shame that had crept into his bones over the remarks he'd made to her that night in the foyer receded quickly to be replaced with a look of scorn. It didn't take much to bring the worst out in her. He would just make sure to settle the score later that evening.

Tyler watched discreetly when Emma walked away from the intimate group of friends. The slim line of her back was presented to his wandering eyes. The mere sight made his blood quicken. He ran a shaky hand through his dark, wavy hair wondering why she had the power to make him think and act differently than usual. Maybe it was because it'd been such a long time since he'd enjoyed something so simple as watching a woman move.

The music halted when Edward Sanders stepped up to the podium to be better heard by the crowd. "I'd like to thank all of you once again. As you know, the purpose of this reception is to introduce Mr. Tyler Wilkins to those of you in the business community who have yet to meet him. I'm sure you all have managed to figure out that the tall, dark-haired man being monopolized by my Board members is the guest of honor."

The crowd searched for Tyler and witnessed him nod his head toward Edward.

Emma spotted him at the same time. Instant heat suffused her cheeks. The group applauded, and then Edward raised his hands for silence.

"Now, I'm sure you all would enjoy it if I just stood here all night and gave speeches..." more than one guest guffawed at his attempt at humor, "but let's begin the dancing. In fact, I'd like to start the evening by inviting my lovely daughter to join me on the floor." His searching eyes finally spied her in the crowd. "Emma, come dance with me!"

The crowd applauded again and moved aside as Emma crossed the floor to her father with the sound of a whimsical waltz in her ears. Edward gathered her into his arms, and other couples slowly joined the father and daughter. The evening was officially underway.

When the music ended, Edward spotted Tyler thanking an elderly woman for graciously accepting his offer to dance.

"Come, Emma. Let's save Tyler before another old society dowager drags him out on the floor."

"But Papa—" Her father grabbed her by the hand and dragged her toward Tyler before she could object further.

"We came to save you, young man!" Edward chortled.

Tyler chuckled in return. "Thank you, Edward, but there's no need."

"Well, I know Emma would rather dance with the dashing guest of honor than an old man like me."

"That's not true!" she sputtered. "I love dancing with you."

"You young folks enjoy yourself." Edward handed his daughter over in a flash. "I feel the need for a glass of champagne. Get your dance in now, Tyler. All the young bucks will have her dance card filled shortly!" He saluted his guest, kissed Emma on the cheek and disappeared into the crowd as the soft strain of a waltz began.

Emma simply stared up at the man before her.

Tyler studied her quietly for a moment, then bent at the waist in a gallant bow. "May I have the pleasure of this dance, Miss Sanders, or do the other young *bucks* get you first?"

Emma was tempted to slap his sun-darkened cheek. "I'm sure my father would be upset if I didn't dance with you. After all, you *are* the guest of honor." She stood stiffly before him and waited for Tyler to make the next move. She wasn't about to encourage him further.

His jaw twitched. Forcing his ire down, he took her hand in his and gently placed his opposite palm on the small of her back. Slowly, he moved them around the floor.

His hand was firm and warm against her satin-covered skin. Without provocation, an indefinable emotion hit Emma with the force of a summer storm. Heat radiated from the spot on her back where he touched her. Her breath suddenly and surprisingly came in disjointed rasps.

She forced down both sensations, suddenly aware of his dancing expertise. For such a large man, Tyler moved gracefully. Neither spoke as they moved in unison, allowing the floating strains of the waltz to propel them into a world where the other dancers ceased to exist.

Even Tyler fell prey to the moment. He guided her body a little closer to his.

The sudden contact with his hard, firm chest weakened Emma's knees. Never in her twenty-two years had a man infuriated her in one moment and churned her insides the next. She hadn't known him long enough to make any sound judgments, yet she was acting like some smitten schoolgirl, all aflutter with his mere touch. Her eyes drifted shut as they glided about the floor.

Tyler felt her chest rise and fall against him in a contented sigh and cursed silently. He'd done nothing but think of her all week and now, to actually hold her in his arms made his blood boil. The feel of her soft breasts as they brushed his chest, the curve of her tiny waist beneath his hand and the light scent of her perfume, all combined to affect him in ways he hadn't experienced in a long time.

Despite the fact that Tyler still reserved his opinion Emma wasn't the person she portrayed herself to be, he couldn't get past the sensations that ran through his body. It felt good to hold her. She was so delicate, so beautiful, and he could feel the envious stares of the other men in the room.

He gently whirled her to the subtle beat. Emma's breasts brushed his chest again. It shocked his senses to realize that, at that very moment, he wanted nothing more than to whisk her into his arms, carry her from the ballroom and relieve the building tension in his body on the first bed he came across.

He hadn't even thought about having sex in two years, yet now, as he held Emma in his arms, every carnal urge that had been buried, emerged.

Guilt settled on his shoulders like a leaden weight. The sudden desire to flee to his room and wallow in thoughts of his beloved Sara were swallowed up by Emma's overpowering allure.

He gripped his emotions in a fierce hold, fought against the ones that led him farther from his dead wife and finally won the battle that raged inside him. His tortured mind demanded that he remember Sara and, when the music ended, so did his dance with Emma. He stepped back and glared down at her through guilt-ridden, disgust-filled eyes.

Emma blinked and gradually became aware that the melody no longer filtered through the room. Her mind had gone blank. Her body had moved to the gentle rhythm of the music of its own accord as she'd basked in the feel of his strong arms around her. Tipping her head back to thank him, she suddenly recoiled from the contemptuous expression that marred his rugged features.

"Thank you for the dance," he muttered abruptly, then turned on booted heel and walked away.

Bewildered, her confusion quickly turned to rage. She trembled with the extent of her anger. How dare he leave her standing alone? A quick glance around the ballroom further fueled her ire. Women whispered behind their fans, furtively watching her next move.

Emma raised her chin a notch. Desperately needing some fresh air, she walked with as much aplomb as she could muster toward the open doors that led to the balcony.

Once outside, she crossed to the edge of the gallery and grasped the railing tightly in an attempt to stop the shaking of her hands. Her thoughts tumbled one over another.

What had happened? One minute, she was being held in the arms of a tall, dark stranger who made her insides jump crazily. The next? He scorned her as if *she'd* done something wrong.

Drawing in steadying breath, she swiped a tear from her cheek with the back of a hand. The night was just beginning and already she yearned for the solitude of her room.

Finally, the warm night air gently embraced her, and her churning thoughts calmed. She lingered to gaze out over the moonlit gardens in the hotel plaza and sort out her confusion. What was it about Tyler Wilkins that stirred her emotions so? Most of her waking thoughts had centered around him since the disastrous afternoon they'd met. He'd awakened something inside her that she'd never experienced before. Emma wasn't like most of the girls she knew, immature females who were all agog over the opposite sex. In fact, up until this week, she'd never given men much thought at all.

A soft sigh escaped as she contemplated all the strange feelings. Mystified, she shook her head and decided to let thoughts of Tyler Wilkins rest for the time. Turning from the railing and intending to go back inside, she nearly collided with Samuel Fontaine. His lips held the same, brittle smile.

"I saw you leave the ballroom and thought this might be a good time for us to 'catch up' as my mother put it." His fingers brushed his mustache as his eyes wandered the length of her body again.

A quickening of fear stabbed at Emma's insides for the second time that evening. "I'm sorry, Samuel, but I've been gone from the party far too long already. Maybe some other time." She attempted to skirt him, but he reached out to clutch her wrist tightly.

"Why don't you just stay a while and talk? Or are you afraid to be out on a dark veranda with a man?"

His sneer catapulted her back in time. Samuel was still the bully. He still enjoyed hurting her. She tried to shake her arm free, but his firm grasp only tightened.

"Let go of my arm."

"I don't think so, Em. At least not yet."

She raised a defiant chin and tried once again to rid herself of the uneasiness that spread through the pit of her stomach like an incoming tide. "To answer your question, yes, I might be afraid to be on a dark veranda with a man—if there were a *man* present, that is." She hurled her retort with more bravado than she felt.

"You're still the snotty little bitch, aren't you, Emma?" he gritted.

"Let me go! I'm no longer the little girl you used to torment. Grow up!" She yanked her arm hard enough to be free of his grasp this time and rubbed the soft skin on her wrist, which was already turning red. "Go pick on someone else. I'm an adult now, not a child, and I won't put up with the likes of you."

She moved to step around him, but was suddenly and unexpectedly shoved against the wall with enough force to rattle her teeth. Her heart slammed against her ribs. She struggled to take a breath.

"Listen, you little red-haired bitch. No one talks to me like that and gets away with it. You haven't changed one bit. If you think you can look down your nose at me, *you are wrong*." He punctuated the last three words with small shakes of her body.

"You haven't changed a bit either," she tossed back. "And if you don't release me this minute, I'll scream. What will your parents think about their prodigal son then?"

"Oh, so you think you'll scream? Well, my dear Emma, you might find that a little difficult."

His mouth plummeted to capture hers. His lips ground against her tightly closed ones cruelly, sadistically.

Emma shrieked her outrage against his mouth as she struggled to free herself from his steely hold. Her anger quickly turned to panic when he changed positions and the hard stucco wall of the building bit into the soft flesh of her back. Samuel held her prisoner with one arm now, as his free hand moved to her breasts.

Emma attempted to twist her head away from his punishing lips, but his strength was far too much for her. He ravaged her mouth for what seemed an eternity. His hands continued to paw the rest of her body until she went limp with defeat.

The kiss stopped as abruptly as it began.

Samuel reached up to cover her trembling mouth with his hand and glared into her wide, frightened eyes. Emma gasped for air through the slits in his fingers. Her visible fear lit a spark of excitement in his eyes. "I'll say one thing, Emma, you were right. You *are* definitely the woman you claim to be." Her body jerked when his free hand moved to her breast again. Squeezing the soft mound mercilessly, his last words were a warning. "I'm going to let you go back inside now. You better not breathe a word of this to anyone. This is *nothing*—" he crushed her breast slightly harder between his fingers and enjoyed her whimper of pain "—compared to what I'll do if you even think of opening that beautiful mouth of yours. You can be assured no one would believe you anyway."

She bucked against his hold again, her eyes burning with hatred.

"Let's see," he mused. "What do I need for insurance? Ah, I know." His lips curved in a cruel grin. "Strange accidents can happen to people in foreign countries. You remember that if you care at all for my pansy ass brother. I'm not above hurting him." He removed his hand from her mouth. His knuckles moved to gently brush her cheek. "You remember, don't you, Emma?"

"You are a pig!" she spat, knowing from experience that he was only too capable of carrying out his threat. "So help me God, if anything ever happens to Jacob—anywhere, anytime—I'll expose you somehow. Now, let me go!"

Samuel released her with a caustic chuckle, then watched as she hurried to the door. She paused to cast one last murderous glare over her shoulder while she took a moment to smooth her gown with shaking hands.

My God, she thought, *he hasn't changed at all — and he's even more dangerous now than he ever dreamed of being as a child.*

"Remember, Emma, I'll be right behind you. Better for you to keep your mouth shut." The quiet words held an ominous tone.

She took a deep, cleansing breath, pasted a wide, counterfeit smile on her lips, stepped into the ballroom and nearly bumped into Tyler. He stood just inside the balcony doors conversing with a young woman who had waylaid him when he was on his way to the veranda to apologize to Emma for leaving her alone in the middle of the dance floor.

He stared at Emma's state of dishevelment. Two bright spots of color stained her cheeks, the beautifully coiffed tresses were slightly askew and her smile was much too forced to be genuine. It didn't take long for him to put two and two together when a blond man entered on her heels, the same whose eyes boldly raked Emma's body earlier in the evening. The man paused inside the balcony doors as he straightened his jacket with an irritating nonchalance.

"Oh Emma," the young lady said. "You must come and congratulate Priscilla Stanaway. She's just announced that she's having a baby! Isn't it thrilling?"

She grasped Emma's hand and dragged her from the doorway, but not before Emma saw disgust spring into Tyler Wilkins' seething eyes.

Samuel glanced from Emma's slim back as she disappeared within the crowd, then back to the man beside him. Here was a perfect opportunity to malign the little witch's character.

"You must be Tyler Wilkins, the guest of honor," he began. "I'm Samuel Fontaine, a friend of the Sanders family. My father owns the mill that supplies the iron for Edward's company. I'm pleased to say that we'll be seeing much more of each other in the next three weeks. It's nice to finally meet you." He extended a hand.

Tyler could do nothing but return the handshake—however warily—and attempt to ignore the other man's smug grin as he nodded in Emma's direction.

"I saw you dancing with Edward's daughter earlier. Quite the little bit of fluff, isn't she?" Samuel leaned closer and added for Tyler's ears alone, "and a damn good kisser, if I do say so myself." He threw another leer in Emma's general direction as she exited the ballroom. "My, but it was good to get," he paused for effect, "reacquainted with her."

Tyler withdrew his hand slowly and lifted a skeptical eyebrow. Samuel chuckled and clapped a hand on the other man's shoulder.

"Allow me to give you a little piece of advice, friend." He leaned close again. "She comes across as a sweet, innocent little thing, but in truth, she's quite the man-eater. She'll gobble you up in one bite, so watch yourself." His laughter became downright vulgar. "Not that such a thing would be *all* bad."

Samuel sauntered off then, leaving Tyler's jaw to harden with an uncustomary rage.

Chapter Six

Tyler glared at the brandy in his glass with a steely gaze. A foul curse left his lips as he tossed the amber liquid into the cold ashes of the fireplace. Jerking open the buttons on his shirt, he flopped into an overstuffed chair, rested his weary head on the back of it and went over the evening in his mind once again.

The night had dragged on for an eternity after his short conversation with Samuel. He'd danced until his feet hurt, smiled until the curve of his lips more closely resembled a pained grimace and answered questions until he was tempted to strangle the inquirer. He'd pretended to have a grand old time when all the while, he'd watched for Emma to reappear. Strangely, he'd found himself both frustrated and happy when she didn't.

Tyler stood, tossed his shirt to the expensive carpeting and paced between the bed and the fireplace as he attempted to sort out his feelings.

One moment he'd want to make love to her and the next, he'd wanted to shake her for being so damn fickle. He let out a mystified sigh. Had she really been out on that veranda allowing herself to be kissed and pawed and God knows what else?

Edward had mentioned at one point that his daughter was twenty-two years old. Evidently, she planned to remain single, but did that mean that she'd already experienced the delights that a man's touch could offer?

Probably — and why does that bother me so? A week ago, I didn't even know she existed. Now, I can't get her out of my mind...

Two years! He started pacing again. *It's been two goddamn years, and I haven't thought of another woman besides Sara. But now — now I'm walking around like a lovesick pup! Dammit!* He stared up at the ceiling. *Is it just her I want or would any woman do?*

His fists balled in self-deprecating anger. He damn well would never find out because bedding his new business partner's daughter wouldn't be a prudent thing to do.

Mentally shaking himself, he shrugged off his pants and climbed into bed. Rubbing his eyes with the heels of his hands, he forced thoughts of Emma Sanders from his mind. His determination lasted all of five seconds.

Damn, but it felt good to hold her when they danced. He could've easily hauled her out of there and had his way with her. His stomach muscles constricted with the thought.

"God, I need to go home," he groaned loudly.

* * * * *

Emma lay curled into a tight ball on the canopied bed. Hours had passed since her dreadful encounter with Samuel, yet she still felt nauseous.

She'd managed to escape the reception early, pleading a fearsome headache. Upon arriving home, she'd ordered hot water for a bath. She'd scrubbed her skin until it was raw, but couldn't wash away the bruises on her upper arms where Samuel's cruel fingers had bit into her flesh. Her lips were still tender from his crude kisses. Emma had vowed then to speak with Jacob the next day. The discoloration on her arms should be enough to convince him of the abuse she'd suffered at the hands of his brother.

Now, as she lay in the darkness though, she knew she would say nothing. Samuel was evil enough to make good his threat if she spoke out against his character. Jacob would pay—maybe with his life. He would be unsuspecting prey for anyone determined to do him harm—even his own brother. She would stay clear of Samuel until she could figure out what to do.

Emma suppressed another shudder, then firmly turned her thoughts to the dance she'd shared with the guest of honor and all the conflicting emotions that came with it. What had she done to anger him? Emma shook her head. She came up against a brick wall every time she encountered the man from Minnesota.

Tossing her agitation aside, she rose from the bed and crossed to the open window. The warm air whispered across her skin, helping to relax her tangled thoughts as she stared out at the quiet night. What is it about Tyler Wilkins that drew her like a moth to a flame? And why, even when he evoked constant anger, did the man not frighten her like Samuel? She could still feel Samuel's groping hands on her body. The mere thought made Emma's stomach churn again.

Being held by Tyler was totally different.

Her eyes fluttered shut. The thought of his strong arms about her, the clean male scent that emanated from every pore, his gracefulness as he whirled her effortlessly around the floor made her heart quicken. She wasn't quite sure what it was about the Minnesotan that turned her knees to jelly, but she wasn't willing to just toss it away. She was twenty-two years old and attracted to a man for the first time in her life.

With a determined squaring of the shoulders, she turned and padded softly back to the bed. Tomorrow, she would seek him out. She would see just what that *something* might be. He aroused a curiosity in her. If nothing else, Emma felt compelled to find out more about the man behind the aloof exterior that was one Tyler Wilkins.

* * * * *

The food tasted like sawdust in Tyler's mouth. The restlessness he'd awakened with the following morning was still a constant companion. It was Sunday. There would be no business negotiations and a long, boring day stretched out before him. Edward had invited him for Sunday dinner, but claiming that he had some paperwork to catch up on, Tyler declined. The truth of the matter was that he needed some quiet time. He had wrestled with his emotions all week due to Emma's unnerving presence. After last evening's fiasco, he had no desire to see her again.

Now, however, he wasn't so sure he'd made the right decision. Even a few hours of sparring with the uppity Miss Sanders would be preferable to an entire afternoon and evening spent alone.

He mentally checked off a list of New York City attractions as he chewed on a piece of steak. There were museums to visit or various historical buildings to tour. He shook his head. The thought of spending another day cooped up inside four walls, no matter where they were, didn't appeal to him in the least. Maybe he should rent a horse and visit the famous Central Park.

The decision made, he attacked his food with vigor as he anticipated spending an entire afternoon in the warm New York air.

His hand froze midway to his coffee cup a few minutes later when he glanced up from a nearly empty plate. Emma Sanders stood across the room, her green eyes doing a delightful dance as they searched the crowded room.

"What in the hell..." The thought froze as abruptly as his hand when his gaze scanned the blue taffeta dress that hugged her petite body in all the right places. A matching hat was perched jauntily atop her auburn curls.

Emma spotted him at the same moment. Her step momentarily faltered. The resolve to speak with him suddenly didn't seem like such a good idea anymore. But, she was determined to see this thing through. Lifting her chin, she continued forward with an aplomb she didn't feel.

Tyler set his napkin aside and rose from his seat when she approached the table. He cleared his throat uncomfortably. "Hello...Emma. It's quite a surprise running into you here."

"Hello, Tyler." Her responding smile was apprehensive. "I hope I'm not interrupting your meal."

"Oh, no, I...was just finishing up, as you can see. Would you like to sit down, or are you meeting friends?"

She fidgeted with her purse strings for a moment before looking up to meet his questioning gaze. Her heart flipped in response to his handsomeness. She took a deep breath to calm the erratic beat of her heart. "No, I'm not meeting anyone. In fact, I came expressly to see you." His eyes clouded with a guarded expression, and she rushed on. "Could you give me a few minutes of your time?"

Tyler's gaze continued to hold a decided wariness as he moved around the table to pull out a chair for her. She sat down. He stared in total confusion at the back of her head for a moment before resuming his own seat.

"Is there something I can do for you? Your father is fine, I hope."

"Oh, yes, he's quite well." Emma took another deep breath and continued. "I came of my own accord to discuss last night—"

A dark brow rose at her statement. "Last night?"

"Yes. I…ah…wanted to apologize if I did something to offend you. I have thought and thought about it and am at a loss as to what I might have done. I know a look of reproach when I see it, Tyler." She met his gaze directly. "Did I do something that I'm unaware of?"

Other than turning me into a horny old bull, and then carrying on a ribald flirtation with a man out on the veranda, no, he answered silently. Aloud, however, he spoke carefully and with the utmost politeness. "I'm sorry for my behavior, Emma. It wasn't you. It was me—for reasons I prefer not to discuss at this time."

She smiled with visible relief. The twinkle in her eye and sudden softening of her porcelain features rammed him in the chest, momentarily robbing him of breath.

"Well, if you're telling me the truth, then I'll rest much easier tonight."

The previous evening's tension melted away bit by bit as they conversed for the next fifteen minutes about the weather and daily happenings around New York.

Tyler was impressed with her knowledge of the city. It didn't take long for him to realize that she was highly intelligent and was forced to reverse his original impression of a woman who played her days away without a care in the world or an ounce of sense in her head. He still wondered, however, if she was as virginal as she appeared.

"So, what are your plans for the day? Papa said you declined his dinner invitation because of some work you must catch up on. Am I keeping you from something?"

Tyler decided a little white lie was in order. "I couldn't keep my mind on business, so I've decided to lease a horse and see a little of this fair city of yours."

Emma leaned forward, rested her elbows on the table and gave vent to a sudden, wild idea. "I'd like to make it up to you for my uncomplimentary remarks at our first meeting." Her cheeks colored to a becoming shade of pink with just thinking about that horrible day.

Tyler's stomach clenched at the sight of her blush.

"If you wouldn't think it too forward of me," she continued in a rush, "could I show you around the city this afternoon? I have an afternoon stretching out ahead of me. New York is always better when seen through the eyes of a local resident."

The look of genuine surprise on Tyler's face, followed by an emotion she couldn't quite read, was enough to make Emma backtrack quickly. "I'm sorry, Tyler. I didn't mean to put you on the spot. If you can't, it's quite understandable. The invitation *is* rather last minute—"

He held up a hand to silence her. Staring at her with a mixture of pleasure and disbelief, it suddenly came to him that there was nothing he would rather do than spend the afternoon in her company. Something about her had caught his interest from the first moment they'd met and demanded he find out what kind of person she really was. "I'm honored that you asked me, Emma." He stood, tossed some bills onto the table, then moved to stand behind her chair. "Shall we go then?"

Another blush—a happy one this time—flushed Emma's cheeks as she rose. She took a step away from the table, then paused when she felt Tyler's hand on the small of her back. Her heart knocked against her breastbone as she glanced up at him. His responding smile served only to heighten the beat.

* * * * *

Chatting about Emma's beautiful mount was the one subject that helped to ward off the initial awkwardness between them. They soon discovered they had much in common. Both enjoyed discussing their individual state histories, spending time outdoors and pitting their intelligence against others when it came to business acumen.

Emma also proved to be the perfect tour guide, having lived in New York her entire life. Tyler had to smile more than once when her expression grew animated while telling him little tales about the city's history. It became obvious that she wanted him to appreciate New York as much as she did.

He couldn't hide his amazement that a city as big and populated as New York could boast such a place as Central Park. The wide open, tree lined space brought the ranch to mind along with a pang of homesickness.

"You should see Minnesota, Emma. It's a lot like this, but extends for miles and miles."

"Isn't it rather lonely though, when the nearest neighbor could be miles away?"

Tyler chuckled. "You have to understand that my home state is a very new, very virgin territory. People are just discovering what a wonderful place it is to live. At present, it's still wild and untamed. I live in the northern part of Minnesota, and the natural resources have barely been tapped." A regretful smile curved his lips. "But I suppose our secret will be out before too long."

"What makes you say that? What secret?"

"There've been rumors that entrepreneurs from the East will be buying up land rich in the natural ores used to make steel. Underground mining will soon follow. It's still a long trip inland from the Atlantic coast, but I imagine there might come a day when people will be shoulder to shoulder—sort of like here in New York." He glanced sidelong at her. "I hope it doesn't happen too soon, though. I'm rather selfish about my space."

She watched his face soften. Tyler was a man who would never be comfortable living in a city such as New York. The entire afternoon, he'd compared her home to his own. In his eyes, New York always came up short of his expectations. He needed the wide-open spaces of Minnesota. A city such as this would slowly suffocate him.

A pang of regret jabbed at Emma's heart. Strangely, she wasn't at all happy with the idea of him leaving for his home in a few short weeks.

He'd coaxed near hysterical laughter from her several times during the course of the afternoon with his sometimes ribald tales about growing up in Minnesota. Emma's favorite story though, concerned his little sister, Carrie. Tyler and his brothers, Cole and Trevor, had convinced the little girl that if she entered the smokehouse, she would turn into a piece of ham and be served for dinner. Thus, for an entire summer, every time a platter of pork was placed on the table, Carrie was certain it was one of the hired help.

"You know, Emma," Tyler explained as he wiped a tear of laughter from his eye, "what we did to Carrie that summer might sound mean, but I guarantee you that if anyone touched a hair on her head, they dealt with three irate brothers."

Emma had no doubt. If nothing else, his stories that afternoon proved his love of family.

"Can I make a suggestion?"

Tyler's question brought her back to the present with a jolt. "Of course."

"Could we visit Castle Garden? A lot of my workers came through there when they arrived in the States." From past conversations with his hired help, he knew that Castle Garden was the receiving station for immigration located at the Battery in lower Manhattan.

"Are some of your workers immigrants, Tyler?"

"Almost all of them," he returned. "They're hardworking people, doing their best to carve out a life here in America. It's a tough life, but my brothers and I do our best to help them meet their goals. We pay a fair wage and provide housing and meals when needed."

Emma was amazed at his kindness, or rather at the kindness of his family. "Well, I can guarantee that's not something you would see here among the factory workers. I tend to think most of them are quite underpaid."

He shrugged. "It's a different life out West. Without our crew, my brothers and I couldn't operate the mill. We expect the men to work as hard as we do—and most comply, because they've worked for other companies that didn't treat them as fairly."

They entered the austere grounds of Castle Garden's processing center a few minutes later by way of a circular cobblestone driveway that led to the front entrance of the red granite building. The pair reined their horses to the right and paused before a side platform to be out of the way of the quickly growing crowd.

Tyler pushed back his wide brimmed hat, leaned back in the saddle and watched intently as a ship unloaded its cargo of foreign speaking men and women. The immigrants reached the landing stage at the shore's edge and were then herded as one up a corridor and into the interior of the building. Their boxes and baggage were taken from them and removed to the luggage warehouses for examination.

He stared in thin-lipped silence as an Immigration Commissioner ripped a filthy rag doll from the arms of a blonde-headed little girl. Her pleas and accompanying tears were to no avail. The toy was tossed carelessly onto a pile of crates and baggage that awaited inspection.

Tyler's brittle green eyes continued down the line to another foreign family in the midst of dealing with their three sick children who vomited uncontrollably onto the wooden planking. Their haggard parents could do nothing but watch through sunken eyes that attested to their extreme exhaustion as they patted each child haphazardly on the back.

Finally, he could stand the sight no longer and looked away. Dismounting, he helped Emma from the back of the mare. Taking her elbow, he guided her through the doors and into the station. They watched quietly as individuals were processed through the terminal. Tyler was humbled by the thought of his own men arriving alone in a strange country, unable to speak the language, wondering where their next meal would come from and missing their families.

He knew what it was like to miss someone…

Keeper of the Spirit

They left the building without a word a few minutes later and strolled down to the dock. Another old frigate anchored in the harbor waited its turn to deposit a second load of immigrants.

Tyler stared out through narrowed eyes. "I think I finally understand the awful conditions my men were forced to abide just to make it to the New World. It must be devastating to be packed like cattle into the hull of an old ship, not to mention being deprived of decent food and even safe drinking water. My men told me they were allowed to go topside for fresh air only at certain times of the day."

Emma shook her head sadly. "I guess you can't help but respect them for all the hardships they had to endure."

"That's for sure. You can bet I'm going to see that we do more for our own workers when I get home."

They strolled in silence back to where the horses were tethered. Their lives were settled. They had roofs over their heads, plenty of food in their bellies and those who loved them close by. The immigrants though, had no idea what lay in store for them in a strange and unfriendly world.

They mounted again and plodded down pedestrian and carriage-filled streets.

Tyler shook his head and glanced down at the beautiful woman who rode beside him. "All right, Miss Tour Guide, how many people actually live in this city?"

She smiled with her newfound understanding of his disapproval. "Would you believe over one million?"

"You've got to be joshing!" The sheer numbers boggled his mind.

"Uh-uh. New York's populace has doubled from five-hundred-thousand to over one million just in the last thirty years."

"How can all these people live together in such close proximity?"

Emma laughed. "I guess if you've never experienced anything different, it doesn't bother you."

"I guess," he returned, though his tone was far from convincing. More than ever, he longed for home. His wide shoulders lifted in a shrug when his gaze turned back to her. "Someday, you and your father will have to come visit my home. The wide-open spaces and friendly people will get under your skin. I guarantee it."

"Is that an invitation, Mr. Wilkins?"

Twin sets of green eyes locked. A second later, a man hawking his wares claimed their attention.

Chapter Seven

Two mornings later, Tyler was in Edward's office, going over some figures for the refurbishment of the man's ships. He glanced up when a bell tinkled above the door, happy that the woman who never left his thoughts had just shown up in person.

"Good morning, Emma." Tyler stood upon her entrance, then paused to glance at Edward when he noticed the tears in her eyes.

Edward rose and rounded the desk to stand before his daughter. "What's the matter?"

"I've just come from seeing Jacob off." Her gaze shifted to Tyler. "You remember Jacob, don't you?"

He nodded.

"He left on a passenger liner for Africa this morning and will be gone for quite a long time. I know it's foolish to act this way, but Jacob is my best friend and has been from the time we were children." She swiped at her moist eyes. "I don't know what I'm going to do without him."

A sympathetic smile curved Edward's lips as he gave her a quick hug, then directed his comments to Tyler. "This little gal and her friend, Jacob, used to get in more scrapes than two small pups on the loose in a china shop. Why, I remember one time when they decided to play pirate and chose one of the ships docked for repairs here at the factory, as their vessel. Well, the ship had already been patched up and was about to leave port." Edward watched Emma's face flush slightly with his words. "You can well imagine the captain's surprise when he discovered that he had two small children on board—and that one of them was *my* daughter. He lost an entire day's worth of travel, because he had to turn around and bring them back home."

Tyler's appreciative laughter filled the room. "And here I thought I had astounded Emma a few days ago with tales about my brothers and me."

"No, you definitely bested me, Tyler." Emma's eyes turned to him. "At least *I* didn't slink around a house of ill repute and peek in windows."

Edward warmed up to the more animated look on his daughter's face. "No, you didn't—but if I remember correctly, you and Jacob once stole some sailors' clothing from the beach while they were swimming next to their docked ship."

Emma's blush deepened to a color near scarlet when she caught Tyler's raised eyebrows. "It wasn't my idea!" she spouted. "It was Jacob's!"

"Don't believe that for a second, Tyler." Edward struggled to keep his laughter in check. "I saw the two of them run by my office window—both with an armload of pants and shirts. By the time I got outside to see what was going on, Emma had dropped the clothes and stood on the dock, whistling and waving her arms to gain the sailors' attention." His twinkling eyes bored into his daughter's. "She didn't think the prank was so amusing though when the two sailors leapt onto the dock and tore after them—buck naked I might add—to retrieve their clothes. She and Jacob lit out like the devil himself was chasing them!"

Emma wiped tears of laughter from her face as she gazed sidelong at Tyler who was doing the same thing. "Stop it, Papa. What is Tyler going to think of me?"

"That there's more to the sweet and innocent Emma Sanders than she's willing to let on," Tyler answered softly. The laughter left his eyes in an instant and darkened with an emotion that Emma was rapidly becoming familiar with.

Her cheeks colored again, but she refused to lower her gaze. Her own eyes glittered with boldness. "You haven't begun to discover my deep, dark secrets, Tyler."

He stood and swept an arm before himself in a bow of supplication. "I fold, madam, under the weight of your superior childhood feats—and I look forward to hearing more."

The light banter helped Emma to forget the pain of Jacob's leave-taking earlier that morning. It also erased Samuel's image as he had stood on the dock beside his parents with concealed hatred etched into his face. His mere presence had put her on edge, but she had managed to stay as far from him as was physically possible during the departure.

*****

The companionship Emma discovered in her father's office over the days was a balm that soothed her mind from missing Jacob. She would often arrive unannounced and shortly be as engrossed as Tyler and Edward in the plans to refurbish the four ships that would carry Minnesota lumber to Europe. More space would be needed in the vessel hulls, and blueprints were spread out on every table in the room.

It was such a day that Edward watched quietly as his daughter and Tyler put their heads together. It would be difficult, but not impossible, to devise a way to move the interior iron crossbeams and create additional space, yet not jeopardize the integrity of the vessel.

Edward found it refreshing that, unlike many of his other clients, Tyler actually took Emma seriously and bowed to her years of experience in the fundamentals of shipbuilding. He smiled inwardly as he studied them, wondering if Emma had any idea that she just might be falling in love.

He continued to watch as Emma leaned over one of the blueprints and showed Tyler exactly how the ship's galley could be moved to provide extra storage space. He didn't miss the look of awe in Tyler's eyes when he responded that she was right.

So, Mr. Wilkins, what about you? You clearly look enamored with my Emma, but there's still something I can't put a finger on. Why do you always manage to quietly back away from a conversation when it becomes too personal? You don't act like a man ready to strike up a relationship with a woman on a permanent basis. Yet your face gives you away every time you look at her...

Edward was not above trying his hand at matchmaking, but somehow he felt that Emma and Tyler wouldn't take kindly to his intervention. He longed to see his daughter settled with a husband and a safe and secure future, instead of whiling away her days as a spinster and businesswoman. Up to this point, however, she had never even shown an interest in a man.

But maybe the right man just hasn't come along until now. And you, Mr. Tyler Wilkins, are just the sort of man I would pick for her.

* * * * *

Tyler stormed into Edward's office a week later, a terse look emblazoned on his face.

"You're here early," the elder man said as he glanced up from the paperwork that cluttered his desk. "By the look of it, you're upset about something. Anything I can do?"

"I'd like to visit the Fontaine mill, Edward. They are the only ones supplying iron for the ships' crossbeams, correct?"

"Yes. Is that a problem?"

Tyler sat in one of the chairs before the desk, rested his forearms on his knees and paused momentarily. "I have a lot of faith in you, Edward. I believe you conduct your business honestly and that your ships are built to exact specifications, but I heard something last night about Fontaine Ironworks that I want to check out personally."

Edward leaned back in his chair. "Go on."

"I was talking to some men about the pros and cons of using wooden beams versus iron beams in a ship's hull. As the evening progressed, they started to tell me about some of the practices being used in area mills. One of those practices regarded the substitution of cheaper alloying elements in the initial mixture. Another questionable practice comes into play during the cooling process. Instead of allowing a long, slow cooling period for the beams, some mills are quenching them rapidly. This saves additional cost when it comes to heating fuel, since the fires really should be gradually cooled along with the beams. It gets the product out faster." His unflinching gaze met Edward's. "The gentlemen I spoke with insinuated that Fontaine Ironworks may be using some of these questionable practices."

Edward sat forward again and folded his hands on the desk. "Just what are you getting at?"

"This quick method of cooling sets up internal strains in the metal. Internal strains I can't afford to deal with. What happens if the ships run into rough seas and the beams start to snap under the strain? According to your daughter, the crossbeams are a fundamental part of a ship's overall integrity. Add the weight of all that lumber, and what happens? We have four ships sitting at the bottom of the ocean. As I said before, we can't afford to lose the ship's integral strength before we're even at sea."

"Let me assure you, Tyler, that I've done a lot of business with John Fontaine over the years. Never once has he done anything behind my back in the name of saving money."

"I don't think it's *John's* business ethics we're talking about. The men I spoke with said that Fontaine Ironworks just started employing these shoddy business practices within the last couple of weeks—after John literally handed over management of the mill to his oldest son, Samuel. It appears that this man's character leaves something to be desired. The men I talked to don't think John has any idea of what's happening. It was also implied that Samuel Fontaine has a bit of a gambling problem, so therein lies a probable reason as to why the sudden cheaper methods in milling. I just wonder how he's managing to make it all look good in his father's eyes, and on paper, if that's what's actually happening."

Tyler ran a hand through his dark hair and heaved himself out of the chair. He crossed to the window, pursed his lips and finally turned back. "If this turns out to be true, I'm afraid I'll have to withdraw from our partnership. It's a decision I feel I must make for the good of my brothers and myself. Europe was just another way for us to expand the business, but we aren't willing to risk the lives of a ship's crew—or our investment—to do it."

Edward stood, closed the ledger in front of him and raised his hands palms up in a plea. "Let's not jump to any conclusions before we know the facts. We'll go find John right now and discuss the problem with him. We may find that there's nothing to worry about."

As they left the office and entered the churning throng of pedestrians on the street, Tyler's thoughts turned again to Samuel Fontaine. According to the men he met with last evening, Samuel was a simpering, gutless man who'd never done a decent day's work in his life. He lived off his parents' money, and now it appeared as though he was stealing it, too, from right under their noses.

His thoughts immediately led him to Emma's connection with the man. On the night of the reception, she'd allowed Samuel to openly ogle her and, later, spent time on the veranda with him apparently enjoying his advances once again.

Tyler had done his best not to think of that little episode since the night it happened—or about the fact that Samuel and Emma both disappeared after they returned to the ballroom from the veranda. Were they together then, too?

* * * * *

Tyler and Edward waited in the main office of Fontaine Ironworks. To their surprise, Samuel sauntered in through the open doorway instead of his father. Dislike for the man roiled in the pit of Tyler's stomach once again, though he had little evidence to base the reaction on. He'd always been one to trust his gut instinct, however, and his gut told him that this man wasn't to be trusted. He hoped like hell it had nothing to do with any relationship the man might have with Emma.

"Well, Mr. Sanders, Mr. Wilkins," Samuel said as he nodded to each of them. "I was informed that you were here to see my father on business. I hope you won't mind discussing the matter with me since I'm the operating manager at this time. Please, come into my office." He strutted like a peacock through an adjoining door. Tyler and Edward were left to follow as the man took a seat behind a large oaken desk.

"My father and my lovely mother left yesterday for a four-month tour of Europe. It's a holiday well deserved for both of them. My brother is on his way to discover the adventures of Africa, leaving me in charge of the mill." He smiled. "Of course, I'll eventually be taking over complete management of the company anyway, so my father wasn't concerned about leaving me with the reins now."

Tyler caught Edward's eye.

Edward cleared his throat and leaned back in his chair before he directed his comments to Samuel. "I'm surprised your father left the country without informing me when he was well aware of my venture with Mr. Wilkins. He did mention an upcoming trip to Europe a while back, but I didn't think he would be leaving so soon."

Samuel laughed lightly. "I almost hate to admit this, but I was supposed to notify you. Everything happened so fast. There were only a few ships leaving for Europe. In order to secure tickets, my father was forced to make a quick decision. He felt I could handle any last minute details concerning your project. Unfortunately, I've been so busy running the mill that I guess it slipped my mind to let you know he was gone. A minor infraction, if I do say so myself. Now, what can I do for you gentlemen today?"

Tyler settled back in his chair, perfectly content to let Edward handle the situation.

"It came to our attention recently that some of the iron working mills in the area have changed their production procedures, perhaps to save expenditures. If that's the case with Fontaine Ironworks, then I think we deserve an explanation. Mr. Wilkins is concerned, and so am I, that the changes may result in a weaker product. Since *you* are the operating manager now, hopefully you can allay our fear."

Samuel's brow furrowed in a show of consternation, but it was gone as quickly as it appeared.

Tyler thought Samuel looked like he'd just gotten caught with his hand in the candy jar.

Samuel smiled succinctly at both men. "Gentlemen, I hope you're not insinuating that Fontaine Ironworks would sink so low as to follow in the footsteps of some of our competitors and sell a lesser quality product. I've also heard rumors of late about such unsavory practices, but I can assure you it's not happening here." He looked Edward squarely in the eye. "Mr. Sanders, my father has been doing business with you for years and has always provided you with the best product possible. I plan on continuing in his stead. Once again, I assure you that such unsavory practices would not be tolerated in our factory. Now," he stood, "I hope this issue is resolved and that I've set both your minds at ease." His gaze moved to Tyler. The look in his eye dared the other man to challenge him further. When Tyler said nothing, Samuel continued. "If there's anything else I can do for you, please let me know. I realize that there's a lot at stake here. I want to assure you that I would do nothing to jeopardize the partnership on our end."

He moved around the desk and extended a hand to Tyler, signaling that the meeting was at an end.

Tyler ignored the parting gesture and remained in his seat. "Mr. Fontaine, if you wouldn't mind, Edward and I would like a tour of your operation. Now, if possible. Since the three of us will be entering into what could be a very lucrative partnership, I'm sure you wouldn't mind giving us a little more of your time." Tyler's tone held nothing but politeness, but his eyes dared him to refuse.

Samuel knew he was trapped. Hadn't he just stated that he would do nothing to jeopardize their business relationship? Wilkins was a cunning bastard and had just intentionally backed him into a corner.

The smile that creased Samuel's face revealed nothing of his inner turmoil. "Well, then, gentlemen, shall we take a tour?"

* * * * *

The three men entered the main mill through the front entrance and encountered a heat so fierce that its force slammed them in the face. They were also met with the stench of sweaty, unwashed bodies.

Tyler was appalled at the sight that met his gaze. The workers were stripped to the waist in deference to the intense heat, their glistening bodies packed into a large, unvented room. They stood over slabs of hot metal, hammering them into various shapes, mindless of the nearby kilns that shot out flames and ashes that nearly licked the skin from their arms. The few men who bothered to look up upon their entrance displayed no emotion and quickly returned to their duties.

A large man in his early forties with the stamp of his Irish forefathers marked on his rugged features, stepped up to the platform on which they stood. Sweat ran from his body in rivulets. "Mr. Fontaine! I didn't realize you'd be back today. Are there new orders?"

"Step back, O'Malley!" Samuel snapped. "Can't you see I have guests viewing the plant? Your unwashed stench is making our eyes water."

Samuel pulled a handkerchief from his pocket and made an issue of shaking it open and placing it over his nose. The huge man quickly stepped back and away. His head sank forward with embarrassment, but not before Tyler spied the look of contempt that burned in his eyes.

Tyler shifted uncomfortably as beads of perspiration became rivers and trailed down his own back beneath the jacket. How in hell could Fontaine expect these men to work in such harsh conditions?

"Mr. O'Malley, is it?" Tyler took a step toward the other man and spoke above the din. "Save your concern for where it's warranted. Any man working in this kind of heat would be hard-pressed to smell like he'd just stepped out of a bath." He swung to face Samuel and the words of reproach tumbled from his mouth. "The conditions in this building are appalling, Mr. Fontaine. How do you expect to get a good day's work out of these men when they're treated like animals? I'm of a mind to tell you to go to hell, but it would do little good, because I feel like I'm standing in the middle of it already."

Samuel's jaw hardened murderously as he returned Tyler's glare. "How I run my mill *and* how I interact with my workforce is none of your concern, Mr. Wilkins," he railed through clenched teeth. "You're here to purchase the product I sell and the conditions under which that product is produced shouldn't concern you!"

"I'm sorry to have to disagree, Mr. Fontaine—"

"Look," Samuel rudely interrupted. "Granted, this is not an ideal place to work, but the men are paid well for the sacrifices they make. All *you* should be concerned about, *Mr.* Wilkins, is that you receive a high quality product from their labors, and you will."

The Irish foreman's head came up with a jerk. He stared through wide, incredulous eyes at his employer. Samuel's responding glare was enough to make the man quickly drop his gaze again.

"I think it's time to end this tour," Samuel gritted. His eyes bored into the foreman again, and he couldn't resist getting in one more reprimand before he left the building because all work had stopped as the laborers shuffled uncomfortably. "You, O'Malley, get back on the job. You've wasted enough of my time and money standing around. Make certain the current order is filled before you or any of the others even think of leaving for the day—even if it means working through the night. If the job isn't completed when I show up tomorrow morning, not a one of you will be paid."

He swung back to Tyler. "Since I'm sure you wouldn't want these men working in such *deplorable* conditions any longer than is necessary, I suggest that we end the tour." His chin came up another notch. "I have other business to attend to. I'm sure you'll be able to find your way out." He turned on his heal and left Edward and Tyler standing just inside the door before he completely lost control.

Edward met Tyler's gaze with a slow shake of the head. "I think we had better go back to my office and discuss this further. I have a sinking feeling that you might have assessed the situation correctly."

Tyler paused to look over his shoulder before he left the building. His searching eyes settled on O'Malley. He tipped his head in a respectful nod.

The foreman straightened his back in a show of pride and returned the gesture, then gave Tyler a quick, two-fingered salute.

* * * * *

Samuel charged through the door to his father's office and slammed it with such force that the adjoining wall shook with the impact. Crossing to a large cabinet, he threw open the heavy doors, unmindful of the dent his anger created when one banged the antique desk. He filled a snifter half full of cognac, tossed it down with one swallow and reached for the bottle again before stomping to the window that overlooked the plant yard. He stiffened when he saw Edward and Tyler speaking to a man on the loading ramp.

I need this partnership. Shit, I shouldn't have lost my temper... He would have to stay alert when it came to dealing with the likes of Tyler Wilkins. The man had proven himself to be a worthy adversary in the world of business. *That smart-assed bastard was after me before he ever reached the office...*

Samuel slowly sipped the cognac as he watched the tall, dark-haired man. How in hell had he gotten wind of what was going on? His jaw hardened. Wilkins was dead wrong if he thought he was going to waltz in and ruin everything.

Things were finally falling into place, including his simpering brother's trip to Africa. Hell, Jacob had jumped at the chance to give his brother complete control of the mill so he could pursue his own life. Samuel finally had the little fop out of the way. After achieving that end so easily, Samuel wasted no time in talking his father into a European holiday—a move that put him in charge of the family business.

Upon returning home from Washington, D.C., it hadn't taken Samuel a long time to figure a way to siphon money from the company. In fact, he'd covered it up so well that his father was totally ignorant of the theft. An errant smile touched Samuel's lips as he remembered the many things he'd learned at Howard University that were not taught in class, including the art of error-proof embezzlement.

A thoughtful frown furrowed his brow as he sipped the drink. Cold, hard cash—that's what he needed to resolve his gambling debts. A few changes at the mill, along with some well-placed threats to keep certain workers quiet and he'd furthered the advantage for himself.

I need that cash to keep the wolves at bay... His hand trembled with the thought.

"Christ, I've already banked on the credit this new venture with Wilkins and Sanders will bring." The words were muttered quietly, but echoed inside his head. He just needed time to sort out the details. If Wilkins backs out now, he could lose everything.

His gaze returned to the window to see Edward and Tyler climb into a waiting coach. *I'll get you, you son of a bitch. If all the walls come crashing down before I get things resolved, I'll get you…*

* * * * *

A few questions on the street and some well placed currency was all it took for Tyler to discover where the Fontaine Ironworks foreman lived.

Dougan O'Malley didn't give Tyler another thought until the next night, when the man appeared on his front stoop.

"Good evening, Mr. O'Malley. I hope you remember me. I toured the mill the other day. Would it be all right if I step in for a moment? I won't take up too much of your time."

Dougan's weathered brow wrinkled in confusion upon the request, but he hurriedly ushered Tyler inside. His wife stood by the table chewing her lower lip in concern. "Uh…let me introduce my wife, Katherine, Mr. Wilkins," O'Malley stuttered as he pulled out a chair for his guest. "And please, the name's Dougan. If the neighbors heard a gentleman like you calling me '*Mr.*' O'Malley, they'd laugh themselves right into their graves."

Tyler chuckled before he tipped his head again in a respectful nod toward Dougan's pretty wife. "Nice to meet you, ma'am. I hope you don't mind my stopping by at such a late hour, but I have a matter of importance to discuss with your husband."

She gave a little bob of her head and a tentative smile touched her lips. "Please sit down, Mr. Wilkins. I'll be about perking some fresh coffee while you menfolk tend to your business."

* * * * *

Dougan, Katherine and their late night guest still sat at the kitchen table an hour later. It took a little persuasion on Tyler's part in the beginning, but the foreman finally confirmed that Samuel Fontaine's business ethics were not up to his father's standards.

"I can't believe Samuel thinks he can get away with this," Tyler exclaimed.

"Methods to decrease the cost of producing beams started almost as soon as the devil arrived. Since Samuel took over management, he's received credit against revenue sure to be generated by yours and Mr. Sanders' partnership." Dougan shook his curly head in despair. "My men are the salt of the Earth, sir. Now he's got them working longer hours for the same money, and what they were making before was a mere pittance. None of 'em dare complain though, 'cause they need the job. The heat does take its toll, though. There've been more than a few accidents these past weeks."

"And you can be sure that the money he's received will go to pay his gambling debts," the formerly quiet Katherine O'Malley shot out. Her nose wrinkled in a distinct show of distaste before she continued. "And to pay for the services of any prostitute he can lay his hands on. And lay his hands on them he does, to be sure. The man has an evil streak, he does." She crossed her arms over her slim body. "Just this week, he battered another poor girl down the street who demanded payment for her services. Instead of money, he paid her with the back of his hand." Her jaw set in stubborn determination. "And even though whores they may be, Mr. Wilkins, that don't give no man cushion to beat a woman. Gambling and whoring, that's the only thing that devil knows. If God were to show any justice at all, he would make Samuel Fontaine rot in hell someday."

Dougan blanched at her words. "Mind your mouth, woman," he mumbled as he glanced warily at Tyler, judging his reaction.

"It be God's truth, Dougan O'Malley, and you know it! Every morning I watch you leave for that hellhole. I pray all day long that you'll return to me safe, instead of having one of the men show up at my door to tell me you've had an accident. The man can go to hell, like I say!"

Dougan reached across the table and took his wife's hand in his. He smiled. "Katy, my girl, I'll always return to you. Have no fear on that account. Besides, who would you beller at to take off his boots, wash up and hurry and sit down to eat the meal you've been preparing all day?" He rolled his eyes heavenward and released a heavy sigh. "I wait patiently all day for the whistle to blow just to hurry home to your abuse."

"Oh, go on with you, you big, redheaded lump of a man." She squeezed his hand with love shining in her laughing eyes.

A bittersweet pang shot through Tyler as he sat and listened to them. He missed sharing his life with that one special person. He missed the teasing banter, the day-to-day conversation and the intimacy shared like the couple before him.

Deciding that he'd overstayed his welcome, he stood to leave. "It's getting late. Thank you for all the information, Dougan." He paused on his way to the door and turned back just as the O'Malleys both rose from their chairs. "If you'll forgive my curiosity, just how much do you make working for the Fontaines?"

The large man's eyes dropped to his dusty boots. "Fifty cents a day," he muttered, obviously ashamed to admit the meager amount.

Tyler forced himself to contain his surprise. On impulse, he reached into his breast pocket to pull out a money clip. He laid an amount on the table that was equal to three months' wages for the Irishman.

The O'Malleys' eyes widened in simultaneous expressions of surprise. Never in their lives had they seen that much money together in one pile. They had eked out an existence for the past twenty-two years and had come to terms with the fact they would never be rich.

"It would make me extremely happy if you two would take this money." Tyler drew their attention to him again. "With it, I'd like you to purchase two train tickets to Minnesota and any amenities you might need for the trip." His gaze shifted to the Irishman. "I'm offering you employment at my family's lumber company, Dougan. Believe me, we could use a man like you."

He turned to Dougan's wife next. "Katherine, we've had the same housekeeper for years. She's getting on in age. I'd like to see her do less work and enjoy life more. Your responsibility would be to help her with the cooking and cleaning. She can be rather overbearing, but has a heart of gold. I'm sure with your candidness that the two of you would get along fine. I'll also provide a cabin for you to live in," he continued in a businesslike manner that he hoped wouldn't offend the couple. "It's rather rustic, but all our employee's houses are sound and can stand up to any weather Minnesota has to offer. Tomorrow, I'll send a messenger with all the information you'll need to get to my home."

He fell silent then and took in the astonished faces before him. The room was so quiet that he could hear the ticking of a clock from somewhere else in the house. "If you can't see your way clear to accept my proposal, please feel free to keep the money as a thank-you for all the information and for your hospitality tonight. The insight you gave me into Fontaine Ironworks will help to save a lot of money down the road. It's already helped me make a difficult decision."

The O'Malleys stared at him, then at the money, then back at one another, and then at Tyler again. A soundless chuckle shook his insides. He'd wager on the spot that it was the first time 'Katy' O'Malley had ever been rendered speechless.

"I don't expect an answer tonight," he concluded. "I'm sure you want to talk it over. It's a big decision. If you decide to accept my proposal, I'll plan on seeing you no later than the end of September. I'd like to see you settled in before the first snow." He bade them both goodnight and quietly closed the door on his way out.

The sound of Katy's ecstatic yelp met Tyler's ears a moment later.

Chapter Eight

෩

Emma drowned in emotions she couldn't sort out. It was Tyler's final night in the city. Whether it was fate or her father's ability to influence, he would spend his last night at their home. Edward didn't want Tyler to deal with checking out of the hotel, thus chance missing the cab that would take him to the train station.

Emma mused over the events of Tyler's last days while she finished dressing for dinner. They'd spent most of that time together since all business dealings with her father and the Fontaines were put on hold. Her father, true to his old friend, wouldn't take his business elsewhere until he'd had a chance to speak with John Fontaine personally. That wouldn't happen for another four months when John returned from Europe.

Emma and Tyler had spent their last days together visiting museums, riding, lunching and even took in the current opera in town. She'd held her breath more than once when he'd dropped her off at the door, thinking that he might attempt to kiss her, but he'd always retreated at the last moment.

She grabbed a pewter brush from the dressing table and took her frustration out on the long tresses curling down her back as she paced. She would miss him desperately. She wanted more carefree days to gaze at his handsome face and bask in his dark eyes. Tossing the brush back onto the vanity, she sank into a chair and stared at her melancholy reflection. Grabbing a handful of hair, she wound the length around a shaking hand, swept it to the crown of her head and jabbed pins through the silky thickness.

She didn't even know how he felt about her, but his green eyes were always watching. A few days earlier when she'd stumbled on the steps leading to the front porch, he'd caught her. Emma was sure she'd felt his heart racing when she leaned against his firm chest. She'd actually thought he would kiss her then, but instead he'd let her go as if his fingers burned. And she'd wanted him to kiss her.

Tonight would be one of the worst evenings of her life, but Emma was determined to see it through with an air of aloofness. If that's what he wanted, then fine—she could do it. She was happy that he could finally return home, because that was all he ever talked about.

Let him go. You don't need him! A single tear escaped. *Why then does my heart feel like it will break when he leaves?*

Tyler had never mentioned if he even had a sweetheart back home. His private life was a closed book, and he never let anyone peer between the covers. Emma's father could not shed any light on the matter either. It was a subject that Tyler had taken pains to avoid.

Emma swiped at the tear, braced herself for the coming evening and, again, repeated her earlier thoughts aloud.

"If that's how he wants things to be, then I'll have to live with it." The softly spoken words held little conviction. Still not fully understanding her heavy heart, she proceeded downstairs.

* * * * *

"Son of a bitch…"

Tyler sat on the bed in the guest room and tugged at his boot, then swore again with impatience when it refused to slide over his heel easily. He stared at the ceiling. "Why in hell did I agree to stay here tonight?" he groaned.

It was a simple question to answer. Edward had refused to take no for an answer. Now his bags sat in the corner of the room, ready to be picked up in the morning. It was going to be a long night—one final night of fighting to keep his hands off of Emma—and, with her in such close proximity, it would be a difficult task.

More than once over the course of the last few days, he'd wanted more than anything to pull her into his arms and kiss her. To hell with every other man she might have been with, and to hell with Edward and any business relationship. He wanted Emma physically and emotionally, and the thought of leaving her behind settled in the pit of his stomach like a leaden weight.

So what is it, my man—love or lust? He snorted at himself. Probably the latter, but it didn't matter. She did things to his insides that he hadn't experienced in a long time.

His weary shoulders sagged. He just had to hold out for one more night...

* * * * *

The evening proceeded miserably for both Emma and Tyler. Edward had the cook prepare a sumptuous meal. Neither of them did it justice.

She picked at her food, trying to maintain control over her emotions.

Tyler filled his cup with brandy more times than he could count.

Conversation was about the mundane. It was only when the subject turned to his home in Minnesota did Tyler show any interest in the discussion.

Emma gritted her teeth with frustration. She yearned for just one private moment with Tyler. One moment in which to say goodbye.

She eyed her father scornfully when he filled their glasses with brandy again. She was sick of her father's attempts to monopolize Tyler in conversation. And she was sick of Tyler looking so forward to leaving, when all the while she ached for him to stay.

Tyler struggled to not stare at her. But when she'd reached up to rub her furrowed brow at the beginning of the meal, he'd longed to rub the tender spot himself. Instead, he poured more brandy into his glass.

He'd watched her when she cut a small bite of pheasant, put it in her mouth and chewed it slowly. The simple act was erotic as hell for him, so he refilled his glass to cool his heated blood.

When she'd leaned forward to reach for the plate of bread, he'd been sure her breasts would spill from the top of her dress. Or had he only hoped they would? Regardless, that little maneuver almost sent him toppling over the edge of restraint and deserved two more glasses of brandy.

She's ignoring me, he decided. *Probably for the best. I can't afford to give myself away at this late date.*

Emma stared at Tyler over the rim of her own glass as he laughed at yet another of Edward's drunken jokes. It was pretty obvious that her father held his interest better than she could. She willfully straightened her shoulders. *Remember, you can live with it.*

Tyler's bleary gaze wandered from the empty brandy bottle that Edward had just slammed down on the table to his host's ruddy colored cheeks. He blinked. Had they drank all of it?

"Well, young man," Edward garbled out. "It looks like we need to find another bottle—"

Emma bolted from her chair and nearly sent her wineglass flying across the table. Both men gazed at her through liquid eyes, as if she'd just materialized in the room.

"Well, I see the two of you are enjoying yourselves immensely, so I think I'll retire for the evening." Her hesitant gaze shifted to Tyler.

Please ask me to stay, she pleaded silently.

He rose unsteadily from his chair. "Thank you, Emma, for the tours of your beloved New York. They certainly helped me get through the days."

Please don't go, his heart unknowingly answered back.

Edward stood on wobbly legs and weaved a crooked course around the table. He snatched his daughter to him in a bear hug and gave her a loud, smacking kiss on the cheek.

"G'night, kitten." He turned a lopsided grin toward Emma, and then looked back at Tyler. *Funny,* he thought, *it's taking time for my eyes to catch up with my head.* "I think we'll have one more to cap off the evening, eh ol' boy?"

"Sounds good to me, sir," Tyler replied with a slight dip of his head and a rather sickly smile on his face.

Emma swallowed back the lump that formed in her throat and forced a bright smile before reaching out a hand toward their guest.

Instead of the impersonal farewell gesture that she planned, however, Tyler encircled her fingers with a warm, gentle hand and brought the back of her palm to his mouth.

The familiar smell of her perfume floated to his nostrils. He steeled himself, and then kissed her soft skin gently as his eyes searched hers. Were those tears sparkling in the emerald depths or was it the candle's glow shining back at him?

Wishful thinking, he speculated.

"It's been a pleasure meeting you, Emma Sanders. I wish you well with your future. If I'm ever back in this fair city of yours, I'll be sure to look you up and renew our acquaintance."

Emma blinked back the forbidden wetness. *Just say goodbye and get out of this room!* "Well…goodbye then, Tyler. I hope you have a safe trip home."

He swallowed convulsively. *Stay where you are. Don't touch her again or you'll be lost…* "Goodbye to you, Emma, and thank you for the nice sentiment."

She turned and walked from the room with measured steps. But upon reaching the staircase, she slapped a hand over her mouth, stifled a sob and raced up the stairs. Her tears flowed freely by the time she slammed the bedroom door behind her. She fell across the bed and wept into her pillow.

* * * * *

An hour later, Emma rolled onto her back and stared at the ceiling. His face floated before her mind's eye. The full force of her feelings hit her squarely.

She was in love with him—it was as simple as that. How would she survive without him? Why hadn't she recognized her emotions for what they were?

Why hadn't she told him?

"Because you were afraid he'd throw your feelings back in your face," she spoke to the darkness. And what if he didn't return those feelings? Or, even more frightening yet…what if he did?

Rising from the bed, Emma trudged across the room to the small table that held the pitcher and basin. She dipped a washcloth into the water and pressed it to her swollen eyelids.

She wanted to die.

She loved him, and it had taken his imminent departure to finally make her realize it. Drawing in a ragged breath, she stripped the clothes from her body and donned a silken nightgown before returning to her damp pillow.

* * * * *

The duo moved to the library after Emma's hasty exit. The final nightcap of the evening turned into a full bottle of wine. They laughed loudly, told drunken, ribald stories and all the while visions of Emma flitted on the edges of Tyler's hazy mind. The casual observer would never have guessed that the calm, confident—and very drunk—Tyler Wilkins was falling apart. He couldn't stay. He had a family and a daughter waiting for him.

And nothing melded in his brain except the fact that he wanted Emma in his arms.

Finally, Edward asked Tyler to help him to his room. The twosome zigzagged a path through unknown hallways and finally found the correct one. Tyler pointed the older man in the general direction of his chambers and headed out for his own.

"Helluva note when you can't find your own room," Tyler mumbled.

Two more turns and he'd finally reached his own. Fumbling drunkenly with the knob, he shouldered his way inside, closed the door and cursed the darkness that surrounded him. His hand fumbled along the edge of a dresser, nearly knocking over the hurricane lamp before he found some wooden matches, struck one and lit the lantern. He stared at the burning stick in his fingers, mesmerized by the glow until it burned his fingertips. Muttering another curse, he tossed it onto a tray and turned to squint into the dimly lit room.

"Who the hell changed the furniture around…"

* * * * *

Emma awoke to the sounds of someone fumbling with her bedroom door. She sat up slowly, her mind still groggy with sleep, until a shadowy figure entered her room. Throwing back the covers with a soundless squeal of fright, she poised herself with one knee on the bed and the other foot touching the floor. Her breath caught in her throat when a male voice mumbled curses—a voice that was not her father's.

A match flared. The hurricane lamp cast its glow across the floor.

"Tyler!" she exclaimed over the beat of her pounding heart. "What are you doing in my room?"

"Emma?" he slurred as he took a few unsteady steps toward her. He squinted into the shadowed far corner of the bedchamber where the huge canopied bed loomed in the semi-darkness. "I...I don't know. I must have entered the wrong room."

Son of a bitch, he chastised himself and caught himself as he stumbled over a shoe.

"Well, that's easy enough to believe when you drank enough to drown a horse," she threw at him.

"Madam, I think you may be right." A crooked smile reached his eyes. He leaned forward, then swayed slightly with his effort to peer more closely at her. A vision in sheer chiffon with auburn tresses draped over barely concealed, creamy white breasts met his blurred gaze. He shook his head, but the apparition didn't go away.

Her green eyes sparked as she glared back at him, angry because he had the power to make her heart beat wildly. "I think you'd better leave."

He stood frozen to the spot. His appreciative gaze boldly scanned her sumptuous form. "Emma?" He wavered again. "Do you know what a fetching sight you are in that nightgown?"

"You'd better go before somebody hears you." Her voice came out in a raspy whisper.

He moved another step closer and gazed down into her wide, questioning, incredibly beautiful eyes. *To hell with it*, his mind screamed. *To hell with everything...* His features softened and responded with an equally hoarse voice.

"Ask me to stay. Please, Emma. I want you in my arms. I want to kiss you and never let you go."

Emma scrambled backward across the bed, ignoring the unsettling thrill that raced down her spine. "You have to get out of here—now!" She said it, but it was the last thing she wanted.

He stood at the edge of the bed, his face a constant plane of changes as he stared down.

"I *said* get out of here, Tyler!"

He closed his eyes, pursed his lips and stood quietly before her. When he looked at her again a moment later, he released a heartfelt sigh of defeat. "Such a beautiful face," he whispered. "Dear, sweet Emma. I'd love to stay, but know I must leave."

He turned on unsteady legs and crossed the room. *Don't look back, just look forward.*

Emma watched his retreating form as it neared the door. Her heart splintered into a thousand pieces. *Isn't this what I wanted earlier? Didn't I want him to kiss me, to hold me?* The thoughts raced through her mind. *No! He wants more! He wants...*

She clamped her eyes shut against the conflicting emotions that constricted her chest. It didn't matter! He wanted her, even if it was only for this one night... She couldn't let him leave without at least once feeling his arms around her and his kiss upon her lips.

"Tyler!" His name exploded in the quiet room before she had a chance to pull it back.

He swayed with his hand on the doorknob and didn't dare look back.

He would not, could not ask again, only to be turned away. His eyes closed, his head swirled in a fog—and he waited. An eternity passed before her voice whispered from directly behind him.

"Don't go. I want you to stay."

He kept his eyes closed for a moment longer, willing the effects of the alcohol to leave his brain.

"Please, turn around, Tyler. Stay with me. I need you…"

He swung slowly to face her. His eyes locked with hers. His heart pounded madly. "Are you sure? Once I've got you in my arms, Emma, I won't let you go."

She stepped closer and stared up into his burning gaze. Slowly, her arms encircled his neck. She guided his mouth close to hers. Going on instinct alone now, she raised on tiptoe to fit her body intimately against his. Her answer whispered across his lips. "Stay…"

A muffled groan left Tyler's throat just before his mouth devoured hers. He pulled her against his hard body. "I need you, Emma," he rasped against her silken mouth. "I've needed you for so long."

All inhibitions fled as her body became awash with desire. Their mouths shared the glorious kisses they'd both been denied for too long.

Tyler hands drifted to her buttocks as he coaxed her mouth open once again. Exploring the moist depths within, the sweet taste as her tongue meshed with his as he pulled her firmly against his hardness.

He heard her moan as she pulled away slightly.

"I told you I wouldn't leave," he whispered close. His hands left her body for only as long as it took to shrug off his shirt completely.

Emma stared wide-eyed as he unbuttoned his pants.

"Touch me…"

She continued to stare. He reached for her hand and pressed it against his beating heart.

"Touch me…"

Emma's hesitant fingers explored the warm, lightly furred skin of his chest.

Tyler's eyes closed as her fingertips moved lower and grazed over his belly. His hand found her wrist and gripped it tightly before his gaze burned into hers. His other hand clutched the open waist of his pants. He was hard and throbbing, but… He swallowed and wished his head wasn't so goddamn fuzzy.

"Are you sure?" As difficult as it would be, he would leave if that was what she wanted.

Emma's decision was already made. Her hand kneaded the taut flesh of his shoulders and back. She pressed closer to sprinkle butterfly kisses against his chest. Slim, feminine hands traveled the length of his muscled arms and full, moist lips followed with tantalizing half-bites, half-kisses.

Tyler groaned. His mouth moved quickly to the hollow beneath her ear. His eager hands found the lacy straps of her gown. Slowly, he slid them over her shoulders, following the same path with light, feathery kisses. He tugged at the front of the satiny gown, revealing her breasts. Lowering his head, he kissed one of the pink-tipped mounds as the gossamer material slipped to the floor.

He wanted her. It had been so long since he'd experienced the sensation that throbbed inside him like a building flame. Bracing his feet wide, he swept Emma into his arms, kissed her long and hard and, with two long strides, placed her gently on the bed. He removed his pants with anxious, shaking hands and kicked them away.

Emma stared up at him through shuttered, passion-filled eyes. His body was perfection at its finest. Shuddering at the sight of his boldness, she pushed her initial fear aside. She wanted him beside her. A tremulous smile played about her parted lips as she reached out to beckon him nearer.

Tyler sank onto the bed and gathered her tenderly to his side. They didn't speak. There wasn't a need. They communed as only man and woman can—with their hands, their eyes, their mouths and their bodies. They'd fought their attraction to one another for the last four weeks. Now, with the moment of joining so close at hand—a moment neither thought would ever be—words were insignificant.

She didn't know if he loved her and, at that point, she didn't care. His hands washed over her body with an exquisite slowness and, wherever his palms touched, a trail of heat was left behind. Soon, her entire body was aflame, tumbling her emotions until she clutched frantically at his body, yearning for something she couldn't quite comprehend.

Tyler existed in both heaven and hell at the same moment. It had been too long since his body experienced carnal relief, and the woman in his arms was hot with excitement due to his touch and his touch alone. He couldn't maintain control much longer, yet he knew what the consequences would be if he did not.

He was past caring. His hand left her breast and traveled lower, over the smooth silkiness of her stomach, then slipped between velvet thighs. She froze for a quick, surprised instant, then strained against his hand. Stroking her warm, moist center, her hips swayed with passion against his fingertips. Emma urged him on with eager lips and clutching hands until he could no longer stave off the surging emotions.

Rolling her beneath him, he poised himself on strong arms and stared into the green eyes that so mirrored his own. His lips searched for hers and, as his tongue delved into her mouth, he entered her with the passion of a man totally fixated on the woman beneath him. Her muffled scream reverberated in his mouth, but he was beyond knowing if the cry was one of pleasure or of pain. He continued the slow, rhythmic movements and was rewarded by the tightening of her muscles around him and the sensual rise and fall of her body.

Emma entered a world of skin against skin and tongue against tongue. The initial pain of his entry faded away, only to be replaced by a delicious sensation that grew by leaps and bounds. Instinct demanded she increase the power of her own thrusts, to rise and meet his body, and she waited—waited for something she had never experienced before.

She held her breath. The flicker of heat that suffused the core of her being intensified into a flame. She moaned as an excruciatingly intense inferno exploded and engulfed her entire body. Her breath came in wild gasps, mingled with small cries of ecstasy. It carried her to a high crescendo and then, slowly, the flame flickered to a warm glow. And she returned to a bed and a room and a man.

He heard her groans, and then her cries of fulfillment somewhere in the recesses of his mind. It was the turning point for him, the moment when all reason was lost. He stroked harder, seeking his own release now, and finally spilled into her depths to a rapturous fulfillment.

Like a feather dipping in the soft breeze, they floated back to reality. Tyler rolled carefully from her sweat-slicked body and gathered Emma's silky form into his strong arms. With her head nestled against his shoulder, his breathing finally slowed to a regular rhythm, and hers followed suit.

They lay quietly, their bodies and their fingers entwined in the aftermath of the storm they'd created. Neither knew what to say, so they spoke of nothing. They simply held one another until sleep carried them into a world of blissful contentment that only lovers can share.

* * * * *

She was tucked into the crook of his arm, her back against his chest, her elfin, yet supple body unconsciously seeking his for warmth. Carefully settling his hand against her trim waist, Tyler pulled her against him, relishing the feel of her luscious backside as she snuggled even closer. A soft, contented sigh escaped her lips when he nuzzled her neck and inhaled the clean, perfumed fragrance of her hair.

He would never forget the scent of her hair... He yearned to passionately kiss her mouth once more, but feared waking her. His heart clamped shut against the pain that seared him.

Janie was waiting...his life back home awaited his return.

He stared vacantly into the half-darkened room and came to the conclusion that it would be impossible to act the mere acquaintance in front of her father now.

Quietly, so as not to awaken her, Tyler untangled his limbs from Emma's and slipped from beneath the covers. He stood beside the bed for a moment, stared longingly and wondered if he'd ever see her again.

Would she even care? They'd never spoken of love. It would be better to just leave...

Quietly he gathered his scattered clothing and slipped on his pants. Sheer will was the only thing that got him across the room and soundlessly out the door. It was all he could do not to look back as he pulled it shut and hurried to the guest room. Once inside, he rushed to change.

It could never be. They lived in two different worlds. His was back in the wilds of Minnesota with his family and his daughter. Emma's was in the hustle and bustle of New York. He stared numbly across the room. It simply could never be.

Chapter Nine

☙

Emma drifted toward wakefulness slowly. The sound of chirping birds filtered through an open window, bringing a lazy smile to her lips. Silken arms stretched languidly across the soft pillow as she pondered the feeling of contentment that threaded through her body—and then the events of the night before sifted into her fuzzy brain.

Green eyes widened. She sat up abruptly, then grabbed for the sheet to cover her exposed breasts. A heated flush reddened her smooth features when her gaze settled on the nightgown that lay in a heap on the floor. The telltale ache between her thighs only confirmed she had made love with Tyler.

Sinking back into the pillow, she stared at the ceiling, her cheeks hotter when she remembered the things Tyler had done to her—and how she had asked for more. He'd awoken her sometime during the night with light kisses and hot, searching hands that had moved with a seductive slowness across her stomach. He'd taken her hand in his and guided it to him, showing her the gentle rhythm that resulted in him growing hard again beneath her gentle touch. He'd rolled onto his back, taking her with him and, when neither could contain their need any longer, he'd let her lead the way to another glorious communing.

Emma's stomach muscles clenched with desire. She remembered his tenderness. She remembered her shamelessness. And she remembered the exact moment she knew she loved him without a doubt. The emotion now floated through her body with a happy sigh. Her slender fingers covered her mouth in amazement.

Glancing at the indented spot on the pillow beside hers, she drew the fluffy softness to her nose and breathed in his lingering scent.

The memory of his demanding mouth pressed against her lips and his gentle, calloused hands sliding across her body brought on a rush of liquid desire.

She stretched lazily as her gaze strayed to the window, flitted past the clock on the armoire, and then quickly returned to the brass timepiece. It was a few minutes past eight—the time Tyler had planned to leave.

Leaping from the bed, she grabbed her robe. "Damn!" she muttered as she struggled to get her arm into the sleeve.

He can't be gone—her frightened mind insisted—*not after last night!* She ran to the door, threw it open with a bang and raced down the hall to the guest bedroom.

The door was open to the chamber he should have slept in, but didn't. Emma skidded to a stop in the center of the room. Her chest heaved, more from panic than the exertion of the dash from her bedroom to his. Frantic green eyes darted from the made-up bed, to the empty bureau top, to the vacant corner where he had placed his bags when she showed him to the room the day before. Her throat constricted with dread as she whirled to face the door again.

Voices filtered up through the open window. Spinning again, she rushed across the room, then stiffened when she saw Tyler standing on the cobblestone street below, shaking hands with her father.

Look up! her mind screamed. *Don't go away without even telling me goodbye!*

He climbed into the waiting carriage. She pressed white knuckles to her mouth to keep herself from calling out his name. He never looked back.

Tears slid down her cheeks as the buggy lurched forward and carried him away.

* * * * *

Edward sauntered up the staircase a few minutes later to check on his daughter. Emma was usually up and about by this time of the morning. He'd been totally surprised when she didn't come downstairs to see Tyler off.

He shook his graying head. *I would have thought something might spark between those two.*

Heading down the hall toward Emma's room, he paused when a muffled sob came from the guest room. Glancing through the doorway, the sight that met his gaze made his blood run cold.

Emma huddled against the far wall with her arms wrapped around her robe-covered knees, her face buried in the soft fabric. Her shoulders shook with silent, heart wrenching sobs. Edward rushed forward, knelt before her and reached out tentatively to touch her shoulder.

"Emma? Honey? What are you doing in here? What's wrong?"

She simply continued to weep.

"Emma, tell me what's wrong. You're frightening me."

The breath caught in his throat when she slowly lifted her head and looked up at him through swollen, saturated eyes. Her chin quivered and a new batch of tears streamed down her face.

"Papa…" she whispered through a choked sob "He left…and he never even said goodbye."

Edward cradled her in his strong embrace and absorbed the shuddering sobs that racked her slender body. "Honey, I'm so sorry," he murmured as he gently rocked her. "I didn't know. I didn't understand how you felt."

He continued to hold her until the weeping subsided. Leaning back, he gently cupped her face. His understanding gaze searched her grief stricken eyes. "So, you love him then?"

Emma's quivering lips worked to form words. "Yes…Papa, I do, but now he's gone, so it doesn't matter." She wiped her face with the back of a trembling hand.

"Why didn't you tell him?" he asked softly.

"I…I couldn't. I didn't know how much…not until…I saw him climb into the carriage and leave. It's too late." Her head lolled in abject misery. She turned lifeless eyes upward. "I'll never see him again, will I?"

"Come, Emma." He helped her to her feet. Settling her beneath his arm, he led her back to her room. Easing her into her bed, Edward tucked the blankets around her, and then retrieved a wet cloth from the washstand. He sat quietly while she wiped the tears from her face. His heart ached with his own inability to ease her pain.

"I wish there was something I could do for you." He brushed a kiss across her brow. "I love you, honey."

Her smooth features sagged with exhaustion as she sank back into the pillow with a grief stricken sigh. "There's nothing you can do. He's gone, and I'll never know if he loved me or not. It doesn't matter. It's too late." She closed her eyes and rolled onto her side to face the wall. An awkward silence followed.

Finally, Edward stood and gently brushed the tear-dampened hair from her cheek. "You rest, kitten. We'll talk later. Remember how much I love you."

Edward crossed the room to the door, but paused to gaze over his shoulder. Emma had curled into a fetal position, as if the pose would ward off further pain. His heart broke as he closed the door quietly behind him.

* * * * *

Tyler stared out a grimy window and watched the scenery fly by as the train took him further from New York and closer to Minnesota. He should be excited. But the image of an angelic, sleeping visage in the early hours of the morning would haunt him for a lifetime.

I never should have taken her, he berated himself. But the alcohol and his overwhelming need to hold her had taken all of his restraint. He'd been lost when she asked him to stay.

Now, as the train took him further away from her with every spin of the wheel, his thoughts turned to the long night of lovemaking. Emma had been uninhibited and had even urged him on. She had been a wonderful partner in love.

Tyler tried to recall the exact moment when he'd entered her. What was her reaction? He remembered her muffled cry, but was it a cry of pain or pleasure? Had she been a virgin or not?

Samuel Fontaine's words echoed in his brain, but was the man believable?

Damn! I had such a head full of liquor, I couldn't tell. A part of him hoped that he'd been her first lover, but Tyler seriously doubted that he was. She was simply too willing—and too knowledgeable. He would never know for sure.

He closed his eyes again and slowly rubbed his stubbled face with his hands. The idea of going home was not as appealing as it had been four weeks earlier.

He couldn't look back. He needed to look forward.

* * * * *

The locomotive hissed and spat great billows of steam as it pulled into the Duluth, Minnesota train depot. Grabbing his bag, anxious to be off the rumbling, lurching mass of iron, he was up and moving toward the exit before the train came to a complete stop. His daughter, Janie, was on the other side of the door. He could hardly contain himself, knowing that shortly he'd be able to hold her in his arms.

The conductor cast him an impatient glare as he reached to unlock the iron door. Tyler threw him an equally scathing look in return. He'd had enough of the bouncing train filled with June humidity, of the obese woman beside him who told endless stories about her family, and of the cramped, dirty leather seats. He missed Janie and everyone else at the ranch and just wanted to go home.

The door finally opened. Tyler was the first to step off the train. His weary eyes swept the length of the crowded platform, but didn't see any of his family members. Shouldering his way through the milling throng, he made his way toward the station house to see if any messages awaited him.

"Tyler! Over here!"

He spun at the sound of Cole's voice. Janie raced toward him with arms outstretched. Tyler sank to one knee just as the little girl flung her body into his embrace. He clasped her tightly, loving the feel of someone who was a part of himself. "God, I missed you, Janie…" She buried her face in the crook of his neck. The familiar scent of the little girl's soft, blonde locks reached his nose.

God, it was good to be home.

He watched over the top of his daughter's head as Cole and Carrie worked their way through the crowd with huge smiles of welcome. He stood with Janie still in his arms and reached out to take his brother's hand in his.

"Cole, you are a sight for sore eyes!" Tyler's lips, too, curved in a huge grin as he accepted the firm handshake. A moment later, he wrapped his free arm around his sister's shoulders.

"It's so good to have you back home!" Carrie squeezed his waist tightly in return and batted tears from her eyes. "We've all missed you terribly." She glanced at Janie, then whispered for his ears only. "Especially one of us."

"It's good you're back, Ty," Cole murmured. "It hasn't been the same since you left for New York."

Janie finally loosened her hold on Tyler's neck and patted his shoulder to regain his attention. Tyler met her excited gaze and couldn't imagine any other place he'd rather be.

"Honey, I sure missed you. Did you miss me?" Setting her down, he quickly dug inside his bag. A moment later, he pulled out a package wrapped in brown paper and handed it to his daughter. "Go ahead, honey, open it. It's from a big store in New York called *Woolworth's*. You and I might go to New York someday, and I'll take you there."

Janie slowly pulled the string that held the package closed and unwrapped the parcel. Inside lay a soft, cuddly doll with a mop of red hair.

"Do you like it?" Tyler asked, hoping he'd selected the proper gift. He received his answer in the form of a vigorous nod. She wrapped her tiny arms around his neck once more in another fierce and loving hug.

Cole and Carrie watched the exchange in contented silence. It had been a long, sad month for Janie. She'd existed with a total disinterest in every idea the family came up with to distract her from Tyler's absence. As the days and weeks passed, her disposition had only worsened—something Tyler need never know. He'd needed the time away.

Tyler stood and gathered up one of his bags as Cole reached for the other. "Let's get out of here. I've had enough of train stations to last me a lifetime."

The cheerful group left the depot platform and headed for the carriage, and all the while Tyler rambled on about his trip, more animated than they'd seen him in a long time.

Cole and Carrie's eyes met behind Tyler's back as he lifted Janie into the waiting buggy. Hopefully, his mood would last. It seemed that the old Tyler had returned. Only time would tell if the change would be permanent or not.

* * * * *

That evening, the entire family celebrated Tyler's return amidst continual discussion about the sawmill. Mamie outdid herself by preparing many of his favorite dishes. When Tyler pushed himself away from the table, he groaned with pleasure and rubbed his full stomach.

"Mamie, not even the fanciest restaurant in New York can hold a candle to your cooking. I'm totally miserable."

Her round cheeks dimpled in a smile as she paused behind him to lovingly pat his shoulder. "Tyla, it be a pleasure cookin' for you—and knowin' someone appreciates what I do 'round here. Why, your two brothers, they do nothin' but complain every time I put food on the suppa table. Yessiree!"

Trevor jumped up, his face twisted in a comical display of outrage and grabbed Mamie's bulk when she sashayed past him. "Mamie, I'll never complain again. You're the best cook in northern Minnesota. Why, just feel right here. Look at how you're expanding my waistline."

He grabbed her hand and held it against his flat stomach as the group around the table burst into laughter. Mamie smacked the middle Wilkins brother on the shoulder.

"Aw, go on with you! There ain't got an ounce of fat on that body of yours and you knows it! You be tall and porkchop lean like them brothers of yours. You ain't foolin' no one."

Trevor seated himself again as Mamie poured coffee. With a raised eyebrow, he leaned back in his chair and met his eldest brother's gaze.

"Enough about the sawmill—let's hear some more about New York. Too bad this new venture with Edward Sanders didn't work out."

With the mention of Edward's name came a vision of Emma's red hair and sultry green eyes. Tyler pushed the image aside with decided difficulty and brought his attention back to the conversation at hand.

"Edward Sanders is very forthright and honest. I think we'll eventually be able to forge some sort of business relationship. For the time being though, as I said earlier, the timing just wasn't right."

"I just can't understand why this Sanders won't go to some other mill for his iron," Trevor stated the easy solution to the problem. "Why is he so intent on buying exclusively from Fontaine Ironworks?"

"You have to understand what kind of man Sanders is," Tyler replied. "He's been a close, personal friend of John Fontaine's for years. He's not the type to walk out on their business relationship without discussing the reason of his forfeiture to another company." He stifled a yawn and continued. "And, with John conveniently out of the country, Edward feels he must wait."

"Well, I guess you do have to admire the man's loyalty," his brother agreed, however grudgingly.

Tyler nodded. "There's a lot more involved here than a simple business arrangement, Trevor. It seems that John's oldest son, Samuel, might be embezzling from the company. Edward feels obligated to protect his friend's interests until John returns from Europe. Samuel is the operating manager of the mill in his father's absence—something both Edward and I feel Samuel deliberately orchestrated in the first place. Samuel now has free rein over the company funds and operating procedures."

"He must be quite an ass to do that to his own father," Trevor grumbled.

Tyler nodded his agreement. "I respect Edward's business ethics and really don't want to go elsewhere for our shipping supplier. He's already put a lot of thought and hard work into the proposition and deserves some time to straighten out this mess." Tyler's shoulders lifted in a tired shrug. "In truth, I didn't want to make the decision on my own to go elsewhere."

Trevor eyed his brother with an admiring glance. Tyler had always been the cautious type and ever watchful over their best interests. Since their father's death, the eldest Wilkins son had taken it upon himself to oversee their financial future. Money accounts had been set up so each of them would be independently wealthy in their own right, even their little sister, Carrie. Now, the four of them worked together to increase both their individual and cumulative wealth via the family logging business. The fact that they all lived together in the same, sprawling ranch house only strengthened their commitment to one another.

Sara had been surprised by their obvious family unity. When she'd married Tyler, the question of where the two of them would live never came up. She'd embraced them all as her extended family. When Janie was born a year later, the family bond deepened even further.

"So," he continued his questioning, "what did you do for entertainment while in New York? Did you have a chance to enjoy a little of the nightlife?" His eyes twinkled into his brother's. "What about the women?"

The always observant Cole noticed a sudden flash of remembrance—or was it longing—that softened his eldest brother's rugged countenance momentarily.

"It seems the citizens of New York are hell-bent on enjoying whatever the city has to offer—and into the wee hours of the night as well. I've never been forced to make up so many excuses just to escape another evening out. It's definitely a different world than the one we live in."

"And what about the women?" Cole's repeat of Trevor's earlier question was prompted by the fleeting look he's seen on his brother's face.

Tyler paused to choose his words carefully before replying. "I really didn't meet many women while there. Most of the introductions were social. Edward's daughter, Emma, seemed to be pleasant enough. She reminded me of you, Carrie." He smiled at his sister. "She's very interested in the family shipping business and has notions of continuing in her father's stead when he's gone. You two are about the same age, I think. You'd get along well. In fact," he teased, "if we were to put the two of you together in the same room, you'd create a formidable force for anyone to deal with."

Tyler promptly changed the subject to New York City's historical sights, but his evasiveness when it came to Edward Sanders' daughter did not go unnoticed by Cole.

"I forgot to mention that I offered jobs to one of the Fontaine mill workers and his wife," Tyler continued, interrupting Cole's train of thought. "They accepted immediately and can't wait to get out of New York. I hope to see them arrive sometime in September."

"What kind o' *job* offers?" Mamie questioned immediately with heavy suspicion. "We always got room here for one more man, but what would his woman be doin'?"

"Helping around the house," Tyler replied promptly. Inwardly, he cringed as he awaited her reply. He hadn't planned on Mamie discovering so quickly that there would be another woman entering her domain.

"I don't need no help."

"Mamie..."

"Said, I don't need no help."

Tyler took a deep breath and continued. "So, what was I supposed to do? Tell her husband to leave her in New York? Come on! These people were in dire straits. Dougan O'Malley makes little or nothing in wages. He's honest and hardworking. We need his type on the ranch."

"So he be needin' the job and maybe you needs him. But you got other men workin' in the loggin' camp who got wives, and none o' them is takin' over *my* house."

Tyler sighed. "Come on, Mamie. I thought you could use the help. You work too hard. You'll like Katy. I told her about you, and she's most anxious to have you as her supervisor."

The pout on Mamie's face immediately lifted. "You mean I's gonna be her boss?"

"You're the only one around here who knows the complete workings of the household." He nudged Carrie's knee beneath the table. His sister cast a discreet, yet knowing glance in his direction. "You'll love her, Mamie. Her house was spotless when I visited it. She also said that she couldn't imagine someone actually running a household as big as this single-handedly. She can't wait to meet you and learn all that you can teach her."

The praise worked. Mamie's chin came up in a show of pride. "Yas, I do have lots to teach her at that." She passed by Tyler's chair and patted him on the shoulder again. "Boy, you do me proud with your goodness. Iffn' that woman has a hard time, we'll just have to find a little patience with the poor thing." The old Negress turned away.

Carrie leaned over to whisper close to her brother's ear. "You're good. She never had a chance."

* * * * *

The conversation continued late into the evening. Janie slept nestled within her father's arms.

"Well, it's getting pretty late," Tyler finally gave into his own fatigue. "I'd better get her to bed."

He stood carefully so as not to awaken his daughter, then bid his brothers and sister goodnight and trudged up the staircase. Entering Janie's room, he crossed to the bed and tucked her gently beneath the covers. Straightening, he studied her cherished features.

She looks so much like her mother. A heavy sigh lifted his chest. He bent to press one final kiss on Janie's forehead, then left the room and slowly closed the door behind him.

He shuffled toward the master bedroom he once shared with Sara. The emptiness — the loneliness — surrounded him when he entered the room. He'd managed to stave off the feelings since returning home, but they crept into his being now and wrapped around his heart. Crossing to an overstuffed chair near the window, he sank into it — not yet willing to climb into bed alone.

His gaze stared into nothingness, wondering what his homecoming would've been like if Sara were still alive. Closing his eyes, his mind conjured up a vision of her face, flushed with the excitement at his return, then later, provocative and filled with the promise of what was to come when they were alone within these four walls.

He grasped at an invisible thread and held on until the burst of pain subsided. Being home, being back in this room after a month's time, was worse than he'd ever imagined it could be.

Life had dealt him an awful hand two years ago, but he couldn't go on like this. It was time to move on, time to steer himself in a more positive direction.

His thoughts slowly shifted to Emma and the weeks spent in New York. *Has she thought of me at all?*

"Of course, she's thought of you, you idiot," he muttered into the darkness. "You got drunk, climbed into her bed, had a walloping good time, and then left without even saying goodbye."

His thoughts tempered a bit. He'd been so drawn to her. Why did he long for her as he had for no other woman since Sara's death?

Tyler shook his head. He'd almost made it through that final week without touching her, but that last night his fledgling control was stretched to the breaking point. But could he really blame his high consumption of alcohol as the reason behind why he finally took her? Or, more realistically, had he simply suffered an unconscious need to hold a woman again, a woman who meant something to him, and finally move on with his life?

A woman who means something to me...

The thought came back to haunt him. *What the hell is it? Loneliness, lust? Love...?* Tyler knew one thing for sure—those four weeks in New York with Emma were the happiest he'd experienced since Sara's death.

Too exhausted to further battle his emotions at that point, he forced himself out of the chair and crossed to the bed, leaving a trail of clothes in his wake. He dropped down onto the soft surface. Lying alone in the darkness, he wondered if he would ever lose the sadness that followed him throughout his days.

Chapter Ten
August 31, 1880
New York City

※

Emma entered her bedroom, crossed to the pink ceramic bowl that rested on the wash counter and dipped a washrag into the tepid water. She dragged the cloth across her brow, and then down into the opening at the bodice of her cotton dress. A groan of pleasure escaped her throat at the small relief the dampened rag offered.

August was quickly waning and, hopefully, so would the string of dreadfully hot days. She looked forward to dusk, when she could retire to the terrace and bask in the cool night air as it flitted across her skin. The summer heat, combined with the depression she'd not been able to shake since Tyler left, had brought Emma to her wits end. It had been nearly three months since he'd walked out of her life—and she still couldn't force the image of his face from her mind.

Her slippered feet padded back across the Aubusson carpet. Settling onto the window seat, she blinked back the seemingly endless flow of tears. He was gone from her life—but she would love him forever.

Emma reached for a small wooden bird that perched atop the windowsill and studied the piece's intricate carving and elaborate workmanship. Tyler had purchased it for her during his last week in New York on one of the many days they'd toured the city. They'd strolled through an open market until coming to a table of beautiful, handcrafted wooden items, each created by the gnarled hands of a wizened old Indian brave. The man's body was small and shriveled, yet he sat cross-legged on the ground with an aura of what he'd once been still surrounding him. Emma sighed sadly as she recalled the strange afternoon...

Tyler stood quietly, ever patient while Emma perused the objects on the table, as well as the ones spread out across the ground. His own interest was piqued, however, when his eye caught a small, wooden figurine that sat among others like it on a brightly colored blanket. Meeting the old man's piercing gaze, he silently requested permission to examine the carving. The old warrior nodded his approval and spoke in broken English.

"It is the loon," he said, proud eyes never leaving Tyler's.

"Yes, I know. There are many of these birds on the lakes near my home."

Emma watched quietly as Tyler's gentle, almost worshipful hands clasped the carved figure. He examined the intricate detail before his gaze returned to the Indian's. "You've captured his spirit very well. It's beautiful."

The old man's lined and weathered features remained the same, but his eyes now held a different light than of a moment earlier. "I once sang like the loon. I once flew free like my spirit friend." His gnarled fingers formed a fist. He gently held it to his breast. "I still carry him here in my heart."

"It's a very honorable spirit you carry with you." Tyler's eyes rested on the small, broken man. He glanced down at the figurine in his hand, and then back at the Indian's fiery gaze again. "I'd like to carry this spirit back to my home with me. It can be near the lakes and forests where it belongs. May I buy it from you?"

The old Indian straightened, clasped his knees with steady hands and closed his eyes. Emma waited breathlessly for him to speak.

It was a full minute before he surveyed his surroundings again as if seeing them for the first time. He then focused on Tyler's rugged features once more. "Take the loon, my friend. Take the spirit home. I will not accept payment if you will do this thing for me."

Tyler reached down to grasp the noble man's wrinkled hand. Rheumy black eyes locked with the younger man's green ones in a shared experience that excluded all others around them.

"The spirit will go home. I'll see to it in your honor, sir."

Emma strained to hear Tyler's quiet words, but he placed his hand on her elbow and led her away before she could question him about the bizarre exchange. The old man watched them depart through clouded eyes.

The couple had reached the corner of the marketplace before Emma was able to grab Tyler's arm and halt his determined march from the square.

"I can't believe he just gave that carving to you. What happened back there?"

"One second, Emma. I'll explain shortly." He grasped her elbow again and led her to where their coach and driver waited. She watched in amazement when Tyler handed the man a wad of bills, even more dumbfounded by the words that came out of his mouth.

"I want you to go to the middle of the marketplace and find an old Indian peddler whose wares are spread on a brightly colored blanket." Tyler pulled the wooden loon from his pocket. "I want you to purchase another one of these carvings—and make sure you give him all the money."

The driver shrugged, took the money and left to do as Tyler asked. Tyler then handed Emma up into the coach.

"What's going on?" she asked. "That's far too much money for even two of those carvings."

Once he was settled beside her, he finally answered.

"That old Indian back there was once a proud man who lived freely on the land he loved. He cared for and protected his family until most likely the white man forced him from his home. Now, he sells his handmade wares in order to survive. He's alone, Emma, except for the spirit he carries within him."

"Spirit?" Her brow furrowed with her level of confusion.

"All Indian braves seek a 'spirit' when they reach manhood. They derive strength and direction from it throughout their lives until the day they die. This man's spirit is the loon. It's a beautiful bird and hard to describe if you've never seen one or heard its cry." He paused for a moment as he struggled to find words that would help her understand. "Emma, that old man is dying. I'm taking his spirit home because he can't go there himself. Do you understand now?"

Her eyes swam with tears as the full impact of his words finally sank in. "You live in such a completely different world than me. What a wonderful thing to do for him. How did you know he wanted you to take his 'spirit' home? I think I understand what you're doing, but...how did you know?"

"I can't really explain it. It was just a feeling. I've come in contact with many of his people back home. Through the years, I've learned their customs. Most people think the Indians are savages out to kill every white man, but it really isn't like that at all. They're just protecting their land and their homes from acquisition by the federal government as civilization spreads westward." A gentle smile touched his mouth as he glanced down at the glittering green orbs before him. "Indians are a mystic people. How that old man got his message across to me so quickly, I'll never quite understand. But I do know that, in some unspoken way, he asked me to bring him home so he could rest in peace."

He rolled the carved loon in his hands, contemplating the life of the old Indian—a life the proud and distinguished man would never know again. Finally, he placed the carving back in his pocket.

The driver returned a short time later with another wooden loon and handed it to Tyler. He paused though, before climbing up onto the front seat. "Mr. Wilkins, it was the oddest thing. I just gotta tell ya. As I walked away from that old man, he called out to me. He said, *'Tell the keeper of my spirit to think of me when he hears the loon sing.'*" He scratched his balding head as he moved to scramble up onto the front seat of the coach. "Darndest thing I ever heard tell."

Tyler and Emma exchanged knowing glances.

"See, Emma, you just have to believe."

"I've never experienced anything like that in my life. He knows you sent the driver to buy the other loon, doesn't he?"

"Oh, yes, he knows." He eyed her closely, and then reached for her hand. He placed the second loon in her tiny palm. "Here, this one is for you to keep. Consider it a thank-you for bringing me here in the first place." He wrapped her slender fingers around the figurine. "Now you have a 'spirit' too, and, every time you look at it, you'll be reminded of that proud old man."

Emma didn't think so. She knew that every time she looked at the carving, she would think of the kind, gentle man who had given it to her...

Now, weeks later, as she studied the little wooden bird in her hand, she knew she'd been right. The carving would always remind her of Tyler. Once again, a flood of tears ran down her cheeks.

* * * * *

A week later, Emma reluctantly dined at a posh new restaurant with her father. He was worried about her. Since Tyler's departure, Emma remained depressed, pale and disinterested in everything around her. Tonight was the first time in weeks that she'd even left the house.

Edward sat making small talk with his daughter when a business associate approached their table. He was both relieved and irritated at the same time. Adam Tinker was a known gossip, but manners were manners. He forced a sick smile to his lips and greeted the gentleman. "Hello, Adam. It's nice to see you again."

"Edward, it's been awhile! Miss Sanders, you look beautiful as always." He took Emma's hand and kissed the back of it.

She smiled politely before pulling her fingers from his grasp and tucking them securely into her lap.

"It's been weeks since we last met up, Edward. I imagine things have slowed down a wee bit since the halt on that project with the fellow from Minnesota."

Emma's head jerked up at the reminder. Edward gritted his teeth. The ingrate had no way of knowing, of course, that even Tyler's name had become taboo.

"I still have all my other customers to take care of." Edward was already regretting the man's presence, knowing that Adam was only fishing for information to spread to the next table.

"Speaking of your other customers, are you still doing business with the Fontaines? I heard just this morning that the mill is in quite a bit of financial trouble. Samuel has dug himself in pretty deep. With his father out of the country, some vendors are stopping shipments due to lack of payment. Did you hear about that?"

Edward had heard murmurings in the past week about the very same thing, but wasn't about to add fuel to the fire. "I'm sure it's all speculation," he replied. "You know how people are. There isn't much going on in the city lately, so they make up something to get tongues wagging. With Samuel testing the 'manufacturing waters' for the first time, it gives everyone something to ruminate on." He hoped his comments would end the conversation. Apparently, Adam took the hint. It took him only a few moments more to say his goodbyes and move on to another party seated across the room.

"What was that all about?" Emma sat forward in her chair, showing interest in the conversation for the first time that evening. "Is it true? Is the Fontaine mill in trouble?"

"I'm really hoping it *is* just speculation, Em. For John's sake. But I don't think so. I've been trying to keep an eye on the situation. It looks like the mill is headed for big trouble. There's nothing I can do for John at this point, though. It was his decision to put Samuel in charge." He ran a hand through his thinning gray hair and sighed. "Lord, I hope my letter reaches him soon."

* * * * *

The news broke three days later. Fontaine Ironworks closed down. Two hundred and fifty men lost their jobs, and Samuel Fontaine was nowhere to be found. Vendors filed liens at City Hall against any impending profit and the story was splashed across every newspaper in the city.

Emma closed the morning paper, sick at heart for all the displaced workers who had families to feed, hoping John Fontaine did not have all his money invested in that one venture. She couldn't help but wonder how long it would be before her father heard from John or Jacob. And more importantly at this point, where Samuel had disappeared to.

She had been right about him all along. Now she wished that she'd risked her reputation that night and exposed Samuel for what he truly was. As it stood, the Fontaines could lose everything.

Edward entered the sitting room in search of his daughter. He spied the paper on the table before her and saw the concern in her green eyes.

"It's terrible, Papa. What do you think is going to happen now?"

"Hopefully, John will get home soon and straighten out this mess. If Samuel reappears though, I'll be hard-pressed not to physically harm him myself. I don't know what he was thinking. Tyler was right about him, and so were you. I just wished I had listened to the both of you."

Emma rose from her seat and laid a comforting hand on her father's arm. "Papa, you're a wonderful friend to John. Don't blame yourself."

Edward pulled her into his arms and silently gave thanks for his own business acumen. Still worried about his friend, he left for his office.

* * * * *

Emma dallied about the house that morning but by late afternoon, the idleness wore on her nerves. She stepped out onto the back veranda and glanced in the direction of the stables, thinking she should walk down to the building and check on her horse. It had been weeks since she'd even taken an afternoon ride and felt slightly guilty for having put her life on hold for so long. Jim had exercised the big white mare and she owed him a personal thank-you for attending to Bonne.

The smell of fresh hay surrounded her as she entered the cool building. Strolling past the empty stalls and not finding Jim anywhere, she headed in the direction of the estate's small pasture. Lost in thought within the quiet surroundings, she was taken completely by surprise when a strong arm snaked around her waist from behind and a sweaty hand clamped over her mouth. She was yanked into the empty box as she clawed at the suffocating hand that tightened over her lips. Any attempt to scream for help was useless, so she lifted a foot and brought it back with ferocious intent. An angry oath hissed beside her ear as she hit her mark. Still, her captor refused to loosen his grip. Her attacker pulled her into the far corner of the stall before he whirled her around. A cruel hand still covered her mouth.

Emma's eyes widened in horrified shock.

Samuel!

Fear curled through her belly.

"I was beginning to think you'd given up riding forever," he sneered. "I've waited two days for you to come out of the house." He pressed her further into the corner in an attempt to halt her struggle, then leered down into her frightened eyes. "I was almost hoping you wouldn't come out today. I had planned a little visit to your room tonight."

Her heart lurched. She struggled to keep her body from trembling, but to no avail.

"Are you cold, Emma? My, and it's been so warm out, too. Hell, maybe we just need to warm you up a bit." He slammed her down into the bed of soft straw, flung himself across her body and sneered into her pale face. "This is where you belong, Emma. Beneath a man." He shoved his groin against her pelvis. Emma shrieked into his hand.

"Were you under Wilkins like this?"

She shook her head, her eyes pleading to be released.

"No? Well, too bad for him, that arrogant bastard. He ruined me, Emma. Because of him, I lost everything. He pulled out of the deal when I needed him the most. Were you in on it, too?"

She denied his assumption with a groan, which caused Samuel to press his hand even tighter over her mouth.

"Don't lie to me, you bitch! I saw the two of you together more than once. Did you go whining to him about the night of the reception, thinking he would be your knight in shining armor?" His eyes took on a devious, feral gleam. "He's not here now though, is he? And, since I can't bring him down, I've decided that you will pay the debt for the both of you. What have I got to lose anymore? I have no business—no friends. The two of you managed to take away everything I ever had."

Emma's eyes widened in disbelief. In his twisted mind, Samuel had managed to lay the blame on her and Tyler for all his own transgressions. Even more frightening, his warped sense of justice would allow him to make her pay.

His hand left her mouth. In the split second it took for him to move his lips closer to hers, Emma gasped for air, turned her head away and screamed before he smothered her terror with his own mouth. His groping hands made his intent all too clear. She bucked beneath him and beat at his shoulders.

A muffled thud echoed around her.

Samuel's body tensed in pain as he rolled away. Unbelievably, Jim stood above them, a shovel raised and ready for a second blow if needed. Emma scrambled from Samuel just as he rose to his knees. Her trembling hand stifled the sobs that clogged her throat.

"Miss Emma, you all right?" Jim's frightened eyes darted from Samuel to hers. "You get away from here! Please, Miss Emma, go now!"

"Jim," she sobbed. "Come with me!"

Samuel rose slowly, his eyes never leaving the stable hand or the shovel. Emma's instincts told her to run for help, but her legs were too frozen with fear.

The three of them stood in the quiet of the barn, unsure of what to do next. Suddenly, Samuel sprang in Jim's direction. The younger man swung the shovel again, but Samuel was ready for it this time. He raised his arm to fend off the blow, then knocked the shovel free of the boy's grasp. Grabbing the front of Jim's shirt, he flung the stable hand against the side of the stall.

"You little bastard! I'll teach you," Samuel seethed and pummeled the boy's midsection.

Emma frantically sought something to stop the abuse. Her gaze settled on the shovel. Racing to it, she snatched it up and swung ferociously at Samuel's back. "Samuel!" she screamed. "Stop or you'll kill him!"

She kept up her attack, making contact with his body on every stroke, and, finally, Samuel fell to his knees, clasping his head. They both panted hard from the exertion. Their hate-filled gazes locked as Jim's body crumpled to the straw-covered ground.

Samuel's eyes took on the same sadistic, feral gleam as he staggered to his feet. Emma gripped the shovel ready to swing again just as a horse thundered up the driveway toward the open door of the barn. A piercing scream for help left her throat.

"This isn't over by any means, you slut. Someday you'll be totally alone, and you'll pay." His battered body staggered in the direction of the back door. A moment later, he was gone.

Emma dropped the shovel and hurried to kneel beside Jim's writhing body in the corner of the stall. She helped him to a sitting position just as her father ran through the front entrance of the barn.

"Emma! Where are you?" His voice rose with fear. "Emma!"

"Papa! Back here! Hurry!"

He bounded into the stall, then stopped short when he saw his daughter's disheveled state and the injured Jim in her arms.

"Thank God you came! Samuel was here and..." She choked back a sob. "He tried to...hurt both of us. Jim hit him with the shovel, and now he's hurt!"

"Miss Em, I'm...fine," Jim mumbled. "When I saw that man and what he was doing to you...I grabbed the shovel." He looked into her eyes and pleaded for forgiveness. "I'm just sorry I didn't get here sooner."

Edward assisted the boy to his feet. Jim bent at the waist, clutched his ribs to ease his pain.

"You need to see a doctor, boy," Edward stated with a worried frown.

"I'm...fine, Mr. Sanders. It's...Miss Emma I'm worried about."

Edward's frantic gaze swept his daughter's trim form. His eyes turned to stone when they settled on her tangled hair and the torn bodice of her dress. An unspoken question rested in his gaze.

Emma opened her mouth to reassure him, but the words became as hazy as the spots that formed before her eyes. Her world slowed as her father's arms reached out. Just before everything went black, his muffled gasp of alarm echoed in her ears as his hands caught her.

* * * * *

"Emma, wake up. Come on now, young lady. Concentrate on opening your eyes."

Her sluggish mind struggled to obey. It took a huge effort to lift her lids. She lay in her own bed and the strange voice belonged to Dr. Benton, the man who'd taken care of her since she was a little girl. He sat on a chair beside her and smiled down at her over the rim of his glasses.

"Well, young lady, it's nice of you to rejoin us. You had me wondering there for a while if you were ever going to wake up today."

She blinked—and suddenly remembered events of the afternoon flooded her mind.

"What happened? Did I faint?" A quizzical frown furrowed her brow. "I did faint, didn't I?"

The old doctor reached over to pat her arm. "Yes, you did—and almost gave your father a heart attack in the process. How do you feel?"

"I'm all right, I guess. How is Jim faring?"

"He's fine. He'll be rather sore for the next week, judging by the color of his bruises, but nothing is broken. He took quite a beating, Emma." He patted her arm again. "He explained to your father and me what happened. Jim arrived just in time, didn't he?"

Emma's face flushed hotly even though this man was a doctor and had personally attended her throughout her entire life. She swallowed for composure before speaking. "Yes, he did. Thank God it's over." She closed her eyes for a moment against a sudden bout of queasiness.

Dr. Benton stood and poured a glass of water. "Here, drink this." He sat in the chair again and leaned forward to rest his forearms on his knees. "Emma, as your doctor, I need to ask you something else of a personal nature." His questioning gaze held hers.

Emma sat up straighter, confused by his words and his actions.

"Emma...when was your last monthly time?" He kept his eyes on her face as he asked the question.

She shook her head in total bewilderment. "What does that have to do with today's events?"

He reached for her hand, clasped it between his warm ones and continued. "I examined you for broken bones, felt along your ribs for any bruises and prodded your stomach." He sucked in a breath. "I'm quite sure, Emma, that you are in your first three months of pregnancy. That's probably the reason why you fainted today, combined of course with the traumatic events you experienced."

Her mind went blank.

Pregnant?

She sagged against the pillow. She'd been queasy in the mornings and had even emptied her stomach a few times. She'd also been overly emotional, terribly fatigued during July and August, and had missed her monthly flow twice — but attributed the symptoms to Tyler's leaving and the hot days of summer.

But, it wasn't because he'd left and it wasn't the weather. It was because she was pregnant — with his baby...

"I guess your silence means you know what I'm talking about." Dr. Benton sighed heavily. "Please understand that I'm not judging your morals. I'm just concerned with your overall health."

Her gaze strayed to the small wooden loon that sat on the windowsill. Thoughts of Tyler and the night they shared sifted through her mind. The repercussions of their actions slammed into her chest. She was going to have his baby.

Her hesitant gaze found the kindly doctor's again. "Yes, Dr. Benton, there is every possibility that I'm pregnant. I'm sure you're right."

"You need to discuss this with the baby's father before too much longer," he stated firmly. "And you need to make your father aware of it. There are plans to be made."

"I will talk to Papa today. But, as far as the baby's father is concerned, he won't be told. He made it clear he doesn't want me." The last few words were laced with pain and accompanied by a quivering chin.

Dr. Benton's shoulders fell with a heavy sigh. Emma was a beautiful young woman who clearly was being torn apart by the rejection of a man she'd given herself to freely. He'd done his part. How Emma handled the situation was out of his hands.

Gathering up his medical bag and supplies, he explained the need to set regular appointments to keep watch over the progression of her pregnancy. He reminded her once more to talk to her father, then slowly closed the door behind him as he left the room.

Emma left the bed and crossed to the window seat. Bewildered green eyes scanned the front yard of her home. The last time she'd seen Tyler, he'd entered a coach that took him out of her life forever and away from the memory of a beautiful night—the night when the baby she now carried was conceived.

Her eyes fluttered shut. If only the child had been conceived in love...

Her hand lowered to her slightly rounded stomach. Pregnant! She had never even given it a thought after he left.

Reaching for the wooden loon, she clutched it to her heart. Would he even care? A foolish question. Of course he would. Tyler was a kind and gentle man, the type to take care of his responsibilities. His innate wholesome character would demand that he love this baby.

But can he love me? She returned the loon to the sill with a heavy heart. The decision was in her hands.

He would never know. She didn't want to be in his life just because of some sense of responsibility he'd feel toward her and the baby. If she told him now, she'd never know how he truly felt about her, and Emma couldn't live with that. She would love the child and do well by it on her own.

She would be the talk of the city's gossipmongers—a single, pregnant woman who refused to tell anyone who the father was. *It's my mistake—not the baby's. I'll get past the gossip.* It was all she could do.

Emma stood, took a deep breath and crossed to her bedroom door. She was scared to death of what her father's reaction would be, but keeping the secret would do no good—for either of them. She swallowed down her own shock at her wanton actions of nearly three months ago and willed herself to continue downstairs to talk to Edward.

* * * * *

"What do you mean you're not going to tell him!" The words exploded from Edward's mouth as he paced back and forth between Emma and the fireplace. "That's one of the stupidest things I've ever heard! If Tyler is the father, then he should own up to his responsibilities!"

The discussion had been going on for the last twenty minutes. Up to this point, Edward had been surprisingly calm. He'd handled the news of his unwed daughter's pregnancy with grace and compassion. When he asked what her plans were, however, the dam burst.

Emma pressed her fingers to her temples, knowing that if she lost her patience now, she'd never be able to sway him.

"Please quit pacing and just sit down and listen to what I have to say."

Edward tossed her an angry glare, opened his mouth once more, and then thought better of it. He dropped into the chair directly across from her and waited silently for her to speak.

"Papa, please understand how I feel. From the first time I met Tyler in this very room, something happened to me. I just didn't know what it was—that I had fallen in love with him—until the night before he left."

A vision of his brokenhearted daughter on that long ago morning flitted through Edward's mind. He believed her beyond a doubt.

"I asked him to stay with me that last night. I think the amount of alcohol the two of you consumed throughout dinner was probably the reason he accepted so readily."

A stab of guilt pierced Edward's heart for the part he had unwittingly played in his daughter's current situation. He opened his mouth to speak, but she held up her hand and continued.

"You have to understand that, even if I love him still, I don't think the feeling is reciprocated."

"Your mother and I didn't—"

"I know you and Mama tried hard to have a normal life. And I know the two of you loved each other only as friends do. But don't you see? I can't have that kind of relationship with my husband. I want a deeper love than that—the kind of marriage I know is possible. Tyler never once alluded to the fact that he might truly care for me. If he's forced to accept me now as his wife—because of the baby—I will never know if he could've loved me for *me*. I'll never know if he would have come back. I don't want him to feel just responsibility toward me, Papa. Can't you understand that?"

Her father's lack of interruption throughout her long explanation filled Emma with nothing short of amazement. Feeling more confident, she rose to look out the window. "You know that if Tyler were to find out about the baby, he would do what is right—because that's the type of man he is." She hesitated, took a deep breath and went on. "I want to keep this from him. He left, Papa, without even looking back."

Edward sat in the chair, studying the straight line of her back. He loved Emma more than anything in the world. Because of it, he had to do what was right, no matter how difficult.

While Dr. Benton attended her earlier, Edward took the opportunity to talk with Jim about that afternoon's episode. When the boy spoke of Samuel's last threat to his daughter, Edward had made a decision. She needed to be hidden some place out of harm's way until Samuel could be found. She was in real danger, and the thought made his stomach turn.

"Come here and sit down, Em." The pleading look in her eyes tore at his heart. He reached out to take her hand in a gentle grip when she sat beside him. "Honey, I do understand how you feel.

But do you honestly think you're being fair to Tyler? He has a right to know that he's going to be a father."

She opened her mouth to object, but he squeezed her hand to silence her.

"No, let me have my turn to speak. I love you. I respect your opinion. In fact, I'd probably agree with you and just let it be done, but there are other factors to deal with. Jim informed me about Samuel's threat to you. Both you and I know we can't give him the chance to hurt you again. He *will* be back."

"And I can just stay here in the house and not go out alone. Surely he'll be caught soon and things will return to normal—or at least as normal as they can be until the baby is born."

"Emma, he hid on our property for two days and we didn't even know it! What if he were to get into the house when you're home alone? Are you willing to risk the baby's life and your own?" Again, he refused to give her a chance to speak. "Well, I'm not. You are too dear to me. I refuse to give that madman another chance to hurt you. I'm sorry to go against your will, but in the morning I'm going to send Tyler a telegram telling him of the pregnancy—and informing him that you'll be arriving in Minnesota within the week."

She was out of the chair and on her feet before the last words left Edward's mouth. Never had he seen such anger in her gaze before—anger directed at him.

"How dare you plan out my life for me?" Her green eyes glittered dangerously. "Do you think I want to be some sort of excess baggage Tyler accidentally left in New York? Do you think I want to show up on his doorstep, pregnant and looking like I need someone to care for me? I can just hear the conversation. 'Please take care of me, Mr. Wilkins. After all, you jumped in bed with me and had a smashing good time between my legs, so now it's time to pay up!'"

"Emma!" Edward was more shocked at her choice of words than at her outburst. He stood quickly. "This is for your own safety! Can't you see that? You need to be away from here as soon as possible. Tyler is your baby's father—so what better place to send you? Samuel will never find you if you move that far away. Being with Tyler is far safer than here in New York."

He reached out to clasp her arms in a gentle hold, hurt beyond belief when she tried to break free. "Honey, God knows I'll miss you terribly. But the threat Samuel poses cannot be ignored." His hands fell to his sides again. "I'll be sending that telegram in the morning. If you feel you must stay angry with me, then so be it, but I will not leave you in harm's way. That's the end of it."

Emma searched his familiar face that seemed older now than of an hour ago. "Papa, please don't do this to me." The tears rolled down her cheeks. "Please don't send me away—especially to Tyler."

"It's the only recourse I have, honey. I will not let the people in this city shred your reputation. And I will *not* allow Samuel another opportunity. Besides, Tyler needs to know he's going to be a father."

Blinded by tears, she whirled and ran from the room. Edward felt the traitor. He knew in his heart though, that he would stick to his decision. She and the baby must be protected from Samuel Fontaine, and he couldn't do it here in New York.

He crossed to the mahogany writing desk, pulled out his personal stationery and took pen in hand. Sinking down into the swivel chair with a tired sigh, he stared at the white surface of the paper. He would be at the telegraph office in the morning. He had to believe that Tyler would accept his proposition, especially with a baby on the way. If not, he would force the issue. Emma's safety remained uppermost in his mind.

He sighed heavily once more. Hopefully, the love she held for Tyler would help carry them both through the storm that was sure to follow.

Edward dipped the pen into the inkwell and sealed his daughter's fate.

Chapter Eleven

ಸಾ

Tyler sat atop his black steed as it cantered past the house. His sagging shoulders gave away the fatigue of many hours spent in the saddle to the north end of the Wilkins property. Normally, it was a trip to be made over the course of two days—a progress check of the skidding crews—but Tyler had done his best, since arriving home a month ago, to never to be gone overnight. Janie had hardly left his side when he'd first arrived home from New York, and he despaired at ever getting back to a normal work schedule. He was infinitely thankful for the one event that changed her sudden clinging tendency. He'd been home for just over a week when he'd taken Janie with him to the foreman's cabin to discuss a problem with one of the big saws at the mill...

The evening was spent in the cozy home around Tom and Mary Jenson's kitchen table. Janie sat on the chair beside him, always assuring some part of her little torso touched her father.

Tom's two young sons entered the cabin, each with a yellow, floppy-eared pup in their arms. Janie's interest piqued at the sight of the tiny dogs, but she still wouldn't leave her father's side. It wasn't until one of the boys crossed to her, held out his charge and offered it for her to pet that Janie was coaxed to join them.

By the time Tyler concluded his business, Janie sat quietly with a tired pup in her lap, stroking the velvety ears with a contented smile. Tyler stooped down to her level and scratched the dog behind the ears.

"He's cute, isn't he?"

Janie nodded her head in agreement.

"It's time we get a move on, though. Mamie's going to wonder why we're so late."

His daughter threw him a pleading look and cuddled the pup close.

Tom called one of his younger sons to him during the exchange between Tyler and his daughter. After a whispered conference, the young boy returned to Janie's side, hunkered down in front of her and offered the pup to her for keeps.

Blue eyes glowed with excitement as she sought her father's permission. Tyler knew the battle was lost before it even began. Janie never asked for much. How could he resist giving her this one little bit of happiness?

A rueful smile touched his lips. "Having a pet is a big responsibility. It'll be up to you to make sure he's fed all the time and your job to watch him until he's big enough to take care of himself. Do you think you can do that?"

Her blonde head bobbed yes, and the small round face glowed with pleasure.

Tyler smiled again. "Well then, I suppose this little fellow will be getting his first horse ride tonight. Up you both go now." He lifted the two of them into his arms while saying goodnight to the Jensons along with a hesitant thank-you to all of them for the pup…

The acquisition of the animal had actually helped his work schedule return to normal. The month away from his daughter had been hard on her, but now Janie threw herself into the care of the puppy and had stopped clinging to him. Tyler was able to resume his usual timetable as far as the business was concerned without the accompanying guilt.

Reaching the entrance to the barn, he wearily dismounted the massive black Arabian and thought longingly of a warm meal.

Earlier, his brother tried to talk him out of the one-day trip or at least to allow him to ride along, but Tyler had declined. He'd needed some time to himself, even though he knew he must return that evening. His mind screamed to escape the confines of his daughter's needs, yet Tyler's love for her always pulled him back. He dealt with it by driving himself to the physical brink each day so when he entered his own private hell at night, he'd have the chance to sleep part of it away. Now, the long, hard, self-imposed workdays were evidenced in sunken cheeks and dark circles beneath his eyes. His family did their best to help him, but only Tyler could come to terms with his emotions. So far, he was still in the midst of his own battle.

He led the horse into the soft glow of the gas lantern and entered an empty stall. From behind, he heard Clancey's voice coming from the tack room.

"Evenin', Tyler! Been waiting for you to show up. Didn't expect you for another couple of hours, though." The hired hand slung his elbows over the wooden gate.

"Hello, Clance. I was able to head for home earlier than I thought."

The man looked at his boss, studied the weariness etched on his face and made a quick decision. "Here, let me take care of that black beast for you. You go on up to the big house. I'm sure Mamie has a plate warmin' for you."

"I think I'll take you up on that offer. It's been a helluva long day. I'm hoping to see Janie before she falls asleep."

Tyler gave his horse one more pat on the neck and left the stall.

"I stayed around, Ty, to let you know that the New York couple you offered jobs to showed up today. They're in the cabin you had readied. Carrie and Mamie made sure they had some food supplies and got them settled in."

"Thanks, Clancey. I'm surprised they're here already. I didn't really expect them for another month. Good thing I listened to Carrie about preparing the cabin."

"They seem like a nice enough couple. Both wanted to dig in right away, but your sister insisted they just set up housekeeping on their own for now and talk with you in the morning."

"I'll do that." Tyler left the barn as Clancey's laughter-filled voice followed after him.

"Hey, Tyler! You'd better go in duckin'! Mamie was madder than a wet hen earlier! Seems that pup of Janie's pulled her clean sheets off the line and dragged them through the mud. Also earned himself a good swat on the ass from the end of Mamie's broom. The little shit had the audacity to lift his leg and pee on the leg of her kitchen table!"

Tyler could hear his cackle halfway up to the house.

* * * * *

The scene he observed wasn't what he'd imagined it would be when he opened the back door. Mamie sat at the kitchen table with her ever-present basket of mending. Janie scribbled on her chalkboard, and the pup stretched lazily on his back in a basket placed by the stove. All four legs sprawled out in different directions, and he was sound asleep. The mayhem of earlier seemed to have disappeared.

Janie scooted off her chair and ran to her father to be lifted up and clasped in a bear hug. She promptly gave him a loud, smacking kiss on the cheek.

"You have no idea how I needed that, Janie. So, how was your day today?"

He caught her telltale glance darting to Mamie and then to the waking pup. Father and daughter watched as he sat up, yawned indifferently and padded clumsily to them for a scratch behind the ears. Tyler accommodated him. "Heard tell that someone got his little yellow butt in trouble today."

Janie's blue eyes widened along with another quick, darting glance in Mamie's direction. She raised a tiny finger to her lips to shush him. It was all to no avail. Mamie heaved her bulk from the chair and shook a pointed finger at Tyler.

"Put that yellow beast outside before he pees in my kitchen agin! He be walkin' a thin line 'round me today! Tyla, don't know how much longer I can be puttin' up with the likes o' him. He be pee'in on my floors and dirtying up my laundry. Yessiree! Things be comin' to a head 'round here afore long." She continued to mumble as she moved about the kitchen to ready Tyler's late dinner.

Tyler stifled the small chuckle her words evoked and whispered to Janie to let the pup out before Mamie started to rant again. He sat at the table, gave the steaming food in front of him its due and asked about the O'Malleys.

"Carrie took care o' everythin'. She shot orders to them brothers o' yours about gitten the O'Malleys belongin's inside," Mamie chuckled.

"I can just imagine Carrie. I know what she's like when she takes charge." Humor at what his brothers probably went through made him grin.

"I don't think those O'Malley people ever had anyone waitin' on them in the whole of their lives. That poor Missus wrung her hands whiles Carrie told her to be sittin' back and enjoyin' her tea. And Carrie wouldn't take no for an answer! Yessiree, she had them two brothers of yours a-hoppin'. Clancey insisted on takin' care of the hired trap and horse for the Mister O'Malley. I thought his eyes would pop plumb outa his head! We left both of 'em with smiles reachin' acrost from ear to ear, we did. Yessiree, we surely did."

"I wish I could've been here to greet them on their first day." He looked forward to visiting with them in the morning and couldn't wait to hear their account of their first day on the ranch.

Janie reentered the kitchen and Mamie started on the pup once more with a shake of a plump finger in the animal's direction.

"You go on and git back in that basket! There'll be no whizzin' no mores on my clean floor!" Understanding the shaking finger, the pup made quick tracks to his bed, keeping a watchful eye on the old woman the entire time.

"Janie, have you come up with a name yet for the pup?" Tyler asked.

She shook her head no.

"We really should start calling him something, honey. You've had him long enough. Mamie needs to know what to call him when she's smacking his butt with the broom."

A snort erupted from the old black woman. "He don't be needin' no name for me to smack him when he's peein' on my floor."

Janie listened to the exchange and suddenly grabbed the chalkboard. She scribbled quickly and handed it to Tyler, pointed at the piece of slate, and then to the pup in the basket.

Tyler glanced at her suggestion for a name and felt the laughter build inside him. Before long, he let it out along with a slap to his thigh. Mamie and Janie looked at one another in surprise. It'd been a long time since they'd heard that sound come from his lips.

"Look here, Mamie," Tyler chuckled as he pushed the board in her direction. "I think my daughter has come up with the perfect name for the...what do you call him, the *yellow beast*? She has cleverly given him the name of 'Whizzer'."

A huge smile appeared on Janie's face. She'd actually made her father laugh. At that moment, he didn't seem so sad and it was all because of her.

Mamie concealed her delight. "I think that daughter of yours be spendin' too much time with her uncles. She's startin' to sound like 'em now." She softened her statement, however, with a loving smile in Janie's direction.

They watched the newly dubbed "Whizzer" sprawl across the floor. Trying to scratch behind his ear, he'd missed his mark and plopped over sideways with a comical look of surprise.

"Come on, honey—show's over." Tyler said as he stood. "It's time for you to be tucked in."

Janie ran to Whizzer, kissed him on the nose and crossed to Mamie to be wrapped in her comforting arms. She took her father's hand then and they left the kitchen.

Mamie placed Tyler's dirty dishes on the counter. Whizzer eyed her every move, ready to skittle out of harm's way when the old woman crossed the kitchen with a small chunk of meat in her hand and bent over.

"Sit, you little heathen!"

Whizzer quickly plopped his hind end on the ground, his tail swishing a path back and forth across the floor.

"This here is for you—for makin' my Tyla laugh again. And don't be thinkin' I'll ever be tellin' anyone I gives you treats. You be watchin' where you be liftin' that leg o' yours or you and me gonna knock heads. Yessiree. You be one sorry yellow dog then."

She eyed the pup and shook her head at her own actions. After one last loving pat, Mamie extinguished the gas lamp on the table.

* * * * *

Tyler was greeted by Dougan O'Malley's booming laugh the next morning when he pushed open the kitchen's swinging door. The Irish couple sat at the table chuckling about something Mamie had just said.

Tyler glanced heavenward before taking his last step through the doorway. It seemed Mamie was readily going to accept Katy O'Malley into her domain.

"Well, I see you decided to take me up on my offer." He strolled across the kitchen to shake hands with Dougan, who jumped up from his seat at Tyler's entrance.

"Hello, Mr. Wilkins." He pumped the boss's hand vigorously. "Katy and I are happy to be here. This country is beautiful, isn't it, Katy?"

His wife had also left her chair when Tyler entered the room. She now gave a quick little curtsey prompted by her husband's words. "The cabin you prepared for us is so lovely, Mr. Wilkins. We can't tell you enough how thankful we are for the employment."

"Let me grab a cup of coffee and we'll get down to business. First, we need to familiarize you with the ranch."

Dougan and Katy exchanged wonder-filled glances, still unable to believe the opportunity that had been presented to them. The respect being accorded to them was something they'd never before encountered.

The four sat at the kitchen table for more than an hour as the two women's jobs were outlined and easily agreed upon. Mamie left with an excited Katy in tow for a tour of the house.

The men left for the stable shortly afterwards. Tyler brought up the subject of Fontaine Ironworks on their way across the yard.

"How did your leave-taking go over with Mr. Fontaine?"

Dougan shook his head. A look of concern spread across his face. "Not well, I'm afraid. I went in the morning after you left my home. My first reaction was to never set foot in those four walls again, but I felt I owed it to my crew not to walk out on them overnight. I asked for a meeting with Mr. Fontaine and was granted one that afternoon. I explained to him that I was offered another job, but was willing to work until he could find a replacement for me. Mr. Wilkins, I never had an ounce of respect for the man, but was willing to stay on a while longer to help him out. He fired me on the spot. That's why my wife and I got here sooner than originally planned."

"Better for you and better for me, Dougan. I'll expect you to work hard for what I pay you, but you'll never be treated unfairly by anyone on this ranch. It's a policy we strictly adhere to."

Dougan stopped momentarily to fish an envelope from his front pocket. He held it out. "This is what's left of the money you gave us the last time I saw you. There are receipts enclosed for everything Katy and I purchased to get ourselves out here. We talked last night and feel we should give the rest back. If you think any of the purchases aren't warranted, please let me know. Between Katy and myself, we'll work them off."

"That money was given to you and Katy, Dougan. I'll not accept its return. Put it away for something special. We made a gentleman's agreement that night. You've stuck to your end of the bargain and I plan on keeping with mine. Now, I want to hear no more about it. Agreed?"

"Thank you, sir. I promise you'll not be sorry for hiring me. I plan to work hard and treat this ranch like it was my own." Dougan returned the envelope to his shirt pocket and continued on to the barn, listening intently while Tyler explained his duties as if the conversation about the money had never come up.

* * * * *

It was a sunny afternoon during the first week of September when Tyler slammed the door to his home office with as much force as he could muster. He tossed two slips of paper onto the surface of the shiny oak desk, and then reached for the bottle of brandy sitting on the side cabinet. Pulling the cork from the neck of the bottle, he threw it angrily across the room before swallowing a long draught. Ramming the bottle onto the desktop, he dropped into the stuffed chair behind it.

He stared numbly around him, then closed his eyes. A heavy sigh lifted his chest when he leaned his dark head back against the soft cushion of the chair.

Emma was pregnant — and she had named him as the father.

It could damn well be possible, but I don't believe it for a goddamn minute.

As hard as he had tried, he couldn't forget their encounter that last night in New York. The little wanton had gotten herself in trouble and pointed the finger of fault at him. Any feelings he might have entertained toward her were erased by sheer anger.

Leaning forward to take another swig from the bottle, he finally reached across the desk to drag the two telegrams a little closer, settled back in the chair again and studied them with animosity etched across his rugged features. His shaking hand reached out to pick up the one nearest him.

It stated that Fontaine Ironworks had closed down. Edward implied it was for the reasons the two of them discussed before he'd left for Minnesota. The missive also stated that Samuel had dropped from sight, making threats before leaving.

He dropped the wrinkled paper and watched it flutter to the desktop before turning his attention to the second telegram. Tyler took one more slug of courage, and finally picked it up.

'*Tyler — stop — Emma is with child — stop — informed in regards to your last night in New York — stop — I will send her to Minnesota because of threats — stop —* '

"Probably all the damn gossip... Little Miss Emma has been found out and Daddy's going to save the day." His dark brows slanted again at the next words, which leapt off the page.

I expect marriage immediately — stop — your responsibility — stop — dowry funds to be wired within the week — stop — further details to follow on Emma's September 10 arrival — stop — please respond — Edward Sanders.

"A dowry? I don't want your goddamn money or your daughter! What the hell? Marry her? No questions about who she's been with—just marry my princess, or else..." He rose from the chair to pace the room, all the while rubbing his hands through his thick, dark hair. How in hell was he going to explain this to Trevor and Cole? How in hell could he stop it?

He wasn't going to get the chance. Edward was putting Emma on a train in New York at this very moment. He'd made it very clear that he expected Tyler to marry Emma immediately without further questions. Apparently, he believed his daughter's assertion that only he, Tyler Wilkins, could be the father of her baby. Emma would arrive in three days. Further details would be sent shortly as to the exact time she was expected in Duluth.

He pictured her arrival—then he pictured his fingers around her neck.

* * * * *

Tyler was unusually quiet at the dinner table that night. Terse answers to the questions asked him were the only responses. Trevor, Cole and Carrie eyed him closely trying to decide what was wrong. They were used to his quietness on some days, but Tyler had never been openly rude to any of them. Toward the meal's end, Trevor had had enough of his brother's behavior.

"All right, Ty. It seems you're having a problem with something. I'm sure I speak for all of us. What the hell is going on? You've been slamming dishes and answering questions to the point of rudeness. You owe us an explanation."

"Is that right?" Tyler tossed back as he banged his glass down with a glare. "Maybe it's none of your concern. Maybe how I act is none of your goddamn business."

Trevor bounded out of his chair, never taking his eyes from his brother's face.

Tyler followed him up just as quickly. "Back off, Trevor. I'm warning you."

Carrie's gaze swung to her oldest brother. Her mouth sagged open in shock at his outburst. She reached up and rested a gentle hand on his arm. "Tyler, that's enough. We all can see something is wrong. We just want to help you if we can. It's not like you to act this way."

Dark green eyes moved from his sister's face, then to each of his brothers.

They all seemed to hold their breath as they waited for his response. A muscle in Trevor's cheek ticked angrily. Cole looked ready to leap to his feet if necessary.

Tyler breathed an apologetic sigh. "Trev... I'm sorry."

His brother slowly seated himself again. "What the hell's going on, Ty? Christ, I haven't felt like punching you in years. You never treat anyone like you have tonight."

Tyler took a deep breath. A loud whoosh of air followed when he expelled it. "I suppose we should all talk about it, since you'll find out soon enough anyway." He helped Janie from her chair as the other three adults at the table exchanged worried glances again.

"Honey, you go in the kitchen and help Mamie. Daddy's going to have a short meeting in the library, then I'll come back and we'll read a story." He pressed a light kiss to her blonde head and sent her on her way.

* * * * *

The small group seated themselves in the library behind closed doors and waited eagerly for Tyler to fill them in.

Unsure of how to broach the subject of Emma Sanders, Tyler decided to let them read Edward's two telegrams, and then take it from there. He handed the first to Trevor who was closest and saved the second until later.

Coward, he reprimanded himself, using the excuse—if only for himself—that he wanted them to read Edward's message about Fontaine Ironworks before giving them the other. Tyler waited quietly as they passed the telegram between them. All three looked confused.

"There doesn't seem to be anything so bad in this telegram," Cole spoke up. "So, Fontaine is putting part of the blame on you for the mill's closure. Who cares? He's probably blowing a lot of smoke if you ask me."

"There's a second telegram that came with this one. I guess I'll just let you three read that one, too. Then we can talk." He pulled the second telegram from his pocket and felt like he was sealing his fate with the gesture. Handing it gingerly to Trevor, he walked to the open window—and waited for a response.

The ticking of the grandfather clock was the only sound in the room, except for a crumpling noise as the second telegram was handed from one person to another. Tyler felt three pairs of eyes bore into his back, gathered his courage and turned to face them.

Trevor squirmed in his chair, cleared his throat, then rubbed the palms of his hands on his thighs before reaching up to scratch the end of his nose. He cleared his throat again then, at a loss as what to do with himself.

Carrie was suddenly interested in a chipped fingernail.

Cole just sat calmly and waited for Tyler to speak. Finally, he decided to take the lead when it became apparent that his eldest brother wasn't willingly going to offer any sort of explanation. Stretching his long legs out in front of him, he inhaled deeply and plunged in.

"Well, Ty, it seems you did more than just…negotiate…while you were in New York."

Trevor struggled to contain a threatening snort. He immediately dropped his gaze to the floor.

Carrie suddenly lost interest in her fingernail, covered her face with her hands and pretended to rub her eyes. She cast a secret glance at Cole's face. He looked as innocent as a lamb.

Cole's twinkling eyes met his sister's, but the sight of her twitching lips was almost his undoing. A quick forced cough was the only thing that saved him from laughing outright.

Tyler looked askance until their reactions widened his eyes. "Oh, so you all think this is funny, do you? Edward has already judged me to be the baby's father! He's closed the case and sentenced me to marry his daughter…or else." His angry eyes swept the small group. "I can't see the humor at all. Emma is twenty-two years old. How the hell does he know if she's ever bedded anyone else?"

Cole turned in the chair to face his sister. "Carrie, could you leave us alone? There are a few questions I'd like to ask Ty that are kind of personal. I'm sure Trev needs to ask a few things, also."

Trevor waved his hand in the air. "Oh, you're doing just fine on your own, Cole."

Carrie's lips parted in surprise. "If you think the two of you are going to throw me out of here, well, just think again! I'm not a little girl anymore. I can handle this conversation. Go ahead, Cole, ask away." She settled herself firmly in the chair.

Cole shrugged his shoulders, looked at Trevor for confirmation to continue and received an affirmative nod.

"Did you all forget that I'm in the room?"

Upon Tyler's stiff words, Cole leaned forward in the chair and addressed his older brother. "Well, Tyler," he scratched his ear. "It seems to me you should know whether this Emma had ever been with anyone before." He rolled his eyes upward for a brief second. "How can I put this delicately?"

Tyler could stand the dramatics no longer. "I don't know if she was a virgin or not! Is that what you're trying to ask?"

"Well...yeah, Ty." He sniffed before continuing. "How come you couldn't tell?"

"Because I was drunk!" Tyler roared.

With those words, Trevor was lost. He had controlled his laughter thus far, albeit with considerable difficulty, but knowing that his brother had rejoined the living with the rather sordid escapade in New York, the humor burst from his chest. He slapped Cole on the back. Both his younger brother and sister were infected by his mirth and joined in on Tyler's most embarrassing moment.

Tyler stared incredulously at the three of them as if they had all grown a second head. "Don't you understand how serious this situation is? Christ, I'm going to be forced to marry someone who claims I'm the father of her baby! That's not too goddamn funny!"

Trevor mopped his face and was the first of the siblings to regain composure. "Ty, whoever you decided to sleep with is your own business, but I'm sure I speak for all of us—she must be one heck of a lady. You've never been one to hop into bed with just anyone. Besides, she's Edward Sanders' daughter—the man you've spoken so highly of. Surely his honesty and integrity must have rubbed off on his offspring at some point."

"But she's naming *me* as the father!" Tyler repeated what, in his opinion, was the most important point. His appalled expression mirrored his stunned reaction to their response.

Trevor rose and strolled to the liquor cabinet. He grabbed four glasses and a bottle of brandy. Returning to the group, he poured each one of them a stiff belt—each of them except his sister. For her, he splashed only a small bit in the bottom of the glass. "Well," he smiled, "I think congratulations are in order."

Tyler's already disbelieving expression now resembled astonishment. "What? Are you crazy? Don't you understand? I'm going to be *forced* to marry Emma Sanders and claim the baby as mine."

Cole glanced at his older brother. Finally, sympathy set in. "What other recourse do you have? She'll be here in three days. I think among the four of us, we can get a small wedding planned by then."

Tyler slammed his glass down onto the desk making the other three cringe. "Why can't I make you see reason? The baby might not even be mine! For crissakes, she let Samuel Fontaine paw her the night of the reception. Worse yet, she enjoyed it! Why will none of you even consider that she might be a little tramp?"

"Ty—" Cole's voice was altogether *too* reasonable.

"Fine!" Tyler pointed an angry finger at all of them. "You three plan the goddamn wedding and maybe, just maybe, I'll show up. And while you're at it, figure out a way to pick her up in Duluth because, in the morning, I'm heading for the logging camp." He whirled to the door. Just before it slammed, he flung one last caustic comment over his shoulder. "And I don't know when I'll be back!"

His siblings sat quietly as Tyler's last words echoed in their ears. They glanced warily at one another over the rims of their glasses until Carrie's sudden doubt marred her smooth features.

"Maybe he's right...maybe the baby isn't his. I've never seen him so angry."

Cole watched her pace before him. "You could be right, Carrie, but I don't think so. Do you two remember the night he came home from New York? I sat and listened to him ramble on about the trip and was happy to see him finally showing some enthusiasm again, but there was something I couldn't quite put my finger on. Something that bothered me. Tyler was very evasive when we asked him about the women in the big city and about Edward's daughter in particular. Now I know why. He was thinking of this Emma woman that night—and his guilt over what happened between the two of them was nipping at his heels."

"Well, she's got to have some redeeming qualities," Trevor interjected. "Tyler was still in pretty bad shape when he left for New York. But he wouldn't be blindsided by just anyone. There had to be a strong attraction on his part for him to even consider—" his glance darted to his sister "—sleeping with someone. It's never been in his nature to have a quick roll in the hay, and then dump the woman. He had to feel something for her."

"You know what I think the problem is?" A grin tugged at the corners of Cole's lips. "I think our big brother is finally getting over Sara's death, and he's not dealing with it very well. Things are moving a little quicker than he would like and the guilt is setting in. Hell, how would you feel, Trev, if you were a devout widower who was being forced to marry someone—even if that *someone* was a woman you were grudgingly attracted to?" He nodded his head. "That has to be it—Tyler's finally found someone he could love again, but he hasn't admitted his feelings yet—even to himself. He's pissed because he doesn't have time to explore other options since there's a baby involved—and a quick wedding in the very near future."

Carrie raised her chin a notch and crossed her arms. "Tyler has always been a good judge of character. He would never take up with a woman who had loose morals, so I, for one, have to believe that he's the father of that baby. Besides, it's out of our hands. The decision's been made already—she'll be here in three days, so we may as well get something planned. Are we agreed?"

Three sets of eyes met and, once again, Cole's response was as eloquent as ever.

"Hmmm…looks like I might have to oil up my shotgun for the wedding, though."

The three of them broke into near hysterical laughter again at their older brother's expense.

* * * * *

Tyler stomped down the back staircase with a duffel bag slung over his shoulder early the next morning. Katy took one look at his scowl and headed out of the kitchen. Word had spread quickly throughout the house. Mamie simply eyed him as she flipped bacon at the stove, not the least bit intimidated.

"Where you goin?"

His scowl deepened. "To the logging camp."

"No yar not. You got a bride gonna arrive in a few days."

"Well it certainly didn't take long for everyone to find out, did it? Too bad if she's on her way. I never asked her to come."

Mamie's eyes rolled heavenward. "She must be a wonderful gal to put up with the likes of you. Yessiree," she stated with a lopsided grin. "She's got to be if'n she's fallen in love with you—specially when yar acting like a nikenpoop."

"Love doesn't have anything to do with this."

Mamie snorted. "Aw, go on, Tyla. Love gots everythin' to do with it! Why would a nice, upstandin' lady like Miss Em be takin' a chance and gitten hersef with chile if'n she didn't love you?"

"Mamie," he hissed through clenched teeth, "you have no idea if she's nice or not. And you certainly don't know if she's upstanding." Tyler paced before her with clenched fists at his side. "I can't understand why you all refuse to see that there's a very good possibility the child isn't even mine. You don't even know her."

"Don't have to," Mamie sniffed. "If'n you be with her, then she be nice. Tyla, I have faith in you, boy. No ways you be pickin' a piece o' fluff to be lovin' with. Yessiree. That be what I think. Now git if yar gonna be an old crabass! I gots a weddin' to get ready for."

Tyler raised his hands, tempted to wrap them around her beefy neck. Her comment about the wedding though was the final straw that snapped his patience.

"That's it! You all can think whatever you like, and you all can *plan* whatever you like! It doesn't seem to matter how I feel anyway. I'll be back when I'm damn good and ready." He stormed out the back door and slammed it behind him.

Mamie smiled to herself. "Son, you be good and ready afor you know it. Yessiree…"

Chapter Twelve

స్

Emma's contemplating eyes watched the miles slide by the train window on the last leg of her journey to Minnesota. Her father had stood his ground and informed Tyler of her pregnancy and, in no uncertain terms, told her to begin gathering what she needed, or he would pack for her. She had done everything in her power to dissuade him from the deliberate course he'd set, but with no success. In the end, Emma had no choice but to prepare herself for the journey to her new home. They'd slipped out in the dark of night and secreted themselves inside an enclosed carriage in case Samuel was nearby. Saying goodbye to her father at the train station was dreadful. He'd held her close to hide his own tears and whispered how much he loved her.

Emma shifted on the seat. She was sorry now that she'd wasted those last three days wallowing in anger. She could still envision her father standing on the loading platform, his hat in his hands. The sadness in his eyes pierced her heart as effectively as a knife when the train pulled away.

Now, here she was, a few short hours away from seeing Tyler again. She'd spent the entire trip searching a soul that was filled with conflicting emotions. Lowering her hand to where their baby lay safely within her, she wondered if he would ever find it in his heart to love her, or would he always think of her as the woman who forced him to marry against his will? She couldn't imagine that he'd accept her readily — not when the choice had been taken away from him.

* * * * *

He sat motionless beside the blue water on a lake far north of his home, but thoughts of an unknown future raced through his mind. Soon he'd be a married man again, and Tyler greeted the idea with more than a fair amount of anger. Reaching for a small round rock, he pitched it forcefully across the water and watched the waves ripple outward.

What sort of marriage could they build when it would begin with a lie? His first marriage had been built on a solid foundation of love and trust. And still he and Sara had had a few rocky moments. His head sagged against the tree behind him. His eyes winced shut in frustration.

He and Emma came from two separate worlds and now they'd be forced to raise a child together — a child that for all intents and purposes could be some other man's. And what about Janie and her feelings toward a new and unfamiliar mother? Tyler was so angry at his family's reaction to Emma's pregnancy that he hadn't even said goodbye to Janie before leaving her again.

A visit to Sara's gravesite the day before, which should have provided some sort of comfort, succeeded only in agitating him like never before. He realized now that he'd gone there to seek an answer to his dilemma, but the only revelation upon his departure was that for the first time in two years, he'd walked away from her final resting place with less grief in his heart.

Tipping his face upward to bask in the warmth of the evening sun, he chewed thoughtfully on a sweet blade of grass. Counting out the days in his mind, he knew she'd arrive tomorrow.

The familiar trill of a loon calling to its mate broke the peaceful silence. He opened his eyes in search of the bird. A sudden image of the old Indian brave flashed through his brain. He'd kept his promise and released the carving at a lake near the ranch.

Am I still the keeper, or is my job done? He sighed. *I hope the old man found his way home...*

His thoughts shifted to the second figurine he'd presented to Emma. It seemed like a lifetime ago.

His green eyes fluttered shut again. He closed his mind to the old man and Emma, content to simply listen to the forlorn calls of the loon and ignore the urge to return home.

* * * * *

Emma glanced at her reflection in a small, handheld mirror and sighed. Pale and haggard from the long, overland trip to Minnesota, she pinched her cheeks to regain some color before stepping off the train. Her stomach clenched at the thought of seeing Tyler again — and at the loathing that was sure to burn in his eyes.

Panic washed through her when she stood on the platform, her darting green eyes reflecting uncertainty as she inspected the nameless faces around her. A quarter of an hour later, she was still standing alone on the wooden planking. Where was he?

"Miss, do you need assistance with your bags?" A uniformed man stepped forward to gain her attention. "I can carry them inside for you, if you like."

"Yes, thank you. My party isn't here yet to meet me."

Following the steward into the station, she watched silently as he piled her trunks against the wall. Digging inside her reticule, she pulled out a coin and pressed it into his hand before sitting on one of many hard benches that filled the large room. Ignoring her parched throat and the insistent growling in her stomach, she rested her head wearily against the wall as she waited for Tyler.

* * * * *

An hour later, Emma still observed the comings and goings of travelers and station employees, her fear growing by leaps and bounds, blinking back the tears that threatened to burst forward at any moment.

A friendly clerk approached her to ask if she needed anything. She accepted a glass of water with trembling hands, hoping the cool liquid would help to control her flagging emotions.

The afternoon sun was now low in the western sky. Darkness would arrive soon. She certainly couldn't spend the night here. Gathering her purse, she was about to rise from the wooden bench when two men and a woman burst through the doorway to the station, their faces etched with concern.

Carrie spied Emma where she sat alone across the room. It had to be her. "Hello. Are you by any chance Emma Sanders?"

Emma swallowed back the threatening tears of relief. "Yes. Yes, I am!"

"I'm *so* sorry we're late! I'm Caroline Wilkins, Tyler's sister." She waved in the direction of the two men behind her. "And these two scoundrels are my brothers. This is Trevor," she gestured in his direction, "and this is Cole."

Emma easily guessed Trevor Wilkins was Tyler's brother. He bore a striking resemblance to his brother—the man who was *supposed* to be standing before her. Both possessed the same dark, swarthy good looks and bright green eyes. Caroline and Cole Wilkins carried some of the same features, but were lighter in hair color and possessed hazel-colored eyes. Tyler's brothers tipped their cowboy hats in a gallant show of politeness as Carrie continued.

"The carriage threw a wheel on our way here. We're so sorry that you had to wait and wonder if anyone was going to pick you up."

Relief again washed over Emma's face. A hesitant smile lit her gaze. "I have to admit I was beginning to wonder what I should do. It was getting late... I thought I might have to find a room for the night," she murmured as her gaze strayed to the station door.

Carrie immediately noticed the movement, shifted uncomfortably and wondered how she would take the news that Tyler hadn't come to retrieve her. She cleared her throat and charged on. "You're right, it is getting late so we've decided to take rooms here in Duluth for the evening. You've had an awfully long trip. I bet you haven't had anything to eat either. We'll take care of that. After the day we've had, I don't relish the idea of bouncing around in a carriage for another four hours, and I can imagine how *you* must feel. Without the light of the moon tonight, it would be best to wait until morning."

Silence descended on the group when Carrie finished her rambling speech.

"Is Tyler waiting outside?" Emma asked quietly. She watched as three pairs of eyes met and held in an uneasy glance.

Trevor threw her another disarming grin as he picked up one of her bags. "There was a problem at one of the logging camps. Tyler's expertise was needed—so he sent the three of us in his stead." He blinked one eye in a devilish wink. "Besides, you'll have a lot more fun with us. Tyler can be an old stick in the mud sometimes."

Emma's heart sank, not the least bit fooled with Trevor's excuse. But she bravely forced a wan smile to her mouth.

Cole easily read the hurt in her eyes and thought Tyler was a real son of a bitch for disappearing.

Emma allowed herself to be led outside to the waiting carriage. Carrie chuckled quietly to herself as Trevor and Cole tripped over one another in an attempt to help their future sister-in-law into the backseat.

"Watch your step, now. Here—sit right here." Trevor scrambled to take Emma's arm and patted the cushioned bench before her.

She sat, her wide-eyed expression showing that she was a little flabbergasted by all the attention.

"I don't think you'll be comfortable there, Emma. Why don't you sit on this side," Cole insisted.

"I'm fine—"

Before she had a chance to object further, Cole grabbed her elbow and whisked her to the opposite bench. "This way, you can look forward and have a better view of the town." He quickly settled her, ignoring his brother's hidden jab to his ribs.

Emma busied herself with adjusting her skewed bonnet, which now hung low over one eye from the forced flight across the length of the carriage and missed the exchange between the Wilkins men.

Cole stepped to the ground and met his brother's offended gaze.

"She was fine where she was." Trevor muttered.

"Just grab her bags—she would've got sick facing backwards. Use your head." Cole jumped into the front seat and gripped the reins before his brother had a chance to get a hold on them.

Carrie was forgotten as her dubious gaze watched the men go in two different directions. She climbed into the carriage of her own accord, trying to hide the tiny smile that tugged at her lips and wondered what Tyler would think if he could see the two making such asses out of themselves.

She liked Emma already. The fact that she blushed with embarrassment at all the attention showed she was no prima donna who expected to be waited on hand and foot—even in her present condition. Carrie had also noticed the orphaned look on Emma's face when she realized that Tyler wasn't a part of their group.

* * * * *

Trevor kept up a constant stream of conversation on the way to the inn. Carrie and Cole added their own comments in an effort to lessen the pain of Tyler's absence. The laughter and jokes were always at their older sibling's expense, however, and, difficult as it was, Emma relaxed. These three virtual strangers already treated her like family—apprehensively, she could only hope that Tyler would feel the same.

The group reached the hostelry twenty minutes later. They entered the lobby through the front doors.

Carrie's hand held Cole back as Trevor and Emma proceeded to the check-in desk.

"Let's eat immediately. I'm a little worried about Emma. Did you notice how pale and quiet she is?"

"It's hard to miss," Cole replied as his gaze strayed to the now noticeable slump of Emma's shoulders. "That damn Tyler—"

"Well, we'll deal with him tomorrow. That poor woman has been on a train for three days. Right now, I just want to feed her and get her up to her room."

Trevor returned and distributed room keys. "I had the bags sent up. My stomach is growling. How about the rest of you? Want to eat, and then call it a night?"

Emma stood quietly but, inside, she fought a fierce battle to control the wave of dizziness that suddenly threatened to overcome her.

Carrie took in the ashen color of her complexion and the perspiration that beaded her brow, and grasped her arm. "Come, Emma. We'll be quick about supper and get you upstairs."

Sitting in the unadorned dining room, the small group conversed quietly. The Wilkins family let Emma's pregnancy go unmentioned for the time being and concentrated on telling her about the ranch. She, in turn, told them about her life in New York. Her unassuming demeanor and obvious intelligence struck all three Wilkinses.

Cole was convinced her face lit up every time she smiled. Trevor had already fallen in love with her dimpled cheeks. Carrie was simply pleased that her future sister-in-law looked physically better than she did an hour earlier.

Emma listened to the flowing conversation around her. Finally, curiosity got the best of her when the name Janie came up once again. "Excuse me, but I have to ask you a question. You're all talking as if I know this woman Janie, but I don't. Does she live at the ranch?"

The other three sat with fixed expressions of stunned disbelief on their faces. Apparently, Tyler had told her nothing about his personal life. It seemed Emma had no idea that he was once married or that he had a daughter.

Trevor leaned forward, took a deep breath and prepared to break the news. "I can't believe Tyler didn't tell you about Janie."

Emma sat motionless and waited for the bad news. The only thing that she could think of was how Tyler must hate her because she simply walked into his world without being asked.

Trevor's gentle voice brought her out of her self-destructive reverie, "Janie is Tyler's seven-year-old daughter."

Emma's face paled even further to a color that resembled chalk. Carrie silently reached out to squeeze her hand.

"His daughter?" Emma whispered. "He never said anything…" Her voice trailed off as she stared at Trevor, sure she hadn't heard him right. "Tyler has a daughter?" She shook her head, trying to ward of the confusion that threatened to engulf her. "I know this is going to sound foolish, but does he have a wife somewhere?"

She asked the question so softly that Cole had to lean forward to hear the words. "Tyler's wife, Sara, was killed in an accident two years ago. He never talks about it, so that's probably why he didn't mention it to you. Janie is the only child resulting from that union. Please, don't be angry with him for keeping something so personal from you."

Emma stared blankly into his beseeching eyes as the information sank in. *Oh my God...* It was too much for her to take in after the last stress-filled days. Exhaustion, along with Cole's words, helped to initiate a heartache that she feared would never stop.

"Excuse me," she stated quickly when she bolted from her chair. "I'll be ready to leave in the morning whenever you are." Her eyes filled with unwanted tears. She fled the dining room and tore up the stairs to her room without another word.

* * * * *

She lay in the unfamiliar bed, the covers pulled up tight around her neck. Sleep though, eluded her. "How could he not tell me that he's a widower and has a daughter?" she asked the quiet room.

Her eyes widened in sudden horror. *And what on Earth does his family think of me, traveling halfway across the United States, pregnant with their brother's child and not knowing a single thing about his personal life?*

What was she going to do if neither Tyler nor his daughter accepted her? The three of them would be thrust into a family relationship, because of one fleeting moment of passion—but what if they didn't want it? What if they did not want *her?*

Tyler had already proven his unwillingness to have her in his life with his refusal to meet her in Duluth by not meeting her.

She rolled onto her side and thoughts of him flitted through her mind. She pictured his face, the drawn, sallow features at the times when he'd looked so sad. "He's still grieving for Sara..."

What was she going to have to contend with in the next few months? If he was still in love with his dead wife, could the feelings she carried for him sustain her through this mess?

The questions kept coming late into the night. As they raced through her mind, she cradled her stomach where their child lay. She would try her hardest to make this work, because of the baby. It deserved no less. She would love Tyler until he could fight it no longer, and then hopefully he would learn to love her back. She had so much to give him if only he could only find acceptance in his heart.

Settling the situation in her mind as best she could, Emma finally succumbed to exhaustion.

Chapter Thirteen

☙

The next morning proved to have a rather rocky start, but tensions eased though when they headed out to the ranch. The ride took them through some of the most beautiful country Emma had ever seen. As they bumped along the well-worn dirt road, she continually pointed out the maple and birch trees, which were gradually changing to the bright shades of autumn. She'd never before seen anything quite like it—even in the state of New York—and her excitement grew by leaps and bounds. She fooled no one, however. The three Wilkinses knew that her enthusiasm had little to do with the scenery and *everything* to do with the fact that she would soon see Tyler again.

Emma's good humor infected the rest of her party. Green eyes sparkled as her pink cheeks dimpled in continuous smiles. The two men were completely enamored.

Carrie just shook her head. *They're so obvious,* she thought. *Good—she's going to need a few champions, especially if Tyler decides to keep hold of his animosity toward her.*

The carriage finally rounded a last bend in the road. Cole pulled up the reins at the top of a large hill.

"There it is, Emma," he murmured.

Her new home was nestled among some of the largest pine trees she'd ever seen. The sprawling log structure spread out in the form of an elongated "T". A barn and numerous outbuildings filled in the landscape behind it. Emma hadn't known what to expect, but her new home far outweighed even her wildest dreams. The sheer beauty of the homestead took her breath away.

Her wide, worried eyes frantically searched for a sign of Tyler as the carriage rolled slowly down the hill, her heart sending a silent message for him to at least try and give her a chance.

They entered the ranch proper through an immense log gate. Her eyes still sought him. But when the carriage drew to a halt in front of a massive porch, she was forced to hide her disappointment. He wasn't there to greet her. She clung to the slim hope that there really was a problem at the logging camp that demanded his attention—a problem that was more important than his future wife's arrival.

Emma's attention was drawn to an old black woman who waddled out onto the front porch, wiping her hands on her gingham apron before sending a smile and a wave to the foursome.

"Bout' time you be gittin' back! I was worryin' mysef sick there be no souls sittin' 'round my table tonight!" She lumbered down the steps one at a time, never ceasing her banter. "Cole! Trevor! You help them ladies offen that wagon! What's the matter with you boys, leavin' ladies to sit in the sun! Hop to it now. Yessiree!"

Both men leapt to the ground at her command. Trevor lifted Emma down, and then bent to whisper conspiratorially in her ear. "I told you about Mamie, didn't I? Remember what I said. She's got a heart of gold and a lot of hot air to go with it."

Emma allowed herself a nervous muffled giggle as Trevor led her to the foot of the steps and quickly realized that there was nothing wrong with the old woman's hearing when a raucous laugh escaped Mamie's throat along with a swing of her fist in Trevor's direction.

"Pay no mind to that big mouth, young lady! Go on, Trevor, git! And makes sure you got armfuls of Miss Em's belongins. Cole, you get offen your arse and help him!"

Cole and Trevor hustled as Mamie shot out orders. The two men quickly unloaded Emma's bags from the back of the carriage. Tipping their hats to their future sister-in-law, they hurried up the wooden sidewalk and into the house.

"Why, Carrie, this here lady be no bigger than a mite." Mamie's glance swept Emma from head to toe as she rested her hands on her own ample hips. "Yessiree. We gonna take care of that! You come in the big house now, lil' lady, and we'll be gittin' you somethin' to eat and drink. I suppose those two lunkheads didn't even give you breakfast afore leavin' town, did they?"

Emma laughed aloud at the black woman's colorful language as she ascended the stairs to the porch. "Miss Mamie, I've heard a lot about you on the ride north. It's a pleasure to finally meet you in person. And yes, I was allowed to eat something before we left Duluth. Please, don't be too hard on Cole and Trevor. They've treated me wonderfully, and so has Carrie."

"Well, it be a good blessin' then, that they took to my promptin' when I told them two boneheads to be good to our new Miss Em. Figured Carrie be along to smack 'em upside the head if'n they go by the wayside." She folded Emma into her soft bosom with a hearty squeeze. "Welcome, honey, to the Northern Pine Ranch. Now, let's be gettin' you inside and outta this sun so you can be restin' up after your long journey. Yessiree, it be a fine day in the makin'."

Emma offered up a little prayer of thanks that Tyler's family had accepted her so readily.

I only hope that Tyler will feel the same...

* * * * *

He reined Storm to a halt and warily eyed the returning group as he sat astride the black stallion far atop a hill opposite the one the carriage traveled. The cowboy hat rode low on his forehead, hiding a heavy scowl as he watched the buggy pass through the ranch gates.

Emma was here. He met the realization with mixed emotions.

He'd spent four days at the logging camp, purposely avoiding her arrival. He'd planned to make her sit around for an entire day and night, wondering if he would ever appear. Instead, without even knowing it, she'd pulled one over on him. He'd just been riding in when he'd caught sight of the carriage coming over the hill.

Dammit! They must've spent the night in Duluth!

His stony eyes observed Mamie on the porch. His jaw hardened to match his gaze when Trevor effortlessly lifted Emma from the carriage. He knew he was doomed when the old woman took Emma into her arms in a welcoming hug.

Shit! Mamie'll never get off my ass now that she's decided this mess is going to work.

He watched until the entire group entered the house, feeling like an outsider. Tyler turned the big stallion away from the house with a jerk. He'd be damned if he'd go in now. Let her wait until later and wonder where he was.

Kicking Storm into a gallop, he headed north again.

* * * * *

Emma awoke with a long, luxurious stretch. A glance at the clock on the mantel widened her eyes. It was late afternoon. After Mamie fussed over her and fed her a late lunch, she'd barely been able to keep her eyes open. Carrie had insisted she nap.

She sat on the edge of the bed with a groan but, as she glanced about the room, she was struck by the elegance of the Wilkins' home. Carrie had told her that the spacious log dwelling was divided into four separate wings, each housing a different necessity needed by the family. One of the wings contained the living room, library, and office. The second housed the kitchen and dining room and the last two parts of the "T" shaped structure housed the six bedrooms.

Carrie had also explained that Tyler's master suite adjoined hers via a small hallway, with the water closet encompassing half of the area between the two rooms. At one time, the room she now occupied was used as a nursery. Janie was in a different room now though, just down the hall, and the family remodeled this one as a spare room for visiting guests. Now it was hers, to do with as she liked. Had Carrie meant just for the present or for the duration of her marriage?

Emma had spied Tyler's daughter for only a fleeting moment when they'd first entered the house. The little girl had peeked at them from around a corner in the large foyer, then disappeared. Carrie and Mamie quickly assured Emma that everything would be fine. It would just take time for the child to become accustomed to the new arrangement.

Would Tyler get accustomed also?

She sighed and rose to put away her belongings. She opened one of the bags, then gently withdrew the wrapped wooden loon. Removing the tissue, she wondered where Tyler was as she set the figurine on the chest of drawers. Her stomach jumped at the thought. Last night, she'd vowed to make this marriage work, but suddenly she wasn't so sure she could make it happen.

Her eyes settled on the connecting door that led to his room. Chewing on her bottom lip for a moment, the decision was made. She crossed to the door and slowly turned the knob. Feeling like a thief in the night as she passed through the small hallway and an alcove that hid a claw foot bathtub, she paused in the open doorway that led to the master suite.

His room took her breath away. It was spacious and airy and definitely masculine in design. An immense fireplace dominated the west wall, with windows flanking each side. A door stood to the left of one of the windows. A quick peek revealed that it led to a small overhang on the exterior of the house. The oak furniture was polished to such a sheen that Emma could see her reflection in it. A huge four-poster bed sat against the north wall with a beautiful hand-quilted bedspread covering the feather-tick mattress. Two massive overstuffed chairs sat in front of the fireplace atop an exquisitely braided rug. The room was cozy and welcoming.

Drawn to the bed, her green eyes scanned the comfortable surface. Would she ever share it with him?

Lost in thought, she reached out to touch one of the tall posts, but jerked her hand back as if she had touched fire when a cold voice rumbled behind her.

"Find anything that interests you?"

Tyler sauntered into the room, dropped a saddlebag on the floor and never took his eyes from her face.

"Tyler…" Further words refused to come. The sight of him rendered her speechless.

The worn cowboy hat, boots and cotton shirt and pants somehow made him even more ruggedly handsome than she remembered. His face was tanned to a copper color, which defined the dark lashes framing his eyes. His unshaven face gave him a roguish appearance.

Emma's heart knocked in her chest. God, she loved him.

He watched her from across the room with a totally nonchalant expression. Inside though, he struggled fiercely to control the emotions that raced through his body.

She's so beautiful...

The reason why she stood before him though, hit him squarely in the chest. He forced all thoughts from his mind and all feeling from his heart. He wouldn't make this easy for her.

He ambled toward one of the overstuffed chairs in front of the fireplace, casually tossing his hat onto the bed as he passed it. Seating himself, his eyes returned to her face—one that held myriad emotions.

"So, how is our little mother feeling after her long journey? Sorry I wasn't here to greet you." He shrugged his broad shoulders. "I didn't think you'd mind, since you're only here looking for a name for the baby."

Emma's heart lurched at his crudeness. She stood beside the bed, blinked back the threatening tears and struggled with her thoughts before speaking them aloud. "I want you to know I don't blame you for anything. I'm just as responsible for what happened as you are. I'm sorry if you don't want me here, but the decision was beyond my control. When my father found out about the...baby, he insisted on this marriage."

Tyler glared at her through suspicious eyes and said nothing.

Emma took another deep breath, but her words came out in barely a whisper. "I had planned to raise the baby alone, Tyler, and not involve you. My father, however, felt differently. He didn't want it to be raised as a bastard and insisted I come to you. I can see now that it was a mistake. I thought maybe we could make this work, for the baby's sake, but I guess I was only fooling myself. If you'd like, after the wedding—and there will be a wedding, because my father was right that the child deserves a name—I'll leave."

Her heart sank as she spoke the words. Leaving was the last thing she wanted to do. But how could she stay when he'd just made it obvious that he would never come to terms with being the baby's father? He didn't want her or the child in his life.

Tyler eyed her closely. "I want to know just one thing, Emma. Am I really the father, or are you just looking for a place to hide out when your pregnancy begins to show?"

She opened her mouth to respond, but his hand came up to silence her.

"I know it's possible that I could have sired the child, but I want you to be honest with me. Have you been with anyone else?"

His words slammed into her chest. Her eyes instantly glittered with anger. "How dare you even ask me that? Is that what you think, that I've been with other men and don't even know who the father is?" Emma's rage manifested itself in the tears that flowed freely down her cheeks. "A moment ago, I mentioned the word bastard in conjunction with the baby. Well, I was wrong! The only *bastard* in this room is you! You can think anything you like, Tyler. If you want to take the chance that this child isn't yours and throw us out, then so be it."

Blinded by tears, she raced from the room and slammed the adjoining door behind her. Tyler jumped up, ready to follow her, ready to continue the argument, but paused just short of the entrance to her suite. He tilted his aching head forward and rubbed his stubbled face with both hands.

It was an act. It was *all* an act. His initial reaction to the sight of her standing in his room was that of immense joy—joy that lasted only a split second until her condition reared its ugly head and made him doubt her honesty. He wouldn't be duped into claiming a child that wasn't his.

He glared at the closed door before him, his jaw hardening with determination. He had every right to go in there and demand the truth. He wanted her to admit that he was *not* the father of her baby.

The decision was made. He shoved open the door, shouldered his way through the connecting hallway and burst through the entrance to her suite. Emma spun when the door to her bedroom banged against the dresser.

"Get out of here!" she choked through the tears that still clogged her throat.

"Funny," he gritted through clenched teeth, "I was going to tell you the same thing."

Emma's face paled to a sickly pallor. She stumbled back with the impact of his words.

Tyler immediately regretted the caustic remark, but refused to allow the hesitancy to show on his face.

Sinking into a nearby chair, Emma wiped the tears from her face as she stared at him with sad, questioning eyes. She shook her head slowly. "What happened to you? You're not the same man I met in New York."

"What the hell am I supposed to think, Emma? I receive a telegram out of the blue that states you're pregnant with *my* child and that in three day's time you'll arrive for the wedding. Too many questions were left unanswered. Then you arrive on my doorstep..."

"You weren't even here to see me arrive!" she tossed back.

"What? Did you expect me to be waiting on bended knee?" His eyes glittered dangerously again. "Did you think I'd welcome you with open arms?" He ran a hand through his dark hair in utter helplessness and forced himself to lower his voice. "Tell me, Emma...tell me the truth."

The tears swam in her green eyes. "I already did!" She moved her gaze to a spot over his head and waited for him to leave the room.

He didn't budge. His expression became even more resolute.

Emma's chin lowered. She inhaled deeply, and finally met his gaze. "Neither of us is on trial here, Tyler. This baby deserves to have two parents who will love and cherish it. That's the bottom line." Unbidden tears started again. Should she tell him that she still loved him? No. He'd never believe it.

"You have to trust me when I say you are the father."

Doubt shadowed his eyes.

Emma interpreted it as being directed at her. She rose and walked to the window, her stiff back turned to him. "You need to make a decision, Tyler. I need to know if I should make plans to return to New York."

A moment later, the door clicked shut behind her.

* * * * *

Voices filtered out from the family room as Emma descended the steps, silently congratulating herself for finding the nerve. She was about to discover her future. Gathering all the reserve she could summon, she straightened her back and entered the room to find the entire family waiting patiently for her to join them, including a clean-shaven Tyler. She paused in the doorway, unsure of his mood, and was saved when Carrie rose to greet her. Trevor and Cole followed suit. Tyler remained seated and calmly sipped a drink, his green eyes gauging her presence.

"Good evening, Emma," Carrie said. "I have to say, you look much more rested. Come, sit down for a few minutes before we go in for dinner."

Emma felt Tyler's suspicious stare bore into her and swallowed the knot of nervousness that lodged in her throat. "I'm sorry if I kept you all waiting. I fear I slept longer than planned. The afternoon got away from me." Her wary eyes darted in Tyler's direction, wondering if he'd told them all about their argument.

Trevor hurried to show her to the sofa, his ever-present good nature shining through. "Don't fret for a minute, Emma. Tyler was just filling us in on his trip to the logging camp. We didn't even notice the time."

After seating her, he returned to his chair and hoped like hell that someone would follow his lead and start talking. The tension in the room was thick enough to cut with a knife as the three younger Wilkinses waited to see what would happen next.

To stave off the awful silence, Carrie sent an encouraging smile in Emma's direction. "A reverend from town will travel out here tomorrow to perform the ceremony. We know it must seem like you're in the center of a whirlwind, but we all thought it best to be done with the marriage before your...condition begins to show."

It was the first time her pregnancy had been acknowledged aloud. Emma paled at the thought, but her heart sang loudly. Was he going to go through with it?

She waited for him to say something. When it became obvious that he wouldn't, her tentative gaze met his cool one. "Does that meet with your approval, Tyler?" She searched his eyes for even a small sign of happiness.

He set his glass aside and never took his dark green eyes from hers. The others held their breath and awaited his words.

"It doesn't seem like either of us has much of a choice, now does it? If this is the course we're forced to take, then we may as well be finished with it as soon as possible." His answer sounded precise and practiced to everyone in the room.

Only Cole observed the grimace Emma tried so valiantly to hide. His heart went out to not only her, but to his brother as well—even if he was being an ass. The two of them would have to come to terms with the situation in their own good time. He glanced at Carrie and tipped his head toward the dining room. She took his cue and stood.

"Maybe we should go in and eat. Mamie will have our hides soon if we don't do justice to the meal she's been preparing all day."

Trevor stood and offered his arm to Emma. Cole swung his gaze to his older brother. The murderous expression on Tyler's face showed that he was none too pleased he'd been usurped even though he didn't have much to say. Cole hoped the little show of jealousy on Tyler's part was a sign of better days to come.

* * * * *

Tyler's daughter wasn't present at the dinner table. Emma used the opportunity to open up an avenue of communication that would work between them.

"Is there a reason Janie isn't dining with us? I had hoped to get to know her this evening."

Tyler's eyes jumped to her at the mention of his daughter, realizing she wasn't aware of Janie's problem with speech. It must be the only thing his sibling hadn't told her. Hell, according to Cole, they had no problem with telling Emma about Sara's accident.

"Janie has decided not to come down tonight. She had a rather busy day, and I've already tucked her in. I'm sure you'll have plenty of time to get to know her later on."

Emma's eyes widened with his answer, hoping that Tyler wouldn't make her leave after the wedding service. She chanced a small, happy smile in his direction.

The entire Wilkins family, barring Tyler, showed themselves to be an entertaining lot. They laughed and teased one another throughout the meal, drawing Emma into the fun as the evening progressed. When the last bite of Mamie's homemade apple pie had been consumed, the group rose from the table.

"Emma, come sit in the family room for awhile," Carrie invited.

"I'm sorry to decline, Carrie, but I think the last few days have caught up with me again." It was a small lie. The tension between her and Tyler was beginning to take its toll. "Thank you all for the wonderful evening, but I think I'll retire immediately. I'll see you all in the morning." She turned to leave, but was halted by his voice.

"I'll show you upstairs, Emma." Tyler rose and joined her near the doorway. He stood stiffly beside her as Emma bid the others goodnight once more, then followed his soon-to-be wife from the dining room.

Neither spoke until they arrived at her bedroom door. Emma was at a loss for words, so she simply offered a small nod of the head, hoping he would at least respond in kind.

Tyler's gaze lowered to the floor. He took a deep breath, cleared his throat, then raised his chin again. "There's something you should know about Janie."

She read the hesitancy in his gaze. At that moment, Tyler seemed more like the man she'd met in New York, the same she'd fallen in love with.

"Cole told me he explained to you about...the accident two years ago. When it happened...after it happened, Janie changed. You won't be able to visit with her like you would another child. She hasn't spoken a word since Sara's death—not to me, not to anyone in this family. She's the most important thing in this world to me, Emma, and I won't allow her to be hurt by my actions of a few months ago. She's had enough pain in her short life without us adding more. Right now, Janie needs me and nothing will come between me and my daughter."

Emma stood quietly, watching the play of emotions on his tanned face. She'd seen the same pain on Cole's face earlier when he'd told her about Sara's death. It was obvious that the accident had affected them all and that Janie wasn't the only one in this household who'd suffered from the loss.

"I was rude to you this afternoon. I'm sorry," Tyler continued. "I want you to understand something, though. I still don't know if I should believe you when you say that I fathered your baby—for reasons of my own. But it seems fate has stepped into my life again and decreed another change of course. I will marry you, Emma, because there seems no way out for me." He took a step back. "Goodnight. I'll see you at the wedding."

Emma watched quietly until he disappeared down the steps and out of sight. The old grandfather clock in the foyer below ticked the minutes away, and still she stood in the hall—motionless.

It was all for nothing. The trip here, the wedding—all of it would be for nothing. With a trembling chin, Emma entered the bedroom and closed the door silently behind her.

Chapter Fourteen

ಸಿ

Emma's eyes opened to a feeling of dread. Today, her life would be joined with Tyler's. She met the idea with a fair amount of trepidation. She listened closely for any sound from the room adjoining hers. When silence met her alert ears, she shoved the blankets away, lowered her legs over the side of the bed and stared out across the unfamiliar surroundings.

She lowered her face into her upturned hands. There were so many things to straighten out between the two of them—no...the three of them...

Emma's tousled head snapped upright.

All this time, she'd worried solely about herself and Tyler and hadn't even given a thought to how Janie felt about having a new mother—one that she did not even know. Instantly ashamed of her own selfishness for wallowing in self-pity, she grabbed her robe and left the safety of her room to search for his daughter.

Remembering Carrie's earlier explanation of the home's layout, Emma bustled down the hall. Janie's room was somewhere in the area she explored. Luckily, a peek through an open doorway a dozen feet down the corridor from her own room revealed a tiny, blonde girl. She sat on the floor playing with a yellow pup. Emma stood for a moment, studying the child as her heart filled with an amazing realization. This little girl would be her stepdaughter by the end of the day.

The pup's welcoming bark echoed in the large room, giving away Emma's presence. Janie spun about. Her blue eyes narrowed with wariness.

A gentle smile curved Emma's lips as she crossed to seat herself tentatively on the braided rug. The pup bounded forward to lick her face. She let out a startled giggle a moment later when the animal crawled into her lap.

"Oh, my goodness! This must mean he likes me." Emma tussled with the exuberant pup until he calmed, then she turned her smile in Janie's direction. "Hello. My name is Emma, and you must be Janie. Is this your puppy?"

Tyler's daughter stared at her in wide-eyed suspicion for a moment longer before committing to a small nod.

"I saw you yesterday, but I didn't have a chance to say 'hi'. Did anyone tell you I was coming?"

Again she received a small nod. Emma's racing mind struggled for something else to say. She glanced around the room noting that it was every child's dream. A worn wooden rocking horse stood in the corner beside a huge box of toys. An intricately designed dollhouse topped off a small table built with the height of a child in mind. "You have a very nice room, Janie. My room looked kind of like this when I was your age. My Papa bought me a rocking horse once. If I remember correctly, his name was Rocker. Kind of a dumb name, wasn't it?"

Janie's tiny hand covered her mouth and hid a grin as she nodded her head.

Emma laughed. "Oh, I see you agree with me. Does your horse have a name?"

Janie looked at the toy horse, and then back to Emma with furrowed brows of indecision. She rose and walked to the play table to retrieve a chalkboard and a broken piece of chalk. Hesitating to stare at the stranger in her room, she finally returned, sat on the floor again and painstakingly scribbled something on the slate before handing it over. Strands of unruly blonde hair were pushed aside by chubby hands as she waited for a response.

Emma studied the childish scrawl and deciphered the word. "Storm?"

She glanced at Janie, and then at the window with a questioning look. Janie leaned forward, pointed to the board, and then back to the rocking horse that sat beneath the window. Emma still didn't understand. The child released a heavy, exaggerated sigh, took the slate from her new friend and labored once more with the broken piece of chalk. Finally, she held it up for Emma to see. On the board she had written the words "Daddy's horse".

"Oh, I get it now. Storm is the name of your daddy's horse, too?"

Janie nodded her head vigorously.

"I think that's a beautiful name. I used to have a white horse named Bonne. She ran as fast as the wind. Every night I would feed her a special treat, like a carrot or an apple."

The little girl sat with eyes wide and listened attentively to Emma's every word.

"Janie," Emma's voice was filled with hesitation. "Do you think we could be friends? Friends often like the same things. It seems we both like horses and puppies." She scratched the pup's ears as she spoke. "It would be fun if you could show me some of your special places outside. I've never been to Minnesota before. I'm afraid I might get lost if I go out exploring alone."

Janie's blue eyes moved to the pup. Emma sat quietly, letting the child make up her own mind and released the breath she held when Janie finally glanced up. A grin split the little girl's face. She reached out her chubby little fingers to take Emma's slender hand in hers.

Emma's face glowed with her own responding smile. It was so important that she start out on the right foot with this child. She squeezed the small, dimpled fingers, and a pact was formed.

Neither was aware that Tyler watched the exchange in silence from his vantage point in the hallway. He backed away slowly, unwilling at this point to let them know that he'd witnessed their tentative alliance of friendship.

* * * * *

She stood beside him, her hands clammy and her cheeks ashen, as the reverend awaited her response.

"I do," Emma replied in a whisper.

Tyler's back was ramrod stiff as he listened to her answer. A wave of *deja vu* washed over him. How many years had it been since he'd heard Sara say those same two words with such joy in her heart? Sara had been his partner, his friend and his lover. He'd loved her with all his heart and soul and, somewhere in time, it all went wrong.

Now, he repeated those same vows to a woman he hardly knew.

"And, by the power vested in me by the state of Minnesota, I now pronounce you man and wife." The elderly reverend smiled at the pair before him. "Tyler, you may kiss your bride."

Emma turned to face her new husband, stared up through wide, uncertain eyes at his handsome features and waited.

He bent to brush his lips against her cold ones and realized how clammy her hand was. Looking deep into the emerald depths before him, uncomfortable surprise at the anguish he saw there rippled through him.

A resounding round of applause saved them both the agony of speech. They turned as one to meet the happy faces behind them. Other than the immediate family, only three additional people had been invited to the ceremony, an older couple and a handsome, blond man that Emma gauged to be about Trevor's age. She hadn't had the opportunity to meet them before the wedding. Now curiosity got the better of her as she wondered who they were.

Janie, dressed in a lacy yellow frock with matching ribbons in her hair, stood beside Carrie with a wrinkled brow of confusion. Emma smiled at her stepdaughter. A wave of relief washed over her when the child answered with a grin of her own.

Tyler's brothers suddenly crowded before her. Trevor reached for Emma's cold hands. "Congratulations to both of you." His twinkling eyes met his older brother's wary ones. "My dear brother, Cole and I think we should both be afforded the chance to welcome our new sister-in-law to the family."

Tyler's eyes squinted even further with suspicion. "So, go ahead, Trevor. *Say* what you need to *say*," was his curt response.

Trevor's grin quickly became a smirk. "Ah, Tyler, *saying* something just won't cut it. Welcome to the family, Emma." He pulled the surprised bride into his arms and gave her a hearty kiss on the lips. It was followed by a tight squeeze—and a leer directed at his younger brother. "Cole, isn't there something you'd like to *say* to the new bride, too?"

The glower on Tyler's face left Cole with the distinct impression that his eldest brother was ready to punch Trevor. He stepped up for his turn though, with obvious pleasure. "Emma, I never was one for words." His mouth plummeted to capture his stunned sister-in-law's, but all the while he kept one eye on the red-faced man beside her. He ended the kiss with a loud smack, then quickly stepped back.

Tyler ignored his new wife's reddening cheeks and observed his brothers' antics through cool eyes, but, inside, his blood simmered.

Carrie quickly stepped in, before they came to blows. "Out of my way, you two!" She pushed Cole and Trevor aside and took Emma's hands in hers. "Congratulations, Emma. I'm so happy you're with us." She turned to her brother. "And I couldn't be happier for you, Tyler." She reached up to embrace him and whispered for his ears alone, "I love you, Ty. Everything will be fine, you'll see."

He stared back with a doubtful dip of the eyebrows.

Tyler's attention then turned to the family friends who attended the ceremony. He reached to grasp the palm of the blond man. "Hello, Steven. Thank you for coming." He tipped his head in the direction of the elderly couple who'd just joined them. "I would like you all to meet my wife, Emma. Emma, these good people are our nearest neighbors, Gregory and Laura Adams and their son, Steven."

"It's so nice to meet all of you." Emma hid her nervousness with a forced smile and accepted Laura's hand, but her senses were drawn to her husband. It seemed to her that another man had taken over Tyler's body — at least temporarily. The smile on his face produced the image of the typical proud and happy bridegroom. The possessive hand on the small of her back only added to the charade.

"Gregory used to be the local doctor," Tyler continued. "Steven has taken over his practice now since his father's retirement. We're all grateful he decided to come back home and set up shop."

A soft chuckle escaped Steven's throat with Tyler's comment, then he turned his attention to the bride. "It's very nice to meet you, Emma. And the reason Tyler is so happy that I chose to set up my practice in the area stems from the fact that I grew up with him and his brothers. I know all the scrapes they get into. One of us had to become a doctor to take care of the other three."

Emma laughed, but before Tyler could retort, Mamie pushed her way through the small crowd as fast as her girth would allow. She dabbed at her eyes with a lace handkerchief.

"Tyla and Miss Em! I'm so happy I'm leakin' water all over ma' new dress! Come here, the both of you, and gives Mamie a hug!"

Mamie got her wish. She released the newlyweds a moment later, stuffed her white hanky into the pocket of her dress and addressed the small crowd. "Time to be celebratin' the nuptials, it is! We got a yard plumb full of lumberjacks and their families just awaitin' to congratulate the new Missus, and they be ready for some fun. Yessiree. Time to be movin' this party outside." She turned with the expectation that one and all would automatically follow—and they did.

Janie, who'd conspicuously turned up at her father's side during the introductions, slid her tiny hand into Tyler's and gave it a quick tug. He lifted the child into his arms before turning to the very quiet Emma. "The masses await. Mamie will be hollering if we don't get outside soon." He grasped her elbow with his free hand and, as a family, they ventured out onto the front porch.

Emma was taken aback by the large number of people who stood in the yard and by the thunderous applause that accompanied their appearance. A small group of men equipped with fiddles, struck up Mendelssohn's *"Wedding March"* in their honor.

Knowing the people were employed by the Northern Pine Ranch, she was instantly overwhelmed at their unconditional acceptance as they waved and cheered—and wondered if they knew the real reason for the wedding. Forcing the thought from her mind, she raised her chin and gripped Tyler's arm, determined to enjoy the day if it killed her.

Trevor and Cole shouldered their way through the crowd and paused at the bottom of the steps. Each man held a glass of homemade beer in his hand. Trevor hailed the crowd to gain their attention. As the clamor died down, he turned back to face Tyler and Emma with his raised glass. Placing a shiny boot on the bottom step, he prepared to begin his speech. "I'd like to make a toast to the bride and groom! May they be happy and healthy for years to come and grow exceptionally old together!"

The crowd roared its approval. Trevor waved his hand for silence again, then shouted above the lessening din. "May they be prosperous their entire lives, and may they prove themselves forever young by begetting numerous children." He waved his glass of beer in the couple's general direction. "Take a look at them, folks! That shouldn't be too tall an order for either of them, especially Tyler! Hell, he's been tellin' me and Cole for years that he's the *big* man around here!"

The crowd exploded with laughter. Ribald comments abounded. It seemed that every man in attendance had ideas on just how to "beget" those children. Emma blushed deeply. Tyler threw his brother a malevolent look just before the younger Wilkins brothers raced up the steps, linked their hands together behind Emma and swept her off her feet. The crowd hooted its approval as the two men carried her through the gathering and away from the house.

Emma giggled uproariously, her earlier sullenness vanishing. "I beg you!" she screamed. "Please! Don't drop me!" She clung to their necks as the men chuckled and whisked her away.

The noise of the ensuing party was left behind when they rounded the corner of the barn. Cole and Trevor set their burden gently on an upturned barrel.

"Did you see the look on Tyler's face?" Cole laughed as he reached into a well-concealed basket and pulled out a bottle of fine wine and three glasses.

Emma wiped the laughter-born tears from her face and shook a finger at her kidnappers while Cole proceeded to fill the crystal goblets. "You had this planned all along, didn't you?" Her answer came in the form of twin shrugs from her captors. "You two are cads for taking me away from my wedding celebration."

A lopsided grin appeared on Cole's face as he handed a glass to both Trevor and Emma. "We just thought we'd like to spend a private moment with you. We wanted you to know how happy we are to have you in our midst. Besides, the two of us decided years ago that it's great sport to get Tyler's goat."

The trio companionably clinked glasses. The men finished their drinks in one swallow.

Emma sipped at hers thoughtfully. "You two will never know how thankful I am that you accepted me so readily—especially when you consider the reason why I'm here in the first place." Her slender shoulders rose and fell with a sigh. "I know it's no secret that Tyler isn't too happy about all of this. I guess I can't blame him for feeling the way he does. My father didn't give him a choice...neither did I." Her gaze lowered to her lap. She busied herself with brushing imaginary dirt from the front of her dress.

The men exchanged thoughtful glances.

"Don't worry yourself about the future," Trevor stated and reached out to give her hand a reassuring squeeze. "Listen to me—I know my brother. There's no way you'd be here if he didn't want you to be. He would've come up with some reason to keep you in New York, or he would've sent you packing the minute you arrived in Duluth. Time will work things out." He released her hand to pat her shoulder, albeit rather awkwardly. "Hell, look at what you've got to work with. Between Cole, Carrie, myself, and especially Mamie, he'll have to come around sooner or later."

"You two are quite a pair," she responded with a shaky laugh. "I think we should probably be returning soon, don't you?"

Cole retrieved the glass from Emma's hand as Trevor assisted her from the barrel's surface. "Excuse me if this is too personal, Emma, but I have to ask you something. In fact, I've wanted to ask you this since I first met you." His gentle gaze held her wary one for a long moment before he finally voiced the question. "How do you really feel about Tyler?"

The inquiry took her by surprise, but she answered honestly. "When I first met Tyler, I thought he was the most arrogant man I'd ever met. But, as we spent more time together, he did something to my insides that no other man ever has. I couldn't get him out of my mind." Emma swallowed to regain her composure and struggled to find the right words. "The night before he left New York, we...ended up together—I'd rather not get into the details. The next morning, I watched from my bedroom window as he rode out of my life. I knew, then and there, that I'd fallen in love with him and hadn't even realized it." She looked up to meet her brother-in-law's understanding gaze. "And yes, Cole, I love him still, with all my heart and soul. I just wish I could tell him that but, until he's ready to accept me into his life completely, I have to keep that knowledge to myself."

"Emma," Trevor rolled his eyes in exasperation, "why don't you just tell him?"

"Because he wouldn't believe me. He'd just think they were empty words spoken to ensure that my baby has a name." She shook her head. "This is the way it must be, Trevor, at least for now. So, please keep this conversation to yourselves. I just wanted to assure you both that I'm not playing with your brother's emotions. I love him. It will be up to me to discover if he can love me back."

Cole shrugged his broad shoulders. "All right, Em, we'll abide by your decision if that's the way you want it. For the record, however, I think you're making a mistake by not telling him." A mischievous grin lit his eyes a second later. "Don't be surprised if we give Cupid a helping hand once in awhile."

Another squeal left her throat when they swept her off her feet once more and carted her back to the celebration.

Trevor and Cole deposited the bride before her husband a few seconds later, then beat a hasty retreat in the direction of the beer table. Neither of them dared to glance back and check the expression on their brother's face. Emma, too, couldn't bring herself to meet his gaze and simply walked off to stand beside Carrie who chatted with guests.

Tyler's brow dipped in a frown as he watched her move gracefully amid the friendly crowd. She was in her element now—the perfect hostess—yet her face was decidedly flushed compared to its earlier pallor. His cool gaze strayed to his brothers, where they chuckled loudly and swilled more beer, wondering what they'd said to her. He looked at Emma again and observed her take Janie's hand as yet another well-wisher offered congratulations. She was absolutely stunning in her white lace dress. The sun glinted off her hair turning it to the deep shade of auburn he'd remembered so many nights since he'd left her in New York.

Ah, hell... Tyler straightened his shoulders and started toward where Emma stood amid a group of merry lumberjacks. *I may as well play the proud bridegroom instead of standing here grumbling by myself...*

* * * * *

The afternoon waned and dusk descended long before the lumberjacks and their families left for their own homes. The afternoon had been filled with music and dancing and enough food to feed the entire lot for a week.

Steven Adams and his parents sat in the large, open living room, enjoying one last nightcap with the Wilkins family before heading home themselves. Emma's mind wandered as she listened to the different conversations around her. Thoughts of the day floated through her mind.

Earlier, when the guests insisted that the newly wedded couple dance the first waltz, she'd held her breath as Tyler took her in his arms. Within his tender embrace, the more than one hundred onlookers ceased to exist. As they slowly moved to the music, she recalled another dance and another time.

Tyler had seemed to be attentive all afternoon. Now though, he sat on the opposite divan with Steven and discussed inconsequential happenings around the area. It was as if she wasn't even present in the room.

She had absolutely no clue where the night would lead—but she desperately hoped it would be in his room. Emma craved the opportunity to talk with him alone, to tell him of her dreams for their marriage, but didn't want to appear eager in front of the neighbors. So, she sat patiently, playing the obedient wife and waited for Tyler to make a move. She pushed her uncertainties aside, using the opportunity to study the other personalities in the room.

She observed Carrie accept her drunken brothers' biting comments with good humor. Strangely, though Steven Adams was only too willing to add a comment of his own now and then, Carrie totally ignored him.

Tyler watched his new wife secretly from the corner of his eye. He'd done everything possible to delay going upstairs. In fact, he'd had even gone so far as to invite Steven and his parents in for a nightcap.

He wouldn't spend the night with her. It didn't matter that they were married now. And he damn well planned to stick to his guns. They hadn't even talked about the baby any more. How could he take her to the marriage bed with the parentage of her child still hanging over their heads?

The moment of truth fast approached when their three guests stood, offered a few last words of congratulations and left for home. Trevor and Cole, never ones to be discreet, winked at Tyler, and then headed for the stairs. Carrie, in turn, hugged both the bride and groom and whispered words of encouragement in their ears before retiring to her own room.

Once they were alone, Tyler poured himself another drink before he cast a hesitant glance in Emma's direction. "Would you care for a nightcap?"

"No, thank you," she declined and scurried for something to say. "Mamie did a wonderful job with the wedding."

"Yes, she did. She was determined to make it a nice day for everyone involved."

"Tyler?" Emma eyed him closely, determined to begin the conversation that could make or break their future. "I have to ask you something." She swallowed convulsively, then her words came out in a rush. "Do you want me to stay or would you rather I begin plans to return to New York?" She held her breath as she awaited his answer and prayed he wouldn't send her away.

The minutes ticked by as he swirled the brandy in his glass. His silence resounded off the four walls around them.

He had watched her closely today — and he had watched his family. What did he want? Yesterday, the answer had seemed so clear. It was obvious that they already were enamored with her. Even Janie walked around with a smile pasted on her face — the type of smile he hadn't seen on her little features since Sara died.

Thoughts of New York, of how he'd felt about Emma that last night, tugged at his mind. She was so damn beautiful and it would be so easy to carry her up to the bed.

But did he believe her? Did he believe that she'd been with no other men? Did he believe, unequivocally, that the baby was his?

No, he didn't.

The evening of the reception in New York flashed through his brain. Emma, alone on the terrace with Samuel Fontaine — her disheveled condition when she returned to the ballroom after apparently enjoying his advances. It was a scene that would be forever imprinted in his mind. They'd both disappeared after returning to the ballroom. Were they together then, too? Samuel said he was going to find her and finish what they started.

How many other men were there that I don't know about? Will I ever be sure that the baby is mine? He sighed heavily. There were just too many unresolved issues between them that couldn't be settled in the space of one evening.

Tyler rubbed his forehead with a shaky hand. "I don't know what to tell you, Emma, because I don't know how I feel right at this moment, and that's the way of it." He watched the glimmer of hope fade from her eyes. "Go to sleep. It's been a long day for you. I still have a few things to check on that might take me awhile." He set his glass on the table and glanced at her defeated expression one last time. "Goodnight. I'll see you in the morning."

Crossing the room, he left without looking back.

Emma sat and numbly stared at nothing. Tyler had thrown his decision at her feet. The pain of his rejection flowed through her body as surely as the tears that rolled down her cheeks. She had no way to prove to him that she'd never been with another man. He would never trust her, never want her completely.

She rose and shuffled up the stairs only moments later.

Chapter Fifteen

୫୬

Cole and Trevor stabled their horses late the next evening after spending the day with one of the cutting crews. Their tired gazes were drawn to the barn's entrance when Carrie stomped through the open doors with a scowl etched across her face. She marched straight toward them.

"Shit," Trevor muttered to his brother. "She's carrying a head of steam."

Cole ducked behind his horse. "You handle this one. I'm too damn tired to explain why we're late."

"Hi, Carrie," Trevor jumped in before she had a chance to say anything. "Don't nag at us for being late and missing supper. We've had one helluva day and just want to get cleaned up, eat and get some shut-eye." He settled his saddle over the wooden gate with a grunt and proceeded to fill the feed bin with hay.

She stared at them with arms crossed while her foot tapped a rapid beat on the straw-covered floor. "I've been waiting for the two of you all day. Did you by any chance run into Tyler on the trail?"

"No. Why, is there a problem?" Trevor turned with an armful of straw and met her gaze.

"Only that Tyler and Emma slept in separate rooms last night. He took off this morning and hasn't returned yet. He left Mamie a note to tell the two of you he might not be back until tomorrow or the day after. Poor Emma was on the verge of tears all day. What are we going to do with him?"

Cole stepped from behind his horse and moved out of the stall. "How do you know they slept apart last night?"

"Because Mamie brought a breakfast tray up to Tyler's room, and he was alone. He nearly snapped her head off, then told her he didn't need it, but to check on Emma in the *other room* to see if she was hungry. When she knocked on Emma's door, she didn't get an answer right away. Thinking Emma was asleep, Mamie opened it. The poor thing was still in her wedding dress, curled up in a chair, and the bed wasn't even mussed. Some wedding night, huh?"

The two brothers glanced at each other with a shared realization. Tyler had created an awful situation for himself and for Emma.

"What in hell is wrong with him?" Trevor shook his head, then tempered his words. "Look, all we can do is support both of them, I guess, and see what happens. Christ, with the mood Tyler's been in lately, if Cole or I say anything, he'll likely take a swing at us."

"Well, Mamie is ready to start swinging in Tyler's direction. She mumbled all day about second chances and him not knowing what he's got. She's been slamming pans around in the kitchen like there's no tomorrow. Between Mamie's ranting and raving and Emma's tears, I couldn't take it anymore. I finally took Janie out riding just to get away for a while. Poor Katy said the afternoon was horrible."

Cole squeezed Carrie's arm as he walked by her. "You keep talking like that and I'm gonna saddle up and head back north." He pushed his hat further back on his head and sighed. "Let's just wait and see how this develops. Tyler will come to his senses eventually."

"Well, he'd better hurry before he makes Emma sick. She doesn't deserve this. She's got enough to worry about with keeping herself and the baby healthy."

Trevor doused the light in the barn, and the three siblings walked back to the house.

"I wonder if things will ever return to normal around here." Cole's words echoed the thoughts of his family members.

Carrie shrugged as she took his arm. "If Tyler would only open his eyes and see what he could have, he might be truly happy again."

Trevor swung a jacketed arm over his sister's shoulders. "They've got to figure it out on their own, Carrie. Let's just give them time."

* * * * *

Tyler poked at his small campfire and added another piece of wood. As the flame flared, he remembered her beautiful smile and how it became wider and more frequent yesterday as the afternoon progressed—a smile that charmed just about everyone in her wake. He also remembered the pained expression on her face when he'd told her to go to bed alone, and it had just about killed him.

It was not in his nature to be cruel to anyone, but when she asked what he wanted, it had scared the hell out of him. Had she expected to spend the night with him? He jammed another chunk of wood into the fire and watched the smoke carry the sparks upward.

His chest tightened again with the memory and, to make matters worse, instead of staying home this morning and taking the opportunity to apologize, he'd ridden out to fight his demons alone.

Laying back, he rested his head against the saddle, then gazed up into the night sky filled with thousands of stars. His throat clogged with emotion as he focused on one that sparkled brighter than the rest.

"Is that you, Sara? I wanted so much for us. I wanted a long, happy life with you and Janie, but fate stepped in and stole you from me. When I met Emma, the last thing on my mind was the thought of spending my life with another woman. Hell, it took me weeks just to get over my guilt for betraying you that last night in New York." A heavy sigh lifted his chest. "I never planned on there ever being anyone but you. I never planned on Emma moving into my heart…"

He tucked his hands beneath his head and continued to stare at the ebony sky above him. "I'm sorry, Sara, but I don't want her to leave. I don't know what, if anything, is going to happen between us. But I do know that I need her to stay at the ranch if we're to ever straighten this mess out. I can't let her go."

And what about the baby? What if the child wasn't his? He didn't know if he could put aside his anger and love another man's child as much as he loved Janie. His daughter's happiness meant everything to him. She'd already made it clear that she'd accepted Emma unconditionally, and he didn't want her hurt again simply because he couldn't figure out his own mind.

He shook his head again. "I don't know if what I feel could ever amount to loving her. Hell, I don't even know how she feels about me. She just said that she refused to raise the baby without a name. We just need to find the right time to discuss everything rationally, I guess. I want to believe in her—it's the only way this marriage is going to work. Janie deserves some happiness and the chance to have a mother again." Sudden tears glistened in his eyes. "You can never come back, Sara. As hard as that is for me, I know in my heart that I need to let go of you."

His thoughtful gaze swept the sky above him one last time, wondering if maybe Sara, in some divined wisdom, had sent him and Janie their second chance at happiness. The simple thought eased his mind considerably.

Tyler threw one more chunk of wood into the fire, reached for a blanket and settled himself on the hard ground. "You could be sleeping in a soft bed," he muttered as he bunched his jacket into a makeshift pillow. He lay his head down, readjusted the coat when a button poked his ear, and then flopped onto his back. "You goddamn idiot. You could be in a warm bed with a soft woman beside you."

He tossed his thoughts away quickly. No. He wouldn't lay a hand on her until he got the situation resolved in his mind. He needed to find the trust.

He watched the bright star twinkle above him again and thought of Sara. His dead wife would've wanted him to create a new life for himself. He hoped though, that she'd understand the future course of events.

* * * * *

Emma stepped onto the front porch and hugged the woolen shawl tighter around her slim shoulders to ward off the chill of the night air and her acute disappointment. The canter of horses' hooves in the yard earlier was due to Cole and Trevor's return, not Tyler's, and her spirits had plummeted even lower with her husband's continued absence. Granted, they probably wouldn't have spoken to one another that evening, but just the knowledge that Tyler was home would have done wonders to raise her lagging spirits.

She'd waited for her brothers-in-law to settle themselves in for the night before quietly escaping the house to sit on the porch swing. Listening now to the croak of distant frogs and the song of a nearby loon, she pondered the life she'd been thrown into so quickly. She found it hard to believe that he could so callously omit her from his life—especially after what the two of them had endured in the last forty-eight hours.

A wolf howled in the darkness. The lonely cry combined with the cool night air raised goose bumps on her skin. The stars that twinkled overhead had a calming effect though as she absorbed the beauty of the night. Was Tyler close enough to hear the haunting bay?

She rose from the wooden swing, stepped down off the porch and into the yard. Her gaze moved from one twinkling star to the next, but even the peaceful night could not ease the frustration that came racing back.

"I'll make you want me, Tyler. I know that you'll hold Sara's spirit close to you forever, because the life you shared with her can't simply be forgotten." She laid her hand on her chest. "But I am flesh and blood, and I am here. I won't let you throw away what we could have. I don't care if you never return my feelings. I'll love you forever, and that's the way of *that*, Mr. Wilkins."

She stood in the middle of the yard, her eyes closed and her face turned upward. She willed her whispered plea to reach him. The stillness of the moment engulfed her until the minuscule fluttering of butterfly wings quivered within her womb. Her eyes widened with wonder. Slowly, she brought a trembling hand to her stomach, the shawl forgotten as it slipped from her shoulders and slipped to the ground. She waited, breathless, and soon it came again—the barely discernable, featherlight touch deep within her.

Her child.

A gentle smile touched her lips. "Oh yes, Tyler—someday, you'll want me."

* * * * *

The next morning, Emma was dressed and ready for the day by seven a.m. Filled with energy for the first time since arriving in Minnesota, a new resolve formed within her mind. She would no longer press Tyler for a resolution to their problem, but neither would she permit him to walk away from her or their marriage. She was determined not to lose her temper again. As hard as it might be at times, she would simply get him used to her presence in degrees. If her plan worked, he would eventually come to accept her.

She opened the kitchen door and stopped dead when she saw the object of her thoughts sitting at the table. He conversed with his daughter, whose tiny chin rested on the palms of her hands atop bent elbows while she listened attentively.

Mamie stomped across the kitchen with two plates full of pancakes and bacon. She set Tyler's dish before him with a bang, causing the contents to jump on the platter's surface. Janie received hers considerably quieter.

Emma hid a smile. Mamie was making a fine show of retaliation for his behavior of the last few days. When she spied Emma standing in the doorway, however, her mood changed dramatically. The old woman immediately ignored Tyler and hustled the young bride to the table.

"You jes sit yoursef down and Mamie'll cook anythin' you wants for breakfast!" She pulled out a chair, laid her gnarled hands on Emma's shoulders and forced her to sit. "What be soundin' good to you this fine mornin', Miss Em? I gots ham, eggs, whatever your lil' heart desires. Yessiree!"

Tyler eyed the bowl of pancake batter on the counter and the bacon that lay on a tin plate atop the woodstove, and couldn't help but remember the words he'd heard come out of Mamie's mouth countless times while he was growing up.

I don't run no restaurant where people can pick and choose their food. You swallow what I put in front of you, or you go hungry!

Now, there she was, ready to go out back and kill a chicken if that was what Miss Em wanted to eat.

Emma, well aware of Mamie's game and still holding firm to her new resolve, thought it best not to start the day by antagonizing her new husband. "Those pancakes look so tasty that I think I'll just have to try them for breakfast, Mamie." Her eyes instantly widened in horror when the old black woman whisked Tyler's plate from beneath his nose and set it before her.

"Here, Miss Em, you eat offen this here plate. It be spankin' hot and fresh as you'll ever get it. And Tyla, he can just be gentlemanlike enough to let his lady eat first."

Tyler sat with his fork held in midair. Now, Mamie poked a finger at his shoulder, the other hand on her hip. Her stern expression dared him to disagree. "Ain't that right, boy? You gentlemanlike enough this mornin' to let your *wife* eat first?"

Emma lowered her eyes to the traveling plate of flapjacks in an effort to hide her amusement at Mamie's obvious performance. Tyler's gaze burned the top of her head. Finally, she peeked up from beneath long eyelashes. Her eyes met the twinkling emerald ones before her. A hesitant smile curved her lips.

Satisfied, Mamie turned back to the stove. Tyler, in turn, rolled his eyes for Emma's benefit. He released his breath in a long sigh. "That's fine, Mamie. I can wait a few minutes longer." He reached for his coffee and waited patiently for another helping.

Sensing that her husband had set aside his intolerance of her, at least for the moment, Emma broke the impending silence. "I wanted to ask if you have a horse that I might borrow. I wanted to go riding yesterday, but didn't feel I should just take one without your permission. You weren't here for me to ask... I promise I won't go too far until I know the lay of the land." Her steady gaze met his as she continued. "And I really do miss riding on a regular basis."

Tyler set his cup down. "You're free to use any horse on this ranch, Emma. In fact, you can use anything you want, without my...permission. All I ask is that you be careful and keep a sedate pace. Please stay on either the main roads or the well-used trails. It's very easy to get lost when the landmarks so closely resemble one another."

Her smile brightened with his answer, and she attacked her pancakes with gusto. "Thank you, Tyler. I haven't ridden in a long time. I can't wait to explore the ranch." She turned to Janie who sat quietly listening to them. "Do you have a horse?"

The little girl nodded her head vigorously. Emma swung her gaze back to her husband. "Do you think Janie could ride along with me? I won't let the house out of my sight."

He glanced from one eager face to the other and made a quick decision. "You know, I have a quiet day today. How would you two like it if I tagged along? Then I could show you where to ride safely."

Emma's heart pounded wildly in her chest as she looked at the little girl again. "What do you think, Janie? I think it's a grand idea!"

The girl's head bobbed with enthusiasm.

Mamie placed a new breakfast plate on the table before Tyler with a huge smile creasing her dark face. "Well, that be one of the better ideas I seen planted around here in a long time. Yessiree! Tyla, you take Miss Em down to the barn and let her pick out a horse. Meantime, I be packin' a picnic lunch. After Janie changes her clothes, I be sendin' her down with it. Yessiree. It be one fine day for a ride."

Tyler's eyes followed the old black woman as she bustled about the kitchen humming a happy tune. He shook his head slowly before turning his attention back to Emma. "Did you want to change clothes, too, before we leave? I'll wait here for you, and then we'll go down to the barn."

Emma leapt up from her chair. "I'll be right back!"

* * * * *

With Tyler in the lead, Emma and Janie turned off the main trail and moved slowly down a brush-covered slope. Little by little, a small lake came into view as they neared the bottom.

"Tyler, it's beautiful!" Emma's green eyes scanned the quiet clearing that lay before them. Huge pine trees edged it, enclosing them from the rest of the world and all its problems.

"I thought you might like this place. Janie and I come here all the time." He dismounted Storm, then moved to help Emma from the back of a gentle mare. Their gazes met for one heart stopping moment before her feet found the ground. He quickly stuffed his hands inside his pants pockets as he took in her excited expression.

Emma grasped Janie's hand and led her to the water's edge. Small ripples glistened in the sunlight. Across the lake, a doe and her baby drank. The sun warmed her cheeks as she glanced up at Tyler when he joined them. She had to smile.

He had to grin back. Her face literally glowed in the morning sun. He had all he could do to bring his attention back to the present and the reason he'd brought them there in the first place. Ripping his gaze from his beautiful wife, he ruffled the soft hair on his daughter's head. "Why don't you get the picnic basket, Janie, and we'll eat lunch."

She immediately turned and raced to her pony to free the basket from where it was securely attached to the saddle. Tyler busied himself with spreading out a blanket on the fragrant earth. Soon, the three were eating the lunch Mamie prepared for them.

Emma picked at a cold chicken leg, glancing secretly at her husband. The change in him was nothing short of amazing. He was funny, attentive and, again, more like the man she met in New York, not like the stranger who'd greeted her so cruelly only a few days before.

"This is my favorite place in the world." Tyler leaned back on his elbows. A lazy, contented smile curved his firm lips.

Emma's eyes scanned the cozy clearing again and finally rested on Janie's slight form where she played by the water's edge. "I can understand why. It's so quiet and serene." She took another sip of Mamie's homemade wine. "Do you come here often?"

"My brothers and I used to camp here all the time when we were kids. We'd build a big fire and sleep under the stars. I guarantee you though, it wasn't all that serene when the three of us were here together. Trevor never shut his mouth."

A giggle escaped Emma's throat. "He does like to tell stories, doesn't he? He's quite the character."

"Hell, what you've heard come out of his mouth is nothing compared to when he was a boy. We had this hair-brained idea that we were going to breed horses when we grew up. He could go on about it for hours."

She tipped her head in his direction, and the simple movement caused her thick braid of hair to fall from her shoulder and lay across an ample breast. "Tell me more."

The innocent display was enough to make Tyler's heart jump in his chest. "It was always our dream to raise fine riding stock some day. We used to sit right here and draw pictures of foaling barns and riding paddocks in the sand."

"Why didn't you ever do it?"

He shrugged. "There just never seems to be enough time to make it happen. We still talk about it from time to time, but it would mean backing off from the lumbering business, and many of our men would be without jobs." He rolled onto his side and propped himself up on an elbow. "They're lumberjacks, not horse breeders. What would they do for a living?"

Emma was overwhelmed once again at the generosity of the Wilkins men. They had put a lifelong dream on hold for the sake of the families who worked so hard for them.

Tyler reached to pour himself another glass of wine as he reflected on his own words. "Maybe it'll happen someday. There'll come a time when there won't be enough timber to harvest, and we'll have to branch out into other areas. Conservation has always been high on our list, so we continually replant and replenish the forests, but it'll take years for those trees to reach cutting age. So, maybe in the meantime, Trevor, Cole and I can finally achieve the thing we want most to do."

"I couldn't help noticing what beautiful stock you keep on the ranch." She glanced at her husband's horse. "Storm would make a wonderful sire."

"I agree, but we've already used him as stud to most of the mares on the ranch, so we'd have to bring in fresh brood mares with good sturdy lines. If we ever decide to look at this project seriously, it would mean taking time away from the ranch and the mill to do it right." His green eyes watched his daughter stack rocks beside the shoreline. "Maybe someday. I know one thing—it's been discussed a thousand times, mostly when we were young and right here in this very spot where we sit."

Emma listened to the cadence of his voice. She would never tire of it. His story captured her heart. It was easy to imagine the three Wilkins men as young boys, dreaming of their future and making a pact to be together always.

Her gaze swept the clearing again—a place where dreams were made—and noticed for the first time an area where a campfire had recently burned. She brought it to his attention. "It seems someone else has discovered your secret place—and in the last few days or so, no less."

Tyler, who busily packed the basket for the ride home, finally glanced up at her. "It's my fire. I spent the night here recently." He stood, casually brushed off his pants, and then crossed to Janie's pony, checking the cinch to cover the instant silence.

Emma sat on the blanket and watched after him for a moment. Her gaze moved to the water and the ripples formed by rocks Janie threw into its center. *So, this is where he was last night—even though he won't admit it. Does the fact that he brought me here today, to his special place, mean something?*

She decided not to question him further. This was a day she would always hold dear to her heart, and she wouldn't ruin the memory by bringing up the fact that he'd left her the morning after their wedding.

She stood, brushed off the back of her skirt, called for Janie and walked to the horses to return home.

Chapter Sixteen

ಸಿ

The middle of October found Emma firmly ensconced within Tyler's home. She'd been in residence for only a month, but already had become an intricate part of the ranch by helping with the household chores, much to Mamie's contrary wishes. The old woman stated firmly that she received enough help from Carrie and the new woman, Katy O'Malley. Emma shouldn't bother with such day-to-day tasks in her condition. Emma staunchly held her ground, however, and informed those around her that it was her home, too. Mamie finally gave in and steered the easier tasks in the young woman's direction.

Emma was an avid pupil. The women of the ranch taught her how to can the vegetables they harvested and, when Carrie showed her how to milk a cow, they both ended up with tears of laughter streaming down their faces at Emma's inept attempts to fill her pail.

In New York, she'd never had to participate in the actual management of the household and now found her days busy from morning to night. Janie taught her how to sneak eggs from the nest of a roosting chicken. They also spent hours together gathering the last of the harvest from the numerous vegetable gardens on the property. In the end, it was those first weeks in Minnesota that helped form an unbreakable bond between the two females in Tyler's life.

The air turned cooler and colored leaves fell from the trees. Tyler spent most of his time now with Trevor and Cole at the logging camps. The brothers feverishly pushed the logging crews to complete the necessary harvest before the rivers clogged with ice.

The nights when the men returned home were few and far between, which only served to make Emma long for her husband more. Most times, they were able to send a message ahead of their arrival. Emma, Janie and Carrie always prepared a special celebration in honor of their homecoming. Those evenings were always filled with laughter. Trevor never failed to regale them with stories about their days spent in the woods.

Emma's pregnancy was obvious to the casual observer now. Steven Adams came by the ranch often to check on her welfare. Consequently, doctor and patient struck up a comfortable friendship. One day, he also became her confidante when he surprised her with a personal question as he packed his medical bag.

"Is there a reason why you and Tyler have separate bedrooms? I'm not trying to pry, but, as your doctor, I just want you to know it's perfectly safe to have intimate relations with your husband."

Emma cheeks colored to a bright, rosy hue as she sat quietly in the chair, pondering how to explain their situation. When she offered no information, Steven pulled up a chair and took her hands in his.

"You can talk to me, Emma. I'm not only your friend, I'm your doctor. Anything you say will be confidential." He watched Emma's expression change from embarrassment to uncertainty and, finally, to determination.

"I suppose you don't know the full circumstances surrounding our marriage, do you?"

"What I know is that you and he met in New York. You became pregnant with his child, then traveled here to marry him." He squeezed her hand gently. "Don't be embarrassed by the situation you've found yourself in. Do you think you're the first decent woman to become pregnant out of wedlock?"

"I know, Steven, but there are so many other factors in our case." She rose to stand before the window. He patiently waited for her to continue.

"Tyler and I have not occupied the same bed since the night we conceived this child. We spent that last night in New York together by a trick of fate. Tyler was pretty well intoxicated, entered my room by mistake and...I asked him to stay." She turned to seek his understanding gaze. "I want you to know that, Steven. I want you to know that this whole mess is just as much my fault as his."

"Go on, Emma. I'm trying hard to piece together your story, but I fear I don't know everything yet, do I?"

She shook her head. A bittersweet smile curved her lips as she turned back to the window. "Tyler doesn't believe the baby is his. He thinks I've been with other men and that I chose him because he was my best prospect for a safe and secure future." She shrugged her slim shoulders. "At least that's the only theory I can come up with after trying to piece it together in my own mind. I can't seem to convince him he's wrong. Because of that, he refuses to treat me as his wife and invite me to his bed."

Steven sat quietly and mused over her words. Her response reflected the current situation to a tee. "How does he treat you when the two of you are alone? From what I've seen, he's pleasant enough when we're all together."

She turned back from the window with a sigh. "The first few nights after I arrived were really rough. He was angry and felt cornered. My own behavior was none too ladylike, either." She shook her head and raised a rueful eyebrow. "I seem to recall telling him that he was more of a bastard than this baby could ever be. He left the morning after the wedding and didn't come back until the following day. Since then, we've been like strangers forced to live in the same house. Amiable and polite, yet distant. It never goes beyond that." She crossed back to the chair, sank down and gazed at her friend with sad, defeated eyes. "I know Tyler needs time to accept me as his wife, and I'm willing to wait as long as it takes. He's still grieving for Sara. I would expect no less from a man who loved his wife as deeply as Tyler did. She's been gone only two years. I'm hoping though, that someday he'll love and trust me as much as he did her."

The young doctor's thoughtful, understanding gaze moved over his patient's beautiful features with an invisible shake of the head. *You're a damn lucky man, Tyler, and you don't even know it.*

* * * * *

The thwack of axes biting into hardened tree bark and the whine of double-handled saws echoed through the forest. Those sounds mingled with shouts of the workers and constant whinnies from the draft horses to create an atmosphere of organized chaos. The logging crew was almost finished culling the last stand of timber. Two more days would see them home again with their families. No more timberline shacks. For most, it would mean home and hearth, working close to home during the day and their wives beside them at night. For Tyler and Cole, it simply meant the end to another cutting season, one that had grown agonizingly long.

"I'm glad I listened to Trevor and hired extra men to clear this stand of trees," Tyler commented as he and Cole oversaw the beehive of activity below. "We wouldn't be near this close to finishing up if we hadn't. I'm ready to go home and just stay put for a while." An image of Emma's smiling face flitted through his brain.

"I have to agree with you there. We should really see about keeping this last bunch of guys working, though. They've more than proven themselves in the last week." A sly smile lifted the corners of Cole's mouth. "I'm not only getting good and ready for some of Mamie's cooking, but a soft bed at night. Hell, I'm even more good and ready for someone soft to share that bed with."

Tyler pretended not to hear Cole's last comment. Instead, he stretched his long arms above his head in a casual show of disinterest, then trudged back up to the top of the hill to watch the line of men who readied the trailer of logs that were to be sent down the embankment and into the river.

He yearned to get home. He was ready to make peace with Emma. He'd been at the camp for the past week and, not once, had quit thinking of her. She had even invaded his nightly dreams.

He lifted his hat and swept a hand through his thick hair thinking about the past month. Constant agitation had plagued him since they'd been back at the ranch. When he couldn't take her close proximity inside the house any longer, he'd urge Emma and Janie outdoors, where he could put a little distance between them.

The ruse also provided a means to observe his wife and daughter together. He could find no fault with Emma's attitude toward the little girl. She always made sure Janie's needs came before her own. Most importantly, the child adored her.

The rest of his family, too, seemed entranced by her bright outlook in everything she did. Wherever Emma went, her good nature followed, and her admirers grew by leaps and bounds. Tyler actually found humor in the fact that if a decision had to be made for one of them to leave the ranch, his family would pack his bags without a second thought.

He'd gone over and over his marriage and finally came to the realization that he wanted Emma in his life. He had to believe that the baby was his. Emma deserved her own past just as he did.

Tyler felt a weight lift from his shoulders with the decision. Only two more days—two days that would seem like a lifetime now that he couldn't wait to go home to her. He would court her as she'd never been courted before—until she was weak with desire.

He walked down the hill toward the shore with a much lighter step, then paused when Trevor hollered to him from above. He turned and waved to let his brother know he was listening.

Trevor shouted above the din. "Get the men ready! We'll send the logs down in a minute. Whistle when you're set and we'll let 'em loose!"

Tyler waved again in confirmation, and then continued down the trail beside the treeless skidway.

The Earth shuddered. Nearly at the bottom of the incline, Tyler whirled just in time to see logs crashing down the earthen ramp. His alert gaze swung back to the water's edge where three men worked unawares, trying to break up a jam that had backed the logs up more than thirty feet from the shore. He waved his arms wildly and bellowed a warning above the deafening roar of river water as he raced toward them. If he didn't get their attention, they would be killed.

Tyler leapt onto the first of the congested logs. His feet flew over their cut lengths in an effort to reach his men. His startled mind raced in wonder that Trevor had given the go-ahead to release the trailer without his signal. He was within fifteen feet of the three loggers when one glanced up to see the gigantic timbers barreling toward them.

The man frantically motioned to the other two and leapt out of harm's way.

Tyler recklessly picked his way across the logjam as fast as his feet would carry him, then jumped to safety himself and spun to check the whereabouts of his men as the barreling timbers rolled down the hill less than six feet from him. Suddenly, one log bounced off another and shot through the air. It clipped Tyler on the side of his head, knocking him to the ground.

* * * * *

Tyler awoke in one of the logging shacks to a headache so fierce he could barely move his head. His eyes fluttered open. A second later, he tried to sit up.

"Jesus Christ, Tyler, you scared the hell out of us!" Trevor railed. He laid his hands on his brother's shoulders and held him down. "Don't sit up. Just stay where you are. The men are bringing a wagon around and we're going to get you home." His face was the same pale shade as Cole's.

Tyler struggled to remember the events leading up to the accident. Trevor was supposed to wait for his signal, giving him time to clear the area beside the shoreline.

Ignoring the throbbing in his head, he squinted at his brother. "What the hell were you doing up there? You were supposed to wait for my whistle. I wasn't even to the bottom of the skidway yet. I could've been killed, along with three other men."

Relief flooded Trevor's eyes. Tyler's memory seemed to be intact, but he still had a nasty, blood-oozing bump on the side of his head. They needed to get him home so Steve could stitch it up. "We were ready at the top of the ramp. When I saw you were still making your way to the bottom though, I walked over to Cole and Jack. The next thing I knew, I heard the logs roll off the trailer. It was so damn noisy that we couldn't get your attention." His masculine features blanched once more at the thought of the possible outcome. His voice lowered. "One of the men saw somebody from the new group cut the main holding rope."

Tyler's fuzzy brain digested his brother's words. Someone had purposely tried to kill him and three others? His stomach churned at the thought. "Did you find out who it was?"

Trevor shook his head. "He's gone. With the logs rolling down the hill, everyone was just worried about getting your attention. Whoever slit the rope took off." He peered closely at his brother. "So, do you have any enemies we don't know about?"

Tyler pondered the question. Finally, his glassy eyes met his brother's concerned ones. "Well, apparently I must." He winced. "Jesus, my head is pounding so hard that I can't even think."

At that moment, the foreman stuck his head through the open door. "The wagon's here, Trevor."

"Thanks, Jack," he replied over his shoulder, then looked at Tyler again. "Okay, let's take this nice and slow."

Cole and Trevor helped Tyler sit upright. Immediate concern clouded their gazes when his eyes rolled back in his head and the bandage on his head soaked with blood. They carefully pulled him to a standing position.

Try as he might, Tyler couldn't keep his legs straight beneath him. His body dipped in the direction of the floor. Everything went black.

* * * * *

Emma and Carrie hung laundry on the clotheslines, both of them giggling about something Mamie had said earlier. Emma reached for another sheet and automatically handed one edge to her sister-in-law.

Carrie's eyebrow rose when she glanced across the length of white material and saw the happy sparkle in Emma's eyes. "You sure are enjoying the laundry today."

The other woman's smile simply widened as she threw her end of the sheet over the line.

Carrie placed her hands on her slender hips. "Okay, you look like the cat that lapped the cream. What's going on?"

Emma's face flushed with excitement. "I'm just happy that the men will be home for good in a few days."

"You mean that *Tyler* will be home for good. You can't honestly tell me you're looking forward to having those other two idiot brothers of mine underfoot."

The sound of Emma's laughter rang out in the brisk afternoon air. "Trevor and Cole are wonderful, Carrie, and you know it.

You're right, though. I'm really looking forward to having Tyler around. It will help my mood immensely to see his face every day."

Emma and Carrie had just finished hanging the last of the towels when the door to the kitchen banged open and Katy waved her arms frantically to gain their attention. "Carrie! Emma! Come quick! A rider just came in! There's been an accident at the logging camp!"

Both women bolted for the house, then skidded to a stop just inside the kitchen door when they confronted a man with wood shavings stuck to his shirt. He nervously fingered the hat in his hands.

Carrie immediately took charge. "Who's hurt? What happened?"

The man's gaze rested on Emma. "I'm sorry, Mrs. Wilkins—it's Tyler—"

She clutched the back of a chair for support. "Tell me what happened!"

The man's eyes softened with compassion in light of her concern. "Ma'am, he took quite a blow to the head from a rolling log. It knocked him out for a time, and he's got a wicked cut. Cole and Trevor are bringing him in. Cole told me to ride ahead and notify you. He says to send someone for Doc Adams, cuz Tyler needs stitches. Ma'am, I'd be happy to start out for the doc now." He shuffled his feet nervously and waited for her answer.

Emma remained mute with fear.

Carrie instantly spoke up. "Katy, show him down to the barn and ask Clancey to saddle a horse immediately." She looked at the lumberjack again with a shaky smile. "Thank you so much for your help. Hurry now, though—tell Doctor Adams to come immediately."

Katy left with the logger in her wake. Carrie turned to Emma. The sight of her sister-in-law's pale face was enough to make her pull a chair away from the table. She guided Emma down onto it. "Just take a deep breath, Em. The man said Tyler was fine, except for a cut on his head."

"But he said he was unconscious."

"Yes—for a time. I'm sure Tyler is fine." She spoke the words to allay her own fear, as well as Emma's.

"I'm so scared, Carrie. If something ever happened to Tyler, I don't know what I would do."

"Well, you won't be doing anyone a favor if you make yourself sick." She patted Emma's trembling hand, and then gave her a quick hug. "Come on. We'll get out what medical supplies we have here, and then go out front to wait for them. It's going to be all right. I promise."

* * * * *

The two women stood on the front porch and scanned the horizon for any sign of a wagon. The better part of an hour passed before they spied the buckboard as it lumbered down the hill. They hurried to the entrance gate. When the wagon approached, Emma hopped into the back with Trevor's help. She crawled to Tyler's side and touched a controlled hand to his shoulder.

"Tyler?" she whispered softly when he slowly opened his eyes. "You're home now. Steven will be here soon to take care of that cut."

The distraught woman of earlier was gone. Emma was now calm and in control, reacting to the situation with a composure she found somewhere in that space of time. Only she could feel the frantic thud of her heart against her ribs.

Tyler focused on his wife with some difficulty, his head swimming with the effort. "'Scuse me," he mumbled, "if I don't talk much. It's not you…my head hurts."

She bit down on her lower lip in an effort to hold back the tears at his slurred words. "Then don't say anything. You're alive. That's what counts."

The wagon stopped in front of the house. Cole helped Emma down, then turned back to aid Trevor in getting Tyler out of the back. The two men sat him upright, then assisted him to a standing position.

Tyler was forced to lean against the wooden side of the buckboard until his head and stomach stopped whirling. He hated having Emma see him like this—weak as a baby and dependent on someone else to help him walk—but the situation was out of his control. If his brothers let go of him, he would be facedown in the dirt.

Steven raced into the yard astride his horse just as Cole and Trevor helped Tyler up the stairway to the second floor. He leapt from the saddle, ran through the open doorway and met them on the steps.

Cole smiled a grateful welcome. "I think he's going to live, but he's got one helluva gash on the right side of his head. We figured we'd put him to bed. I don't think he'll be going anywhere for a while."

Steven glanced up at Emma and Carrie's pale faces where they stood at the top of the stairs. "Carrie, do you have bandages laid out?"

"Of course I do. Do you think I've been sitting around here for the last hour doing nothing? And it's a good thing I did, too. It took *you* long enough to get here."

Emma's gaze swung in Carrie's direction, but didn't dwell on her attitude toward the good doctor. Cole and Trevor had finally reached the top of the staircase with their burden and now carried him into the master suite.

Emma ran ahead to pull back the covers on the bed. The two men carefully laid Tyler on the white sheet. Steven unpacked his medical bag while Cole and Trevor began to undress their brother. No one noticed when Emma slipped quietly from the room and sank down onto a chair in the hallway. She hadn't seen Tyler naked since the night they'd made love in New York and wasn't sure her presence would be welcome in the room. So, instead, she fidgeted anxiously in the chair and listened closely to the muffled voices that came from the other side of the door, hoping she would be summoned soon.

Emma counted the passing minutes with a sick feeling of dread and clutched her hands in her lap to control their trembling. A sudden noise drew her attention. Glancing up, she saw Janie standing at the top of the stairs with the pup at her side. The child's pale expression and rivers of tears tore at her heart. Emma opened her arms and the child ran to her, clinging to her neck in a silent plea for comfort.

"I'm sorry I didn't come looking for you, Janie."

The girl's small shoulders shook with an almost tangible fear.

"Honey, don't cry. Your daddy is going to be just fine. I promise."

Janie shook her head "no" against her stepmother's shoulder. Emma held her at arm's length in order to meet her gaze directly. "Yes, he will," she stated with more conviction than she felt. "As soon as your Uncle Cole and Uncle Trevor say it's okay, we'll go inside and you can see for yourself."

Gently pulling Janie onto her lap, she held her tightly, willing away the child's certainty that she was about to lose her last remaining parent. She rocked the little girl slowly and waited for the quiet sobs to cease before pushing damp strands of blonde hair away from her wet cheeks. "Listen to me. Your daddy isn't going to go away. We won't let him, because we love him too much. He's just got a bad cut on his head and Dr. Steve is stitching it up." She hugged her closely once more. "You sit here with me and we'll wait together. How does that sound?"

Janie wiped her face with the back of a chubby hand and nestled her head close. As Emma gently stroked her soft blonde locks, she realized how much she had come to love Tyler and Sara's child.

* * * * *

Cole opened the door to Tyler's bedroom three-quarters of an hour later and stepped into the hall. Emma gently placed Janie on the carpeted floor and rose from the chair. He threw a quick smile in her direction before squatting to pat his niece's shoulder.

"Hi, Janie. I think your daddy needs a big hug from you. Make sure you don't forget when you see him, okay?"

A tremulous smile appeared on the child's face before she raced into her father's room.

Cole straightened. "Would you like to go in, Em?"

"How is he? Is he going to be all…right?" Her voice broke.

Cole pulled her into his arms. "He's going to be just fine. Probably a little ornery for a while. I'm sure his head feels twice the size it should be. Steve stitched him up good."

She leaned back to stare up into her brother-in-law's handsome face. "What happened? You all are usually so careful…"

"It was just a dumb accident," he responded with carefully chosen words. There was no need for her to know at this point that someone might be out to target Tyler's life. "I'm just thankful he's still alive. That's all you should concern yourself with, too, at this point. Why don't you go in and see him?" He smiled. "Especially since it's easy to see that you'd rather be in there than talking to me in the hallway."

Emma entered the bedroom and met Trevor as he was leaving. He gave Emma's arm a quick squeeze. "He'll be fine. Go see for yourself." He nodded toward the bed where Steven placed the last of the blood-spattered clothes into a bag.

Emma's stomach churned at the undeniable proof of Tyler's injury.

The doctor grabbed the last of the rags and forced a stern look onto his face for his friend's benefit. "I'm warning you, Tyler. You stay in that bed until at least tomorrow afternoon. You've got a concussion." Steven cocked an eyebrow in Emma's direction and tried to lighten the gloomy mood in the room. "Make sure he doesn't escape and go bronco riding or some other crazy thing."

His statement produced a small, relieved laugh from Emma.

Tyler tenderly ran his fingers over the bandage. "Get the hell out of here, Steve. Your rambling is making my head hurt worse." But his expression sobered as he met his friend's gaze. "Thanks, for everything. I'm serious."

Steve patted his buddy on the shoulder. "I know you're serious, Tyler. You don't have to thank me. Besides," he added with a cheeky smile, "you probably won't be so grateful when you get my bill."

"Go on, get out of here," Tyler chuckled softly. "I'll see you tomorrow."

Tyler held a hand out in a silent invitation for his frightened daughter to climb up on the bed beside him. Emma whispered a thank-you to Steven on his way out, then turned to help the little girl up onto the feather tick.

Once she was settled, Tyler tapped the bandage wrapped around his head. "Pretty nice, hey, Janie?" he quipped, trying to ease the fear he saw in her wide, blue eyes. "Uncle Trevor is mad that he didn't think to wrap his head up so he could get out of work."

A smile tugged at the corners of Janie's mouth. He took her small trembling chin in his hand. "Come on, let's see that smile you're hiding. Daddy is just fine, honey." Relief washed over him at the sight of her grin. He pulled her close.

* * * * *

Emma spied the fatigue in her husband's eyes a short time later and reached out to pat Janie's hand. "Honey, why don't you go wash up for dinner. I'll be down shortly."

Janie bounded down from the bed and left the room. Once she'd disappeared, Emma pulled a chair to the bedside and sat down. Tyler shifted in search of a more comfortable position for his head. Seeing his struggle with the pillow, she stood again to lend some assistance.

"Here, let me help you with that." She reached across the span of the big bed. "Lean forward and I'll straighten the pillow."

The scent of his clean washed hair reached her nostrils as she adjusted the headrest behind him. Her stomach flipped.

In turn, her perfumed fragrance caused his heart to beat a little harder. Their gazes locked.

I love you so much, her mind betrayed her. She threw caution to the wind as she pressed her lips to his.

Her impulsiveness drew a raised eyebrow from Tyler. He reached up to gently caress her silky cheek with his roughened fingers. The kiss deepened. Two hearts beat as one for a breathless and extremely fragile moment. The spell was broken when Tyler slowly pulled back to stare into the sultry green eyes above him.

"What was that for?" His words were barely a whisper.

"Because you're still alive. I was so scared, Tyler."

"You were?"

Her eyes widened slightly with disbelief. "Of course, I was." She sat back in the chair again. Her gaze dropped to her lap. "Tyler...we really need to talk."

"I know we do." He closed his eyes for a moment against the agonizing pounding in his head. "Please don't think I'm turning you away, Emma, but can we talk tomorrow? I can hardly keep my eyes open, and I ache all over. I know we need to talk. I want to, but I can't give you the attention you deserve right now."

She stood and her dimples deepened in an understanding smile. He was willing to discuss the situation between them. She couldn't ask for more. Squeezing his hand gently, she bent to press a kiss against his stubbled cheek and ignored the surprise in his eyes. "I'll stop by after supper and check on you. Maybe then you'll feel like eating something. See you later."

She floated from the room with a song in her heart.

* * * * *

Tyler opened his eyes with a start to find Janie standing beside the bed, patiently waiting for him to waken. She held a tray with toast and juice in her tiny hands.

"Well, hello there." A questioning dark brow slanted over his left eye. "Are you the new maid Mamie hired?" His answer came in the form of a nod and a smile that creased Janie's face from ear to ear. "Is that for me?" Again he received a quick nod. "Okay, but I'll only eat it if the maid shares it with me."

He sat up with slow and measured movements, plumped the pillows behind him, ignoring the dull thud in his head. Taking the tray from Janie's hands, he waited while she scurried up beside him. Balancing the food on his lap, he proceeded to hand her one of the pieces of toasted bread and their makeshift party began.

* * * * *

Emma entered the room through the connecting doorway fifteen minutes later and was greeted by the sound of Tyler's deep laughter and Whizzer leaping through the air to catch the small piece of crust thrown to him from the bed.

"This certainly doesn't look like a sickroom, now does it?"

He glanced up with a welcoming grin. "Come on in, Emma, and join us. My beautiful daughter graciously brought me breakfast in bed. I think I'll have to jump in front of rolling logs more often if this is the sort of treatment I'll receive."

"Don't even joke about that," she chastised as she crossed the room. "You scared everyone half to death. If you want breakfast in bed every morning, I'll be happy to comply. You don't have to get hit in the head with a log to get it."

A dark, sensual spark lit in his eyes. "I can't think of anything I'd like better." Emma's face blushed a deep red. Tyler chuckled softly at her reaction and at her meager attempt to find something to occupy her attention so she wouldn't have to meet his gaze.

She finally returned to his bedside. "Why don't we go downstairs, Janie, and let your dad wash up. We can come back later."

"You'd better." Tyler's gaze held hers and, again, his hidden meaning was clear. They had much to discuss, not the least of which was whether or not she would share his bed that night.

Emma's cheeks flushed again as she took Janie's hand in hers and exited the room.

Chapter Seventeen

ಐ

By noon that same day, Emma was hard-pressed not to snap at anyone foolish enough to get in her way. Tyler entertained one group of workers after another the entire morning. Though Emma knew she should be touched by the concern for their employer, it didn't make her growing frustration any easier to bear. She wanted to talk with Tyler herself without interruptions and plan the future she hoped he wanted as much as she.

She finally escorted the last of the visitors to the door, and then bounded up the stairs to his room before anyone else could intrude. Janie, with a fair amount of coaxing on Emma's part, finally agreed to ride with Carrie to a friend's house. They wouldn't return to the ranch until just before dark. Mamie and Katie were busy in the smokehouse, and Trevor and Cole were at the mill. She and Tyler had the house to themselves.

She knocked softly on his half-open door, then peeked around the corner to see him sitting in one of the overstuffed chairs placed before the fireplace.

He glanced up and motioned for her to join him. "There isn't anybody else waiting in the wings is there?"

Emma shook her head as she seated herself across from him. "The house is finally cleared out."

A moment of tense silence ensued as each waited for the other to speak first. Emma fidgeted in the chair, amazed that she couldn't think of one thing to say after waiting half the day for this moment.

Tyler's expression was just as uneasy. He took a deep breath though, and started the conversation. "I thought a lot about our situation during the last month I spent up in the woods."

"I know. I've also agonized over it." She couldn't make herself meet his gaze and sat with her head tipped slightly downward.

"Let me back up a minute, Em. I haven't asked you how you're feeling lately, with the baby and all, I mean. I can see you've changed your style of clothing slightly. I hope that means things are progressing well."

It was the first time they'd talked in a civil manner about the child. It did Emma's heart good when he asked the question.

"I'm feeling well. Steven says he's very happy with how things are going and expects the baby to be born sometime in March." She met his gaze. "I can feel it moving now."

It was Tyler's turn to drop his gaze to his lap. He was so out of touch on the subject of the child. The issue hadn't come up again since that first awful night after she arrived in Minnesota.

"Emma," Tyler leaned forward in the chair and clasped his hands together, "do you think…"

"Hello!" Steven's voice echoed through the upper floor. A second later, he entered the bedroom. "There you are. Sorry I didn't get here sooner to check on you, Ty. I had an emergency and was tied up most of the morning." His glance swept to Emma. "How are you doing today?"

"I'm fine," she murmured through clenched teeth.

Steven was oblivious to the pained expression on her face as he turned to his patient. He set his medical bag on the table between the two chairs and rummaged through it for a stethoscope. "And how's the head today, Ty? Do you still have a headache?"

"I didn't until a moment ago," his friend muttered beneath his breath.

"I'm sorry, what did you say?" Steven asked as he pulled the instrument from his bag and clipped it around his neck.

"Never mind," Tyler groaned.

"Okay," Steven replied slowly. "Come over to the bed so I can check you over."

Emma stood with a look of consternation at having to wait yet one more time to settle the matter at hand. "I'll leave you with Steven for now."

She started to leave the room then, but paused to turn back. "Steve, would you have a moment to speak with me before you leave?"

"Sure, what's up?"

"Oh, nothing. I'll wait for you on the front porch."

Tyler's quizzical eyes followed her slender form as she left the room.

* * * * *

The October sun warmed Emma's face as she sat and waited for Steven. She used the tip of her toe to move the wooden swing and mused about the fact that she was witnessing one of those rare days of Indian summer. Soon, they would have snow.

Steven finally strolled through the front doorway and onto the porch thirty minutes later. Spotting Emma on the swing, he crossed and sank onto the wooden surface beside her.

"Not many of these left before winter sets in. An October day that's this warm is very rare in these parts." He paused, then turned to look at her. "So, what was it you wanted to talk to me about?"

"How is Tyler doing? He's going to be fine, isn't he?"

"Yeah—be assured he'll come out of this completely unscathed. I left him in the library. He said he needed to get up for a while and wanted me to let you know that's where he'll be." Steven glanced in her direction. "I've come to know you pretty well, Em. What else is bothering you?"

"Tyler and I are finally going to settle this matter between us. In fact, we were talking about it when you came in."

Steven winced. "Ouch—I thought something was going on. I'm sorry my timing was so bad."

She waved her hand in dismissal. "It wasn't until I saw you that I realized I needed to ask you something. I'm hoping most of the issues between us will be resolved today." Emma stared straight ahead and finally found the courage to voice a question. "I wanted to know if Tyler is well enough to..." Steven watched the blush spread across her smooth cheeks. She struggled to continue, but couldn't find the right words.

Steven couldn't suppress the chuckle that rose in his throat. He nudged her shoulder in a show of friendship. "If you're asking me what I think you are, then my answer is yes. Tyler will be ready for anything he decides he wants to do, barring another near miss with a rolling log. If you two can fix this thing, then I'm happy for the both of you and say go right ahead. Does that answer your question?"

She covered her burning cheeks with her hands. "I can't believe I asked you that—even if you are a doctor! I hope you don't think ill of me for questioning you about something so personal."

"Come on, Em. Walk me to my horse." He grabbed her hand, pulled her up from the swing and they left the porch together. Steven released his grip on her hand and slung an arm over her shoulder. "I could never think ill of you. If for some reason things don't happen tonight though, don't give up. I've known Tyler my whole life. Sara's death sent his world into a relentless spin. I've always respected him for his ethics and the love of his family. Trust me, you already are included in that select circle. You have to believe that." He squeezed her shoulder. "Quit worrying. Things will work themselves out."

They reached his horse. She watched him untie the reins from the hitching post.

"Thank you, Steve, for everything. I'm truly lucky to have you for a friend. You've always been willing to listen with an understanding ear and have never been judgmental. That means so much. It was such a relief when I saw you coming up the stairs yesterday. I knew you'd take care of him. I love him so much… I don't know what I would've done if I'd lost him." She reached out to rest a hand on his forearm, her eyes glistening with unshed tears. "Thank you for being his friend, too."

Steven hugged her slender body and pulled her close. "Go find him, Em. Just go in there and tell him how much you care. You might be surprised by his response."

"What's that supposed to mean?"

"It means that he loves you, too. Good luck to you, hon, but I don't think you'll need it."

She stood on tiptoe to kiss him on the cheek. A bright smile lit her eyes. "Thank you—from both of us."

"Go to him and be happy. I'll be back tomorrow to check his stitches." He mounted his horse and wheeled the animal around before waving goodbye.

Emma watched after him until he was out of sight, then turned back toward the house. Her future awaited her in the library and nothing was going to come between them now.

Her heart took on an erratic beat as she hurried through the foyer. Stepping into the library a moment later, her voice floated across the room to where Tyler stood before the window.

"Hi. Would you like something to drink before we sit down? Mamie has some fresh squeezed juice in the kitchen." He didn't turn at the sound of her voice. "Tyler?"

It was then that she noticed his stiff back. Her eyebrows dipped in concern as she crossed to him and laid a gentle hand upon his arm. "Is something wrong?"

He jerked his arm free of her touch. Cold, uncaring eyes stared blankly through the windowpane and into the front yard. His square jaw clenched with anger. "That was a touching scene I just witnessed." His voice was as brittle and unyielding as his gaze.

"What are you talking about?" Again, he didn't respond. She gripped his arm once more, tighter this time. "You're scaring me, Tyler. What's wrong?"

"I'll tell you what's wrong. I just stood here and watched you say a very *tender* goodbye to my best friend."

He turned to face her, his hateful gaze making her recoil in shock.

"I was ready to bare my soul to you, Emma—to work out a solution to our problems so we could be happy. I've been up in those goddamn woods for the last month, fighting with myself, telling myself that I had to trust you, that I had to believe in your honesty!" The words tumbling from his mouth became seething, caustic. "And how do you repay me? By carrying on with another man—a man who is *my* best friend! I saw you walk Steve to his horse, and I saw him put his arms around you. You not only hugged him back, but you *kissed* him. You could've at least had the decency to be a little more discreet instead of flaunting your affair in broad daylight."

Shock and disbelief raced through her wide eyes.

"Don't look at me like that. Your pleading and your lies won't do any good—not anymore." He whirled and stalked toward the doorway.

"You're wrong, Tyler!" Her words stopped his exit from the room. "Steve has become a good friend. I was simply thanking him for taking care of both of us! You can't honestly believe that we've been seeing each other?" She ran to his side and gripped his arm in a frantic hold. "Please, don't throw away what we could have! I love you! I've loved you from the moment I met you!"

He spun to face her again. His eyes, filled with anger and pain of betrayal, bored into hers. He grabbed her upper arms and pulled her to within inches of his face. "How can you speak of love? You don't even know what it means. Your idea of love is letting some man maul you."

Emma closed her eyes against the tears that threatened never to stop.

His voice lowered to an ominous timbre. "What happened that night on the veranda with Samuel Fontaine? Where did you go when you left the ballroom? Were you with him? Do you think what he did to you was an act of love? Well, believe me, it wasn't. Love believes in someone, Emma! Love is *trusting* someone! Love is making a commitment to *one* person for the rest of your life, not passing your favors around freely, like you seem to do."

"No! You've got it all wrong! Samuel attacked me that night on the veranda because he's hated me his entire life! I didn't tell anyone because he threatened to hurt Jacob if I did. When I left the ballroom, I went home—alone! Please, Tyler, you have to believe me! I love you!"

He released her with a jerk and shook his head slowly. "I already told you. You don't know the meaning of the word. You proved that a few minutes ago. True love is what I once had with a beautiful, gentle, caring woman—a woman I would've gladly died for if I'd been given the chance. But fate took her away from me." His voice cracked with the forbidden agony of the past two years. "I thought fate had handed me another chance—with you—but I was wrong." Pain darkened his eyes further. "This marriage will never work. I want you to leave as soon as you can make the arrangements. I don't want you here anymore. I refuse to raise Samuel Fontaine's baby."

Emma's eyes widened in horror. "Tyler, listen to me, please! This baby is not Samuel's! You're the only man I've ever been with. Don't make me leave—don't make a mistake you'll regret for the rest of your life."

He rubbed the back of his neck, trying to ease the throbbing tension and shook his head. His voice came in a near whisper. "No more explanations. I'm done with your lies, Emma. I have to believe what I saw with my own eyes. I won't let you do this to me anymore."

Intense anger at his ignorance welled up inside of her. Emma balled her hands into fists and pummeled his chest in a futile effort to let it out. Tyler flinched as he took the blows, but his icy gaze never softened as she screamed into his face.

"Do *what* to you? I have done *nothing*, except love you with all my heart! Well, I'll tell you something, you stupid, ignorant man! I won't give up! I won't leave you! I won't throw away the first and *only* love of my life!"

She stumbled back, her glittering eyes darting wildly around the room for an escape from the excruciating pain that seared her heart. The walls closed in as she ran past him, through the foyer and out into the yard.

She raced to the barn to escape the house, to escape Tyler and to flee from his accusations.

Inside the barn, she yanked a saddle off a rail, dropping it twice as she dragged it to the stabled horse that eyed her warily. Quickly, she threw a blanket over the mare's back and followed it with the saddle—and a sob. Sensing her agitation, the animal sidled away in fear.

"Stand still, you stupid beast!" She brushed a sleeved arm across her face to wipe away the blinding tears, yanked a bridle over the mare's head, then tied the horse to the gate and fumbled with the girth strap. A sudden voice from behind was enough to nearly make her jump out of her skin.

"Miss Em? What're you doing?" Clancey's voice held an edge of uncertainty.

"I'm saddling this stupid horse! What does it look like I'm doing?" She swiped the tears from her face again and muttered a curse when she couldn't get the buckle fastened, refusing to meet Clancey's eyes.

"I can see something is wrong, Miss Em. Maybe you should calm down before getting on that animal."

She threw him a scathing glare over her shoulder as she led the chestnut mare past him and out of the stall. "Maybe you should attend to your own business and leave mine alone!"

Emma grabbed a whip that lay atop a hay bale, lifted her foot into the stirrup and heaved herself up by the saddle horn.

The hired hand reached up to grab the bridle. "Please, Miss Em, let's talk about what's wrong. If something were to happen to you out there with you in such a state, Tyler'd have my head."

Sparks shot from the depths of her glittering green eyes. "Let go of the horse, Clancey, or I'll run you over. This is your only warning."

He tightened his grip on the bridle. "I can't let you go like this. I'm afraid for your safety."

Emma raised her hand, brought the whip down hard on the mare's rump and simultaneously dug her heels into the animal's ribs. It leapt forward. Clancey lost his grip. Once she was clear of the doorway, she kicked the horse on to an even greater speed. Clancey raced after her and watched helplessly as she charged down the driveway, then reined the animal through the open log gate at the entrance to the ranch. Auburn hair whipped around her face as she left a cloud of dust in her wake.

A sinking feeling settled in the pit of Clancey's stomach. Emma was riding wildly and hell-bent on going as fast as the horse could carry her. He shook his head, his fear allayed only by the fact that he knew she was an excellent rider. There was nothing he could do but wait for her return.

* * * * *

Tyler sat behind the large oaken desk in the library, eyes closed and fingers against his throbbing temples. He couldn't summon the simple strength to stand, let alone trudge up the steps to his second floor bedroom. Being emotionally exhausted and physically ill after the horrific argument with Emma had forced him to sit for the better part of an hour going over it in his mind.

He'd heard Emma ride out at a breakneck pace earlier. Even as hurt and angry as he was, he'd almost followed her. Her safety was still his responsibility, but it was quite obvious that she wanted to be alone—and away from him.

Recalling his final ultimatum, the mere thought of spending his days without her had his emotions in a turmoil.

You stupid fool!

He cursed himself and his bout with jealousy. One angry swipe of his arm sent the contents of the desktop flying. Staring numbly at the broken glass on the floor, his throat closed in fear.

I'm going to be alone for the rest of my life...

* * * * *

Cole discovered his brother sitting behind the desk in the library ten minutes later. Broken objects and strewn paper covered the floor. Tyler sat in the midst of the melee, his head slumped forward.

Cole's worried eyes observed the clutter, then darkened with something akin to unbridled fear. Clancey had informed him of Emma's state of mind and her wild ride out of the yard. "Ty? I went to your room and you weren't there. What's going on here?"

Tyler's chin rose slowly. He stared at Cole with dull eyes and a mindless shrug of the shoulders. "I'm still trying to figure that out myself."

Reading the look of bewilderment on Tyler's face, Cole's brow deepened with his growing concern. "Clancey told me that Emma rode out of here in quite a state. Did the two of you have words?"

"Christ...*having words* is putting it mildly." Tyler's confused expression tempered to one that held a question. He rubbed a hand slowly through his thick, dark hair. "Cole, what do you think of Emma? Do you think she's trustworthy? Do you think I can trust her with Janie's happiness?"

"What the hell kind of question is that?" Cole took a step closer to the desk. "What happened here today to make you ask something that stupid?"

"We had one helluva row...and I told her to pack her bags."

"You did *what?*" Cole kicked a nearby chair in a rare show of temper and sent it sliding across the floor. "Dammit, Ty, when are you going to open your eyes and see what's standing right in front of you!"

Tyler leapt from the chair. His arm shot out toward the window, his weak body swaying with the effort. "Yeah, well I *did* see what was standing right in front of me. I saw it through *that* window! Steve came by to check on me earlier and ended up outside with *my* wife in his arms in a tender scene that turned my stomach."

A flicker of doubt sparked in Cole's eyes. "What do you mean?"

"She *kissed* him, Cole! Right out there in the driveway in broad daylight!"

"On the mouth?"

"No, on the cheek, but it doesn't matter. He also hugged her, and she happily hugged him back."

The doubt slowly diminished as Cole continued his questioning. "What did Emma have to say about it?"

"She said she only kissed him out of gratefulness for helping both of us."

"And you didn't believe her," the younger Wilkins brother stated rather than asked.

"No, I didn't believe her and neither should you!"

Cole stalked across the room. "You know what? I'm going to tell you something about *your* wife. She loves you with a passion, Tyler. If you'd take off your goddamn blinders, you'd see that you feel the same way!"

"I know exactly how I feel—"

"Just shut up!" Cole roared. "You asked my opinion, and you're damn well going to get it! I've seen the way you look at her. I've read every damn emotion on your face. I've also seen how she looks at you. How in hell can you doubt her anymore? You weren't there to pick her up at the train station when she arrived from New York, but she let it go, hoping like hell you'd be here at the ranch waiting for her. But you weren't, because *you* decided to play the goddamn injured party here, because *you* felt cornered after jumping into bed with her. You took off after you married her and left her alone *again*, and she let that go, too. And, now what do you do? You come home from the camp periodically over the last month, throw her a few crumbs and she's ready to get on her knees and beg for more, because she loves you! If you hadn't been so damn out of it when we hauled your ass home yesterday, you would've seen the sheer terror on her face. She was scared, Tyler! She was scared she was going to lose you. Why, I have no idea, because you've given her *nothing* to miss!" Cole took a step closer to his brother with a tight fist. "You know what you need, Tyler? You need your stupid ass kicked!"

Before Cole could continue with his tirade or throw the first punch, Trevor barreled through the library door with an amazed look on his face. "Jesus Christ! I could hear you yelling all the way outside, Cole!"

"Good! I hope the whole goddamn place heard what a stupid bastard Tyler is. Let the pissant explain to you what he told Emma today. I'm getting the hell out of here!" Cole stormed through the open doorway without a backward glance. The room reverberated a moment later with the slam of the front door.

Trevor took one look at Tyler's pale expression and rushed across the room. "Sit down before you fall down, Ty. You're white as a sheet and bleeding through the bandage again."

Tyler sank into the chair behind the desk.

"So what the hell's going on? Why is Cole so angry?" Trevor asked.

Tyler sat forward, propped his elbows on the desktop and rested his head in his hands. "Because I might have made one of the biggest mistakes of my life. Emma and I had an argument. I thought there was something going on between her and Steve. I told her to pack her things and leave."

Trevor opened his mouth to bellow louder than his brother, but Tyler held up a hand in an appeal for quiet.

"Don't even start. Cole already gave it to me with both barrels, and I know he was right."

"So, what're you gonna to do about it?" Trevor asked through a stiff jaw as he struggled to control his own anger. "We've all kept our mouths shut about this whole goddamn thing with you and Emma — our mistake. We know how Sara's death affected you, but I'm not going to keep my mouth shut any more. You've been given a second chance at happiness here, Ty — a chance most people only dream about."

"I'm just beginning to realize that…"

"Then grab it, Tyler, and hold it close. What the hell's the matter with you?"

Trevor moved around the desk and rested a hip on the edge. He crossed his arms before his chest and looked his brother straight in the eye. "When Sara died, you and Janie weren't the only people in this house who lost something. Cole, Carrie and I also cried many times. Not only for you, but also with our own personal pain. She was part of our lives, too. We mourned her death for a long time. But Emma has changed things. She's brought sunshine back into this house — sunshine that's been missing since Sara left us. You can't let yourself feel guilty for loving again. You know as well as I do that Sara would be the first one to kick you in the ass if you push Emma away."

Before Tyler ducked his head, Trevor spied tears on his brother's cheeks. He had all he could do to control his own emotions and swallowed the quickly formed lump in his throat. "You need to let go, Ty. You need to grab what life is offering you.

You need to take Emma in your arms and love her for all you're worth."

A sob burst forth from somewhere deep inside Tyler. Trevor immediately wrapped his arms around him in brotherly love, amazed that it had taken two years for Tyler to face his past loss. The tears escaped his own eyes as the two grown men clung to one another. One desperately needed comfort, the other gave it.

The pain of the last two years rocked Tyler to the core. "Sara was my life..." Tyler choked out.

"I know, Ty. I know. But Emma is here now, and she loves you more than you ever dreamed would be possible again. Don't let fate win again and take her away from you. Sara can never come back. You have to accept that. You have to look to your heart. You need to admit to yourself that you can love again and not let the guilt consume you. We can all see how you feel about her. You have to let yourself see it, too. Look closely, Ty. Look deep within yourself and you'll find the answer."

Trevor held his brother tightly, willing Tyler's anguish to be washed away. Minutes passed before one brother finally let go of the past and reached for a bright new future. The other gave silent encouragement for him to follow that path.

Tyler finally leaned back in the chair and wiped the wetness from his face.

Trevor, trying to lighten the mood, laid a hand on his brother's shoulder and smiled ruefully. "A fine pair we are, hey, Tyler? Two big rough and tough cowboys crying on each other's shoulders like babies. What would the ladies in town think?"

"Thanks, Trevor. I think I'll go find Cole."

Trevor laughed with a little more humor evident in his tone. "Good luck, but you better plan on doing all the talking. I think he's said his piece and won't say another word."

Tyler chuckled along with him and wiped again at the tears that hadn't dried. "Emma sure has had an effect on him, hasn't she?"

"She's had an effect on all of us." Trevor's eyebrow lifted in question. "So, what are you going to do when you see her next?"

A weak grin preceded Tyler's next words. "I'm going to start my new life—if she'll forgive me. And, if she does, I'm going to carry her up those stairs and not come down for a week."

"Good! I'll run interference so no one bothers you." Trevor chuckled again. "Now, go find that pissed off brother of ours and make peace."

He watched Tyler leave the room. When he disappeared, Trevor's smile faded into a look of concern. Would Emma forgive him? He sent a silent request to her wherever she was.

"Honey, you've gotta give him one more chance."

Chapter Eighteen

ಐ

Emma ceased her relentless prodding of the horse's flanks and finally allowed the poor beast to slow its pace. The mare's sides heaved with exhaustion. Froth bubbled from its mouth. Emma's anger had overridden better judgment. Now she was ashamed for treating an animal the way she had this one.

She reined the mare down a sloping trail, not even realizing that she'd unconsciously ridden to Tyler's special place—the same peaceful haven he'd brought her and Janie to after the wedding. Since then, they'd visited the secluded lake on numerous occasions.

Even in her distraught state, she couldn't ignore the beauty that surrounded her as she dismounted. Late autumn presented itself in the form of brittle, colored leaves, which lay scattered atop brown grass tinged with small traces of green. Snow would cover the landscape soon. She wondered if she would be here to see it.

Heading for the water's edge, she seated herself on a log Tyler had placed there for her and Janie during one of their many visits. A sob caught in her throat. How could she leave Janie and the others? Trevor with his ready and ever-present smile, Cole and his innate ability to read her emotions better than she could herself, and Carrie—who treated her like the sister she'd never had. Emma loved them all—Mamie, Janie and most of all, Tyler. They were her family now. But because of his distrust, she was in danger of losing them all.

Memories of the first time Tyler brought her there whispered around the edges of her mind. Tracing her finger along the bumpy edges of the small rock at the shoreline, she realized with sudden clarity that the rough surface was much like her relationship with Tyler. Would she ever be able to smooth things out? Would Tyler even give her the chance?

Her jaw hardened with determination. She would make him. They were connected now, both by the baby she carried and the love shared by all. A wry smile curved her lips as she thought about the direction her life had taken—a totally opposite turn from the path she'd thought it would always follow, but in a direction she wanted wholeheartedly. Somehow, she would make him believe in her love and maybe, just maybe, he would be able to respond in kind.

Forever the optimist, that's what Papa always says…

Emma raised her face to the afternoon sun, closed her eyes and pictured Tyler's square cut jaw, the black wavy hair and the green eyes she loved so much. She envisioned Janie and the rest of the family and knew she could never leave.

She vowed to go back to the ranch and recruit his brothers' help, if needed. She would even send for Steven and allow the good doctor to beat some sense into his best friend's stubborn head. Tyler had been ready to bare his soul, so, surely he must feel something.

She rose with determination, turned with a lighter step and a steady resolve and walked back to the horse. She paused halfway across the small clearing, however, when a twig snapped on the trail.

The hair rose on the back of her neck.

She watched the trail with wary eyes. Deciding she was overreacting, she continued toward the horse—and froze when a man stepped through the thick foliage.

"Samuel!" Emma's heart sank as she stared into the face of the devil himself.

Samuel Fontaine leaned a shoulder casually against the tree beside him and crossed his feet at the ankles, almost unrecognizable in his disheveled state. His hair was long and greasy. Filthy clothes hung limply from his much leaner body. He glared through glassy eyes.

Emma paled and took a step back.

"If it isn't the fine Miss Emma Sanders, lately of New York." His indifferent glance swept the clearing before his burning eyes again fell on her. "Fancy meeting you in a place so remote."

Her blood ran cold. As he spoke, she mentally measured the distance between herself and the horse. There was no doubt in her mind as to what would happen if he managed to get his hands on her. She took a slow, deep breath and prepared herself for the coming leap onto the mare's back. She had to keep him talking and unaware of what she planned.

"What are you doing here, Samuel? How did you end up in Minnesota?"

The sneer on his lips widened into a leer as he studied her. His stance became more rigid. "No big welcome? Do I frighten you, Emma?" He chuckled evilly. "I should, you know. Did you think that I'd let you and that upstart Wilkins get away with ruining my life? That I would forget everything you did and just let you go on your merry way?" He shifted his weight to the other leg.

Emma flinched unwittingly with the subtle change.

"I have to admit that finding you here with him surprised me though. Hell, when I was finished with him, I planned to go back to New York and make you pay for your part in my ruination." The leer appeared again. "Now, I won't have to."

"What do you mean when you were *finished* with him? He did nothing to you and neither did I. Anything that's happened to you, you did to yourself."

"Oh, I beg to differ with you, Emma. I lay the fault for my downfall directly on the two of you."

Emma's gaze strayed to the mare again. She had to keep him talking...

"Where have you been all this time?"

He took a few steps in her direction. She would have to act quickly if she was to escape. Once more, she counted out the steps between her and the horse—and fought to control her trembling.

"I was busy making plans to come here—to get Tyler. It was so easy. I simply answered an ad for the extra crew your big man was looking for to log his stupid timber." A nonchalant shrug raised his bony shoulders. "I gave a false name and work history and was hired on the spot. I had so many chances to end his life up there in the woods, but every time the possibility arose, my plans were foiled. That is, until I sent the logs rolling in his direction yesterday." His jaw hardened. "But, of course, dumb luck was with him again. Now, I'll have to try again."

"*You're* the one who let the logs go?" Emma choked out.

He dipped at the waist in a gallant bow. "One and the same."

Emma's stomach rolled at the thought of this demented man laying in wait for Tyler—waiting for the perfect opportunity to kill him for something he had no hand in.

"Tyler must pull a lot of weight around here. Wherever I went yesterday, people were talking about how he narrowly escaped death in a freak logging accident. They also talked about his poor Missus Emma and how terrified you must have been to almost lose your new *husband.*" His voice took on a deceptively soft note. "So, you married the bastard, did you?" When Emma failed to answer, he raised his voice to a shriek. "*Did you?*"

Emma bolted to the waiting horse. Samuel's lunging body was a blur as her hands touched the saddle horn at the same time her left foot found the stirrup. Pulling herself up onto the horse's back, she kicked it in the ribs and fumbled for the reins.

She could only find one!

Samuel held the other in his hand, already subduing the circling animal just as Emma's free hand closed around the hilt of the riding whip. Raising it above her head, she brought it down on Samuel's shoulder with as much power as she could marshal.

A strangled cry escaped his throat, but sheer insanity strengthened his hold.

She fought to keep her seat atop the frightened horse as the mare danced sideways and Samuel screamed into its face.

Emma was crazy with panic. Repeatedly she brought the whip down onto Samuel's head and arms. More than one blow ended up meeting the horse's neck and flanks. The mare reared in objection at the brutal treatment. Samuel lost his hold on the bridle as Emma slid sideways in the saddle.

She clung desperately to the pommel, but Samuel grabbed hold of her leg. She slipped sideways with his last powerful yank as the mare bolted.

Emma's body collided with the ground. Dazed and struggling for breath, she lay helpless on the hard earth.

The mare paused in its frenzied flight a short distance away. Samuel threw up his arms, screamed at the animal and watched with a crazed gleam in his eye as it wheeled around and charged back up the path.

Emma rolled slowly onto her side, staring through terrified eyes as a wheezing Samuel bent at the waist, rested his hands on his knees and glared at her from beneath lowered lids. Finally, he straightened and brought his hand to his cheek. The whip had lain open a wicked gash. His fingers came away covered in blood.

"You bitch!" he ground out. "You've finally met with the day you'll regret for the rest of your life. Do you hear me?"

Emma still gasped for air and fought valiantly to ward off the darkness that threatened to engulf her. Samuel staggered in her direction. Hatred etched itself deeply into his features. Totally out of control now, he kicked the toe of his dirty boot into her midsection.

Air rushed from her lungs.

A lurid smile curled his lips. "There's no one here to come to your rescue now..."

She crawled from him, spurred on by pain and a burgeoning instinct that insisted she escape the man who inflicted so much physical abuse.

Samuel threw his head back and laughed like the madman he was. Feeling the thrill of victory already, he kicked her down every time she regained her balance and tried to sit up.

Emma sank to the earth, curled into a ball and gritted her teeth against the cramping sensation that shot through her abdomen. Her hoarse plea was barely audible in the crisp morning air. "Please...don't do this..." She winced as another wave of pain rushed through her womb. "I'll give you anything you want... Please, don't kill me..."

"You still don't understand, do you? There's only one thing I want from you, Emma, and I've waited a long time for it. If you ask me, Tyler is a very selfish man. I think it's about time he learned to share." His hands moved to the buttons at the front of his dirty, stained pants. "Besides, I like my women broken and pleading for mercy."

He grabbed her roughly by the arms and hauled her to her feet, then dragged her across the quiet clearing to a rock wall. Slamming her already bruised body against the hard surface, he peered into her terrified eyes. "Do you like it standing up, Emma?"

Emma groaned, barely conscious as a rush of warm liquid seeped from between her legs. The contractions came one on top of the other now. Her barely whispered words begged him to show even a hint of compassion. "Don't do this. Please, Samuel. I'm...pregnant...and—" She doubled over in his arms and groaned her agony.

Samuel snapped her limp body upright. His scathing gaze scanned her pale features. He shook her until her teeth rattled. "You're *what*? You let that son of a bitch get you pregnant?"

His right hand balled into a fist and connected with her jaw, then the backhand caught her across the mouth. Emma spun free of his hold and landed in a heap on the ground. She felt his weight upon her only seconds later.

Samuel ripped open the front of her dress and tore at the underlying camisole, exposing her pregnancy-swollen breasts. His eager hands and mouth mauled her tender flesh, but Emma couldn't find the strength to scream. Another contraction gripped her a few moments later as he clutched at her skirt and shoved it up and out of his way.

Her weak attempts to stave him off brought little result. Black spots flickered before her eyes now. The pain in her jaw rivaled the agony in her womb. She pleaded for her life in hoarse, choked sobs, but Samuel silenced her with yet another round of blows to her head and torso. Emma tried not to choke on her own blood.

The undergarments were torn from her body. Samuel paid little attention to the blood that seeped between her legs as he positioned himself, and then thrust into her body time and time again.

Her feeble whimpers mingled with the song of a far-off loon. Her tears merged with the blood on her face.

Samuel peered into the almost unrecognizable face beneath him. The power that surged through his veins spurred him on. "Does he do this to you, Emma?" he panted. He grabbed her limp arms and trapped them above her head, never ceasing the rhythmic pumping motions that ripped her body apart. "Scream, Emma... I want to hear you scream..."

One final, desperate sob escaped her lips as a horrific agony knifed its way through her lower abdomen. A vision of Tyler's smiling face floated through her spinning mind as she spiraled into a tunnel of darkness, falling...falling...until there was no more Samuel and no more pain.

* * * * *

Tyler found Cole mucking out stalls with a vengeance. He took a tentative step forward, then hooked his arms over the wooden gate and flinched when his brother viciously stabbed a fresh bale of hay with a pitchfork.

"I'd hate to be that bale of hay right now."

Cole spun, threw him a malevolent look over his shoulder, and then turned his attention back to the fodder that he scattered on the floor of the stall. "Be goddamn glad you're not."

"Cole..."

Cole ceased his actions abruptly, whirled on booted heel and glared into Tyler's eyes. "What the hell's the matter with you—"

"Stop right there," Tyler returned with a raised hand. "I came out here to tell you that you're right. I don't know what the hell got into me. Both you and Trevor made me realize that I've been an ass as far as Emma is concerned."

"Being rather easy on yourself, aren't you? Personally, I'd dub you a goddamn son of a bitch who doesn't know shit."

Tyler's chin sank to his chest. He reached up a hand and ran it through his tousled hair, carefully avoiding the sutures near his temple.

The gesture was enough to make Cole relent, if only slightly. He stabbed the pitchfork into the bale of hay again and leaned against the side of the stall. "You still gonna make her leave?"

"No..." Tyler's eyes rose. "I couldn't let her go. I'd see her everywhere and be even more miserable. I just hope she accepts my apology and doesn't *want* to leave. I'm going to make it up to her. I should never have accused her of the things I did."

"Well, I'm happy to see you finally realized that neither Emma or Steve would do anything to jeopardize your marriage. Steve is your best friend, Ty, and now he's Emma's friend, too. You should be happy they like and respect each other so much."

"I know. It's just that when I saw her hug him, and then kiss him goodbye, I got so insanely jealous that I spoke before I thought about it."

"Emma treats everyone that way. If you spent more time around her, you'd know that."

Tyler nodded. "All I want right now is to find her and tell her how I feel and to apologize for being such an ass. I'm going to make this work, Cole, if she'll only forgive me one more time."

Both men paused when the sound of horse's hooves racing through the front gate caught their attention. Hurrying to the open doorway, they saw the riderless mare with reins trailing as she veered past them, then came to a prancing halt near the paddock.

Cole ran to the frightened animal with a weak Tyler following in his wake. Both men had their arms spread wide to corner the animal before it bolted. The mare reared with wide panicked eyes. Cole spoke in a soft, soothing voice and inched his way closer to the quivering animal until he was able to grab the reins.

Clancey raced around the side of the barn and stopped dead in his tracks at the sight of the frightened mare. The horse's chest was sticky with blood. Air whistled across his teeth when his gaze met Tyler's frightened one. "Christ almighty! That's the mare Miss Emma rode out on."

"Saddle Storm for me—now!" Tyler ordered. "Get me some blankets and send someone for Steve. I need to get my gun, then I'm going to find her."

Cole grabbed Tyler's arm as he turned to make his unsteady way toward the house. "Let Trevor and me start out. How in hell are you going to stay on top of a horse? You can barely walk across the yard."

Tyler jerked his arm free. "If you think for one minute that I'm staying behind, you're crazy. She's my wife, and she might be hurt. We've got to find her before it gets dark."

Cole knew they didn't have the time to argue. "All right. Let's get ready, then. Saddle all of our horses, Clancey, and then get your ass to Steve's place and explain what happened."

Clancey led Emma's mare into the barn as the two brothers hurried to the house to spur everyone into action.

Fear was evident in their tight expressions. Emma was a superb rider, but the bloody whip marks on the horse boded an ill wind as they both tried to contain their quickly growing panic.

* * * * *

Only minutes later, Tyler, Cole and Trevor were mounting up just as Dougan O'Malley raced his horse through the log gate and reined in their direction. Dust billowed up as his horse skidded to a stop.

Dougan's eyes immediately found Tyler's. "I was riding down from the camp. A few miles back, I passed a man on the trail riding a beat-up Appaloosa. He was movin' like the devil himself was on his tail and headed north. Most people 'round here I know, but I didn't recognize this fellow until he passed right by me. I swear to you, Mr. Wilkins, it was Samuel Fontaine!"

Tyler nudged Storm closer to the Irishman. Concern coupled with fear in his eyes. "What in hell would he be doing in Minnesota? He dropped from sight in New York months ago."

"I know, sir, but I'm positive it was him. And I'm sure now he was the man I seen at the logging camp. He's been keepin' away from me, maybe because he thought I'd recognize him and tell you. When I went in for supper last week, he got up right away, kept his face hidden and left the shack. I wasn't sure it was him then, so I didn't say anything. On the road, I recognized that horse, though. In fact, I took a rock out of its hoof. The owner had the same greasy, long blond hair as the man on the road did. I got a good look at him this time, sir—it's Fontaine. I'd know that bastard anywhere." Tyler looked sicker with Dougan's every word. "I wanted you to know, Mr. Wilkins, because you said Samuel blames you for him losin' the mill. I think he might be responsible for the strange happenings at the camp. It makes sense, don't it?"

There was no need for the last statement. It made perfect sense to the other three men. Samuel Fontaine had to have cut the ropes the day of Tyler's accident. He was probably responsible for a few of the smaller incidents that had happened in the last week also—incidents that never failed to jeopardize Tyler's safety.

"Stay here, Dougan, and watch the place until Clancey gets back with Steve." Tyler gathered Storm's reins as he shot out the orders. "Emma's horse came in without her, and we've got to start searching. Have Mamie give you a rifle in case Fontaine shows up. Get a buckboard ready. We might need to come and get it. Fire off a few rounds if she comes back." He wheeled the horse, gave it a swift kick and charged down the driveway. Cole and Trevor followed suit.

* * * * *

The three brothers methodically searched every path that led from the main road. When no sign of Emma was found, they moved onto the next path and began again.

Tyler was wound as tight as a bowstring and blamed himself at every turn when they failed to find her. His head ached from the jarring ride, and he was sick to his stomach with worry.

He ran the conversation with Dougan over and over in his mind. *Samuel Fontaine! Emma tried to tell me that he attacked her that night in New York. Edward stated in his telegram that she had to get away from the city because of a threat to herself and the baby—a threat from Fontaine?*

If Samuel had tried to kill him, what would stop him from harming Emma? If she was hurt by his hand, he would hunt the bastard down and kill him with his bare hands.

Once more, Tyler called out her name and heard his brothers do the same.

* * * * *

Another hour had passed since they'd left the ranch. The men met up again with worry etched deeply into all their faces. Dusk was near. Soon the sun would sink on the horizon. Consequently, the late October temperature would drop quickly. No one in their group knew if Emma even had a jacket with her to stave off the cold night air. And what if she was hurt? Not one of them voiced their thoughts aloud.

"Where in hell is she?" Tyler was beside himself with worry and guilt.

"We'll find her. She couldn't have gone that far." Trevor did his best to keep his brother calm. His eyes took in the fresh blood that seeped through the bandage on his head again. Tyler grew more unsteady in the saddle with every passing moment. "You look like you're ready to fall off that horse, Ty. Why don't you head back to the ranch and see—"

"Dougan would've fired shots. I don't care if you have to tie me to this damn horse—I'm staying out here. I'm the goddamn reason she left, for crissakes!" His words brooked no argument.

"All right." Cole nudged his horse closer. "Trevor, you ride with Ty and watch for any tracks leading off the road. I'll go north toward the camp. We've still got a little daylight left."

A wolf howled woefully in the distance. The hair rose on the back of Tyler's neck as he listened to the mournful cry. The sudden realization of where she was hit him hard in the gut.

He wheeled Storm about.

* * * * *

Tyler rode Storm at a breakneck pace all the way to the lake. He cursed himself for not thinking of it sooner. If Emma was riding as hard as Clancey had said she was, it wasn't difficult to imagine that she could have gone that far out from the ranch.

Branches scratched his face when he reined Storm off the trail and headed down the steep slope. He pushed the horse to its limit, knowing in his heart that he would find her when he reached the clearing.

The immense black horse crashed into the clearing. Tyler leapt from the still moving animal and raced to her side. He dropped to his knees beside her, and one look at her tattered clothes told him all he needed to know.

She lay on her back, arms outstretched above her head. Her face was covered by long auburn tresses, which were now matted with dirt and dried blood. The bodice of her dress was torn away from her body, the skirt hiked up, and she lay in a pool of blood. The insides of her thighs were stained with the color red.

"Emma! Jesus Christ, Emma, please don't be dead. Please, Emma!" Gathering her into his arms, he tenderly swept the matted hair away from her face, all the while mouthing a silent prayer. The air left his lungs in a quiet hiss. The left side of her face was severely swollen and bruised to a dark purple. Her lower lip was split at the corner and dried blood marked a trail down her neck. He tucked her limp body close and rocked back and forth as tears slid down his cheeks.

"I love you, Em," he sobbed. "Don't leave me. Come on...stay with me." Her shallow breath against his neck sent relief running rampant through his body, but she remained unresponsive to his pleas. "I'm sorry... This is my fault. I need you. Janie needs you. Please, stay with me. Emma, you've got to hear me."

Tyler continued to murmur repeated pleas in her ear and pressed countless kisses to her clammy forehead. He didn't realize that Cole and Trevor had arrived in the clearing until a hand gently touched his shoulder.

"Here's a blanket, Ty. Let's cover her up."

Tyler's head jerked up. He gazed at his brother through pain-filled eyes as Trevor gently covered Emma's bruised body with the blanket.

Tyler whispered hoarsely as his eyes moved back to her pale face. "He did this to her—Samuel Fontaine. I'll find him, I swear, and I'll kill him. I'll kill him slowly and make him suffer like she did. I swear it. I'll kill him…"

"And we'll help you. We'll help you find him." Cole placed a shaky hand on Tyler's shoulder. "But, for now, we need to get her back to the ranch. She needs attention."

Tyler looked up into his brother's eyes and nodded. "She's losing the baby, Cole. There's so goddamn much blood. He beat her, then raped her and left her to die. I'll kill him when I find him."

"We'll get him, Tyler, I promise." Cole spoke softly.

Tyler snapped out of his shock-induced stupor. Struggling to his feet with Cole and Trevor's help, he moved on a wavering path toward his horse with Emma still in his arms. Carefully handing her to Cole, he mounted Storm, then reached down to take her back into his arms. Settling her gently on his lap, he allowed his brothers to tuck the blanket around her motionless body.

Cole leapt onto his horse's back and raced up the path ahead of them to ensure that Steven was waiting at the house. He kicked the horse into a swift run once he reached the main road, and then he prayed for Emma's life. *Please, God, don't let it happen to him again… Don't let it happen to any of us…*

He repeated the prayer all the way to the ranch.

* * * * *

Tyler held Emma against his chest in a firm, yet gentle grip, never allowing Storm to surpass a slow, loping gait. Wrapped in the blanket, her body was icy cold, yet still the warm blood seeped from her body. The fact that he was the reason she'd left the ranch in the first place, sickened him. The attack was his fault. With every plod of the horse's hooves, he berated himself—and pleaded with God for her life.

Both men carried fear in their hearts. Trevor gripped his rifle and closely watched the thick stand of pine trees along the trail. Samuel wouldn't get another chance. If Fontaine came back for Emma or Tyler, he'd be ready.

They had traveled a full mile before Tyler finally voiced his fears aloud.

"She can't die, Trevor. She's just lying here and she won't wake up. If she dies, my life won't be worth living. I can't take it again. I…can't take that pain again. I love her too much."

"She's going to be all right. You have to believe that." Trevor hoped his reassuring words would prove true because when he'd first approached Tyler at the lake, he'd thought Emma was dead.

"I'll kill him," Tyler vowed again in a quiet, lifeless tone. "His life is worth nothing. No jury will ever get a chance to put him on trial because I'm going to kill him—quietly and slowly—and nobody will be the wiser."

The look on Trevor's face revealed his shock. Tyler was not a cold-blooded killer—but then, neither was he, yet he agreed wholeheartedly. "I'll help kill Fontaine myself—if the opportunity presents itself. Cole will have a hand in it, also."

The two weary travelers finally reached the bluff that overlooked the ranch house. Light spilled from every window, flooding the front yard.

A rider galloped toward them and, when he yelled out, the voice identified him as Cole.

"Steve is here and ready with everything." He reined his horse up alongside his eldest brother and studied his pale and drawn face in the moonlight. "Do you want me to take her?"

"I'll make it. She…she hasn't regained consciousness yet." His harried gaze moved from Emma's ashen features to his brother. "Did Carrie come home with Janie yet?"

"Yeah, they arrived just before dark. We've tried to keep Emma's condition from Janie, but I think she knows something's up, what with Steven being at the house and everyone on edge."

"Go back and make sure she's not there when I bring Emma in," Tyler's voice was close to a plea. "There's so goddamn much blood… I don't want her to see it again. Do you understand?"

"Carrie already had Katy take her back to their cabin. She's going to spend the night with her and Dougan."

All the Wilkins siblings shared Tyler's concern. Janie had witnessed her mother's death. They would do everything possible to keep the little girl from seeing Emma as she was now.

They reached the yard. Steven, Carrie and Mamie waited at the bottom of the steps. Mamie murmured to herself and dabbed at tear-stained cheeks. Carrie stood beside her with an arm around the old woman's shoulders.

Tyler repositioned Emma's battered body in one arm, then held her carefully against his chest as he dismounted. Help was now at arm's length, yet he was still reluctant to hand her over. Somewhere in the back of his ravaged mind, to let her go would mean losing control over whether she lived or died.

He continued to hold her close against his own body when his feet touched the ground. Glittering eyes dared anyone to take her away from him. Steven understood the distraught man's dilemma and without a word moved to open the front door to the house.

Tyler was visibly staggering by the time he reached the top of the staircase. Instead of carrying Emma through the entrance to her bedroom, however, he walked past it, kicked at his own door and entered the master suite. He trudged across the room and laid her gently on the big bed. Sinking to the surface, he took her limp hand in his.

"Emma, can you hear me? Please, honey, stay with me. Fight this. Janie and I need you. Emma? Can you hear me?" His heart lurched when she moved her head slightly on the pillow and moaned. "Emma, it's me, Tyler…"

She lay motionless again, her skin ominously pale beneath the bruises.

"Tyler?" Steven placed a hand on the frightened man's shoulder. "Let me help her now. I can't do anything with you sitting beside her." His eyes had seen the unmistakable evidence of hemorrhaging and knew how critical it was to stop the flow of blood. Emma's life depended on it.

Tyler stood, slowly backed away from the bed and turned pleading eyes to his friend. "Don't let her die…"

"I'll do everything I can, Ty."

Tyler's frightened gaze scanned Emma's broken body once more before he left the room.

Cole and Trevor waited in the hallway. When Tyler weaved precariously, they each grabbed one of his arms. The shaken group met Carrie as she hurried to the second level, arms piled high with linens. She leaned her head into Tyler's firm chest as he pulled her close.

"We have to pray she'll make it…" His voice cracked when Carrie pressed a kiss to his rough cheek.

"I've already been doing that for two hours, Tyler. We're not going to let anything happen to her. We'll do everything we can to pull her through this, I promise."

His bloodshot eyes followed Carrie's form up the rest of the stairs and stumbled back against the stairway wall when a wave of lightheadedness washed over him. Cole and Trevor grabbed hold of his shaking limbs again and led him the rest of the way down the steps and into the library.

"Lay down before you fall down." Cole instructed, then watched as Tyler sank heavily onto the leather sofa.

He leaned forward and rested his throbbing head in his hands, but stayed in an upright position.

Trevor hunkered down before him. "Why don't you lay back and rest that banged-up head of yours. I'll wake you immediately when Steve comes down."

"I can't." Tyler's tired, defeated gaze sought his brother's worried one.

Trevor patted his brother's knee with understanding. "Okay, then we'll all just sit here and wait together. How does that sound?"

Tyler managed a slight nod of the head.

Cole moved to the liquor cabinet, poured each of them a stiff shot of bourbon and passed the glasses around. Each man silently contemplated the horrific events of the day.

They waited and watched as the clock ticked on.

* * * * *

The hour grew late. Tyler was up pacing the room like a caged animal, ignoring the pain that pounded inside his head. Fear had now pushed him beyond the brink of his own injury.

"What the hell is going on up there? Why don't they come down and tell us something!" He marched on wobbly legs to the doorway, looked up the staircase for the hundredth time, then trudged back into the library.

Tyler's agitation brought him to the window. He closed his eyes and breathed deeply as his immediate reaction to the wolf's howl came to mind. It had been a simple gut instinct that urged him to the lake. Never in his worst nightmares had he thought he would find her as he did—beaten, raped and near death. Fontaine would pay dearly, whether Emma lived or died, and the revenge would be sweet.

* * * * *

Another thirty minutes passed before Steven entered the library. Tyler still leaned silently against the windowpane. The doctor's sleeves were rolled up around his forearms, and his face carried an unnatural pallor. Cole and Trevor bounded to their feet, but before any of the occupants of the room could utter a word, he raised a hand for silence. Crossing to the liquor cabinet, he poured himself a drink and tossed it down with one swallow. Sitting on the edge of a nearby chair, he took a deep breath before meeting Tyler's eyes.

"Is she alive?" He asked the question in a near whisper—and dreaded the answer.

"Yes, she's alive—just barely." Steven struggled for a moment. "I did the best I could for her. She miscarried, but at least the hemorrhaging has finally stopped." He reached up to rub his face, then continued. "I've got to be honest with you, Tyler. I've seen men twice her size take less of a beating and not make it. She doesn't have any broken bones though, which is a miracle in itself. That bastard beat the hell out of her." He shook his head. "Her entire body is bruised. The only thing any of us can do right now is pray—and hope she makes it through the next twenty-four hours. I left a bottle of laudanum with Carrie. If she wakes up, see if you can get her to take some for the pain. You can go up and see her now, if you like. Mamie and Carrie are still with her..."

Tyler was out of the library before Steven finished speaking.

* * * * *

He paused outside the open door to his room and inhaled deeply to clear his head. Stepping into the room, he saw Mamie and his sister in the process of cleaning up bloodied rags, but it was not that gruesome sight that made his blood run cold.

Emma's dreadfully still body lay beneath the quilt in the massive bed, her pale face and slender arms covered with bruises.

I'll kill him, Tyler vowed again, *with my bare hands if necessary...* He passed the quiet Mamie and Carrie and lowered himself into a chair by the bed, then gently clasped Emma's cold hand in his and brought her fingers to his lips to seal the promise.

His sister came up behind him, wrapped her arms around his broad shoulders and laid her face against his wavy hair. "She hasn't awakened yet. Maybe if you talk to her, your voice will bring her back to us."

He felt the wetness of Carrie's tears slip from her cheeks and onto his neck. Reaching blindly, he squeezed his sister's hand.

She tightened her hold momentarily, then kissed his whiskered cheek. "We'll let you sit with her for a while by yourself. Keep believing that she'll be fine—and make her believe it, too." Carrie squeezed his shoulder. Mamie did the same before both women left the room, closing the door quietly behind them.

Tyler studied Emma's ashen face and listened to his own agonized whisper. "Will you be fine, Emma?" If she lived, the bruises would heal. But would her spirit be as resilient, or had Samuel taken something from her that she would never be able to recover? "Emma, can you hear me?" he whispered again. "I'll help you, I promise. I'll help you find your way back if you'll only wake up."

He received no response, but he refused to give up. He spoke to her of their future together, of all the things they would do and the places they would go—and he repeatedly told her how much he loved her. Still, she lay incognizant, lost in the healing sleep of a beaten soul.

Chapter Nineteen

ಸಿಾ

Steven settled himself against the chair's soft cushion and stared blankly into the room. Cole and Trevor had not uttered a word since he'd entered the library and broke the news of Emma's precarious condition to Tyler. The two men now stared into their drinks, each lost within their own horrific thoughts.

"Christ," Steven said to no one in particular. "I can't believe she's still alive. That son of a bitch had to have been kicking her. She's one big bruise." His tired gaze swung in their direction. "I'm telling the two of you something right now—when you go looking for that bastard, you had better include me."

Cole sat quietly and contemplated Steven's words. He didn't want anyone else to look for Fontaine. He wanted the man for himself. He wanted to plan a slow, agonizing death befitting such an animal. Since Emma had entered their lives, he'd seen a change in the household—a step forward that was long overdue after the last agonizing years. He'd come to love and respect her in a way that surprised even himself. Tyler and Janie would have a future again and that opportunity was something Cole wanted desperately for them. He would avenge Emma if it took him the rest of his life.

Trevor ran a weary hand over his jaw. "What's your real prognosis, Steve? Were you just sugarcoating it for Tyler's benefit? Can someone actually come out of a beating like that?"

Steven took in the frightened look in Trevor's eyes. "I don't know. It's a miracle that she's lived this long, but Emma's a fighter—let's just hope she has enough fight left in her to get through the night." He rose tiredly. "I've got to go outside and get a breath of fresh air. I'll be back in shortly and check on her once more before I leave."

He walked out onto the front porch, rested his forearms on the log railing and studied the outline of trees against a moonlit horizon. Thoughts of Emma and Tyler and what they would endure over the next few weeks — that is if she lived to see tomorrow — bounced around in his brain.

"Do you think she'll make it?"

Steven spun to find Carrie perched on the porch swing, cloaked in a thick woolen shawl to ward off the chilly night air. He couldn't see her tears, but he knew they were there — he could hear them in her shaky voice.

"I didn't know you were out here." He hesitated. "Do you mind if I sit with you a moment?"

She moved over slightly on the swing to make room for him.

Steven sank onto the hard surface with a sigh. "To answer your question, I don't know. But, if all the love being directed toward her can help, then she's got one helluva fighting chance."

"You were wonderful with her. Don't forget about your skill and what you did up there."

His surprised gaze swung in her direction. He and Carrie had been at odds since his return from medical school. Something had changed in their relationship during those years away, and he was never quite able to put a finger on the reason why.

As she stared silently into the night, he remembered her as a child, skulking around him and her brothers, always wanting to be part of their escapades. They'd let her, because she was the Wilkins' little sister. She never complained when they ganged up on her and had steadfastly stayed by their sides.

He also remembered how, wherever the young group went and whatever they did, she'd always materialized at his side. Her big hazel eyes would watch his every move. Difficult as it was at times, he'd never discouraged her presence.

"Do you realize, Carrie, that this is the first time since I returned home that you haven't tried to take my head off? Come to think of it, we worked together pretty well tonight. So, why the change of heart?" His brow knitted in a perplexed frown. "In fact, what did I ever do to you in the first place?"

Carrie rose from the swing and stepped to the railing, then turned to lean back against the sturdy log banister and study his handsome face in the window's filtering light.

Her mind returned to the day he'd left for St. Paul to attend medical school. Her child's heart had broken that morning because of it. When he'd found her in the library, a young girl of eleven, she was crying out her frustration over the seventeen-year-old friend of her brother who didn't know she was alive. He'd crouched down before her that last day and asked her to wait for him. She had promised that she would.

It was a promise that Carrie never forgot. When Steven returned home for Sara's funeral, her heart had thudded madly at the sight of him. He was a handsome man of twenty-six then, and she was Tyler's little sister — a little sister just turned nineteen who was as much in love with him as the day he'd left.

Now, two years later, he still couldn't see that she was a woman in her own right. She suspected that, to Steve, she was still Tyler's little sister, to be looked at as just another member of the Wilkins clan. Her pride hadn't allowed her the luxury of fawning over him. Consequently, she was waspish at every turn.

How could she answer his question now without giving herself away? Steven saw other women, escorted them to various functions and didn't consider her in the same vein as he did them.

Carrie managed a mental shrug. Maybe she was wrong to hide her feelings from him. Maybe it was time to put all the years of anger and hurt aside and make him see her in a different light. Tonight they'd worked side by side, Emma's life being their prime focus. She'd gained a new respect for him during those long hours — and her love grew tenfold.

"Do you remember the day you left for school?"

He shrugged. "How could I not? It was exciting to finally be on my way to college. But what does that day have to do with the way you've treated me since I got home?"

"Do you recall finding me in the library that day?" She watched his brow crease in thought.

He nodded slowly. "I remember finding you curled up on a chair — you were crying. I came looking for you because I wanted to say goodbye. That was a long time ago, Carrie. I'm still confused as to what made you cry that day."

"You spent a lot of time at this house when we were younger. You've been a part of this family forever, just like Mamie. You and my brothers always included me in everything you did, even though I must have been a hindrance at times. You, though, were always patient with me. You were always kind and gentle when the other three teased me mercilessly." Carrie straightened and pulled the shawl tighter around her shoulders. "You've had your own separate life since you returned. You have your practice and your other…friends." A small, wry smile touched her lips. "I guess we all grew up, didn't we?"

"I'm still not following you, Carrie."

Her shoulders lifted in a sigh. "You told me that long ago day in the library that you wanted me to wait for you, that I was to hurry and grow up. Well, Steven, I did grow up. I did wait for you, yet you haven't given me the time of day since you came home."

Her words swirled in his mind, along with the implications they presented. He hardly remembered the conversation and had probably said those words to ease a little girl's heart.

"What are you saying, Carrie? That you took the words of a seventeen-year-old boy to heart and waited for my return all these years?" Suddenly, he saw Carrie as a woman, not a child—and much to his dismay, she crossed the porch to the front door.

"Goodnight, Steven. It's been a long, grueling day. I'm sorry for the way I've acted toward you." She entered the house then, and was gone.

He sat for a long moment, his mouth hanging open in slack-jawed amazement. In the short space of thirty seconds, Carrie had become a different person in his mind. She wasn't a little girl anymore. She was a competent, full-grown woman who had worked beside him tonight trying just as hard as he to save Emma's life. She wasn't little Carrie anymore. She was now Caroline, and she had feelings for him—strong feelings.

"Who would've ever believed it?" Steven muttered. Rising from the swing, he let out a tired sigh and entered the house through the same door Carrie had only a moment before.

* * * * *

Emma floated across soft pillows of darkness, her pain lessening with each step she took. She was drawn to a distant brilliance—a light that beckoned her into the euphoria of its comforting center. As she neared the brightness, warmth and peace engulfed her. A contented smile curved her lips. It was a wonderful place.

Yet, there was something else, an equally strong force that pulled her back, but she didn't want to return to that other world filled with so much agony.

A young, virile Indian brave stood at the outer edge of the light. A black-feathered band encircled his brow. His strong, brown hand rested companionably on the head of a large, gray wolf that sat by his side.

"Emma," he spoke in a voice that was faintly recognizable, "you have come too soon."

"Am I not supposed to be here?" She gazed without fear into his vibrant dark eyes. "I feel safer here." She glanced down at her silken arms, now absent of bruises and held them before her. "I don't hurt anymore." Her eyes mirrored her confusion as she looked at him again. "Do you know how badly I hurt before I came here?"

"Yes, I do. I was with you then, too. But it is not yet time for you to come home, Emma. You have so much to accomplish. There are those who need you. You must return and help them find their way."

"But I'm at peace here. Nothing can hurt me now. Why must I go?"

Another figure materialized in the swirling mists of light—a blonde-haired woman sheathed in flowing white robes. The muscular brave turned to face her. "Emma does not want to leave."

The specter's understanding smile reached Emma through the eddying fog. "Our friend is correct, Emma, when he says there are those who need you. You must return to them. It's not time for you to join us. The power that draws you away is the power of love,

Emma, and it's stronger even than death. It's pulling you back as we speak." The woman reached out her arms.

Emma melted into her embrace.

"Go to them, Emma. Take care of Tyler and Janie for me. It was meant to be."

Her arms fell away as she disappeared into the brilliance. The Indian brave followed with the wolf at his side. He paused a moment later when another, softer male voice echoed through the mist. He glanced over his shoulder with a gentle smile.

"Listen. He calls for you. Be happy, Emma. Live your life to its fullest." He raised a hand in farewell. "We will meet again." The light dimmed and blackness surrounded her, and then there was nothing.

* * * * *

Emma's painful moans reached into Tyler's subconscious. His eyes snapped open. Her bruised body writhed weakly beneath the quilt, her head lolled on the pillow and her bruised arms flailed blindly, pushing away an imaginary attacker.

Tyler bounded from the chair. "It's all right, Emma," his tender voice soothed. "It's me, Tyler. Wake up now. You're safe, honey. You're home."

Her thrashing continued. Tyler grasped her upper arms in a gentle hold and pulled her into his arms. A weak, strangled scream escaped her swollen lips.

"Emma, it's Tyler. Please, hear me! You're safe now. I won't ever let him hurt you again. Open your eyes, honey." His heart pounded a rapid beat until she calmed.

He held her at arm's length as she slowly opened her eyes and looked up into his drawn face. Memories rushed in to assault her sluggish brain—Samuel, the beating, the rape...

Tears trickled down her swollen cheeks. She turned her head from him in all-consuming shame.

Tyler tightened his grip on her arms ever so gently. Quietly, but firmly, he spoke. "Look at me."

Her response came in the form of a quiet sob and a weak shake of the head.

"Emma...I'm here with you, and I'll keep you safe."

Emma held her silence, so he simply pulled her close again and held her until he felt the weight of her head slump against his chest.

Carefully laying her back onto the pillow again, he tucked the covers around her shoulders and gently stroked her hair until he was assured that she slept and hadn't slipped into unconsciousness again. Moving to the chair, he watched quietly as her chest rose and fell with slow, even breaths.

I'll make it up to you, Emma. Somehow, I'll make you forget my angry words and Samuel Fontaine's abuse. I'll show you the way back, if you'll only let me...

Leaning his head against the back of the chair, he stared into the semi-darkness. Emma was his future, was Janie's future, and he would love her until the day he died.

* * * * *

Tyler awoke with a start when Mamie touched his shoulder.

"How come you be sleepin' in that chair all night long?" she whispered quietly so as not to disturb Emma. "Come, son. Let's get you cleaned up and be inspectin' that head o' yours."

Paying no mind to Mamie, he leaned across the bed to check Emma's condition. He'd slept fretfully during the past hours, waking often to see if she had moved. He could see now by the way the bedcovers were still nestled around her shoulders that she hadn't wakened again. The swelling on her face was even more pronounced and the darkening bruises more noticeable in the light of day.

"Why in the hell did this have to happen to her, Mamie?" he asked, never taking his eyes from Emma's ashen face. "Where is the justice in this world? She wouldn't intentionally hurt anyone and now look at her."

"That be a question, Tyla, that many ask in times like now. It's not somethin' that ever be figured out. Not by you, not by me, not by God, but we can conjecture why somethin' like this happens." Mamie wrapped her arms around his shoulders, kissed the top of his head and held him close. "When your mama died, God left four youngins—one, a brand-spankin' new life, without anyone to be lovin' 'em like only a mama can. Way I sees it, the only justice to be found by takin' her away is He gave me four souls to love—four beautiful souls that I probably would never bin' able to make on my own. I ain't been your true mama, boy, but I tried hard my whole life long to do right."

Tyler turned and grasped her gnarled fingers in his own. "Don't ever think you could have loved any of us more than you have."

"It makes my heart feel good cuz you be feelin' that way. See, Tyla? There be a silver linin' to everthin' that happens." Her head of gray curls nodded at Emma. "You love this girl, son?"

He bobbed his head in admission.

"Then be lookin' at the silver layin' in the bed. We all gonna try our hardest to git her through this, then you can be showin' her the love you might not have found any other way. It be the devil's shame she went through what she did, but you and this little gal will be stronger for it happenin'. Do you understand what I'm sayin'?"

"I think I do, Mamie." A sad smile touched his lips. "You always find the good in even the worst situations. How can you continue to do that when life throws so many punches?"

"Because, Tyla, sometimes it can git so bad, that iffin you don't go lookin' for the sunshine, you'll jes always be in the dark." She kissed his unshaven cheek and squeezed his upper arm reassuringly. "Now, let's be lookin' at your cracked head and clean up that bandage. Carrie'll be comin' up shortly to sit with our Miss Em."

Tyler turned to gaze at Emma's broken body for a moment longer before leaving the room. He *would* help her find the sunshine again.

You're in there somewhere, Emma. I swear I'll try my hardest to bring you back and make a life for us. I'll carry the load, honey. Just come back to me...

* * * * *

Janie entered the house through the side door to the kitchen, hesitated a moment as she peeked around the corner into the dining room, and then ran across the living room toward the wide staircase that led to the upper floor. Something was wrong—and it had to do with Emma. She'd slipped away from Katy's earlier that morning, unable to bear her own fear any longer. Her Uncle Cole had looked so worried the night before when he raced into the yard on his big brown horse...

She had strained to hear what was being said among the adults in the household, but then Cole pulled Carrie and Mamie into the kitchen. Nobody had said anything to her yesterday about having to sleep at Katy's, yet suddenly Auntie Carrie had packed her a bag.

Then Dr. Steve arrived, looking more scared than she'd ever seen him.

She heard Whizzer's telltale scratching at the front door and hurried back to let him in. Patting his head to keep him quiet, she scurried to the steps again and motioned for the dog to follow.

Janie reached the second floor and peered around the banister. Seeing only an empty hallway, she tiptoed on to Emma's room and pushed open the door. The room was empty and the bed made. Her heart beat faster.

Whizzer sniffed at the closed door that led to her father's suite. Janie hurried across the room. She grabbed at the dog's scruff to hold him back and crept through the short connecting corridor. Pushing the other door open a crack, her curious eyes settled first on Carrie. Her aunt sat in one of the overstuffed chairs, which had been drawn close to the bedside, and dabbed at her eyes with a handkerchief.

Janie pushed open the door a little more until her father's bed came into view. Emma lay beneath a quilt on the soft expanse, her face swollen and discolored. In between the bruises, her stepmother's face was as pale as the white pillowcase her head rested on. Janie began to tremble with the height of her fear.

A vision of the horse racing toward her and the tight hold of her mother's hand on her arm as she pushed her aside, assailed the child's frightened mind. In her mind, she heard her mother's scream rent the air just before she lay on the dirt road with blood dripping from her open mouth...

Her face had been an ashen gray—the same color as Emma's was now.

The nightmarish memories rushed in at her from all sides. Janie heaved the connecting door open with a bang. Carrie jumped at the sound.

The little girl clawed at her clothing, trying to escape the exploding pain that closed her throat. Emma would go away like her mother had.

Janie stared at Emma through bulging, frightened eyes. Carrie approached quickly, with outstretched arms and tears still wet on her face, but Janie bolted around her and raced to the bed. A strange sound vibrated in her throat—a sound that turned into a strangled scream as the little girl draped herself across Emma's still form. She sobbed out her anguish and repeated Emma's name over and over again.

Carrie stood dumbstruck upon hearing the forgotten timbre of her niece's voice. More than two years had passed since Janie had spoken, but now the child cried out her agony. She thought Emma was dead.

* * * * *

Emma fought the darkness that engulfed her. The sound of a child's weeping reached through the fog. Was the little one's undisguised anguish for her? Was she back in that special, soothing place she'd visited not long ago?

No. The pain was overwhelming—the peaceful bliss was gone. There was no light now. Only a frightening darkness.

Drawing strength, Emma struggled to open her eyes. It took a moment for her to focus on the small, blonde head that rested against her chest. The child's tears dampened her nightdress. Slowly, Emma lifted a hand to stroke the little girl's silky soft hair.

"Janie?" she whispered in a hoarse voice.

Janie's head jerked up. Bewildered eyes stared.

"Janie...why are you crying?" Emma struggled against her nausea and concentrated on the realization that Janie had spoken her name aloud. "Did you say...my name?"

Janie scrambled up to sit beside Emma, then reached out a trembling hand to gently touch the bruised face before her. "I thought you went away, like my mama did." The scratchy voice was foreign to Emma's ears, but she had never heard a more beautiful sound. Ignoring her own bruising pain, she wrapped the little girl in her gentle embrace and closed her heavy eyelids. A weak hand rubbed the child's back. "Honey, I'll never leave you. I just...fell off my horse and got hurt. I love you too much to leave. Don't...be scared."

Janie's head lolled against Emma's neck. "I'm not scared anymore, Emma. I love you, too."

"It's good to finally hear you say it." Emma managed the words in spite of her bruised jaw and sapped strength. "Can you tell your Daddy that? He needs to hear you say it."

The little girl sat up, pushed the strands of blonde hair away from her face and leaned forward. Her eyes sparkled with childish excitement. "I can talk, Emma."

Emma fought the darkness that summoned her once more. "I can hear you. Will you come back and...talk to me again later? I'm really sleepy now." Emma's eyes closed and her head moved slightly into the pillow.

Janie backed off the bed carefully. As her tiny feet touched the floor, she turned to see her father standing in the middle of the room. He sank to his knees. She ran into his outstretched arms to be pulled into his shaking embrace.

"Daddy, don't be scared. Emma is just sleeping now—she's going to be fine. Daddy?" Her eyes rounded in surprise. "I can talk."

The raspy voice went straight to Tyler's heart as he hugged her tightly. He'd heard the awful screaming from the kitchen. Thinking Emma had awakened again, he'd bolted up the steps. When he'd entered the bedroom, his fear quickly turned to disbelief.

Carrie slipped past them to check on Emma. Realizing she was asleep again, she motioned for Tyler to take Janie from the room. He stood with his daughter in his arms and carried her out into the hallway.

Mamie reached the top of the stairs at that moment, her face etched with concern. "Tyla, what's happenin'? My Gawd, how's Emma?" she panted out from the exertion of climbing the steps at such a rapid pace.

"Emma's sleeping again, Mamie, but it wasn't her we heard. It was Janie." He tousled his daughter's hair with a trembling hand.

The little girl hid her face in the folds of his shirt. Finally, she peeked up at everyone through wide eyes.

"Janie?" the old woman whispered her shock.

"You heard him right." Carrie exited the bedroom and crossed to Mamie. "I'll tell you all about it later, but I think Janie got so upset when she saw Emma that she just started to scream."

Mamie waddled over to her youngest charge and held out her hands. Janie moved from her father's arms and into the housekeeper's comforting embrace. She cuddled close to the old woman's ample bosom.

"I can talk, Mamie."

"Yes, you can, chile, and it be the most wonderful sound God ever be creatin' for us." Deep brown eyes found Tyler's. Mamie held out a hand to him. He clasped her fingers firmly. "See, Tyla? There be a silver linin' to everythin' that happens. Yessiree…"

* * * * *

Tyler stoked the fire, sighing heavily. Emma had slept most of the day, yet still he didn't leave her side. He straightened, set down the poker and turned to find her awake and staring at him from across the room. Her eyes held a distant blankness as she watched him move to sit in the chair beside the bed.

"Would you like a drink of water?"

She nodded, however hesitantly. Tyler reached for the pitcher, filled a glass and handed it to his wife. She sipped slowly, her eyes downcast, then handed the half-empty container back to him, careful not to let her fingers touch his.

His heart reached out to her as he studied the bruised face before him. "I'm going to go get Carrie. She can help you get up for a minute. I'll be right back." Emma nodded again as he left the room with measured steps.

As soon as the latch clicked shut, Tyler raced to Carrie's room and banged on the door. His sister opened it immediately.

"Emma's awake!" He ran a trembling hand through his dark hair. "Could you help her get up? I don't know what to do. She's been lying in that bed all day. Maybe she needs to...take care of some personal needs. See if you can get her to talk to you. She still hasn't said anything about what happened. I don't know if she even realizes that she lost the baby. Steve said she was sleeping when he checked on her today, and they never had a chance to talk..."

"Slow down, Tyler. Of course, I'll help her." Carrie was already moving down the hallway with Tyler in her wake.

"I'll just wait out here until you're finished helping her."

Carrie's gaze swept her brother's disheveled appearance. He hadn't shaved since his own accident. His eyes were bloodshot after the long, sleepless hours at Emma's bedside. She rested a hand on the doorknob to the master bedroom and paused. "Go throw some water on your face—you look terrible. Use Trevor or Cole's razor. I'll stay with Emma until you get back. Tyler, if she doesn't ask about the baby, I'm not going to bring it up."

Carrie entered the room to find Emma struggling to a standing position. She rushed to the battered woman's side, grasped her arm and helped her to her feet—then noticed her sister-in-law's overwhelming effort to hold back the tears. Carrie fought to control her own emotions and lent her strength to assist Emma in crossing the room to the water closet.

Emma emerged from the small alcove a few minutes later, her skin a shade paler from the strain of being up and about. Her eyes still downcast, she quickly raised an arm to halt Carrie's steps when the other woman moved to help her. Emma's lurching gait carried her back to the bed of her own accord.

The painful grimaces on Emma's face told Carrie that each step was sheer agony, but the physical evidence of her abuse was not what worried the other woman. The tight control of her emotions and the reserved expression on her sister-in-law's face were far more troublesome.

"Is there anything else I can do for you?"

Emma pulled the blanket up and eased her bruised body back onto the mattress. "No... I'm still rather tired after my visit with Janie earlier." A poignant smile touched her swollen lips. "Now that she's found her voice again, she has a lot to say. I'm happy for her."

"It's a miracle, Emma. I never thought we'd hear her speak again." Carrie sat on the edge of the bed. "Would you like to talk? I really don't know what to say about what happened, but I'm willing to listen."

Carrie could almost see the shell encase Emma again.

Emma's gaze fell to her lap. "I can't. Not now. Not yet," she whispered.

Carrie enveloped her in a gentle embrace, willing Emma to feel her love and concern. Emma remained stiff in her arms. Carrie mentally cursed Samuel Fontaine for what he'd done. She leaned back and nervously rubbed her hands together. "Well... I think Tyler is waiting outside, so I'll go now. I'll see you in the morning." She rose from the bed, took a step toward the door, then turned back. "On second thought, would you like me to stay here with you tonight?"

"That won't be necessary."

Carrie left the room quietly. Tyler leaned against the wall in the hallway. He had shaved the stubble from his face, but the haunted look in his eyes remained.

"She's still awake, but very unreachable. Be gentle with her. If you need me, don't hesitate to wake me up, okay?" She wrapped her arms around his middle and hugged him fiercely. "I love you, Ty. I'm so sorry."

He simply hugged her back, and then entered the bedroom. Casting a comforting smile in Emma's direction, he stoked the fire again before returning to sit carefully on the edge of the bed. The facts of her brutal attack still remained unspoken between them. She needed to talk about it if the healing process was to begin, but he understood that she had to take the lead, and would be patient for as long as it took.

"Steve left some laudanum for the pain. Would you like me to get you some?"

She shook her head, her eyes still downcast. She studied her hands, which fidgeted nervously in her lap. "I don't want anything. I just want to sleep, if that's all right with you."

"That's fine, Emma. Sleep is the best thing for you right now."

She finally met his gaze when she settled back into the pillow. Her chin quivered with her effort not to cry. She was unsuccessful. A lone tear escaped and traveled down her swollen cheek.

"There is no more baby, is there?" Her statement was filled with anguish.

Tyler released a heavy sigh, hating what he had to say next. He shook his head slightly and never took his eyes from hers. "No, Emma, there isn't."

He reached out to gather her into his comforting embrace, but she pulled the blankets up tighter around her shoulders and rolled away from his sorrowful gaze.

"Emma—"

"Goodnight." She dismissed him with just the one spoken word.

Tyler's hands froze in midair. He squeezed his lids shut.

I'll do this for us, Emma. I'll get you through this, I promise...

"Good night, then. I'll come back and check on you later." He left the room and closed the door silently behind him.

Emma caught the sob that rose in her throat before he heard it. She was in her own private hell now, and she would bear the suffering alone.

Chapter Twenty

A full week passed. Emma refused to speak to anyone about the attack. She remained sullen and withdrawn, acting reasonably normal only when Janie visited her.

"I don't know what to do anymore," Tyler's voice was filled with desperation as he paced the library. His worried gaze moved from Steven, to his brothers, and then back to the doctor again. "She won't talk about it. She just sleeps, or sits and stares out the window. She's hardly eaten a thing." He stopped before his lifelong friend and spread his arms wide in supplication. "None of us can find a way to reach her. What should we do?"

"Be patient," Steven's eyes scanned all the faces in the room. "Emma's sleeping so much because it's her body's way of healing itself. As for why she sits and stares out the window, I'm sure she's just trying to come to terms with all of this herself. Give her time — it's only been a week. When she's ready, she'll open up. Emma's one strong lady, but after what she's been through, you can't blame her for being distant. I don't mean to sound like I'm preaching, because I know she's received a lot of support from all of you, but you need to let her come around in her own good time."

He noticed the thin set of Tyler's lips and felt a pang of sympathy for the man, but there was nothing he could do for the family or Emma's emotional state — except maybe discover Samuel's whereabouts. "Tyler, have you heard anything on Fontaine?"

Tyler shook his head in disgust as he poured drinks at the sidebar. He passed them along to Steven and his brothers as he spoke. "I got another message from the private investigator yesterday. It's as if that bastard has dropped off the face of the Earth. The trail has gone cold."

"I think Trevor and I should start looking for him." Cole sat calmly and sipped his drink. "We know this country like the back of our hands. Your investigator doesn't."

"I agree." Trevor captured his older brother's gaze. "We might have more luck. Cole and I discussed it—we both want that bastard."

Tyler shook his head. "I need the two of you here. I've been giving this whole thing a lot of thought, too. I want to back off from the mill indefinitely. I know it's a lot to ask, but until Emma has completely recovered, I don't want to be far from the house. I can't do that if the two of you are gone."

"I can understand that, Ty," Cole stated. "But what if Samuel's never found? I'd hate to see that son of a bitch walk away without paying."

Carrie entered the room, then paused to glance at the occupants. "I just checked on Emma. She's asleep, so I thought I'd work on the basket of mending I left in here earlier." Her gaze bored into her brothers. "You all look rather serious. What's going on?"

"Sit down, Carrie," Tyler said as he settled into the chair beside Cole. "We were just trying to figure out how to go about running the business over the next few months."

"In regard to what?" She positioned herself on the sofa, across from Steven. She managed a quick glance in his direction, then looked away. His penetrating gaze gave her shivers.

"In regard to the fact that I don't want to stray far from the house and Emma. That means Trevor and Cole can't just up and leave to search for Fontaine. Somebody has to oversee the operation. Secondly," he continued in a no-nonsense tone, "I don't want you, Emma, or any of the other women in this house to be alone. If I stay close to home and to Emma, it will solve that problem, too. We know Samuel will do anything to get to Emma or myself. He's more than proved it." An image of his battered wife flashed in his brain. "I think he's crazy enough to come to the ranch despite what the investigator says."

Cole rose to fix himself another drink. "We've got a lot of good men around here, Tyler. Not a one of them would let Fontaine within a mile of the place."

"I know they wouldn't, but I don't trust any of them as much as I trust the two of you." Tyler's green eyes glittered with hatred. "I want Fontaine. I think the only way we're going to get him is to sit tight and wait for him to come to us—even if it takes months. I'll still keep the Pinkerton agent on his trail, but for now, I want the two of you here."

"I think Tyler's right." Steven had quietly listened to the conversation. "I would hate to think of Fontaine getting into this house with the women—and none of you being around. Let the fox come back to the chicken coop—or at least let him give it a try." His gaze rested on Carrie. The thought of what he might do to her, too, made him sick to his stomach.

"Okay, Ty. Agreed." Trevor set his empty glass on the table before him. "It's your call. Cole and I will figure out a rotating schedule at the sawmill. We'll bring in Jack now that the crews are out of the woods. That way, there can be two of us here at all times."

Tyler nodded. "That's even better. We have to make sure that Samuel Fontaine never gets the chance to hurt anyone in this family again."

The October wind rattled the shutters as the group made plans for the immediate future. It was not long though before Steven stood to leave.

"I guess I'd better head for home. It's getting late. As long as Emma's asleep, I won't bother her again tonight." He glanced at Carrie who still sat on the sofa with Mamie's basket of mending. She picked through it nonchalantly, as if his leave-taking was no great thing. "Carrie, could I speak with you privately for a moment?"

A flush immediately stained her satiny cheeks. She ducked her head to hide from her brothers' view. Steven had arrived daily during the past week to check on Emma and most nights stayed for dinner. Having him constantly underfoot left her feeling like a schoolgirl in the throes of her first love. She had avoided him like the plague, however, since the night on the porch and had no desire now to be called to atonement for her confession—which she was sure was Steven's purpose in asking to speak to her alone. She wasn't about to make a scene in front of her brothers though, and simply rose with a slight nod in his direction and quickly exited the room. Steven was close on her heels.

Trevor's expression was a little nonplussed. "What's that about? Why would Steve need to talk to Carrie in private?"

"At least they're finally getting along," Tyler commented. "I've noticed Carrie has let up on her sarcasm when he's around. I've never figured out why she doesn't like him."

Cole stretched his arms over his head and chuckled aloud.

"What?" Trevor's voice was filled with confusion.

"It just never ceases to amaze me how some people can be so blind."

"What are you talking about?"

"Haven't you two figured out what Carrie's problem is yet? Where Steve is concerned, I mean."

"Like I just said," Tyler repeated, "I know exactly what her *problem* is. She's never cared much for him. Hell, can't you tell that by the way she snaps at him on a regular basis?" His dark brow raised in thought. "Although she has backed off in the last week."

Cole simply shook his head in disbelief. "You two are such total ingrates. She's in love with him—and always has been."

The two older Wilkins brothers stared at him through eyes that mirrored their doubt.

Trevor snorted. "Oh, come on, Cole. If *that's* how Carrie treats the guy she loves, I'd hate to see how she acts around someone she doesn't like."

"Yeah? Well a woman will resort to desperate measures when the guy is too dense to figure it out on his own."

"Carrie and *Steve*?" Trevor leaned forward, his interest piqued.

Tyler, too, could not quite believe what his brother claimed to be true. "Cole, Carrie has never shown any interest in having boys around. Besides, Steve is like a member of the family."

Cole smacked his forehead with the palm of his hand, rolled his eyes heavenward and reached for his hat. "Carrie has never shown an interest in *boys*, as you so aptly put it, because she's always been interested in only one *man*. Wake up, you two. She's not a little girl anymore. Christ, Tyler, she's only a year younger than Emma. And sometime in the last week, Steve has changed his whole attitude toward her." He adjusted his worn hat on his head. "I'm gonna take one more walk around the place and make sure everything is secure." He hesitated at the doorway. "And don't go out on the front porch. I think they're out there."

He left his brothers with slack-jawed looks of disbelief on their faces.

Trevor's gaze swung to his remaining brother as he scratched his head. "How does he do that?"

* * * * *

"We haven't had a chance to speak alone this week." Steven peered through the darkness at the woman standing before him.

Carrie's gaze dropped to the planking beneath her feet as she struggled for an outward appearance of calm. A sudden shiver crawled up her back. Whether it was due to the cold October wind that swirled around them or because she stood alone with Steven on the porch, she had no clue. She lifted her eyes to his again and watched him warily.

"The days have been hectic," she murmured, then sighed, frustrated with her own ineptness and met his gaze squarely. "I'm sorry, Steven, if I put you on the spot last week. It was just a little girl's confession from long ago. Don't take it to heart. Lord knows I haven't."

Instant anger flared inside Steven with her flippant remark. Being at the house all week in her presence had forced him to look at her differently. She wasn't just Tyler's little sister anymore. She was the first thing he thought about when he rose in the morning and the last thing he thought of at night. She'd even invaded his dreams. It took some doing, but he'd finally acknowledged the fact that he wanted to explore her lips with his own mouth. He wanted to hold her woman's body close to his and never to let her go.

Now, she brushed him away like a pesky mosquito.

"So just what the hell is that supposed to mean? You told me that you waited for me. Because I didn't know how you felt up until a week ago, it doesn't mean anything? I've spent the entire week unable to get you off my mind. I've watched you, I've thought about you, I've *dreamt* about you."

"Oh, so that's how it is, huh? Just because *you* finally decided to notice me as a woman, I'm supposed to simply fall into your arms and say, 'Fine, Steven. Whatever makes you happy?'" Carrie's eyes sparked with fury that sprang out of nowhere. She met him nose to nose. "Let's not forget the fact that *I* waited years for you to come home! Then, when you finally did, you were so busy fawning over other women that you *still* didn't know I was alive! And if you think the last few days have been easy for me, you're wrong! How do you think *I* felt all week after confessing my feelings? You've been in this house countless times, but not once did you seek me out. Not once did you even *try* to discuss it with me!"

"Christ, Carrie, your brothers have been with us constantly! Try looking at it from my point of view. How do you think it feels to know those three would throttle me if I tried to do anything *improper* with their little sister?"

"Hah! As if you're afraid of them." Carrie rolled her eyes in a dramatic show of skepticism. "You'll have to come up with something better than that."

"That's not what I'm saying." He balled his hands into fists in a futile effort to control his temper. "I just know how protective they are of you. They always have been. Hell, they'd probably kill me if they caught me kissing you in an unbrotherly manner!"

Carrie snorted at his statement and tossed her head, sending her sandy-colored tresses flying. "Well, I don't think you have anything to worry about. I haven't seen any kissing going on around here. Have you, Steven? Hell, Tyler doesn't even have the guts to kiss his own wife! Now that I think about it, I don't think anything improper is *allowed* on the Wilkins ranch!" She peered around his shoulder. "Nope! I don't see anyone over there doing anything improper. Do you?"

"Goddamnit, Carrie!" He yanked her into his arms and kissed her for all he was worth.

Carrie was so shocked that it took her a moment to realize what was happening. She had wondered for years what it would feel like to be kissed by him—now she knew it was worth the wait. She wrapped her arms about his neck. The chill wind was forgotten, the angry words lost in the blustery air and the years of loneliness drifted away.

They clung to one another until their passion was spent and the kiss became just a playful touching of lips. A lazy grin curved Steve's mouth as he met her liquid, hazel gaze.

"Well, that shut you up."

Carrie's contented smile belied the excitement she'd discovered in his embrace. Her shaky hands spread across his chest to feel the beat of his heart, which was as rapid as her own. "Steven—"

"Shhh, Carrie. If you say one more word, I'll have to kiss you again," he whispered as his eyes danced over her face.

"Then I'm going to keep talking until—"

His mouth silenced hers once more.

* * * * *

Tyler knocked softly on the door to his bedroom three days later and waited for Emma to invite him in. Her quiet voice came a moment later. He entered the suite, his arms laden with a tablecloth, china plates and silverware. She listlessly eyed his load, turned to lean against the windowsill and gazed blankly through the frosty pane at the fresh blanket of white that lay across the landscape.

"You had a long nap today," he commented as he placed the dinnerware on a nearby table, and then moved to stoke the fire.

Her only response was a small shrug of the shoulders.

Tyler stifled the sigh that rose in his chest. "Mamie said she would prepare a tray for the two of us tonight. I thought we could eat together." This time, Tyler wasn't even granted a shrug for his efforts.

I'm not giving up on you, Em, he thought as he stared at her stiff back. *You'll not chase me away with your silence again.*

"What do you think of this weather? It's the first snowfall of the year." He grappled for conversation.

Emma watched the snowflakes swirl outside the window and pulled the dressing gown more securely around her small body, realizing in some part of her mind that the movement didn't hurt as it had a week ago. The first time she'd seen her face in the mirror with its swollen purple marks, she'd been horribly shocked, but the tears would not come. Her body was slowly healing and the bruises lightening in color, but the pain in her heart would not recede.

Emma half listened to Tyler talk about inconsequential matters as he moved about the room doing equally inconsequential things. She knew that he waited for her to speak of Samuel's assault, but she'd pushed the attack to the far corners of her mind, refusing to allow the pain to come full force.

The loss of the baby was something else they needed to discuss. She squeezed her eyes tightly. The child was the one and only reason they were together — the one and only reason he had not callously ejected her from his home and his life. Her jaw clenched in an effort to prevent her chin from quivering. How did he feel about her now, especially after what Samuel had done to her? She was soiled goods.

Tyler's cruel words spoken that awful day in the library just before she'd lost the baby came back to haunt her. The bottom line was that Tyler would never get past the idea that she was a wanton woman.

"Emma?"

She wiped a wayward tear from her cheek and turned to face him.

"I'm going to run down to the kitchen and see if supper's ready. I've got the table all set up in here." Tyler indicated the small table in the corner, which was now covered with a white cloth and held two place settings.

Emma gave his handiwork a cursory glance, then turned back to the window.

He released another silent sigh. He was at such a loss when it came to her. Steven repeatedly told him to be patient, and he had been. But at times like this, he wanted to scream at her to just let him help.

He turned to open the door.

"I tried to get away…" Her strangled whisper reached him.

Tyler forced his heart to slow as he swung back to gaze at her stiff back. He held his breath as he waited for her to speak again.

"I tried to get away…but I couldn't…"

She continued to stare out the window, failing even to turn and see if he'd left the room. Tyler crossed to stand behind her. He hesitated for a moment, and then placed gentle hands on her shoulders.

"I know, Em."

Her body trembled beneath his fingers. Tyler carefully pulled her against his firm chest, slipped his arms around her waist and rested his chin against her soft hair.

"It wasn't your fault," he breathed quietly.

Emma squeezed her eyelids shut in an attempt to stifle the sob elicited by his gentle touch. "I managed to get on the horse and almost got away…but he pulled on my leg… I lost my balance." She began to tremble.

He pulled her even more protectively into his embrace, then tenderly kissed her satiny tresses.

A sob burst forth. Her body convulsed with the ache in her heart.

Tyler lifted her gently into his arms and crossed to a chair, murmuring words to soothe her—words he would be unable to recall later that evening—and tucked her into his lap. He pulled a quilt around her for warmth as she wept against his chest.

"I knew…what he was going to do…"

"It's over, Em."

"When I fell off the horse…he kicked me in the stomach."

Tyler's belly constricted with her words. He gathered her even closer within his embrace.

"I tried to crawl away…but he kicked me down."

"You don't have to tell me. It's over, Em. I know what happened. It wasn't your fault."

She continued though, leaving nothing out. Tyler felt the warmth of his own tears as she told the story between anguished sobs. Emma kept her face hidden in the crook of his neck. She clung to him as her only lifeline in a world gone mad, needing to purge the experience from her mind while he kept her safe and secure in his arms and whispered that he would never let anyone hurt her again.

Tyler gently stroked her back until her head finally slumped against his chest as exhaustion overcame her grief, and she fell into a fretful sleep. Tyler ached for her. He tightened his arms around her and closed his eyes. He wouldn't take the chance of waking her until she was ready to face the world again.

A creaking hinge made him glance up. Mamie stood in the doorway, watching them from across the room. Tears glistened in her eyes. Tyler tipped his head in a nod. His lips curved in a bittersweet smile. The old woman backed from the room, closed the door again and left them alone as the fire crackled and the snow fell against the window.

Chapter Twenty-One

Emma finally left her room to rejoin the family. The bruises had faded and her body recovered from the miscarriage, but a quiet sadness surrounded her. She put up a good façade, working with Mamie and Carrie in the kitchen and playing with Janie outside in the snow, but she didn't fool anyone, least of all Tyler. Emma's former spirit had disappeared, and he despaired that she would ever be able to recapture it completely.

They took long walks with Janie and Whizzer, laughing at the dog's antics as it bounded through the snow. They spent close-knit evenings before the warm fire in the library, playing game after game of chess, with Emma the victor more often than not. One night, she even got a little tipsy along with the rest of the family when they celebrated Trevor's twenty-eighth birthday. She was extremely happy for Steven and Carrie's newfound love, but overall, the melancholy was still with her and nobody knew what to do.

Tyler now slept in Emma's bedroom at night and only entered his suite when he needed a change of clothes or some other personal item. He didn't mention the less than ideal arrangement, however, until late one afternoon when he entered the master bedroom and found it bare of Emma's personal effects. The top of the dresser where he used to push about her combs and brushes to get at his own toiletries was now void of any article that belonged to her.

He rushed to the oak armoire and threw open the heavy doors. Her clothes were gone. His chest tightened with rising panic.

Rushing through the connecting hallway and into the adjoining room, his headlong flight caused the door to bang against the dresser at his entry. A startled Emma shot up from where she sat at a small desk, writing a letter.

"Tyler, you frightened me! Is something wrong?"

His shoulders sagged with relief as his searching eyes spied her brushes on the dresser and her jacket hanging from a peg on the backside of the hallway door.

"I went into the other room and noticed all your things were gone. It just startled me for a minute." He met her hesitant gaze.

She sank back to the chair and straightened the paper and pen before her with a shaky hand. She knew he'd discover at some point that day that she'd returned to her old room, but it simply had seemed less complicated to make the move without informing him.

"It just didn't seem right that you couldn't sleep in your own bed—"

"So you just moved everything back without even discussing it with me? There was no hurry, Emma."

She turned away so he wouldn't see the tears that shone in her eyes. There was every reason to move back to her old room. He would never want her—not after what Samuel had done. She wanted to make things easy for him—anything so he wouldn't send her back to New York.

Taking a composed breath, she struggled for a level voice. "It wasn't a problem to move my things, Tyler. I didn't have much to do today and you're so busy. Katy was more than happy to help me."

She cringed inwardly with the lie. Tyler wasn't busy anymore. He was always just a step behind her this past month, gracious to a fault and solicitous of her every need as she got continually stronger. That morning when she'd discovered he would spend most of the day with Dougan, Emma quickly garnered Katy's aid before he returned. By taking the initiative and moving out of his room, her actions exonerated him from having to ask her to leave.

Not once had he mentioned the conversation they were to have the day of Samuel's attack...and not once had he ever mentioned the word love. As hard as it was, Emma finally understood that she would always be a wife in name only.

Tyler stared at her petite profile and felt his world crumble. He'd spent the last month waiting for her to be ready for him, physically and emotionally. Yet now she'd taken another step away with the simple act of moving from his room. He yearned to take her in his arms and say how much he loved her, but Steven had cautioned him to be patient. He would—no matter how long it took.

He couldn't imagine life without her anymore. His heart raced whenever she walked into a room, and he loved her more with each passing day. He would see her pain through to its end. He would treat her gently and make her understand that all men weren't like Samuel.

Tyler watched her fidget nervously with the paper on the desk, looking as if she was afraid he would demand her return to his room—and into his bed. But, he would wait until she was ready and until fear no longer ruled her mind. Then and only then would he show her how much a man could love a woman.

"Well, then," Tyler glanced around Emma's suite, "I'll just gather up my things and move them back to my room."

She couldn't watch as he moved about collecting his things and held back the tears of rejection once more. Finally, he exited through the short hallway and closed the door quietly behind him. As it clicked shut, her face sank into her hands to stifle her sobs.

Tyler leaned against the closed door. His eyelids drooped along with the heaviness that settled in his chest.

*****

"Hurry, Emma!" Janie stood outside her stepmother's bedroom door and knocked loudly.

"I'm coming! Is everyone waiting for me?"

"Yup! Uncle Cole has the sleigh all hooked up. Uncle Trevor says he's gonna come up here and throw you over his shoulder like a sack of potatoes if you don't hurry!"

Emma giggled at the picture Janie's words created in her mind and quickly snatched up her hat. She had no doubt her brother-in-law would do just that. She joined the little girl in the hall, and they hurried down the steps and out the front door.

Tyler stood beside the shaggy draft horses in the cold winter air. Plumbs of steam whistled from their snouts as the big animals stamped their feet, waiting to be off.

"It's about time!" he laughed. "Trevor was just on his way up."

She threw a saucy smile in his general direction as he hurried to help her into the sleigh. "I couldn't find my hat." A squeal of delight followed when Tyler scooped her into his arms and set her gently on the seat beside Carrie, who was already snuggled beneath a thick woolen blanket. Hot lightning shot through her veins with his simple touch.

Carrie waited for Emma to seat herself comfortably, and then tucked the blanket across her sister-in-law's lap. "It's amazing how they can just toss us around, isn't it? The other day, Steve picked me up and threw me into a snow bank like I was a small child. Got him back though when he wasn't looking! I shoved snow down the back of his jacket!" She laughed heartily.

"And I'm certain you're not telling me the whole story—like what happened when he caught you." The levity in Emma's words belied the ache in her heart. If only she could have a relationship like that with Tyler…

Carrie's eyes twinkled merrily as she whispered for Emma's ear alone. "Just know that my brothers would not have been too happy with him." Her infectious giggle caught Trevor's attention. His curious expression made her cackle even louder.

Emma's attention was drawn from her giddy sister-in-law to her husband when Tyler climbed up beside Trevor on the sleigh's driver seat. At the ranch, no one ever questioned the fact that they slept in different rooms. But in Duluth and at a hotel, it could become awkward.

Her thoughts were forgotten when Trevor slapped the leather reins across the horses' backs. They were off then with harness bells jingling merrily, bound for Steven's house to collect him, and then a Christmas shopping holiday that none of them would soon forget.

* * * * *

The group reached Duluth late that afternoon. Trevor drew the sleigh to a halt before The Clark House. Bundled-up hotel patrons bustled up and down the full-length outside staircase in an attempt to escape the brisk Lake Superior winds. Her eyes danced with excitement when they fell on the ornate front doors, then moved to the white pilasters that lined the front porch. Each was decorated with red ribbons and cedar boughs in honor of the holiday season.

"Makes you feel kind of festive, doesn't it? Here, take my hand. I'll help you out."

She lowered her gaze to Tyler's sparkling one. Before she knew it, she was in his arms again. When her feet touched the ground a moment later, she grasped the first thing that came to mind when the thrill of his latest embrace faded away as quickly as the muscular arms around her. "The hotel is beautiful. I can't believe it takes up almost an entire block."

"Wait until you see the inside." He grasped her elbow and they followed the rest of the family up the staircase and through the front doors.

Emma was awestruck at the beauty of the marbled floors and oak beams in the grand foyer. An expansive, white oak staircase lined with mirrors led to the upper floors. It was as fine a hotel as any that New York had to offer.

Tyler left her and joined Trevor at the front counter to finalize the arrangements for their two-day stay. He returned with three room keys and distributed them among the group. "Okay, Trevor and Cole have a room. Steve, I'll have you bunk in with me so the ladies can have a suite all to themselves." He passed the keys out, handing one to Emma, as if the fact that he and his wife would sleep in separate rooms was perfectly natural.

Emma's heart sank to the floor, but she kept the smile on her face for everyone to see. If that was what Tyler wanted, then she could accept it in good grace.

Tyler also forced a false smile for the benefit of the others.

"I applaud his ability to stay away from her," Trevor muttered to Cole as the group walked away.

Cole shook his head at the helplessness of the situation. "He's not gonna push her until she's ready."

* * * * *

That night, the entire family, along with Steven, met at the top of the grand staircase. Tyler crooked an elbow, and Emma grasped it with a shy smile. He took a deep breath to calm his erratic heartbeat at the sight of her. Diamond eardrops hung to just above her bare shoulders, but Tyler was more interested in her evening gown's daring black velvet décolletage—and the sparkling jewel that rested in the satiny cleavage between her breasts.

"You look beautiful. It's an honor to escort you to dinner, Mrs. Wilkins."

"Why, thank you, Mr. Wilkins. The short rest I had did wonders." She floated down the steps at his side and found herself looking forward to the evening with an excitement she hadn't felt in a long time.

They entered the large dining room as one and every male head in the room turned in their direction.

"Don't look now," he whispered to Emma, "but you and Carrie are causing quite a commotion among the other men in the room."

A giggle bubbled in Emma's throat. "Hah! The women are eyeing you four gorgeous men. Carrie and I won't stand a chance tonight."

"I think not, madam. I promise you my undivided attention for the entire evening."

His husky words spoken close to her ear caused Emma's heart to skip a beat.

As the meal progressed, Emma found complete joy in the fact that Tyler was true to his word. Tyler feasted more on Emma's candlelit face than he did the meal. A soft smile played about her full lips throughout the entire dinner—even during the countless times she leaned over to cover Janie's ears, and then gently reprimanded Trevor for his choice of words.

Later, the table was cleared and the orchestra struck up the first waltz of the evening. Steven stood, bowed gallantly before Carrie and asked her to join him on the floor. The happy couple excused themselves, holding hands as they left the table.

"Hey, Trevor," Cole grinned after his sister. "Can you finally tell that the two of them are in love, or are you still missing the fact?"

He laughed heartily when Trevor leaned over to whisper what Emma was certain was another risqué comment. Trevor stood to follow Steven's lead and ceremoniously asked Janie to dance.

"If you'll pardon me," Cole stated. "I see a beautiful little blonde sitting across the way making eyes at me. I think I'll go introduce myself and see if she'd like me to impress her with one of my many talents."

"It wouldn't hurt to ask her to dance first, Cole," Tyler called after him with a chuckle.

Cole turned to cast a smart salute in their direction, and then he was gone.

Emma had longed to be alone with Tyler all evening. Now that her wish had finally come true, she grappled for words. Her nervous gaze strayed to where Cole now talked with the "little blonde". "Why is it that Cole and Trevor have never settled down? They both make such good prospects. You'd think that women would be banging down the doors at the ranch to get to them."

Tyler shrugged his broad shoulders. "I guess they've always been so involved with the ranch and the mill that they haven't had time for courting. I'm sure when they finally meet the right ones, there will be two women out there who won't stand a chance." It was the only answer he could come up with and not disclose the fact that neither of his brothers were ready to make a lifelong commitment and chose to frequent a local brothel instead. The occasional visits filled a need—albeit a physical one only—but he wasn't one to judge. He'd been lucky. He'd met Sara early on in his adult life and never felt a desire to visit such a place as he was certain his brothers would over the next two evenings.

Tyler suddenly stood. "Let's dance, Emma. I think we both deserve a night of simple fun." He held out a hand and patiently waited for her to make up her mind.

Emma flushed with the invitation. It was a chance to be in his arms even if it would only be for the length of one dance.

But one dance led to another. Before long, the other members of the family ceased to exist. Emma held her breath each time Tyler pulled her a little closer as a new waltz began.

Janie's eyes sparkled up at her Uncle Trevor. Carrie and Steve whispered to each other amid small giggles, and Cole managed to steal the petite blonde from the glare of her parent's watchful eyes, but Emma saw none of it, lost in a dream she hoped would never end.

Tyler simply basked in the awareness that she seemed more like the Emma of old. Secretly, he hoped that she would soon be his in the fullest sense of the word. His greatest desire was to kiss her at that very moment. Instead, he pulled her closer and pressed his cheek against her satiny tresses. Breathing in her perfumed scent, he stifled a sigh.

Emma battled the sudden tears that stung her eyelids because she could never have more than the moment. Tyler would never truly want her because of Samuel's actions. She opened her eyes, looked up at him and saw his warm smile. She returned it shakily, then her head found his shoulder again and her reasonable side took over once more. Yes, she had been used, but she hadn't given herself willingly. Somehow, she had to make Tyler realize that.

She tightened her arms around him, knowing that he wouldn't callously push her away in public. Her jaw stiffened with a newfound determination.

I'm not going to let Samuel Fontaine rule my life any longer. I want a life with you, Tyler. I want to be your wife in every way. I'm not afraid anymore...

The last song of the night ended, and so did Emma's fantasy. Trevor sat at the table again with Janie asleep in his arms. Cole handed his dance partner back to her parents. Steven and Carrie had already left the dance floor to hurry upstairs and say goodnight in private.

Tyler released Emma from his arms, however reluctantly, retrieved his daughter and the contented group ascended the circular stairway to the second floor.

Leaving his brothers and sister in the hallway with Steven, Tyler entered the women's suite. Emma followed him in and closed the door quietly behind them as he carried Janie to one of the two double beds. He gently laid her on the floral spread and kissed her soft cheek. Emma removed the little girl's shoes and tucked her beneath the covers.

She turned to face him with tiny shoes in hand and smiled. "I can't thank you enough for the wonderful evening," she murmured. "I don't ever remember dancing that much." She crossed her arms and the dimples in her cheeks deepened. "You are rather good, you know. I was the envy of every woman in the room. In fact, I saw more than one clasp her heart in despondency because such a debonair gentleman failed to ask her to dance."

Tyler leaned a shoulder against the bedpost. A reckless grin curved his lips when he swept an arm in the direction of the floor. "Madam, these feet were for your use and your use alone tonight. Pity the old bags in the ballroom who are still searching for them."

"Tyler, shame on you!" A giggle burst from Emma at his vain comment. Before she realized what she was doing, she leaned forward to give him a hug. "Thank you again for making this such a memorable night."

He slipped his arms around her slender waist and gazed into the sparkling green depths before him, then pressed a kiss to her cheek. "You are most heartily welcome, madam. I can't remember ever having such a pleasant evening either." She didn't seem to mind having his arms around her. Maybe...

He pulled her closer and lowered his mouth.

Emma held her breath—until the door handle clicked—and jumped back.

Tyler stifled a curse as Carrie entered the suite.

"I got so involved with those two idiot brothers of ours, Ty, that I lost track of time. Those two never know when to quit. Now, they say they're going to check out a poker game or two."

His shoulders sagged with the long sigh that escaped his lips. "I guess I'll head for bed. Make sure you lock the door behind me." He glanced at his wife, where she stood quietly in the middle of the room looking entirely too gorgeous. "Goodnight, Emma. I'll see you in the morning."

He left the room with a decided nonchalance, as if it were perfectly normal to leave her with his sister instead of hauling her back to his room for a night of passionate lovemaking.

Emma locked the door behind him and rested her forehead against the smooth surface with a heartfelt sigh.

* * * * *

Cole and Trevor sat with three other men, chuckling over a lewd joke. Poker chips were stacked high on the table's green felt surface. The air was thick with the scent of expensive cigars. A player piano trilled over the din of raucous voices.

The dealer paused before doling out another hand of cards when a pretty redhead slid a note across the table to Cole.

Picking up the scrap of paper, Cole glanced at his name written in neatly scripted words. It was from Belle—the owner of the "establishment". He'd sent her a message earlier, informing her that he was in town, and then had waited patiently for her to respond. A wry smiled touched his lips.

Trevor saw his brother's grin and shook his head. "It's amazing…"

"What?" Cole's eyes were wide with innocence.

"You two play the same game every time we come here. Belle always lets you enjoy a few drinks, a few games of poker and some time with the boys. I think she actually likes making you sit down here, eager as a lad awaiting her pleasures."

Unflappable, Cole tossed down a half-full glass of whiskey. Trevor wasn't far off the mark. Sitting at the card table gave him time to think about the night ahead, and all the sensations Belle's experienced hands and mouth would awaken in his body.

He reached for his chips, took one more puff off the cigar clamped between his teeth, and then tamped it out in an ashtray. "Well, gentlemen, it's been a pleasure." Standing, he tucked poker chips and some loose bills into the front pocket of his pants. A smug grin creased his twinkling eyes. His dark brows did a little bounce. "Don't wait up, big brother. I got things to attend to and might not see you 'til morning."

Trevor snorted at his brother's cockiness. "Don't be so sure you'll be the last one back to the hotel, smartass!"

Cole simply adjusted his black hat, saluted his brother and lazily wound his way through the crowd. He nodded his head politely at every woman he passed.

Trevor shook his head. The first time Trevor and Cole visited Belle's establishment, she'd taken a shine to the younger of the two brothers and made it quite obvious to the other girls that he was "hands off". Consequently, Cole never asked for anyone else.

His eyes continued to follow his brother to the top of the staircase until he rounded a corner and disappeared. A second later, his hat was whisked from his head. He swiveled on the chair just as a voluptuous blonde plunked the Stetson on her perfectly coifed tresses.

"Hello, cowboy. Care to buy a thirsty lady a drink?"

Trevor chuckled, pushed his chair back and patted his knee. The pretty blonde sank onto his lap and whispered into his ear. His chuckle grew into a full-blown laugh as she toyed with the buttons on his shirt, then nuzzled his ear. Her whispered entreaties heated his entire body. Helping her from his knee, he patted her behind, and then followed her across the room. Grabbing a bottle from the bartender as he passed the bar, he hurried up the same set of stairs his brother had just climbed. Cole was the last thing on Trevor's mind as he watched the round, feminine bottom swing before him.

* * * * *

Cole knocked softly on a door. A sultry voice invited him in. He entered the room and let out a slow whistle when a vision in silk met his gaze. Belle stood in the center of the room clad only in a filmy robe with the sash tied loosely around her shapely body. He closed the door and leaned casually against a fabric-covered wall.

Belle's heart fluttered as she stared. He looked incredibly delectable with his black cowboy hat tipped low, eyes half shuttered in the candlelight and a lazy grin in place. "Hello, Cole. I was beginning to think you'd found some sweet, little virgin to while away your days with. I haven't seen you lately."

"No such luck, Belle. All the virgins I know are home tucked in their beds behind daddy's locked door."

"Too bad for them. How about you come over here and greet a *real* woman." She pulled on the sash, slowly, enticingly, revealing ample breasts and curving hips.

Dark passion leapt from Cole's eyes. Never taking his gaze from hers, he ambled across the room. Reaching into his pocket, he pulled out a one hundred dollar bill, then tossed it onto the dresser on his way by. He reached up to caress her soft cheek. Her quick shudder made him smile when he brushed his thumb across her full lips. Lowering his mouth, the gentle kiss ended quickly, teasingly.

Belle gazed up through passion-filled eyes. "I missed you, Cole. Don't be such a stranger from now on." Her fingers toyed with the buttons on his shirt as he tossed his hat on a chair.

Cole's breath hitched as her hands opened his shirt and kneaded the bare skin beneath, then moved to the buckle on his leather belt. She slid the trousers down and over his slender hips as he shrugged off his shirt.

Their gazes locked in anticipation when he stepped from the wrinkled pile at his feet and reached inside her robe to pull her naked body against his. His mouth found her neck. Her hands slipped to his back, then traveled up and across his muscular shoulders.

"Don't make me wait any longer," Belle's husky voice whispered.

His lips found her waiting mouth.

The passionate kiss sent a chill racing up her spine.

A sharp gasp followed when his calloused hands clutched her firm bottom. In one fluid movement, he lifted her against his chest. Belle wrapped silken legs around his waist as he moved to the bed.

Cole's heart beat rapidly with the familiar sensations she never failed to arouse. Lowering her to the mattress, he entered her with one ferocious thrust, losing himself in the eager body that strained against his.

Their tongues danced and their bodies followed suit as she met each of his rhythmic movements, urging him on with breathless words of desire. He pumped harder. A deep moan escaped Belle's throat a moment later.

The sound pushed Cole over the edge. He thrust deeply one last time and found an explosive release within her body.

They clung tightly to one another as their breathing slowed. Rolling onto his back, he pulled her with him until she lay atop his muscular body. Belle's head lolled against his furred chest and groaned with the sensuous feel of his hands as they moved across her shoulders, down to her firm buttocks and back up again.

"Ah, Belle, having sex with you is a heady experience..." Cole sighed.

There was no coquettishness on her part. She wanted the raw sex as badly as he did and never begged for promises she knew he wouldn't make. Belle sold sex for a living, but, regardless, Cole was her favorite. They both knew that there would never be anything more.

She sighed and snuggled closer. "How come you don't visit me more often? Just think. We could be doing this on a regular basis. Sex with you is always so much better than with anyone else."

He chuckled as he played with her long, flowing hair and contemplated her words. "I don't think I could afford you regularly. Before you'd know it, I'd be penniless and begging to have it for free, and you'd just slam the door in my face."

She raised herself up on her elbows and met his heated gaze, wishing this one time that circumstances could be different. She never faked a response with Cole like she did with her other clientele. His handsome face and lean, sexy body never failed to excite her, along with the gentle boyish charm that always surrounded him. She knew their visits would come to an end someday though, when an extremely lucky and much younger woman snagged him away from her. Until then, however, he was exclusively hers, and she would relish every moment.

"Do you remember the first time you and Trevor came here?" She laughed. "I was bound and determined to get you up to my room one way or another that night."

Cole chuckled again. "How could I forget? I came in to play poker. I was a sweet, young virgin and you totally corrupted me before the night was over."

Belle cackled with glee and slapped him playfully on the arm. "That's bull, and you know it. Why do you think I warned my girls to stay away from you?"

"I don't know—tell me." His smile turned incorrigible. "It must be because I'm so good in bed."

"You're so damn handsome, Cole Wilkins, and you don't even know it." She shook her head. "Once I finally managed to coax you upstairs, I had one of the finest nights of sex I've ever experienced. There's no way I'm sharing that with my girls." The playfulness suddenly left her eyes. "Do you ever visit any of the other houses in town?"

"Nope. Why would I? You and I got a good thing going here. I have no desire to be with anyone else."

She kissed him on the nose and rose from the bed. Completely at ease with her nudity, she strolled to the liquor cabinet to retrieve two glasses and a bottle of cognac she kept on hand just for him. She was well aware of the fact that he watched her backside and was thankful she'd managed to remain firm and trim—even though she was ten years his senior. Returning to the bed, she waited until he had positioned himself against a huge, fluffy pillow before she handed him the glass, and then slid back beneath the covers.

"What's been going on up at the ranch? Word filtered down that your older brother got married again, and then he had some sort of accident. Care to fill me in?"

"Tyler went to New York early this spring on business and ended up finding himself in an…uncompromising position. He got the daughter of one of his business associates pregnant."

A loud, boisterous laugh escaped Belle's throat. She found extreme humor in the fact that the "polite" girls of society had no idea how to keep themselves from getting in the family way. "So, what's she like, Cole? From what you've told me about Tyler and his love for his first wife, it seems strange that he would even consider remarrying. It must have been a rather awkward position to find himself in."

"Oh, believe me, it was. Trevor, Carrie and I had a grand old time with it. Her father sent her out here lock, stock and barrel, and insisted that Tyler marry her immediately. There's a lot more to the story, but it would take me days to tell you about it."

She leaned over to kiss him, enjoying the taste of the fine liquor on his lips. "So, why don't you stay for *days*...and just tell me bits and pieces in between rounds?"

The coarse hair on his chest raked her sensitive breasts. To find him in her bed every morning would be a dream come true. The dip of his eyebrows, though, told Belle that he was lost in thought. She retreated, at least for the moment. "All right, go ahead and finish what you want to say."

"Emma is one hell of a lady, Belle. She loves Tyler like there's no tomorrow, and she treats his daughter as if the girl were her own. She's the best thing that's happened to him in a long time."

"But?"

Cole sipped at his drink. "So much has happened since Emma first arrived. To make a long story short, some bastard from her past showed up at the logging camp. Not knowing who he was, the foreman hired him as part of a temporary crew. This guy felt that Tyler and Emma had a hand in him losing the family business in New York. He tried to kill Tyler by making it look like he'd had an accident. The next day, Emma and Tyler had a bad falling out, and she tore off from the ranch on horseback. This man, Samuel Fontaine, must have seen her pass by on the road because he followed her." He turned his head to meet her gaze directly. "Belle, he beat the hell out of her, raped her and left her for dead. She miscarried the baby and is still recovering."

Belle listened in stunned disbelief. She sold sex for a living—but not once, ever, in her entire life, had someone forced it from her or treated her roughly. "So, why are you telling me all of this?"

"I want you to keep a lookout for him. He's got a habit of frequenting places like this and beating up the woman he's with. By Tyler's recollection, he's just a bit shorter than me. Right now, his blond hair is long and unkempt. One of the hands at the ranch saw him and said he was riding a broken-down Appaloosa. Just be careful. Tell your girls to be careful, too. If he happens to show up here, call the sheriff, and then get a message to me. I'd like to kill the bastard myself, and so would Tyler and Trevor."

"You must be right about this Emma," she observed quietly. "If the three of you are that bent on revenge, she must be something."

"She is, Belle. She sure is."

Belle took the glass from his hand, placed it alongside hers on the nightstand and spread herself across the length of his body. She smiled down into his upturned face. "I think that's enough talk. Did you come here to talk about another woman, or did you come for the kind of fun that only I can provide?" She rubbed her body against his, then kissed him leisurely. "I want you to make love to me again. Make me forget, Cole, that you'll be leaving in the morning."

His hands were already traveling over her firm derriere. Flipping her onto her back, he kissed one pink-tipped breast, and then the other. His hand moved to cover the velvety mound between her legs.

Belle moaned as their passion rose again.

Chapter Twenty-Two

৪০

Tyler opened the door to his hotel room early the next morning to discover his younger brothers stumbling down the hallway. Cole gripped Trevor beneath the arms and frantically tried to shush the crude ditty—about a blonde with a round derriere—that tumbled from his mouth.

Tyler shook his head and chuckled softly as he studied his brother's appearance. Trevor's shirt was buttoned unevenly beneath the open jacket, his hair was tousled and a lopsided, drunken smile appeared when he spotted his elder brother.

"Ty!" he slurred, then stumbled.

Cole almost lost his grip.

"What a fine mornin' it is! I'll be ready for Christmas shoppin' in just a few short minutes."

"Sure you will," Tyler replied dryly. "I don't think you'll be ready for anything but a drunken sleep for the next few hours. The two of you smell like a cross between a whorehouse and a brewery."

Trevor's bloodshot eyes widened in mock horror as he swung his head and poked Cole in the arm. "Pssst! Cole…" He slammed an eye shut to better focus on his brother's face. "I think our secret's out."

Cole just rolled his eyes as Tyler's grin widened, and concentrated on keeping his other brother upright while he dug in his pocket for the key to their room. "Ty, help me get him in the room before Em or Carrie hear him."

Tyler stepped forward, gripped Trevor from the other side and helped to maneuver the drunken man through the doorway and to the bed. They dumped him unceremoniously on the chenille bedspread. Cole tugged off his boots as Trevor mumbled incoherently and continued to chuckle to himself about the outstanding night he'd spent in the arms of an amorous woman.

"Damn, but she was good... The things that blonde could do with her hands and mouth..." He eyed his eldest brother through a liquid gaze. "You know, Ty, you should really try it with Emma... You two...should...be..."

The rest of the words were lost as his eyes fluttered shut and his breathing deepened.

"Don't mind him, Tyler," Cole intervened. "He's as drunk as a two-bit whore and doesn't realize what he's saying."

"Yeah, well, he's not so far off the mark now, is he?"

Cole read the frustration in Tyler's eyes, and shook his head sadly.

"It's not as if I don't desire my own wife. It's just that I don't know if she's ready yet. Emma has been to hell and back, and I don't want to scare her off."

"You need to be nominated for sainthood or something. How much longer can you possibly wait?" Cole stated as he stripped off his shirt. "You have to push her a little bit. To be honest, I don't think she'd be scared. I've seen the way she looks at you. She cares a lot."

"Yeah, and I want her to continue to care, which means that I have to build her trust in me. I'm hoping my Christmas surprise will help to accomplish that." He sighed. "I guess we'll see."

A sudden loud snore from the bed drew Tyler's attention. He cast a rueful glance over his shoulder, then looked back at Cole. "Are you coming with us this morning or do you also have a wild night to sleep off?"

"No, you can count me in. Give me some time to clean up. I'll meet you in the dining room." He stripped off his pants as Tyler left the room and crossed the hall to knock on Emma and Carrie's door.

It immediately swung open.

"Good morning!" Emma beamed at the sight of him. "Come in and sit down a minute — we're just about ready."

Tyler stepped into the room to receive an excited hug from his daughter. A few minutes later, the four met Steven in the hallway, and they proceeded downstairs.

* * * * *

The morning was one of those fine winter days in Duluth when the sun shined brightly and the crispness in the air had taken its leave. Tyler and Emma fell behind the rest of the family, as they strolled past shops decorated for the season. Heated kettles filled with steaming apple cider were placed along the boulevards and hawkers called out to the milling crowds in an attempt to get them to buy their wares. Emma's hand rested in the crook of her husband's arm.

Tyler glanced down at his wife and chuckled. "You should see your face. You look as excited as Janie."

"I am!" Emma did a little skip beside him. "How can you not be? The weather is warm, and I can't wait to go shopping. It's been a long time."

"Well, I think we should start then. How about you, Carrie and Cole go one way, and Steve and I will take Janie. We can meet in a few hours and switch partners." The men had already agreed earlier that Emma would have at least one male escort at all times. Samuel Fontaine couldn't be forgotten.

"I think that's a good idea. Then I can buy Janie's gifts when she's not around." *And yours, too,* she added the last silently.

The two groups separated. Emma, Cole and Carrie discovered a quaint shop a few hours later and ducked inside. Emma strolled leisurely through the aisles, pausing often to search the shelves—and fretted over the fact that she had yet to find anything for Tyler. Suddenly, her attention was drawn to a wide shelf that hung on the back wall. Her heart thudded in her chest as she focused her intent green eyes on a single item mixed in with the other gifts for sale.

An indescribable shiver ran up her spine as she stopped before the display and reached out a trembling gloved hand to grasp a beautifully carved image of an Indian. Turning it slowly in her palms, she examined it in wide-eyed wonder. A bird sat perched on the brave's shoulder and a wolf crouched by his side. The near lifelike face stared back as if the eyes peered into her soul. There was something strangely familiar about the carving, but she couldn't quite place it… It was enough though, that the statue represented what she'd found with Tyler. Hopefully, he would relate to the gift as she did now.

Emma stood rooted to the spot, seeking to discover the reason for her tumultuous emotions. She quickly removed her gloves and ran her fingers over the small statue almost reverently. She nearly jumped out of her skin when Cole spoke from behind her.

"Find something you like?"

"Cole! You startled me."

"Where were you off to just now? I questioned you twice before you heard me."

Emma continued to stare at the Indian's face. "Isn't it beautiful? When Tyler and I were shopping in New York one day, we met an old Indian. This statue somehow reminds me of him, but there's something else about it, too…" She shook her head abruptly, ridding her mind of the eerie feeling that raised goose bumps on her arms. "I think I finally solved the problem of what I'm going to get Tyler. Do you think he'll like it?"

Cole peered over the top of Emma's head to the figurine. "It's nice, but I think he'll like anything you give him, just because it came from you."

Emma ducked her head. *Is that really how he feels?* Tyler was going to kiss her last night—just before Carrie burst into the room. Was he finally ready to see that Samuel had grievously used her? Would he actually accept her as his wife now? She wanted her life back, and she sought to share that life with him. She wanted to be a mother to Janie and stay in Minnesota with the people she cared for so dearly.

Holding the carving close to her body, she turned and met Cole's gaze. "I wish I could feel as certain about that as you do. I think I'll have the shop owner wrap this for me before we leave."

Before he could comment further, she rounded him and headed in the direction of the front counter.

* * * * *

That night, Carrie and Emma sat on the sofa in their rented suite. The family had enjoyed a quiet dinner, then retired to their respective rooms after the long day of shopping. Janie was asleep. The two women visited quietly about the approaching holiday and how quickly the time had passed since Emma had come to live with them.

"I can't believe it, Carrie. I had no clue any of you even existed a year ago. And never in my wildest dreams did I imagine I'd spend this Christmas in Minnesota."

"I know how you feel. I was still pining away for Steven then, and being as rude as a rich old biddy because I felt so invisible whenever he was around. A lot has happened in both our lives this past year."

A flicker of pain crossed Emma's face just before she ducked her head.

Carrie immediately reached for her sister-in-law's hand. "I'm sorry, Em. I didn't mean to be so insensitive. I wasn't thinking."

Emma squeezed her hand and forced a quick, wan smile. "It's okay, Carrie. We can't pretend that it never happened. I'm trying, but I don't think I'll ever forget the pain and the terror I felt that afternoon."

Carrie breathed a silent sigh of relief. It was the first time the two women had discussed the rape, which she hoped meant that Emma was starting to heal.

"Can I ask you something, Carrie? How was Tyler after…after what happened? I was in such a fog that first week that I don't remember much."

"What do you mean, how was he?"

Emma stood and slowly paced the area between the sofa and the bed. "Before I left the house that day and before we fought, Tyler told me he was ready to discuss our marriage." Her eyes met Carrie's. "I really thought things were going to be straightened out that day. But after the…after what Samuel did to me, Tyler has stayed at arm's length. He's been kind and attentive, yes, but he doesn't treat me like his wife…not in the way I would like him to.

It's no secret that we still have separate rooms." Her brows dipped slightly as she turned her back to Carrie again. "He had a rough two years after Sara's death. Then I barged into his life through no choice of his own. At one point though, I really thought he might finally be ready to accept me as his wife." She closed her eyes. "We had such a horrible argument before I left the ranch that day. I can see why he thought I was having an affair with Steve." She whirled suddenly, her eyes wide. "Still, we might have had a chance. But because of what Samuel did, I don't think it'll ever happen."

Carrie rose from the sofa and took Emma's hands in hers. "So, why don't you tell him you love him?"

Emma shook her head adamantly and opened her mouth to object, but Carrie's hold on her hands tightened, silencing her outcry.

"Come sit down and listen to me." Carrie led her to the sofa again. Once they were settled, she continued. "What happened to you was awful, Emma. No woman should have to go through what you did, but you seem to be forgetting that you were the victim, *not* Tyler. And you have to give him a little credit. Do you think he's so shallow that he'd think you aren't good enough for him anymore?"

Emma's eyes shone with tears. "How could he want me? Samuel ruined whatever chance of happiness we might have had."

"That's not true! If you love my brother, and he's too dense to figure it out, then *make* him understand. Emma, he's never said anything that would make me believe he doesn't want you because of what that evil man did. When Tyler brought you home that night, he was beside himself with guilt and fear. He stayed with you all night, pleading for you to wake up. He was terrified that you were going to die. Be strong enough for the both of you. *Show* him what you could have together. Go to him and start the life you want so badly." Carrie gathered her into her arms, hugged her fiercely, then leaned back. "When you think about it, what do you have to lose? Are you even a little bit happy right now?"

The tears finally escaped and rolled down Emma's cheeks. "I'm miserable. I watch you and Steven, and I'm actually jealous of how much the two of you love each other."

"And I had to practically beat it into his head before he finally noticed me as a woman. It worked for me, Emma. There's no reason it can't work for you, too." She lifted her shoulders in a small shrug. "Like I said, what have you got to lose?"

Emma stood to wander the room again as she thought about Carrie's words. What if she was right and all Tyler needed was a little push in the right direction? She wanted desperately to be a real wife to him, to be loved totally with no barriers.

She turned back. "Thank you, Carrie, for understanding what I'm going through. I'll think about doing what you've said, but it scares me."

"Don't let it, Emma. You're one of the strongest ladies I've ever met and, believe me, I know my brother. There's no reason for you to be afraid."

* * * * *

December twenty-third arrived cold and clear. The ranch house was filled with the odor of delectable baked goods that Mamie turned out in pan after pan. The family was gathered in the open living room now, ready to rearrange furniture for the next day's events.

Emma struggled with a small, but heavy table. Seeing her dilemma, Tyler rushed to her side. "Here, let me help you with that."

"When are you getting the Christmas tree?" She watched her husband lift the heavy table and easily move it into the corner.

"You mean when are *all* of us going to get it?" He smiled at her. "Tomorrow morning, we'll take a trek up the hill behind the house. There's a great stand of Norways to choose from. We'll get the tree decorated before the employee's party." He shook his head with a chuckle. "Wait until you see the feast Mamie and the loggers' wives put on. Eventually, one or two of the men will pull out a fiddle, and then the dancing will start."

"It sounds fun. Christmas in New York was always a quiet affair with just Papa and myself." Her eyes filled with an instant sadness.

Tyler lifted her drooping chin with his finger. "I'm sorry your father couldn't make travel arrangements. I know you miss him."

Emma shrugged lightly to cover her gloom and the shiver that ran through her at his touch. "His last letter said he would get out here in the spring." *That is if I'm still here...* She turned, pretending to busy herself with a crate of decorations, and squeezed her eyes to keep the tears at bay.

Tyler's heart fell with her sudden quietness. A moment ago, her eyes had sparkled happily, then the mere mention of her father had ruined the moment.

Carrie interrupted his thoughts a second later. "Tyler, would you lift this crate onto the table? It's too heavy for me."

He did so, then left the women to dig through the box.

"Come see all the decorations, Emma. We've all made something for the tree, or purchased a special ornament." Carrie reached into the box, pulled out a dainty oval frame and turned her gaze to her sister-in-law. "This was my mother's. It's a picture of her and Dad."

Emma took the delicate object with gentle hands and peered at the images inside. "You look like your mother, Carrie. The likeness is amazing."

"That's what everyone tells me. I wish I could have known her," she stated quietly. "You know, you're going to have to come up with something for the tree. It's your first Christmas with us, and we need to commemorate your becoming a member of the family. Can you think of anything?"

"I wish I'd known about the tradition when we were in Duluth," Emma commented. "I'll give it some thought. Maybe Janie and I can go outside later and find a pinecone to decorate."

Tyler listened to their conversation from across the room, not surprised in the least that Emma would include his daughter in her search. His wife had a close bond with the little girl and involved her in everything she did. Without a doubt, Emma loved Janie completely. He thanked God that the little girl felt the same.

He watched quietly as Emma laughed with Carrie, and how she unconsciously reached to give Janie a hug when the little girl approached her. His own need was just as great. Trevor had been right when he'd said that Emma brought sunshine back into the house. Every day when he looked at her, Tyler felt her presence warm his heart.

A twinge of guilt jabbed his insides when Janie and Emma fell back onto the braided rug and laughed at some shared secret.

So much time has been wasted because of my inflated ego and misplaced jealousy. His mind flashed back to the day of Samuel's assault when Emma pummeled her fists against his chest. She'd told him that he was an ignorant man and that she would never give up on the two of them.

That was before she was abused, however, and before she miscarried the baby. How did she feel now? His heart sank at the mere thought that the day might come when she would ask to go back to her former home because there was nothing to keep her in Minnesota.

I won't let that happen. You're mine, Emma, and I'll never let you walk away. No more running. We're going to have this out...

"Tyler! Are you going to pick up your end of the sofa or not?" Cole bent over the other end of the massive piece of furniture and stared in exasperation. He'd watched the play of emotions on Tyler's face as he stared at his wife. Cole pitied the couple, but the two of them still drove him crazy. Any fool could see how they felt about one another. For some odd reason, Tyler and Emma refused to see it themselves.

"What?"

"I said, are you going to help me or not?" Cole straightened and shook his head. "I don't know why you don't just go over there and kiss her." He grinned. "I promise we won't look."

It was Tyler's turn to throw the exasperated look.

Cole chuckled. "Come on, pick up your end."

Tyler still remained unmoving. "Do you think she has any idea about her present tomorrow?" he whispered. "Nobody has given it away, have they?"

"No. Since you made me haul her damn packages that day in Duluth, I had Trevor take care of the details. He could handle that much—even with a hangover."

Tyler nodded his approval, then hefted his end of the couch with a decided grunt. The two men set down the sofa against the far wall.

"So..." Tyler mused with a knowing smile. "I never had a chance to ask you. How's Belle?"

Cole repositioned the couch and thought about how Belle was so much a part of his life, but in the same sense, separate. It was indeed a shame that she would never be a part of his family. It amazed him that Emma and Tyler couldn't settle their differences simply because of Tyler's earlier misguided jealousy. Cole, on the other hand, found no problem in the fact that Belle had a different man in her bed every night.

"She's doing well. I told her what happened to Emma and asked her to keep a lookout for Fontaine. She said she'd get a message to us if he shows up at her place."

"I can't believe that bastard just disappeared into thin air," Tyler said as he sank down onto the misplaced sofa. The hatred rose again as he listened to Janie's near hysterical giggles, where Emma tickled her mercilessly across the room. "I'll never give him the chance to hurt anybody in this family again, Cole. I swear to God, if he shows up, I'll kill him."

"Well, move over and wait your turn," the other man said as he plopped down beside his brother. "Every man on this ranch is watching for him. If he shows, we'll get him."

Tyler glanced up just as Emma and Janie grasped hands and hurried from the room amid a bevy of hushed whispers. A short while later, they returned to find everyone taking a break and Mamie serving sandwiches.

Emma secreted an object in her palm. "I came up with something for the tree." Crossing to Tyler, she held out her hand with a shy smile. The carving of the loon he'd purchased for her on that long ago day in New York lay on her outstretched palm. A small length of ribbon now adorned the neck of the figurine. "Would you mind if this was my donation? Everyone has something special…and this is special to me." She peeked at him from beneath long lashes to gauge his reaction.

He'd seen the loon where it sat in a place of prominence on her dresser top, but the two had never spoken of it. A warm smile flitted across his lips. "I think it's perfect, and you don't need my permission to put it on the tree. In fact, I'm happy that you want to share it with everyone else."

The other occupants of the room observed the exchange with interest, wondering what significance the small, wooden loon held for the two of them. At that moment, it was easy to see they'd forgotten everyone else.

A loud knock sounded on the front door cut short the fragile moment. A cold blast of air preceded Steven into the house. Carrie jumped up to greet him, and the rest of the afternoon was spent working on the preparations for the next day's events.

* * * * *

Emma tossed fretfully in her sleep, kicking unconsciously at the heavy comforter that pinned her to the flat surface.

She couldn't run! Samuel gained ground and she knew, with certainty and fear in her heart, that he would catch her and her torture would begin again. She gasped for air. A blood-curdling scream left her throat as he grabbed her, threw her to the ground and dropped heavily on top of her. He laughed wickedly.

"I'm going to kill you, you little bitch…after I'm done having some fun with you, that is."

"Please!" she sobbed, "not again—" The words froze in her throat when his fist blotted out the sun…

"Emma!"

"No!" she choked out with a sob. "Don't hurt me again!" She struggled fiercely against the hands that grasped her arms in a gentle grip.

"Emma, it's Tyler. Wake up. You're having a nightmare." He shook her gently in an effort to wake her. "You're safe. He can't hurt you now."

Her frightened green eyes snapped open. Beads of perspiration dotted her brow, and her chest heaved with the effort to escape her tormenter. Finally, she focused on Tyler's concerned features, stifled another sob and threw herself into his arms.

"It's all right, Emma. You're safe."

"He was here, Tyler!" She clung to him, her eyes wide with terror. "He's going to kill both of us!"

He pulled her closer, rested his chin on the top of her head and stroked her soft auburn tresses. "It was just a dream, honey. I promise you, I'll never let him get near us. Now, just take it easy. I'll stay with you until you feel better."

He wasn't quite sure if his words had reached her frightened mind, so he continued to hold her until the trembling stopped, reluctant to let go even when he stood to add wood to the glowing embers in the fireplace.

Emma pulled the blanket up around her shoulders to ward off the chill in the air. She watched the glow from the flames flicker across the stretch of naked skin that ended at the waistband of his pants when he hunkered down before the hearth to poke at the charred logs. Just having him in the room was enough to make her feel safe.

Tyler stood, wiped his soot-covered palms across his trousered thighs and crossed back to the bed.

"The fire should be good until morning," he said as he sat on the mattress beside her. "Are you okay now, or do you want me to sit with you a bit longer?"

"I'm sorry I woke you," she replied softly. "But I'm fine now." *Please don't leave me again.*

Tyler ran a shaky hand through his tousled hair. *Ask me to stay*, he pleaded silently.

He bid her goodnight when she didn't say anything else, crossed to the adjoining door and closed it quietly behind him.

Tyler stood in the center of his room. His shoulders sagged. *Why in hell didn't I just climb into bed with her?* His conscience answered him back. *You know full well why you didn't. She's still frightened, and the nightmare proved it.* How would she react if she knew how badly he wanted her?

Cold tendrils of air crept through the room and touched the bare skin of his upper torso. He trudged to his own fireplace to add wood to the dying flames.

Removing his pants, he dropped them on the floor and climbed back between the covers. His sad eyes followed the flickering shadows across the ceiling, then he clamped them shut against the vision of her terrified expression when he finally managed to wake her.

Placing his hands behind his head, he sighed heavily and opened his eyes again, knowing sleep would not come easily. Would Emma ever totally recover from her experience and accept him as a man? Would she ever trust him enough to know he would never hurt her? Rolling onto his side with another sigh, he stared into the fire across the room.

The telltale click of a door opening echoed a moment later. Tyler bolted to a sitting position just in time to see her slender figure step through the doorway.

"Emma…are you all right?"

Even in the muted darkness, he read the hesitation in her eyes as she took one slow step forward, and then another, until she stood beside the bed. His heart pounded against his ribs.

"Tyler," she spoke softly, "I need to tell you something." She wrung her hands nervously as her gaze lowered to the floor.

It took exceptional strength for Tyler to wait patiently, especially when he wanted nothing more than to just pull her into his arms.

She finally lifted her chin and met his understanding gaze. "I know we came to be married through circumstances that were out of our control. I understand why you didn't want me here. But I need to tell you…before you left New York…I had already fallen in love with you."

He opened his mouth to speak, but she stopped him with a raised hand.

"Please, let me say this." She took a deep breath and continued. "I've come to love you more every day since I arrived at your home. But, after I...lost the baby...I realized we have nothing to bind us together except a piece of paper saying we're wed." Tears welled in her eyes now, but Emma blinked them back, knowing she would seal her future one way or the other in the next few minutes. "I have also come to understand that you can probably never love me in return because of what Samuel did, but can we at least try to have some sort of life together, for Janie's sake? I love her as if she were my own. I can't imagine leaving any of you. I can't imagine not seeing *you* every day." The tears flowed freely now. "I want to be with you forever. I want to be by your side at night. If you can't love me, that's all right, but please, don't send me away."

The weight of the last two months lifted from Tyler's shoulders in an instant. He reached out to gently pull her down beside him.

"I've been so foolish." His thumb tenderly stroked the tears from her cheeks. "I've known from the day I found you standing in this room that I could never let you go. You were right when you called me an ignorant man, Emma, and I hate myself because I've caused you so much pain. If you think I've stayed away from you because of what Samuel did, you're wrong. The only reason I've stayed at arm's length is because I wanted you to be able to trust me completely, to know that all men are not like him."

He watched her expression change from doubt, to awe and finally, to happiness—and he saw the love that shone in the depths of her misty eyes. He wanted desperately to kiss her, to love her as she had never been loved before, but instead, he continued, saying the things that had needed to be said for so long.

"When we argued that day in the library and I told you to leave, it was because of my own stupidity. For some reason, I decided to believe that you and Steve had an affair while I was up at the logging camp. I guess that was easier than admitting how much I loved you—and how unfaithful I was being to Sara because of that love. When your horse came in without you though, I was beside myself with fear. I didn't know where you were or what had happened, but nothing else mattered except finding you and never letting you leave me again."

"How did you find me?" she whispered. "The lake is so far from the ranch."

He pulled her into the circle of his arms and leaned back against the headboard. His heart soared when she didn't resist his embrace.

"I can't explain it. Cole, Trevor and I were at our wits end. We didn't know where else to look for you—and then I heard a wolf howl." He shrugged. "I just knew." A vision of her face, as it looked when he'd found her lying in a pool of her own blood, flitted through his mind. "When I first found you, I thought you were dead. I wanted to die myself, Emma. I was terrified that I'd never have the chance to tell you how much I'd come to love you—how Janie and I couldn't live without you in our lives." He pressed a kiss to her forehead. "I also needed to tell you how much I grieved, too, over the loss of our baby."

Her eyes widened incredulously. "Our baby?"

He tipped her chin up until she met his gaze. "Yes—*our* baby. I'm so sorry that I questioned who sired the child. You have never given me reason to think anything else—yet I foolishly held onto that one fact to ease my own guilt over falling in love with you. Do you believe me?"

Tears saturated her cheeks now. She placed her palm over his warm hand and nodded her head.

"I wasn't going to wait much longer before coming to you." His hand stroked the length of her silky arm, and then back up to the drawstring that held the nightgown together across her breasts. His fingers plucked at the lace tie as he spoke. "I was just trying to find the courage, but you beat me to the punch. All I've wanted since the day I left New York, is to hold you in my arms."

She barely breathed as he tugged at the silken string, then shivered when his warm knuckles brushed her skin. He opened the bodice wider.

"All this time, you actually wanted me..." Her voice was filled with wonder.

"More than anything, Emma."

She reached up to touch his whiskered cheek. "I'm here now, Tyler, and I don't ever want to be away from you again."

"I love you," he whispered before he lowered his mouth to hers for one, tender kiss. "Don't ever leave me, Emma. I couldn't bear it."

His lips moved to nuzzle the soft skin beneath her ear. She pulled his face closer. His breath was hot against her breastbone as he pushed the nightgown back from her shoulder and dropped moist, feathery kisses along the satiny path.

Emma gasped with the desire—and wasn't frightened. She groaned when he pulled the nightgown up and off her body and tossed it carelessly to the floor. He pulled her across the width of his body then. She whispered his name as his calloused hands raked the silky skin of her back.

Unable to bear the sweet torture any longer, Emma leaned back and pressed kisses along the broad expanse of his furred chest, reveling in the clean male scent that tantalized her nostrils.

Tyler groaned, shifted their bodies and pressed her down into the pillows. Staring into the face he'd come to love so dearly, his fingers threaded their way through her thick hair. "We've wasted so much time because of my foolish jealousy. It's been so long since I've believed in anything... I swear, I'll spend the rest of my life showing you how sorry I am."

"No, Tyler," she whispered. "Spend the rest of your life loving me."

He pressed another soft kiss against the moist lips that were mere inches from his own. "Promise that we'll never be apart. I believe in you, Emma... I believe in us."

She reached up to gently cup his face in her palm and stared into his eyes. "I'll never leave you. You're my shelter in the night, and the love of my life. To be separated from you would be like severing a part of myself." A slender finger followed the curve of his lips. "I love you too much." Her eyes glistened in the firelight with the solemn promise she spoke aloud.

Tyler began his slow assault against her senses. His palm cupped a swollen breast. Emma gasped when his mouth plundered its twin. She closed her eyes, loving the feel of his touch as it brushed a sensuous course over the velvety skin of her stomach. When he trailed gentle kisses along the same path, she prodded him on with soft, incoherent moans. She groaned louder as he tortured her navel with quick, darting thrusts of his tongue, and all the while his hands elicited a scorching trail of heat from her hips to her knees and back again.

A smile curved Tyler's lips as he moved sensuously across her stomach again, then lowered to taste the succulent skin of her inner thighs. She opened her legs wider, pleading for release from the uncontrollable passion that built by leaps and bounds within her. Emma begged for him to stop, and then implored him to continue. He brought her to the edge of a reeling precipice. Suddenly, he stopped all movement and glided back up and over her luscious body to gaze at her face. Clasping her hands, he held them gently over her head.

"Open your eyes, Em," he commanded softly. "I want you to look at me…"

"Tyler, please…don't make me wait…" She bucked slightly beneath him, pleading for an end to the sensuous torture that shook her to the very soul.

"No, Emma. You have to look at me first."

She opened her eyes and focused with some difficulty on his smoldering green gaze.

"I want you to see my face before we go any further. I'm the man who loves you. I'm the man who would never hurt you because of that love. Do you understand?"

He waited. That moment and her answer would define their future. He would not enter her body without her permission. It had to be her choice. He wanted Emma to remember how beautiful sex could be. He wanted her to remember that with the two of them, the act was an extension of their love—not a vile act of power and violence. He wanted to erase the memory of Samuel's rape from her mind.

When she didn't answer, he spoke softly again. "I want to be inside of you, Emma, but only if it's what you want." His thumb brushed the silky skin of her wrist. "Tell me what you want, Emma – tell me what you desire…"

His words reached out to her and the tears flowed freely down her face again, and onto the pillow. She pulled her hand from Tyler's gentle grip and tenderly touched his lips with shaky fingers. Her eyes met his and widened with wonder. He loved her. She knew beyond a doubt that he would be content to simply hold her if that was what she wanted. That was why she had to give him more.

"How was I so fortunate to find you?" she murmured in a voice clogged with emotion. "Never have I trusted anyone as I trust you now. Make me whole again, Tyler. Make me forget everything but you…"

Their gazes locked. Slowly, languidly, he moved into her warm depths.

"I love you, Emma. Never forget how much I love you…"

She watched the muscles ripple in his upper arms as he supported his weight and moved ever so gently in slow, rhythmic motions.

He, in turn, watched her eyes become shuttered with the height of her passion. Her moist lips parted. He lowered his mouth to run his tongue sensuously over the delectable expanse, then it darted past her lips to taste her sweetness. The pressure of her warm folds around him almost drove him to the brink—but he would wait…wait until she rediscovered what had been forgotten for so long. He pulled back, almost exiting her, then slid into her deeply again, his movements always measured, always languorous, until…she lifted her hips to meet his.

Her increased momentum was what he had waited for. He wanted her to take the lead in their lovemaking. She *had* to take the lead. She had to have control over what they were doing. Never did he want her to think of Samuel again—not when she was making love with him.

Tyler responded to her urgent need by increasing the power and speed of his strokes. The small groans of pleasure that emitted from Emma's throat quickly grew to a rapturous cry of fulfillment. She clung to him as she spiraled toward a crest she thought never to surpass again.

"Tyler…" she groaned as he slipped deep into her body one final time.

Her name, too, burst from his lips in a strangled cry of release.

The thought of physically parting was more than either lover could bear, and he stayed inside her, nuzzling the soft skin of her neck between murmured words of love. Emma clung to him, reveling in the moment as she examined the never-ending tenderness of the man who filled her, body and soul. He had given her a precious gift—one she would cherish for eternity.

"I love you, Em." His warm breath whispered across her neck.

"I love you, Tyler, and I'll never tire of telling you so."

He rolled from her body and pulled her against him.

They whispered late into the night about the wealth of mistaken ideas that had plagued their relationship over the past months. Emma told Tyler of her life in New York and growing up with Samuel and Jacob. He spoke of his days with Sara before the accident.

Emma reached up to caress his shadowed cheek. "I hope you never stop loving Sara."

"How can you say that, Em?" He clasped her hand and pressed a kiss into the palm. "It was my love for Sara, and my clinging grief that caused you so much pain."

"I could never be jealous of her. I would never seek to take away the beautiful memories of the life you shared with her. I respect your grief. I don't want Janie to forget her real mother. Sara was a part of your life. Therefore, she's a part of mine. Is that idea so hard to comprehend?"

He pulled her closer and buried his face into the thickness of her hair. "Woman, you have about the biggest heart of anyone I've ever met. If I had been more like you, we wouldn't have had these awful months apart."

His hands moved over her body again and, just when Emma thought he would put a particularly passionate end to the foreplay, Tyler grabbed her. His experienced fingers tickled her until she shrieked and laughed and begged for mercy.

"Stop! I can't take it any longer!" She threw her legs over the side of the bed in an attempt to escape, then her playful yelp followed his wicked chuckle as he pulled her back and on top of him with a very definite amorous intent. Rolling her beneath him, he whispered all the many things he would do to her before morning. A contented Emma gave herself up to his demands.

Chapter Twenty-Three

℘

Emma wiggled her soft bottom into the solid band of heat that arched against the back of her own body. Immediately, a calloused hand slid upward to cup her breast.

"I'll give you twenty minutes to stop that," his husky voice whispered beside her ear.

A quiet giggle bubbled in her throat. She squirmed even closer. His muffled groan reverberated in the room as he hardened against her.

"One would think you'd be tired after last night," she cooed. "After all, you are an old man of thirty years."

Her delighted squeal rent the air a moment later when his hand moved with lightning speed to pinch her derriere, then flipped her over and began to tickle her mercilessly. Emma struggled to escape, tangling them in the blankets. They both froze when a heavy knock sounded on the door. She blanched when she heard Trevor's voice come from the other side.

"Tyler! You up in there?"

"Pssst!" Tyler's voice hissed in her ear with a wicked grin. "He doesn't know how accurate his question is, Em."

Her playful slap was accompanied by a frantic whisper. "Don't joke around! I have to get out of here before he comes in!" She leapt from the bed, intending to make a hasty exit into the next room, but realized too late that her leg was tangled in the blanket. Her frenzied attempts to free it succeeded only in worsening her ordeal. Her grinning husband was absolutely no help as his warm gaze devoured her naked body.

"Tyler! Get off the blanket! I'm stuck!" Emma yanked her leg free at the same moment she bent to retrieve her nightgown from the floor.

"You better make yourself decent. I'm comin' in!" Trevor called out again.

"The door's open," Tyler yelled in return.

A loud squeak left Emma's throat as she dove back beneath the covers. Her nightgown floated to its former place on the floor. The blanket found her chin just as her brother-in-law stuck his head through the opening between the door and the jamb.

"Hey, are you going to sleep—" The words froze on his lips when he took in Emma's red face and the nightgown on the floor. A grinning Tyler sat up, propped a pillow against the headboard and leaned back, looking like the proverbial cat that had just swallowed the canary.

Trevor answered his brother's smile with a knowing grin of his own before he turned his gaze back to his blushing sister-in-law.

"Morning, Em! And what a beautiful day it is!" He crossed to the fireplace, added some wood and fanned the small flame created by the glowing embers. "I love Christmas Eve, don't you? Mamie always prepares a special breakfast, and then we're on our own until the troops arrive for the party." He cocked his head, picking up the sound of footsteps in the hallway. "Hey, Cole! If that's you, we're in here!"

Emma sank lower beneath the piled covers. Her blush deepened. Even if she and Tyler were married, she was dying of embarrassment.

Trevor made a show of turning one of the overstuffed chairs toward the bed, then seated himself entirely too casually as he waited for his younger brother to enter the room.

I'm going to kill him... Emma tightened the blankets around her slender neck with a glare.

Cole strolled through the open doorway, his attention riveted to a button on his shirt. He secured the fastener and looked up—then managed quite adeptly to hide his surprise, but not the twinkle in his eye. He lowered his gaze to yet another button and spoke to no one in particular. "You know what? I never have liked this shirt. The buttonholes are too small to get it hooked up properly." He raised a dark brow and glanced at the pair in bed again. "Mornin', Emma. When are we going for the Christmas tree, Ty?" He raised his arms high over his head in an exaggerated stretch. "Boy, it's a nice day outside." He turned the other chair to face the bed and seated himself beside Trevor, then stretched his legs out before him with a cocky grin on his face.

Emma wished for a hole to crawl into. Words refused to make their way through the embarrassment that clogged her throat. She remained motionless beneath the covers, which were still pulled up to her chin. Cole and Trevor's nonchalance rankled her to no end. How was she supposed to get up and get dressed if they wouldn't leave? She peeked up at Tyler from beneath long lashes. His obvious effort to hold back the silent laughter that shook his broad shoulders served only to incense her further, most likely because the two idiots were having a grand time with this latest development. She reached over to pinch his naked thigh with vicious intent.

"Ouch!" He looked down at her red face and rubbed the tender spot on his leg. "What did you do that for?"

"You're just as bad as they are!" she hissed.

Tyler's gaze moved from his mortified wife to his grinning brothers. "Okay, you two have had your fun. As you can clearly see, Emma and I finally figured out our differences. Now, get the hell out of here so she can get dressed." A mischievous sparkle lit his eyes just before he peeked beneath the covers. "Yup, she definitely needs to get dressed!"

Loud guffaws exploded across the room before his brothers stood, however reluctantly, and left the master suite.

Emma sat up, holding the blanket in place over her breasts with a decidedly stern look hardening her delicate jaw. "I repeat — you're just as bad as they are!"

Tyler ignored her and concentrated on the creamy shoulders exposed to his appreciative view. Leaning closer, he kissed the one closest to him. His hand moved to the blanket. A quick tug preceded a dip of his dark head. Eager lips nibbled at her now exposed breasts.

She closed her eyes with a sigh. "Tyler, we really should get up," she murmured.

"I already am, so why don't you join me?"

His mouth devoured hers, and he carried her to frenzied heights again quickly before someone else entered the room.

*****

That afternoon, the family worked together on last minute preparations for the evening's party. Each of the Wilkinses noticed the happy smile that turned up the corners of Emma's mouth at least a hundred times that day.

Earlier, after she and Tyler finally left the safe haven of their suite, the family had bundled themselves against the cold and marched up the hill behind the house to find the perfect tree.

The Norway pine was now erected in a place of honor in the living room. Emma quietly placed her contribution on a branch halfway up the tree. Tyler approached from behind and wrapped his arms around her slim waist.

She sighed her happiness as she leaned into the security of his embrace. "Do you ever think of that old Indian we met in New York?" she asked as her gaze took in the small carving that dangled before her.

He laid his cheek against her hair and looked at the wooden loon. "All the time. When I got home, I heard a loon singing and some part of me hoped it was the old man's spirit calling out."

She turned in his arms. "What did you do with the other carving?"

"I did what the old guy asked me to do. I released it on a nearby lake and let it float away. It may sound rather foolish, but I hope his spirit was riding on the back of that little carving, and that it took him home."

"It doesn't sound foolish at all, Tyler. I like to think that everything has happened as it should." She turned back to look at her own *spirit*, where it hung from the branch as Tyler tightened his arms around her. "Every time I looked at that little loon, I thought of you. I thought it was the only part of you that I had left."

"I've made so many mistakes, Em. I'm sorry for causing you so much pain." His soft breath stirred wisps of hair on the top of her head. "When I let the first carving float away, I had the strangest feeling that I would never be able to get you back. Mamie says everything happens for a reason. Maybe we had to go through all that we did in order to get to where we are now. One thing I know for certain, Emma. I love you more than life itself and, if I could, I would take away all your pain."

She turned, wrapped her arms around his waist and rested her head against his chest. "For whatever reason, we're together now, and I'll thank God for that every day for the rest of my life."

Tyler left her a short time later to attend to some business outside. Seeing that she was without her protector, Cole and Trevor resumed their persistent teasing. Emma accepted their shenanigans with good humor, but Carrie finally had enough. She ordered them outside, threatening bodily harm if they didn't behave themselves.

"You can't help but laugh at them, Carrie," Emma said as the front door slammed shut behind the two men. "You should have heard them this morning when they found me in Tyler's room."

"I can just imagine." She moved to give her sister-in-law a hug. "We're all so happy for both of you."

"Thank you for listening to me when we were in Duluth—and for making me realize what I could have with him."

Carrie lifted her slender shoulders in a shrug. "We could all see how much you two cared for each other. You and Tyler just got lost for a while, that's all. I didn't do anything that those two silly brothers of mine weren't thinking of doing." She reached out to give Emma's hands a squeeze. "But give yourself some credit, too. You were the one who finally had the courage to speak up. Okay, enough of that before we both end up blubbering. Let's go see what else Mamie needs."

Tyler and Janie entered the room before Emma had a chance to follow Carrie. Her stomach jumped at the sight of her husband as she moved into the welcoming circle of his arms. Glancing down at her grinning stepdaughter, she reached out to ruffle her soft, blonde hair. "And what have you and your daddy been doing outside?"

"I can't tell. It's a surprise!"

"Oh, a surprise?" Emma cocked a suspicious eyebrow when she took in Tyler's blasé expression. "And just who would that be for?"

"It's a surprise, Emma," Tyler reiterated his daughter's statement, then a devilish grin appeared as he tipped his head to whisper for her ears alone. "But if you come upstairs with me, I just might be convinced to spill the beans."

Emma stepped from his embrace with a shake of her head. "You just don't quit, do you?" she laughed, making it obvious that she didn't object to this new Tyler at all, the one who had showered her with amorous insinuations throughout the day.

"Nope, and don't ever expect me to." He gave her lips a quick kiss, then turned his attention to his daughter. "Janie, run in the kitchen and get Auntie Carrie and Mamie. I think we'll give Emma her surprise before everyone gets here for the party."

The little girl raced from the room, nearly bursting with excitement.

Emma eyed him warily. "What's going on? I can wait until tomorrow like everyone else."

"Well, my dear, you might be able to wait, but your present can't. Now, put on your wrap. We have to go outside."

Janie returned with Mamie and Carrie in tow. All three had donned coats and boots and were ready to brave the elements.

It seemed everyone was in on her surprise. With growing excitement, Emma wondered what her present might be.

Tyler grasped her hand and led her through the gaily decorated living room and into the foyer, then ducked behind her to place his warm hands over her eyes just as Janie opened the immense oaken door that led to the porch.

"I can trust you back there, can't I?" Emma whispered between giggles before they stepped outside.

"I wouldn't if I were you," he whispered back. Before he could act on his words, however, Janie took Emma's hand and led her carefully through the open doorway.

"Are you going to remove your hands, Tyler, or do I have to stand here and freeze along with everybody else?"

"What do you think, Janie? Should we let Emma see her surprise?"

Janie jumped from foot to foot, and a huge grin stretched from ear to ear. "Yes, Daddy! Don't make her wait any more!"

"Merry Christmas, honey." Tyler removed his hands as Emma felt the warmth of his whisper against her ear.

She opened her eyes, squinted into the bright sunlight that reflected off the snow and finally focused on five of the most beautiful horses she'd ever seen. The animals stood in a line at the bottom of the steps, their lead ropes draped in the hands of Cole and Trevor. Their powerful hooves stamped the cold ground. Steam erupted from their noses with each annoyed snort while eyeing the humans gathered around them.

Emma spun to face Tyler. Excitement leapt from her eyes. "Is this my present?"

"Well...part of it."

"Are these horses really mine?" She whirled back to scan the animals before her. One of the mares was as white as the snow she stood in. "If I didn't know better, I'd say that one was the horse my father bought me for my twenty-first birthday. She looks exactly like Bonne."

"It is your horse, Emma!" Janie exclaimed, unable to contain her enthusiasm any longer.

Emma swung back to face Tyler. "But...what...why is she here?"

"Do you remember my telling you that Trevor, Cole and I wanted to breed fine riding horses someday?"

"Yes, but what does that have to do with my gift?" Her eyes widened in sudden dawning. "Oh, Tyler! Are you really going to do it? Are these the horses you said you needed to start fresh?"

"Yes, they are. I remembered the beautiful mare you used to own. Knowing how much you missed her, I had her shipped out. The other horses though, are Trevor and Cole's way of saying that they want you to be a part of this enterprise, too."

"We're really serious about this, Emma," Cole spoke first. "We figured that, with you constantly biting at our heels, the idea just might work. Tyler was the one who came up with the idea of shipping this fine piece of horseflesh from New York, though." He patted Bonne's flank.

"We really want you to be a part of this, Em," Trevor added. "Will you accept our offer?"

"How could I resist the three most handsome men in Minnesota? Thank you all!" She rushed down the steps to hug her brothers-in-law, then returned to throw her arms around her husband. "I really think we can make this partnership work, Tyler. I'm so excited you finally decided to do it."

He pressed a kiss to her lips, and then released her. "Well, I think you'd better go check out that horse of yours. It's been months since you've seen her."

His eyes glittered with sudden anticipation when Emma turned to walk down the steps. His voice floated on the breeze behind her. "Hey, mister, could you please bring the white mare closer?"

Emma noticed a man who stood on the horse's left flank, her earlier view blocked by the animal. As her foot touched the bottom stair, he stepped out from behind the mare.

"Papa!" she cried. "Papa, it's you!" She flung herself into his waiting arms. "I can't believe you're here!"

"I've missed you so much, Em. How have you been, kitten?" Edward held her at arm's length and gazed into her face, then saw her tears and struggled to control his own. "You're just as beautiful as you always were."

Tyler approached them and clapped a hand on his father-in-law's shoulder. "Why don't we go inside, where you and Emma can have your reunion beside a warm fire."

Edward placed an arm around his daughter's shoulders and steered her toward the steps.

She still wiped at tears of joy. "I can't believe you're here to spend Christmas with us." She reached for Tyler's hand and gave it a loving squeeze. "I've never had a gift as special as this. Thank you so much for arranging it."

He kissed her on her cheek as he fell into step, then slipped an arm around her waist. "I just wanted you to be happy. When your father decided to bring the horses out here himself, it was the icing on the cake."

After introductions were made quickly in the cold afternoon air, they entered the house, followed by Mamie, Janie and Carrie.

Cole and Trevor led the string of horses to the stable. Trevor nudged Cole as they entered the barn. "Are you thinking what I'm thinking?"

"That depends. What are you thinking?"

"Well, that's a first!" Trevor chuckled as he led a small, brown roan into the first stall. "You usually know what's going on in somebody's head before they do."

Cole let the other four horses make their own way down the wide space between the stalls, then hooked his elbows on the gate behind him, leaned against it and pushed his hat back on his head. A cocky grin creased his face. "Okay. You're thinking that Tyler is going to be one lucky cowboy tonight when he climbs into bed because Emma is so damn excited about her father being here."

Trevor tossed a glove at his brother and shook his head in wonder. "Jeez, Cole, how do you do that?"

* * * * *

Janie cuddled beside Edward Sanders, still filled with awe at the idea that she had a grandfather like other children did. The two had met each other in secret earlier that afternoon. With the characteristic bluntness of a child, she'd asked him if he was her grandpa. Edward replied that he guessed he was, and they had formed an instant bond.

Emma smiled to herself as she watched the two who sat on the sofa across from her and Tyler.

"When you first wired me about this idea of yours, Tyler, I thought you were a little touched in the head," Edward remarked.

"It's something my brothers and I have always wanted to do. We're financially secure because of the lumber business. It seemed like the right time to try something new." He squeezed Emma's hand. "Trevor was the one who insisted that Emma be a part of the venture, too, with her love of horses and her head for business." He looked down at her and smiled. "I have to admit, Em, that I had a hidden agenda though, in bringing your mare out here. She'll be prime breeding stock. I'm just glad your father decided to come along."

"So am I," she murmured softly.

"I'm relieved to see that you're so happy," Edward grinned at his daughter. "I was concerned for a time—I wish I could have been here when you lost the baby, honey. It must have been very difficult for you."

Tyler gently squeezed his wife's shoulder in gentle support, but his mind betrayed his true feelings. *You have no idea, Edward...*

A telegram a few weeks earlier had broken the news of the miscarriage to Emma's father. Her wishes though, were that Edward not be made aware of Samuel Fontaine's involvement. Tyler had abided by her decision.

"It was hard, Papa," she murmured. "But there would've been nothing you could do even if you were here." She batted back tears and quickly changed the subject. "How did you ever manage time away from the shipyard? This is your busy season, what with refurbishing damaged vessels and new orders under contract for the spring."

Edward cleared his throat and shifted uncomfortably. "Well, Emma, since you brought it up, I guess this is as good a time as any to talk to you about the shipyard. I know you always wanted to take over the operation, but things have changed now. It's easy to see that you're deliriously happy in your new life. Believe me, the knowledge sets my mind at ease considerably." He took a deep breath. "I sold the shipyard, honey. I've decided to retire."

"You sold the shipyard!" Her brow wrinkled in total confusion at the new turn of events. "You never said anything about it in your letters."

Tyler held his silence. This matter was between father and daughter. He remembered vividly though, Emma's interest in every aspect of her father's business.

Edward leaned forward and clasped his hands together. "Honey, I'm not a young man anymore. My entire adult life has been devoted to running the yard and watching over our interests, just as I have always watched over you. Maybe, if I had spent more time at home, your mother and I could have had a stronger marriage. But, with the never-ending emergencies and meetings, I never seemed to have time for her."

Emma's bewilderment only increased with her father's sudden change of topic. "What does Mother have to do with this?"

Edward held her gaze. His own became determined, almost passionate. "I've met someone. Though we haven't known each other long, we're planning to be married." His expression became a plea. "Please, give me your blessing, kitten. I haven't been this happy in years."

Emma stared at Edward through incredulous eyes.

Tyler patted her shoulder in encouragement, hoping that Edward's trip would remain a happy one. He stood and lifted Janie into his arms. "Come on, honey. Let's let Emma talk with your new grandpa alone for a while. We'll go check on some last minute details for the party." He bent to press a chaste kiss to Emma's cheek, then whispered, "Em, remember how happy we are now. Your father deserves the same." He left the room with Janie riding high atop his shoulders.

She watched them go. A year ago—no—only eight short months ago, she didn't even know they existed. Now, they were her whole life. Realizing how fast things could change, she turned to her father again who studied her through nervous eyes.

"Can we start this conversation over, Papa? Let's see, we were at the point where I was surprised at the idea of you selling the shipyard. And even more surprised when you announced that you were going to be married."

Edward was still unable to read her expression—until he saw two dimples deepen in her cheeks. Her green eyes sparkled with amusement.

Emma couldn't contain her laughter at his pained expression. She rose from the sofa and moved to seat herself beside him.

"You look like you're ready to be sick." She took his large hand in her much smaller one. "I'm sorry about my initial reaction. I guess I was a little shocked at first. I mean, to think you would sell the shipyard—your life's work—and then find someone to marry after all these years." Her expression saddened. "You and Mama never had a deep, abiding love, did you?"

He patted their clasped hands with his free one. "It's not that we didn't try, Em. We just never found the spark, at least not the type of spark I think I'm seeing between you and Tyler. Don't get me wrong. Your mother was a wonderful person. I respected her and confided in her as I would a best friend. But a deep love? No, Emma, not anything like what I've found with Clarice."

"This Clarice, what is she like?"

"Ah, she makes me laugh, and I feel like I'm twenty years old again. But I'm not, and neither is she. That's why we decided to marry quickly and not wait through a proper time of engagement. I don't want to be alone anymore. I don't know how many years I have left and would prefer to live out my remaining life with Clarice. Can you understand that?"

Emma examined her father's lined features. If he hadn't been so adamant about her going to Minnesota to marry Tyler, they might both have missed out on the opportunity to find a devoted partner for life. How could she even consider withholding her blessing for him to seek what she had already found?

She squeezed his hand. "I'm happy for you, Papa. My days of wanting the shipping business are over. What I have here with Tyler and Janie could never be duplicated. I'm selfish enough though, to be happy you're here with me for Christmas, instead of back in New York with Clarice. Why didn't you bring her with you?"

"Because I needed to make sure you were settled and happy before I could make the final decision to marry her. I'm sure she's back in the city pacing her kitchen as we speak, waiting to hear from me. I told her I needed to see you before we could finalize anything."

"And how did she feel about that?"

"She loves me enough to understand why I needed to come without her. In fact, she encouraged me to go."

Emma wrapped her arms around her father's shoulders. "Papa, she sounds wonderful. You have my complete blessing—with one condition."

"And what would that be?"

"That you bring her out here as soon as possible, so I can meet the woman who has made my father so happy."

He sat back. "Done! Maybe we can plan a trip this spring if all goes well."

The door cracked open then. Janie poked her blonde head through the opening. "Emma? Daddy said to tell you and Grandpa that our guests are starting to arrive. Do you want to come and meet them?"

"We'll be right there, honey." She stood and pulled her father up with her. "Come on, *Grandpa*. It's time to see what a Minnesota Christmas is all about."

* * * * *

Just as Tyler predicted, the party was barely an hour old when two men pulled out fiddles and another joined in with his harmonica, and the dancing began.

Emma watched her father where he sat in a corner with Trevor, Cole and four other men. They tipped their glasses of ale and laughed heartily, and she knew with certainty that they all would carry around sore heads come morning.

Carrie and Steven never missed a dance, whispering secrets in one another's ears. When partners suddenly changed during a Virginia Reel, Emma ended up with Steven by her side. She laughed loudly when he asked Emma if she thought Carrie's brothers would miss them if he were to sneak his sweetheart away for a few stolen kisses on the porch. Emma winked and assured him that Trevor and Cole were too busy celebrating to notice anything other than the next bottle, and she would keep Tyler busy.

A short time later, she watched as the couple disappeared through the doorway. Tyler's gaze, and then his scowl followed after them—until Emma pulled him into her arms.

* * * * *

When the door closed behind the last of the guests, Tyler gathered a tired Janie into his arm. Slipping his free arm around Emma's shoulders, the three of them headed to the little girl's room. Once they'd settled her beneath the covers, Emma leaned down to kiss her flushed cheek. The little girl's eyes closed even before her father had the chance to give her a hug.

Tyler clasped Emma's hand and led her to their room. She smiled secretly as she passed her old bedroom door and walked with him to the master suite. Once in their room, his eyes widened in surprise when he saw the package that lay in the middle of the bed.

"What's this?"

"It's your Christmas gift. I wanted to give it to you in private."

"I can wait until—"

"Don't tell me you can wait until tomorrow. I seem to remember a certain man who couldn't wait to give his wife a gift earlier today."

She watched intently as he untied the string with a wide grin on his face and opened the cover on the box, then sat beside him as he folded back the tissue paper. The smile drained from his face when he stared at the contents. Reaching inside, he carefully lifted out the statue of the Indian. Slowly turning the figurine in his hands, he examined it closely before meeting her gaze.

"It's beautiful," he spoke softly. "It's our Indian, isn't it?"

Emma let out her breath she'd been holding. "Yes. When I saw him, I knew it was the perfect gift." She reached out to touch the gift with reverence. "When I saw this, I was strangely drawn to it. It was a feeling I couldn't quite grasp. Do you remember when that old Indian called you the keeper of the spirit?"

He nodded.

"Somehow, I think he was right. You've done so much for me, Tyler. You brought me back when I thought I'd never be the same again. You continued to love me, regardless of what happened." She rested her head against his shoulder and stared at the statue cradled in his hands. "I can't help but think that Indian is somehow a part of our lives, and also part of the reason we're together. Do you understand what I'm saying?"

He held the statue with one hand and slipped his free arm around her shoulders. "I feel it too, Em. When I first saw this, I felt something unexplainable, deep inside." He stood to place the statue on the window ledge and returned to pull her up into his embrace. "We'll never know who the credit goes to for us being together. I'm just thankful that you're finally here with me."

He kissed her then. When he drew away, Emma raised a hand to run her fingers through the soft black waves at his temple. "Merry Christmas, Tyler."

"Merry Christmas, Emma," he whispered before he pressed her back to the mattress.

Chapter Twenty-Four

ೢ

Emma stood on the front porch and let the morning sun warm her face. Spring had arrived, and her first winter in Minnesota was coming to an end. She smiled as she remembered the other family members' desire to see the snow and cold leave as they waited for this day.

Three of the new mares were ready to be bred. Hopefully, the other two would come into season over the next few weeks. This newest venture was all the Wilkinses had talked about that past winter. The preparations had been made, and now their dream was about to become reality.

The mill began operations a few weeks earlier minus the presence of the three Wilkins men who had come up with an idea that would eventually work them out of the lumber business. Each of the men who worked for the company had been given an equal share of stock, and the employees hoped that they would be able to buy out the previous owners within the next year.

She leaned a slim shoulder against the wooden porch banister, scanned the few remaining piles of snow that dotted the shaded areas in the front yard. Her stomach quivered as she recalled her and Tyler's most recent lovemaking session earlier that morning. It never ceased to amaze her that their relationship only got better, and their love for one another, stronger. Only one thing marred her happiness, however. She hadn't become pregnant over the winter months.

Emma was still lost in thought when Tyler stepped out onto the porch.

"There you are! I wanted to find you before I headed for the stables. Big day today. I hardly slept." He took one look at the sad dip of her brow and knew something was wrong. "What's the matter?"

"Nothing...just thinking."

"Come on, Em. There's something—I saw it on your face."

Her gaze shifted uncomfortably as she chewed on her bottom lip. "When did you get so good at reading expressions?" She finally glanced up. "I thought Cole was the only Wilkins man who possessed that talent."

Her husband crossed his arms before his muscular chest and stared at her with a raised brow of expectation. Knowing he wouldn't give up, Emma sighed.

"I'm just feeling sorry for myself. Everyone is so excited about the possibility of new foals next spring. What about me? I want a baby, Tyler, and it's just not happening."

He pulled her up and into his arms. "I'm sorry that it hasn't happened yet, too. But you have to quit worrying about it or it never will. Our time will come." He tipped her chin until she met his eyes. "Who knows? By next spring you might be holding our son or daughter." His gaze flicked to the barn. "Do you want to come down to the paddock with me?"

She shook her head and forced a smile to her mouth. "No, you go ahead. I've got some work to catch up on."

"Are you sure?"

"I'm fine, Tyler."

He pressed a hesitant kiss against her lips. "I better get going. I love you, Em."

"I love you, too."

She watched him until he rounded the corner of a storage shed, and then shook her head at her own foolishness. Maybe she would never conceive again, but she still had Tyler and Janie, and the rest of the family. *I should count my blessings...*

Emma entered the house and headed for the office. Flipping open a ledger book, she recorded the date and the names of horses that would be bred.

* * * * *

The mid-July sun baked the landscape. Just when Emma thought she couldn't bear the heat and the doldrums any longer, Tyler invited her to join him on the long ride up to one of the logging camps. The brothers still made themselves available, albeit only once a month, if the new managers had any problems or questions when it came to running the complex operation.

Looking forward to the time she would spend alone with her husband, Emma stuffed a saddlebag with an extra pair of pants, a shirt and a few personal items. The men's trousers were Carrie's idea. The younger woman often wore them around the ranch. Once Emma tried a pair herself, she realized how comfortable they were compared to the riding habits she'd worn all her life. Upon their next trip to Duluth, she had a totally appalled seamstress make her two pair.

A quick glance at the full-length mirror beside the dresser was enough to pause Emma's quick movements about the room. She walked slowly toward her reflection, slightly shocked by the woman who stared back at her. White cotton shirtsleeves were rolled up to the elbows, revealing slender, sun-tanned arms. The garment was tucked into the tiny waistband of tight-fitting brown pants. Instead of the auburn hair being piled glamorously atop her head, it now hung loosely to past her shoulders, held back by combs on either side of her head. Her face, too, was brown—a totally unacceptable malady in proper New York society—and made her green eyes stand out with even more clarity. There was something else though, she realized. Her complexion actually glowed with happiness.

She snatched her cowboy hat from atop the dresser and plopped it on her head just as Whizzer loped through the open doorway. She watched the dog jumped onto the bed, then giggled when he wagged his tail and let out a deep, resounding bark. "Well, Janie can't be too far behind you."

Her stepdaughter bounded through the doorway a moment later, munching on a freshly baked cookie. "Hi, Emma! Daddy says you're going with him to the logging camp, and that I should tell you goodbye." She scrambled up onto the bed, then swatted at the dog when he tried to steal the cookie from her hand. Whizzer's resulting whine was enough to persuade her to break off half of the treat and feed it to him with a giggle.

Emma smiled. "Don't let Mamie see you feeding him the products of her hard work."

Janie rolled over onto her stomach, popped the rest of the cookie into her mouth and watched Emma close the saddlebag. "Mamie's full of hot air."

"Janie!" Emma struggled to control her laughter and maintain a stern expression. "That's not a nice thing to say."

"But, it's true. Uncle Trevor said so! Mamie's always hollering about Whizzer being in her kitchen, and she chases him with her broom." At the sound of his name, the dog cocked his head and stared at the little girl. "Then, when she thinks nobody can see, she gives him treats. She even saves him a plate of scraps and scratches him behind his ears."

Emma had to laugh. "Well then, I guess Trevor is right. Just don't let Mamie hear you say it." She paused to study her stepdaughter's adorable face. "It's all right with you that your dad and I are going to be gone overnight, isn't it?"

"Sure! Auntie Carrie's taking me to Steve's house. We're going to cook him a special lunch because he's been working so hard lately." Her nose suddenly wrinkled. "Do you think they kiss all the time, like you and Daddy?"

Emma snorted, ruffled Janie's hair and reached for the bag. "You're sure full of the dickens today, aren't you. Come on, walk with me downstairs. And, if Auntie Carrie kisses Steve all the time, it's because she loves him as much as I love your daddy."

Janie rolled off the bed, and the yellow dog followed at her heels. She took her stepmother's hand. "You know what, Emma? I'm glad you came to live with us. Daddy is happy all the time, and I like having my best friend tuck me in at night."

As they walked down the steps hand in hand, Emma blinked back happy tears. "I'm glad I came here to live too, honey."

* * * * *

They had almost reached the logging camp when Tyler reined his horse to a halt beside Emma. "Take a look behind you, Em."

She swiveled in the saddle, and the view took her breath away. They sat high atop a ridge. Directly below, endless forests and sparkling lakes came alive in the late afternoon sun. The panorama in the far northern reaches of Minnesota was like nothing she'd ever seen.

"What do you think, Em? Isn't it a sight to behold?"

"It's beautiful…" She nudged her horse closer to his, her eyes still glued to the magnificent expanse. "It looks so wild and untamed." She reached out to capture his hand, her eyes still glued to the vista below. "I was so frightened when I first came here, but now I feel like this land has welcomed me. I feel a sense of belonging that I never felt in New York, maybe because I took my life for granted there. Here, in this country, a person has to work hard to carve out a life. And, if you do right by it, the land grants you the privilege of seeing another sunrise." She sighed and a small smile curved her lips. "It's such an immense feeling of accomplishment to crawl into bed at night knowing that you'll be rewarded for a hard day's work." She finally glanced up. "You've lived here your entire life. Do you ever feel that way?"

"All the time. I remember trying to explain to you in New York what you just so eloquently described to me. This land *is* a gift to be cherished." He squeezed her hand. "I'm glad you feel the way you do."

Tyler studied her sun-darkened features and long, flowing hair. It dawned on him how much she'd changed since arriving in Minnesota on that warm September day so long ago. She'd overcome almost insurmountable hurdles and had demonstrated more courage than most men. She was a beautiful and confident woman in her own right and had made his life livable again. He would treasure her forever.

*****

Emma and Tyler arrived at the camp an hour later. They ate dinner with the crew, and Emma was caught up in the pride necessary to make a success of such a booming lumber company. These men were not afraid of hard work, nor did they let the constant loneliness dampen their determination. They did ask her to give them time to write quick letters to their families, however, and Emma promised to hand deliver them when she returned home.

By the time she and Tyler mounted their horses, Emma's pack was full of scraps of folded paper. She secured her precious cargo, then turned and waved once more before she and Tyler rounded a bend in the trail and disappeared from view.

"How long until we stop for the night?" Emma asked a short time later. She had been surprised when Tyler told her they would sleep away from the logging camp.

"Why?" His lips curved in a lurid smile. "Are you anxious to snuggle against me under only a blanket of stars?"

She rolled her eyes at his nonsense, but her skin tingled with the promise. "I've never spent the night outdoors, Tyler, and, yes, I am excited."

"And here I thought your enthusiasm was due to the fact that we'll be totally alone tonight." His chest heaved in an exaggerated sigh. "Okay. I plan to erect a small tent about an hour down the trail, have a little something more to eat, and then…who knows?"

His smoldering gaze caused her stomach to do a quick flip. Without another word, they both kicked their horses into a faster gait.

* * * * *

Tyler built a fire, prepared a quick bite of venison and then stretched out with his back propped against a log. Emma leaned against his broad chest and stared into the flames as she sipped from the coffee cup they passed between them. They talked quietly about the ranch and the horses, about Steve and Carrie's upcoming wedding and the possibility of a trip to New York to visit her father and Clarice. It was when they discussed how fast Janie was growing up that Tyler noticed Emma's sudden silence.

"What's wrong?" He rubbed her shoulder with his free hand.

She sighed. "You know I love Janie like she was my own daughter. No one could ever take her place in my heart. But…I can't quit thinking about the fact that I haven't conceived again." She leaned forward and wrapped her arms around her raised knees. "I got pregnant so easily the first time. It just surprises me that it's taking so long now." Sudden tears shone in her eyes as she looked at him and voiced her fears. "Do you think that maybe…because of what Samuel did…I'll never be able to have children?"

Tyler pulled her back into the circle of his arms. "Em, you've talked with Steve. He told you that there was no physical reason why you couldn't have another baby, right?"

She nodded.

"Don't dwell on it then. When the time is right, it'll happen. And, if it doesn't, we'll deal with it then." He nuzzled her neck. "I love you, Emma, and that will never change, whether we have children together or not."

She turned in his arms and studied his handsome face. "But I *want* to have your children, Tyler. I want us to create a tiny being to love and protect…"

His kiss halted her words. Gathering her into his arms, he stood and carried her to the small tent. They shed their clothes in frantic haste and came together. As they loved one another through the night, a wolf howled in the distance.

* * * * *

The end of August arrived and, with it, the completion of a new twenty-stall stable that was the first in a long line of projects. The massive dwelling would house the five mares Emma had been gifted with for Christmas and, hopefully, would boast some of the finest horseflesh in the country as the years went by.

Emma and her three partners sat at the dining room table, discussing yet another construction project when Trevor pushed aside his mug of coffee and pulled a stack of papers closer. "Has anyone given any more thought to what we're going to name this new business of ours? We really need to come up with something. It looks like we'll be out of the lumber business by the end of the year."

"How does Lakota Pines Riding Stock sound to all of you?" Emma leaned forward and waited for a response.

Trevor glanced up from the numerous papers scattered before him. "That's a possibility. How did you come up with that?"

"I've been doing some research into the State's history. Since the ranch is already called the Northern Pine, I thought it would be logical to combine the present name with the new one." She looked at Tyler and received a gentle smile when she continued, knowing he understood where the idea had come from. "Lakota means 'allies' in the Sioux language. Now, that's what we all are, aren't we? Allies, who are working together, to create something good for the future." Emma's gaze moved from one rugged face to the next as they pondered her words. The importance of the Indian name went unspoken, but she hoped dearly that they would agree with her.

"What do you think, gentlemen? She might have something here." Tyler rested his forearms on the table as he, too, waited for a response. Cole and Trevor exchanged glances, then tipped their heads in unison and the name was written across a blank piece of paper.

* * * * *

Emma stood at the front of the church, holding a bouquet of autumn wildflowers. Her gaze never left Tyler's masculine form as he escorted his sister down the aisle and toward the altar. Carrie was resplendent in a gown of white satin, her face glowing with happiness. Her eyes moved to rest on Steven, where he stood in a dark suit at the front of the church. Carrie had asked Emma to serve as the Matron of Honor, and Steven chose Trevor as his Best Man.

Emma smiled inwardly as she remembered her own wedding and wondered what kind of toast Trevor would make at the reception. She forced her attention back to the approaching couple then, as Tyler placed his sister's hand in the groom's much larger one.

She listened quietly as Carrie and Steven repeated their vows, promising to love and cherish one another for the rest of their lives. She also thought about how different their wedding was compared to her own.

A tear escaped and ran down Emma's cheek when the newly married couple turned to face the congregation. She would miss having Carrie around on a day-to-day basis, but, as with the other well-wishers gathered for the nuptials, she wanted only happiness for the pair.

The reception was held at a large meetinghouse, built in the nearby town of Colby for just such an occasion. As they crossed the dusty street, Tyler slung an arm around Emma's shoulders and teased her quietly about the tears that still dampened her cheeks. She poked him mercilessly with a pointed elbow.

"Come on, be nice," he wheezed. "Aren't you happy that they don't have to go through what we did?"

"That's exactly what I was thinking during the ceremony. And don't make fun of my tears. I'm going to miss her terribly."

"They're not gonna be that far away, Em. We'll visit often, and they'll probably be out at the ranch more often than we want." He tightened his arm around her. "Now, if I could just marry off those two idiot brothers of mine, I'd have you all to myself."

Emma wasn't in the mood for his levity. "It's not going to be that easy, Tyler. Carrie is going to be busier than she ever was helping Steve with the clinic."

"It'll be fine, Em, you'll see."

* * * * *

Carrie and Steven bid farewell at the end of the evening. The newlyweds would return to Steven's house for the night and leave for Duluth in the morning on a long anticipated honeymoon.

Tyler escorted Emma and Janie to the waiting carriage. Cole and Trevor waited in the driver's seat. The moon was full and bathed them in its glow as they returned to the ranch.

When they arrived home, Tyler helped Emma haul water upstairs to the small antechamber between the two connecting bedrooms. He watched her disrobe through hungry eyes and step into the bath. When she sank down into the warm water, he reached for a scented bar of soap. A grin appeared on his face at her sigh of pleasure when he lathered her back.

"It was a fun day, wasn't it?" He swirled the soap slowly across her skin, hoping the gentle touch would elicit the response he desired.

"Mmmmm," she answered and only closed her eyes.

His brow creased. "Why are you so quiet? Are you still upset because you won't have Carrie around to talk to now?"

"No. I'm just enjoying the feel of your hands on my back for as long as possible before I ask you to climb in here with me."

Emma giggled with glee as Tyler shucked off his clothes as quickly as possible. Stepping into the tub, he plunked down, then pulled her closer for a leisurely kiss. Reaching for the soap again, he lathered her breasts. Emma leaned back with a contented sigh as her eyes fluttered shut.

"Can I ask you something?" Tyler mused.

Emma's head dipped in a small nod.

"You seem to be gaining a little weight. Is there a reason for that?"

"MmHmmm."

His hands froze. "And what would that reason be?"

Emma didn't answer, but a tentative smile curved her lips. Frustrated, Tyler pulled her within inches of his face. Her eyes opened. His heart rapped when he spied a mischievous sparkle in her eyes.

"What?"

"I'm pregnant, Tyler, due sometime late next spring."

"Why didn't you tell me!"

She shrugged her naked shoulders. "This was Carrie's day. I didn't want to spoil it by drawing all the attention to us." She leaned forward to give him a fierce hug. "Isn't it wonderful? We're finally going to have a baby!"

"Well, I guess that explains why you were so moody earlier. You were close to tears all day. I couldn't imagine why you were so upset." He reached up to cup her face in both hands. "I watched you tonight before you climbed into the tub and thought there was something different about you." He pressed a kiss to her lips. "I couldn't be happier, Em. How long have you known?"

"For a while now—well, I suspected it over a month ago. Steven confirmed that I was pregnant last week."

"Steve knew before me?"

"He's a doctor, Tyler. I didn't want to say anything until I knew for sure." She covered his hands. "Please don't be angry. I already told you that I didn't want to take attention away from Carrie and Steven. It was their time to shine." He still looked doubtful. A contrite grin appeared on her face. "I was getting ready to tell you when you asked me."

"You were, huh?"

The tone of his voice assured Emma that he was weakening. She decided to take advantage of his change of heart—quickly. Her expression twisted into a playful scowl. Suddenly, she splashed water in his face, then watched him sputter and flick the wetness away. "And what was that comment about me gaining weight? You're lucky I told you at all after that."

Tyler stayed her hands. The happy grins left both their faces as their gazes locked.

"Em…a baby? I can't believe it finally happened." He kissed her gently, then stood and lifted her from the tub.

Reaching for a towel, he first wiped her body dry, and then his own before leading her to the comfort of their bed. As they cuddled beneath the blankets, his hand drifted to her stomach.

In the darkness, the smile withered from Emma's face. A sudden need to hold it all close, to guard her cherished life assaulted Emma with the force of a thunderstorm—even as a shiver of foreboding trickled down her spine.

Chapter Twenty-Five

෮

An elegantly dressed man stepped through the front entrance of Belle's Pleasure Place. The last vestiges of a wicked March wind followed him in as he shoved the door shut behind him. Peeling the costly leather gloves off finger by finger, his furtive gaze surveyed the large room. Fifty or more men played cards at more than a dozen tables. Piano music mingled with the acrid odor of cheap perfume and cigar smoke to assault his senses. Overall though, he had to admit that this house was a step above the others he'd frequented in the last year.

He crossed to the bar and ordered a whiskey. Sipping the drink casually, his calculating gaze perused the crowd around him. A quiet chuckle followed when he flicked a piece of lint from the sleeve of his pricey woolen coat.

He'd managed quite adeptly to overcome poverty in the last year, gambling and cheating his way back to the point where he didn't have to worry where his next meal would come from. His face had lost its raw, sunken look, the hard edges now filled in. He looked and felt the part of a gentleman again—a lifestyle that was his due. His money belt was full, his clothes were impeccable and not a blond hair was out of place.

Samuel Fontaine had come back into his own. It had been a long, hard year-and-a-half—totally unnecessary in his own eyes. He was back in Minnesota to tie up a few loose ends. If anything, the last months had made him even more determined to end the life of the one person who'd caused him so much grief. He wouldn't leave this godforsaken wilderness until he accomplished what he'd set out to do.

Samuel observed various high paid whores as they picked their next conquest, and then made their way up the staircase. Maybe he'd sample one later on that evening. At the moment, however, he planned to play some cards and further his wealth.

Grabbing his drink, he swaggered to a table and asked to be dealt in. A chair materialized out of nowhere. He sat down, casually throwing a wad of bills on the table before him.

* * * * *

The number of spectators grew around the table as the evening progressed — and the piles of chips grew higher in front of Samuel Fontaine. Word passed quickly that a major gambler was in the house, and that he was winning more often than not. It was uncanny how often the cards turned in his favor. The men in the crowd laughed and slapped one another on the back every time Samuel reached to drag the chips back to his growing pile. The onlookers also made side bets among themselves as to whether or not the high roller would take the next hand.

Belle observed him with a practiced eye, trying to determine if he cheated — and had been doing so for the last hour. If that proved to be the case, she would have the bouncers throw him out on his ear. Not once though, did she see evidence of sleight of hand. He smiled openly in her direction now as he gathered his chips.

Belle sauntered over. "If you'd like, I could have one of my men cash those chips in for you."

Samuel stared at her through heavy-lidded eyes and affected a grin meant to draw her into his web of deceit. "Under one condition — if you consent to join me at a quiet table and have a drink...or two."

She snapped her fingers. A young man appeared out of the crowd. She whispered close to his ear, and a basket materialized. Samuel dropped his poker chips into the container, stood and followed her to a table in the corner.

"I get the impression that you're the owner of this fine establishment. Would I be correct in that assumption?" Samuel never took his eyes from the voluptuous woman now seated across the table.

Belle leaned back in her chair to study the handsome face before her — and the scar that ran from his cheekbone to the line of his square jaw.

"Yes, that's correct. You caused quite a commotion tonight with your adept card playing. I have to admit that I was certain you were cheating."

Samuel laughed with a flash of white teeth. "Ma'am, what kind of gambler would I be if I gave out all my secrets? No, I can assure you, I've just run into quite a streak of luck lately." His eyes held hers. A smile curled his thin lips. "And, if I'm reading your signals right, that streak of luck might include you."

Belle waited as the bartender set down drinks before them, then leaned closer, rested her elbows on the table and slowly sipped her drink as she eyed him thoughtfully over the top of the glass. "I don't even know your name. I normally let my girls handle the *needs* of my customers. Although," she ran a slender finger down the stem of her glass, "with the amount of money you won, you might be able to afford me. That is, if I feel like it tonight."

Samuel's eyes hardened almost imperceptibly, but the smile remained in place. He would screw the enticing bitch if it were the last thing he'd ever do. "Well, if it's just a simple matter of knowing my name, then you can call me Sam. As far as affording you, you're right. The proof of that was seen earlier at the poker table."

She hadn't allowed another man to enter her suite since Cole Wilkins' most recent visit a month earlier and now admitted the urge to have a good time. Sam was handsome. It might be a fun evening…

They sparred for a while longer, both knowing how the evening would end, but enjoying the game nonetheless. Another round of drinks had passed the table before Belle stood and tossed him an inviting glance. Samuel threw some bills on the smooth surface and followed her up the stairs.

He studied her through cool eyes as she sashayed across her room to the small bar to pour them one more glass of whiskey. Samuel took the opportunity to reach behind him and coughed into his hand to hide the sound of the lock's telltale click. Crossing to a chair then, he waited quietly until Belle returned to sit on his knee and hold up her glass to meet his.

"To us," she said with a brief arch of her eyebrows.

His fiery gaze never left hers. "To us."

Samuel took a sip, then set the glass on the table beside him. Pulling her closer, his moist lips devoured her mouth. The kiss deepened as his free hand increased the pressure on the back of her head.

She pushed him away a moment later with a nervous laugh. "Whoa there, Sam. We've got all night."

"I don't want to wait all night. You've been flirting with me for the past hour, and I'm ready for you now."

Belle's heart pounded in her chest. It was exciting to know she could still have that effect on a man.

"I want you to strip for me."

She stood, placed a hand on her hip and looked down at him with a flirtatious smile. "I know we've agreed on a price already, but it'll cost you more for the show."

Samuel's steely gaze never wavered as he dug inside his breast pocket and flung some bills on the table beside him—an amount that was three times the sum they had agreed upon earlier.

"Take off your clothes, Belle. I'm all paid up."

He watched through flaming eyes as she slowly unbuttoned the front of her gown and slipped out of the sleeves, then loosened the waist and let the dress fall around her ankles to reveal a short camisole. His eyebrows lifted in surprise when she raised a slender foot and placed it between his thighs. She proceeded to unsnap the garters attached to her silk stocking, then rolled the sock sensuously down her thigh and calf. Removing the silken hose, she repeated the same procedure with her other leg.

Samuel's breath came in small pants as Belle wiggled out of the camisole and stood naked before him. An inviting smile touched her lips.

"Was that worth the extra money, Sam?"

"I'm trying to decide. How would you like to partake in a little fantasy?"

"That depends on what your fantasy is." Caught up in the moment, Belle failed to read the subtle change in his expression.

"I want you on the floor—on your hands and knees."

The smile left her face in an instant when his eyes took on a devilish glaze. "Look, Sam, I don't go for anything out of the ordinary. If you'd like to go to the bed, we can have some fun there, but the floor, and on my knees, is not an option. I don't run that kind of place."

His features hardened with rage. Bounding from the chair, he snatched her wrist. "I don't give a shit what kind of place you run. You see that money on the table? I paid for you fair and square—now I expect to get my money's worth."

"You're hurting me!" She struggled against his steely grasp, then her own words became as acidic as his. "I think you had better leave and take your money with you."

"Well now, Belle, I don't think you're in any position to be making demands, do you?" His glittering eyes swept the length of her nude body.

She wrenched her arm free of his hold and lunged for the door, realizing too late that he had locked it behind him. Her frantic fingers fought with the latch as Samuel grabbed her from behind. She spun away from him, but there was no place to run. Grabbing a nearby lamp, she swung it with ferocious intent, but Samuel threw up an arm, knocked the object aside and shoved her roughly against the fabric-covered wall. He hauled back his fist and grazed her chin just hard enough to make her more pliable in his arms.

Belle's knees buckled as he dragged her back across the room. His crazed eyes searched wildly for something and finally settled on a silken scarf. He pulled a hanky from the dresser drawer next and stuffed it in her mouth, then tied the scarf around her face to keep it in place.

"You bitches are all alike. You flaunt your bodies in front of us until we can't stand it anymore, then you tell us no. Well, you little slut, that's not going to happen tonight." He laughed into Belle's white face. When he saw the fear in her wide eyes, he slapped her once more. The snap of her head as it whipped to one side excited him further.

Pulling her arms up tight behind her, Samuel shoved her toward the bar, bent her body forward and slammed her face down onto the hard surface. Her muffled whimper was music to his ears as he loosened the front of his pants with his free hand and forced himself into her warmth.

"How do you like it this way, bitch? I paid you for this, and now I'm getting my money's worth. See how it works?" Samuel increased the pressure on her head. Her muted sobs released tears onto the bar. The power of his thrusts increased, until he felt himself finally reach a pinnacle.

Belle slid limply to the floor when he stepped back, pulled his pants together at the waist and reached for his hat. He nudged her with the toe of his boot, then stared down into her pale face.

"Thanks for the good time, Belle. Maybe I'll come back some time and we can do it again." He scooped up the pile of money on the table and returned it to his pocket before sauntering to the door.

Belle heard the latch click shut, but was unable to find the strength to run after him and have one of her employees stop his retreat. Instead, she just lay on the floor with tears flowing down her cheeks.

Fifteen minutes passed before she eased her bruised body to a sitting position and picked at the knot in the scarf. Spitting out the hanky, her gaze fell to the blood that was mixed in with her saliva. She reached for her dressing gown and covered her body before using the chair as support to help her stand. Her trembling hand reached for the still full whiskey glass. She sipped, then spit into a bowl. Tears tumbled down her cheeks again as she gasped for air.

He said his name was Sam. She needed to get to Cole. She needed to tell him that the devil from his sister-in-law's past was back.

* * * * *

Cole stood in the paddock, brushing Janie's little pinto. His niece had extracted a promise earlier that he would tend to the animal, then she'd left with Clancey to spend the day at Carrie and Steve's clinic.

When the sound of a carriage rolling up the drive reached his ears, he shouldered the pony out of the way, walked to the fence, squinted into the sun and watched as the buggy pulled to a stop at the end of the wooden walkway that led to the house. His eyes narrowed in recognition.

"What the hell is she doing here?" he mumbled his thoughts aloud, hooked the brush on the fence and hurried toward the house.

Belle was halfway up the sidewalk before she heard Cole call out her name. She waited for him to approach, but couldn't meet his gaze. Now that she was there, she wasn't so sure it was the right thing to do. She'd tell him about Samuel Fontaine, and then climb into the carriage for the long trip back to Duluth.

Cole acknowledged the driver, rounded the buggy and approached her with a guarded look stamped on his face.

"Belle, what are you doing here?"

She lifted her face.

Shock bolted through him when he saw her bruised and swollen jaw. "My God, what happened to you?"

She placed a hand on his arm and found the words she'd practiced all the way to the ranch. "Cole...I had a run-in with a customer last night. It wasn't until he'd left that I realized there's a very good possibility he was this Samuel Fontaine you warned me about."

He raised her chin with his gloved hand and examined her bruises again. Anger ballooned in his chest. "Jesus Christ, Belle, did he do this to you? I told you, honey, to watch for him and not let him near any of you."

Her normally carefree attitude was absent when she searched the eyes of the gentle man before her. "I know you did, but the man who was at the house last night was clean shaven and elegantly dressed. He didn't look anything like a hunted man on the run! You said he had blond hair—and this man did. He said to call him Sam. He's sick, Cole, just like you said he was. He came up to my room, and..." She held her breath for a moment, then the rest tumbled out. "You know what I do for a living, Cole, but he hit me, and then he...he raped me. You believe me, don't you? There's a difference, Cole! This man is evil!" Her voice rose as she struggled for the words to explain what happened.

Cole pulled her into his protective embrace, rubbed her back in soothing circles and kissed the soft tuft of hair that rested against his cheek. "Shhh, Belle. It's okay. Of course I believe you."

Her words were little more than muffled tones against his chest as she continued. "I know I shouldn't have come here, but I couldn't send anyone else to tell you. I needed to know you believe me. I'm sure it was him. I needed to warn you, so he can't hurt anyone else."

"Cole? Is everything all right?"

Cole jumped at the sound of Emma's voice, raised his eyes and discovered her standing at the top of the porch steps. His arms fell from Belle's waist in guilty reaction.

How was he going to introduce the two women? They came from completely different worlds and were unfortunate enough to be connected by a monster that had hurt them both.

"Uh…Emma, this is Belle Andrews from Duluth. She's been a…friend of mine for a long time. Belle, this is my sister-in-law, Emma."

Belle's startled gaze rested on the beautiful woman before her, one who was heavy with child. She could see now why the Wilkins men thought so highly of her. She was soft-spoken and one of the loveliest creatures Belle had ever encountered.

"Hello, Mrs. Wilkins. It's nice to finally meet you. I've heard a lot of good things about you." She glanced sidelong at Cole, at a loss for words. She never should have come to the ranch.

"It's nice to meet you, Miss Andrews, is it? If you've come all the way from Duluth, I must apologize for Cole not asking you in." Emma stepped back and indicated the front door. "Please, do come in, where the two of you can conduct your business in comfort."

Belle blanched at the invitation. If anyone ever found out that Emma was entertaining one of the local whores, she would never live it down. Before Cole could utter a response, she spoke up quickly.

"Thank you very much for the invitation, Mrs. Wilkins—"

"Please, call me Emma."

"Emma... I have to return to Duluth and really must be on my way."

"Nonsense. May I call you Belle?" Emma watched as the other woman nodded hesitantly. "I would never forgive myself if I allowed you to climb back in that carriage and make the long trip to Duluth without giving you some sort of refreshment."

Belle decided to put an end to both her and Cole's suffering, despite the fact that she felt drawn to the young woman on the steps. Belle's background created a closed door that would never be open to her.

"Emma, I really don't think you understand. My line of...work...does not permit me to socialize with a proper lady like yourself."

A gentle smile touched Emma's lips as she glanced down at the flustered woman. "I understand perfectly, Belle, what your *line of work* is. It's written boldly across the side of your carriage." Emma indicated the name—Belle's Pleasure Palace—written across the door of the buggy in embossed lettering. She'd passed the establishment more than once while in the city. "You're Cole's friend and that's good enough for me. Now, please come in and rest before you begin your long journey back to Duluth."

Emma turned, walked into the house and waited just inside the door as Cole took Belle's arm and hesitantly led her up the stairs. When they were seated in the library, Emma poured the astounded woman a cup of tea, then settled herself comfortably in the big chair across from her and Cole.

"Excuse me for lumbering around, Belle. I don't seem to be moving as fast as I used to." She rolled her eyes suddenly at her own boldness. "And here I am forcing my company on the two of you without even asking if you would like to be alone."

Belle perched uncomfortably on the edge of the sofa. "This is your home, Mrs. Wilkins. And I have already discussed my business with Cole."

"Do you mind my asking why you would make the trip all the way up here?" Emma saw the pair exchange a quick glance. "I'm sorry to be so blunt, but I have an uncanny feeling it's not good."

Cole left Belle's side and hunkered down before Emma. He took her hands gently in his. "Belle came to warn us about something, honey. She's certain that Samuel Fontaine was in her establishment last night."

Emma's face paled before his eyes. Her hands trembled violently in his.

"Tyler, Trevor and I always thought he might come back. Now that we've been warned, we'll be on guard until he's caught."

Emma swallowed convulsively, squeezed Cole's hand and lifted her frightened gaze to Belle's. "Did he do that to your face?"

Belle nodded.

Emma's chin quivered when she turned back to Cole. "He's come back for me. I know it! We can't let him on the ranch!" Her entire body trembled now with fear.

"It's okay, Emma. We've never let our guard down. Either Tyler, Trevor, or I have always been here with you."

The truth of his statement filtered through the shock waves that assailed her mind. Since Samuel's assault, one of the men was always around—and Emma hadn't realized it until now.

"We'll tell Tyler and Trevor as soon as they get home, Em. We'll watch for him. We won't let him hurt you again."

Belle sat quietly by, horrified by what Samuel must have put this woman through. Tyler's wife physically shook with fear.

Emma's eyes found Belle's. They'd both suffered at the hands of an evil man. As much as she wanted Cole to remain by her side until Tyler came home, her need to speak privately with Belle outweighed her fear. "Could you leave Belle and me alone for a short while?"

Cole stood. "I'll be right outside on the porch. If you need anything, just holler, okay?"

Emma smiled her shaky gratitude as Cole left the room quietly. The door clicked shut behind him.

"Mrs… Emma…" Belle stumbled with her words. "I'm sorry to put you in this position. If word gets out that you invited me into your home, I guarantee you'll be shunned by polite society."

"That doesn't bother me in the least, Belle."

The older woman sat forward and met Emma's gaze directly. "I want you to know something. There are those who would classify me as a *fallen woman*, but I only do what I have to in order to survive. Last night, it wasn't like that. Samuel Fontaine forced himself on me crudely."

"I know he did, Belle. Samuel takes whatever he wants."

"Do you mean you actually believe me?" The tone of Belle's voice made it obvious that she was stunned by Emma's trust.

Emma swallowed to wet her suddenly parched throat and struggled to shake off the feeling of descending doom. "I know what he's capable of."

Belle stared back in surprise. "Not very many women in your position would be so understanding."

Emma shrugged. "This is a harsh part of the country for anybody to live in, let alone a woman all by herself. As I see it, Belle, the only difference between you and me is that I get a home and security for my favors. You get cold, hard cash. I'm just the luckier of the two of us, is all. I have a man who loves me probably more than I'll ever realize. You have your favorites. I suspect Cole must number high on that list."

Belle ducked her head, surprised at the heat that spread across her cheeks. She couldn't believe that she was sitting in a fancy home, conversing with a fine lady about such a subject. She finally lifted her blue eyes. "Cole is special, but I know nothing could ever come of it even though I've known him for quite some time." She lifted her shoulders in a small shrug. "It's what I do for a living." Her gaze encompassed the room in one sweeping glance, wondering if she could ever have anything close to what she surveyed. "Since my encounter last night, the thought of closing the business and just leaving town sounds very appealing. I have a fair amount of money at my disposal. Maybe I could start a new life where no one knows my past," she stated her thoughts aloud.

At the moment, the idea sounded good to Emma, too. She would like nothing more than to just pack up Tyler and Janie and run away. The thought of Samuel lurking somewhere nearby filled her heart with fear.

Belle studied the other woman surreptitiously. She hesitated, then spoke softly. "Was it awful for you?"

Emma knew exactly what she meant. She rose from the chair slowly, unconsciously rubbed her lower back and crossed to the window. "Tyler's sister once told me that what I went through was something no woman should ever have to experience. To be so degraded is almost unfathomable." She hesitated, and then made the decision to bare her soul. "I have never told anybody this, but that first week after it happened, I wanted to die. I could not convince myself I had anything to live for. I had lost my baby and was sure my husband would never want me again. The thought of everyone knowing how soiled I'd become was humiliating. I think I would have found a way to end it all if it hadn't been for this family. It took them a while, but they discovered a way to help me heal."

Emma closed her eyes as the memory of that awful day invaded her thoughts. "Samuel took something from me that he had no right to take—but Tyler gave it back tenfold. I decided then that I would not let that monster rule my life or the lives of the people who love me." She turned a frightened gaze in Belle's direction. "I have fought every day to regain my former life. Now? Knowing Samuel is close, I'm not so sure I'm strong enough to withstand another encounter. I'm frightened and numb at the same time."

Belle pushed herself up from the sofa and crossed to Emma. She reached out a tentative hand and placed it on her arm. "You can do it, Emma. Don't let that evil devil take away what you've worked so hard to regain. You may not believe me, because we've hardly known each other an hour, but I admire you. It takes one helluva strong lady to rise above what Samuel did to you."

"But it's always there, Belle. The possibility that he might come back was always lurking in the back of my mind."

"Well, you've been warned. Do you honestly think these Wilkins men will let him get anywhere near you? You've got their brute power and your own strength of character to see you through." She let out a wry laugh. "How many women in your position would welcome their brother-in-law's *mistress of the evening* into their home, just because they felt it would be unmannerly not to? Emma, you're the first real lady to ever treat me with any amount of dignity. I wasn't so sure earlier that I did the right thing by coming here, but I'm glad now that I did. If I hadn't, I would've never met you."

"You're welcome on this ranch anytime you want to visit, Belle."

"I know that now, but it'll never happen again. Cole needs to find a woman he can share a life with, someone without a past that will haunt him the rest of his life. I care for him too much to ever let that happen."

Emma knew she spoke the truth, no matter how hard it was to understand.

Belle reached out a gloved hand. "Mrs. Wilkins, it's been an honor meeting you. The hour is getting late though, and I need to be on my way. You stay strong. Your husband will know shortly about Samuel's return. He'll keep you safe."

Emma ignored the outstretched hand. Instead, she hugged Belle close and wondered if this would be the last time their paths would cross. "Do what you said, Belle," she whispered fervently. "Leave the city. Don't ever put yourself in the position to be hurt again like you were last night."

"I'll think about it. Goodbye, Emma. Trust in yourself and the life you have. You've earned it." Belle squeezed her hand and left the room.

Emma watched through the window as Cole handed her up into the carriage after a farewell embrace. The front door opened and closed a moment later. Emma listened to Cole's footsteps grow louder as he approached the library.

"Em? Are you all right?"

"I don't know, Cole." She turned from the window.

His heart leapt at the sickly pallor of her face and the fear in her eyes.

"What if he comes back for me? I know that's what he's planning." She covered her face with her hands, unable to control the burgeoning fear any longer.

Cole bolted across the room and pulled her against his chest just as a hoarse sob burst forth.

"He's coming for me!"

He held her gently, knowing she relived the awful experience in her mind. "We'll keep you safe, Em. Everything will be fine."

He held her in his protective embrace until Tyler discovered them a few minutes later. His contented expression floundered when he saw the two of them.

"Cole? Emma? What's happened?"

Emma ran into her husband's outstretched arms. "He's back, Tyler!" She wrapped her arms around his waist and clung to him in desperation.

"Who's back?" Tyler had already answered the question in his own mind though. He could almost smell his wife's fear. His eyes moved to Cole's for confirmation.

"Belle just left. She came here to tell me that a man fitting Samuel's description showed up at her place last night. He roughed her up and…forced her to have sex with him. She wanted us to be on the alert."

Tyler closed his eyes above his wife's head and quickly organized his thoughts. He'd known the possibility that Fontaine would return for either him or Emma was good, but now the threat was real. His mind raced with ways to protect her. Was Emma too far along in her pregnancy to send her away from the ranch? If so, they would have to be extra vigilant—and they would have to be prepared if Fontaine snuck onto the property.

He rubbed gentle circles against her back, then spoke firmly. "It's going to be all right, Em. You have to believe that we'll get him if he shows up here." He lifted her chin and met her watery gaze with a resolute expression. "I told you that I would never let him hurt you again."

"But how are you going to stop him if he's determined to hurt us? He's crazy, Tyler."

"I promised that I would keep you safe, honey, and I plan on keeping that promise. Let me work out the details. You just worry about keeping the baby and yourself healthy." His gaze moved back to his brother. "Cole, find Trevor and bring him back to the house. I left him down at the barn. I'm going to take Emma upstairs and see that she lays down for a while."

Cole sprinted from the room to do his brother's bidding.

* * * * *

Tyler tucked the blankets around Emma's trembling body, then sat beside her on the bed. "I want you to rest. We'll figure out the details. We've got a jump on him, Em. We know he's here and that gives us the advantage."

"You're going to need more than that, Tyler. He fooled us once—now he's had over a year to plan his revenge…"

He bounded off the bed and stalked across the room. "And I told you that I would keep you safe. He'll have to get through me, Cole and Trevor, and there is no way in hell that we're going to let him do that!" His voice lowered with an ominous certainty. "It's our turn now."

Emma scrambled from the bed and yanked on his arm firmly until he turned to look at her. "Promise me that you won't do anything foolish. Evening the score with him is not worth your life! Let the authorities deal with him." She tugged on his arm again. "Promise me!"

Tyler silently acknowledged her fear and admitted that she was right. Evening the score was not worth his life, but he would do whatever was necessary to save hers. No matter what it took, he wouldn't let Samuel near her. And if he said it aloud, she'd never calm.

Gathering her into his arms, he guided her back to the bed. "I won't do anything foolish, Em." He tucked the covers around her again. "You rest now. I've got to go talk to Cole and Trevor." He kissed her, then squeezed her hand. "If you need anything, I'll be right downstairs. I'm not going to leave the house."

After he left to find his brothers, Emma lay staring at the ceiling. She covered her swollen abdomen with both hands when the baby moved inside her. A feeling of doom had hung over her like a thundercloud since the day she announced she was pregnant. She had tried for all those months to shrug off the sense of foreboding, but now with Samuel Fontaine back in their world, everything was about to come crashing down around her.

She rolled onto her side and unconsciously curled up to protect the child within her. Her blank stare centered on the flames in the fireplace. Her mind chanted a single name—Samuel. The devil was coming for her.

*****

"I can't believe the son of a bitch has the nerve to show up in the area again!" Trevor paced the room like a caged animal, remembering only too well their last encounter with Samuel Fontaine. His guts rolled.

"I want every man on this ranch to carry a loaded gun with him at all times," Tyler stated. "We need to stay within eyesight of the house—and one of us needs to be within these four walls at all times. If he's going to make a move, it'll be soon."

"You couldn't get the two of us to leave now if you tried." Cole stood and walked to the liquor cabinet and splashed some whiskey into a glass. "We're going to get the bastard this time." He yearned for the opportunity to wrap his fingers around Fontaine's neck and choke the life out of him—and he wanted to do it slowly. He had two women to avenge now.

Tyler rubbed the back of his neck in agitation and heaved a weary sigh. "Dammit. Emma is too far along to move her somewhere safe. I thought about Carrie and Steve's, but too many people would know she was there."

"She wouldn't leave here anyway. Not without you." Trevor sank into a chair and met his older brother's gaze. "We've got to come up with another plan."

"I know she'll fight it, but what else can we do?" Tyler rubbed his forehead in frustration. "I guess the bottom line is that, actually, I feel better having her here. I don't want to trust her safety to just anybody. I know she'll be safe with the three of us—even if it is like hanging her out as bait." He started for the door. "I'm going to send Dougan to Carrie's with a message and ask her and Steve to keep Janie for a bit longer. She was supposed to come home tomorrow, but I'll feel better if we don't expose her to all this—plus I don't know what Samuel would do if he ever got his hands on her." Tyler's stomach churned with the mere thought as he paused in the doorway. He turned back to face his brothers. His determined eyes bore into them. "We have to make sure he doesn't get to Emma. No matter what it takes, we have to make sure."

* * * * *

The family tried to carry on as if everything was normal. They waited anxiously for the births of the new foals. Emma insisted on visiting the barn every morning to check on the pregnant Bonne. One of the men always accompanied her, yet still she couldn't resist the urge to continually look over her shoulder. Within days, her nerves were stretched taut and the strain started to show, not only on her face, but on the faces of everyone at the ranch. Mamie and Katy kept a rifle in the kitchen at all times, and Cole gave them each a small pistol to carry in their apron pockets when they were away from the house.

Janie continued to stay with Carrie and Steve, but, after four nights of sleeping in a strange bed, the little girl's imagination took over. She started having nightmares. Knowing that Janie was simply terrified about what was going on at home, Emma insisted that she be returned to them.

"I don't care, Tyler!" She paced before him as fast as her pregnant body would allow.

He sat on the bed and let her rant.

"Do you think it's any healthier for her to be experiencing the terror she feels every night? I want her home, and I want our lives to get back to normal! I'm sick of feeling the hair stand up on the back of my neck every time I step out onto the porch. I'm sick of looking over my shoulder every other step to make sure he's not there! And I'm sick of letting that bastard rule my every waking moment!"

"Emma, calm down," Tyler's voice was composed, almost patronizing. "I still feel it's for the best that Janie stay away for now.

If Samuel does show up, I don't want to have to worry about her, too."

"So, what are we going to do?" Emma shot out. "Live in fear for the rest of our lives and deprive Janie of the right to live in her own home?" She moved to sit beside him on the bed and laid her hand over his balled fist. "You've got every man on this ranch alerted and guns all over the place. What do we do if a month goes by and nothing happens? We don't even know for certain if it was Samuel at Belle's place. Are you going to exile your daughter forever?"

Tyler released a sigh that echoed his doubt. "All right. I'll send a message to Carrie's and have them bring her home." He cupped her face with his palms and pressed a kiss to her lips. "I'm just trying to be careful, honey. We know what Samuel's capable of, and I'm just trying to keep the two of you safe."

She leaned her head wearily against his shoulder. "I know, Tyler. I'm sorry for yelling at you, but I'm at my wits end. I just want this whole thing to end." She tipped her head to press a kiss against his neck. "Thank you for bringing Janie home. We'll watch her like hawks. I promise."

Resting his chin on top of her head, it hit him how much he loved her. Emma was so fragile. In less than a month's time, he would be a father again. He sighed deeply. "I'll talk to Cole and Trevor about Janie coming home."

* * * * *

Samuel stared at his reflection in the hotel room mirror and fingered the jagged scar that ran down his cheek. Even after more than a year, it was still painfully visible.

She did this to me. She marked me for life...

He took a pull from the neck of a whiskey bottle, then suddenly swung it into the mirror and watched as shards of glass exploded across the top of the dresser. The spilled liquid wound a lazy course through the pieces of broken glass until it reached the edge of the chest of drawers and dripped to the floor.

That's how I'll kill you, Emma. Slowly. Your life will fade away like drops from a spilled whiskey bottle. And, once your cowboy becomes aware of what happened to his precious little bitch, I'll kill him, too.

He would move on then. He was tired of hiding out and only frequenting places where he wouldn't be recognized. He wanted his life back—the life of a powerful businessman—a life he deserved.

Strutting to the open bag on the bed, he ran his hand across the large wads of money inside. The only good thing about being stuck in Duluth was the fact that he'd hit a lucky streak. He was set to move on now without a care in the world.

He crossed to the window and pushed the curtain aside to peer at the bustling street below. It would be dark soon. He could leave the rented room again. In the morning, he would finalize his plans. He'd been watching the Wilkins ranch, living in the woods for a few days at a time, and then returning to the city to think. As far as he could see, he had only one problem. Tyler and the other men on the spread never left sight of the house and, during the infrequent times that Emma did exit the dwelling, one of them was always at her side.

She was pregnant again. *Very* pregnant.

This one wouldn't be born either.

He knew the layout of the ranch like the back of his hand. He knew Emma's daily routine even better. Still, frustration was beginning to mount. He could almost taste her sweet flesh on his lips and feel the stickiness of her blood on his hands. He'd have her one last time, and then he would make sure…

The curtain fluttered closed.

Patience…

Eventually, someone would make the fatal mistake of leaving her alone.

Chapter Twenty-Six

∞

Steven snapped his bag shut and grinned at his patient. "I hope you have everything ready for the baby. My guess is that you have only about two to three weeks left. How does that sound?"

Emma moved her legs over the edge of the bed with some difficulty, pushed herself upright with her arms and threw him a scornful look followed by a halfhearted smile. "I think it's going to be the longest two weeks of my life. I feel like I've been pregnant forever."

He chuckled as he took her arm and led her to one of the chairs before the fireplace. "You've done remarkably well. You should be proud of yourself." He gave her shoulder a quick squeeze. "I want to talk to you about something. Do you have a minute?"

She waved her arm at the expansive space around her. "I don't think I'm going anywhere. Lately, I haven't been allowed to do much of anything. I'm stuck in this house all the time."

Steven's face sobered into what Emma had come to call his "Dr. Steve" expression.

Her green eyes narrowed. "Is there something you're not telling me?"

"Everything's fine as far as the baby goes. It's your emotional state that has me a little concerned. You're nervous and edgy and snapping at the people who love you. I know the situation around here has been nerve-racking, but you've got to calm down. It's not good for the baby. Can't you see that Tyler is just trying to keep you safe? He loves you and keeping you so closeted is the only way he knows to assure that Samuel won't get to you."

She studied her hands where they lay clasped on top of her swollen abdomen. "So, he's been talking to you?"

"Of course he has. I can see the strain on both your faces every time I walk into the house. The two of you should be happy right now regardless of the Samuel issue. You'll be sharing the birth of your first child soon, and it's going to be a momentous occasion for this entire family. Give Tyler a little leeway — along with Trevor and Cole. They're just trying to protect you. Accept their strategy and concern in this matter. It's their way of controlling the situation."

Emma pinched the bridge of her nose and closed her eyes as she considered Steve's words. With a heavy sigh, she finally tipped her head back. "How come whenever you tell me something, Steven, it makes so much sense?"

"Because I'm always right." He grinned, then patted her knee and helped her stand. "Come on, I'm sure they're all waiting downstairs for supper. Since Carrie and I got married, I miss Mamie's good home cooking. I can't wait to eat!"

Emma actually laughed — the first real laugh since Samuel Fontaine resurfaced. "You'd better not let Carrie hear you say that," she exclaimed, then thinking of the young couple's own announcement a few months earlier, she squeezed his hand. "When she reaches the end of her pregnancy, I hope you'll be as understanding with her as you have been with me. Oh, Mamie may have cooked the meal, but you won't be able to thank her. She and Katy are finishing a quilt for the baby at Katy's cabin."

"Well, my dear, you'll just have to pass on my sentiments."

They walked down the steps together to find Tyler waiting at the bottom with a strained smile on his face. Emma took his hand and let Steve continue alone to the dining room.

"Can I talk to you for a minute before we go in?"

He nodded, and she pulled him down to sit on a small bench near the front door.

"I want to apologize for how I've been acting lately. Steven pointed out a few things that I've lost sight of."

"No apologies are necessary." He reached up to caress her soft cheek. "If anyone should be saying they're sorry, it's me. I've had you under house arrest for the last week, but it's only because I love you so much. You know that, don't you?"

"Of course I do. I'm not going to fight you or your brothers anymore. You don't have to stay by my side every minute, because I promise to follow the rules you've laid down. Does that make you feel better?"

He lifted her chin with a finger so she could receive his kiss. "Yes, it does."

* * * * *

"Well, I don't know about anyone else, but I can't wait for my new niece or nephew to be born!" Trevor pushed his chair away from the dinner table and vigorously rubbed his hands together. "It's going to be great having a baby around again."

"You'd think *you* were the proud father!" Cole shook his head with a wry grin.

"Hell, I *feel* like an expectant father. Between Emma and Carrie and the mares foaling any day, it's going to be a busy place."

The two pregnant women exchanged astounded glances, and Carrie spoke up immediately.

"You can say anything you want about our pregnancies, Trevor, but, please, not in the same breath with the horses! You make Emma and me sound like a couple of brood mares."

Trevor's eyes widened in stunned realization of what he'd just uttered. His mouth opened, but no words were forthcoming. Surprisingly, his cheeks tinged scarlet. The group burst into laughter.

Clancey entered the dining room through the kitchen entrance a second later with his hat in his hands and an excited look on his face. "Excuse me for interrupting you, folks. I thought you'd want to know that Bonne has been laboring hard for nigh on to an hour now. If you all want to witness the birth of the first Lakota Pines riding horse, you'd better come quick. There's a good possibility that the foal will be here before the sun sets."

Instant confusion reigned as everyone rose from the table at once. The events of the past year were finally coming to fruition. Their new future was about to begin.

Emma squeezed his hand. "You hurry on down to the barn. I'm sure Carrie wouldn't mind tagging along with me at a much slower pace."

"No way, Emma. I'll wait for you. After all, it's your horse that's about to foal." Tyler's tone was resolute.

"Oh, don't be silly. You and your brothers have dreamt about this moment your entire life. If any of you miss the birth, I'll feel awful. Go now. I'll catch up shortly. Besides, I left my shawl in the living room. It's a little chilly out there." Her husband remained rooted to the spot. Emma placed one hand on her hip and pointed at the door with the other. "Tyler, go! We'll be fine."

"Absolutely not. I'll walk with you."

"You mean you'll waddle with me. Go!"

The doubtful dip of his eyebrows finally gave way to a wide grin. "Okay, but if you're not there in five minutes, I'm gonna come looking for you." He dropped a quick peck on her cheek, hesitated for a second more, then left to follow the other men through the kitchen door.

Emma laughed as she turned to Carrie. "He looks as excited as he did the day I told him we were going to have a baby." She reached for her stepdaughter's hand. "Come on, Janie. Grab your coat and we'll be on our way."

They walked into the living room. Emma picked up her woolen shawl where it lay over the back of a chair.

Janie balked at the front door. "I've gotta get Whizzer! Mamie made me put him in my room before supper. Please, Emma, will you wait? He wants to see the new baby horse, too!"

"All right, hurry up, honey. We'll wait on the porch. Run fast now. We don't want to miss anything." Emma smiled after the little girl as she raced to the second floor, then she and Carrie headed for the front entrance.

Emma passed through the doorway first. A shriek left her throat when a hand snaked out, grabbed her arm and jerked her to the left of the entrance. Carrie raced through the open door, her eyes wide with alarm.

"Run, Carrie!" Emma screamed.

Her sister-in-law kept coming and swung ferociously at the man who held Emma in an iron grip—a man she knew must be Samuel Fontaine. His animalistic growl preceded the lunge that sent Emma sprawling to the porch. A second later, his clenched fist connected with Carrie's jaw. She spun backwards and sank unconscious to the planking.

Emma lumbered to her feet and stumbled toward the steps, then cried out in pain when Samuel twisted his fingers in her hair. Yanking her back against his body, he wrapped one arm around her waist just above her bulging abdomen and used his free hand to cover her mouth and muffle her screams.

Silently, he dragged her to the edge of the porch. His darting gaze searched the beginning shadows of twilight for any sign that her shrieks had alerted someone to his presence. Seeing no one, he hauled her down the side steps and in the direction of the thick forest that skirted the yard.

Emma stumbled along with him and all the while fought to remove the clammy hand from her mouth.

"Stop it, bitch!" Samuel hissed.

Emma reached back and clawed at his face. Samuel changed her position, forced her flailing arms to her sides and tightened his grip around her waist with a jerk. "I said *stop it*!"

Her muffled screams met his ears as he squeezed his hand tighter across her mouth. He was almost to the trees. Ten more feet and they would be out of sight.

* * * * *

Janie cracked open the door to her room, then paused when a scream pierced the air. Whizzer whined loudly on the other side, stuck his snout into the opening and scratched furiously at the floor. She pushed at the dog's head, attempting to shove him back into her room as another scream filtered up from downstairs.

"Whizzer, *stay*! Mamie will take her broom to you if you're running around and in the way. Emma's having her baby!" The dog's superior weight was too much for the little girl and, once again, he nudged his nose into the space between the door and the jamb. "*Whizzer! No!*"

The dog gave one last, tremendous shove. Janie landed on her backside as he bounded into the hallway and headed down the steps.

She raced after him, almost tripping over her own feet in her haste. "Whizzer, come back!" She chased the dog across the living room and through the open doorway, then stopped dead when she saw her Aunt Carrie sprawled on the porch.

"Carrie! Carrie!" Janie fell to her knees and shook her aunt's unconscious body. "Where's Emma, Auntie Carrie?" Tears of fright welled in the corners of her eyes, then streamed down her cheeks.

The dog sniffed at the inert woman and, with his nose still to the ground, started across the length of the porch. Janie jumped up to follow him. She grabbed at the loose skin on the animal's neck, struggling to hold him back—until her frantic gaze settled on the blond-haired man who dragged Emma into the thick brush at the edge of the yard.

"Whizzer! I've got to get Daddy to help Emma!"

Janie whirled when she heard Carrie's moan as her aunt struggled to sit up. She raced back and fell to her knees.

"Auntie Carrie, I'm scared! A man took Emma into the woods!"

Carrie swayed with the dizziness that assailed her. Her face paled to a sickly pallor. Sagging onto her side again, she reached out with a shaky hand to grab Janie's arm and pull her close. "Janie...run to the barn. Tell...get your dad...tell him it's Samuel! Run!"

Janie leapt up and raced from the porch.

* * * * *

The five men gathered around the laboring horse where she lay on her side in a huge stall. Tyler's dark head snapped up when he heard Janie's frantic screams.

"What the hell—" He tripped over Trevor's leg in his frenzied attempt to get around him and out of the stall, then met his daughter as she tore through the open doors with the yapping dog at her heels. "Janie!"

The terrified little girl flew into his arms. Fear curled in Tyler's belly. He held her clinging body away from his until he was able to see into her face. "Janie! Look at me—tell me what's wrong!"

"It's Auntie Carrie and Emma!" she panted between sobs. "Auntie Carrie said to run get you! She's hurt! She said to tell you...Samuel." Janie clutched at her father's shirtsleeves. "A man took Emma in the woods! Auntie Carrie is laying on the porch!"

Tyler took off at a dead run for the house, his brain registering the sound of boots pounding the dirt behind him. He leapt up onto the porch, raced to his sister and sank to the planking beside her. "Carrie! Jesus Christ, where is she? Are you hurt?"

"Tyler, go! I'll be all right." A sob caught in her throat. "I don't know where he took her, but you can't let him get away!"

"Tyler!" Cole bounded onto the porch. "Janie said he took her into the woods out front! Take the dog. Maybe he'll pick up their trail. We've got about a half an hour before we won't be able to see our hands in front of our faces. We'll get guns and be right behind you!"

Tyler scrambled to his feet, dashed to the edge of the porch and leapt into the growing darkness. In a heartbeat, he was racing toward the treeline. Whizzer raced beside him. "Find Emma! Go boy!" He chanced a quick glance over his shoulder to see Trevor following close on his heels, then crashed through the brush as he tried to keep up with the dog.

* * * * *

Tree branches whipped at Emma's face and arms as Samuel dragged her ever deeper into the woods. She was helpless now, with her arms pinned to her body. Terror pounded into her brain.

It was happening again, but Emma knew beyond a doubt that she wouldn't wake up in the master bedroom this time. This would be her last night on Earth. The eerie sensation she couldn't shake all these months came at her full force now.

They entered a clearing, and Samuel shoved her forward with vicious intent. Emma flung her arms out in an attempt to break the pitching fall. Her hands collided with the pine needle-covered ground. She rolled onto her side, then heaved her ungainly body up again. She hadn't taken two steps when Samuel's arms encircled her burgeoning waist. Hurling her to the ground once more, he rolled her onto her back and dropped spread-eagled across her thighs to pin her body to the earth. A sweaty hand clamped over panicked shrieks. A knife materialized from inside his boot a second later, and he held it only inches from her face.

"Shut up or I'll cut you."

Emma blinked away panic born tears and stared up at him through wide eyes as her heart thundered in her chest. She let her arms fall back to the hard ground, then slowly nodded her head in assent—and never took her eyes from the gleaming blade. A breathless moment passed before Samuel pulled his hand from her mouth, leaving it in close proximity in case she screamed.

"You know this is your last day on Earth, don't you?"

Emma squeezed her eyes shut and stubbornly refused to answer.

"It's over, Emma. I finally have the upper hand," he gritted out. "All those years of you taking the spotlight in Jacob's eyes are done. No matter what you say, I know it's your fault that I lost everything I once held dear. The last year of my life has been hell. It's time you pay. And when I'm through with you, I'm going to kill your husband."

Her eyes flew open. "He's done nothing! Kill me if you feel you must, but let him live. Please!"

"The faithful wife right up until the end, aren't you? Your pleas don't mean shit to me. Do you think I want that bastard hunting me for the rest of my life?"

"Please, Samuel, don't do this! I beg of you!"

"Now, this is a real tender scene, don't you think, Emma? Here you are, pleading for his life and not even worrying about your own welfare or that of your child." He chuckled softly. "I've waited so long for this day."

He jammed the knife into the ground beside her head with a quick jab. His laugh deepened when he saw the growing terror in her widening eyes as his hands encircled her neck. "You'll go slowly. I want you to suffer as I have this past year—breath by agonizing breath. My only regret is that I don't have the time to screw you again." He lowered his head to press a fetid kiss to her lips.

Emma struggled against him. The pressure on her throat increased. She fought for one last breath—enough for one more scream—before his torturous fingers slowly squeezed the air from her body. She was aware of Samuel's weight on her legs and, as black spots danced before her eyes, she heard a wolf's mournful cry amidst a dog's angry growl.

Suddenly, the burden was lifted from her body. She gasped for air. Her eyes widened first in relief, then in horror when she witnessed Tyler fling his body onto Samuel's, raise his fist and smash it into the other man's face.

Tyler's teeth clenched as he hissed out an oath. "You son of a bitch…"

His fist slammed into Samuel's jaw again as Emma crawled out of the way. She watched with shock-filled eyes as her husband pummeled the man who had caused them both so much pain and cringed when the sound of crunching bones flooded her dazed senses, unsure if the noise came from Samuel's face or Tyler's hand.

Another scream left her lips when her attacker wedged his knee between them and pushed Tyler up and away. Both men scrambled to their feet, their chests heaving as they eyed each other murderously across the small clearing. Blood poured from Samuel's broken nose.

Circling his opponent slowly, he spit another red stream from his mouth just before an insane smile touched his lips. "I'm impressed, Wilkins, but your…interference served only to make me change my plans. Now, I'll just have to kill you first and take care of your whore later," he taunted. "Not that this new plan doesn't have its advantages. With you out of the way, I'll have time to screw the shit out of your wife again before I kill her..."

Tyler charged forward and rammed the unsuspecting Samuel in the abdomen with his shoulder. The force of his rage sent both men tumbling to the ground again. Tyler delivered blow after blow into Samuel's writhing body. Bones crunched, and still it wasn't enough. He squared his fist, pulled the other man up by his shirt, beat him back to the ground, then started the process over again.

Emma's sobs finally filtered through the red haze of fury that clouded his brain—just as he pulled Samuel upright again and drew his fist back for the deathblow.

"Tyler! Stop!" she choked out. "You'll kill him!"

Her frantic words sobered him like a blast of cold air. His bloodied hand froze in midair. He turned his head and, for the first time, saw Trevor holding his wife's struggling body in an attempt to keep her from a headlong flight in his direction.

"Let it go, Ty," his brother murmured. "Let the authorities hang him."

"Tyler, please!" Emma sobbed. "Having his blood on your hands isn't worth it. It's over... Please, you have to stop."

Tyler's chest rose and fell with labored breaths. His heart pumped madly. He stared down at the limp and barely conscious man beneath him and, still, he wanted to kill him. He wanted to do it for Emma and for all the pain Samuel had caused her. He wanted to kill him for all the agony she'd suffered after the rape—and he wanted to kill him to avenge her scarred heart.

Instead, Tyler released Samuel's shirt and watched through lifeless eyes as the man's drooping body crumpled to the ground. He hung his head and listened to the breeze rustle through the treetops. It was over.

Rolling from Samuel's body, he staggered toward his wife.

Trevor let her go, then ran a shaky hand through his hair before he dropped his chin to his chest in relief.

Tears streamed down Emma's cheeks as Tyler pulled her into the safety of his embrace.

"Emma..." he whispered against her hair. "I didn't think I'd find you in time."

She ran trembling fingers over his bruised face. "But you did. You found me, and it's finally over."

His forehead sagged against hers, and he breathed in the scent of the woman he loved more than life itself. Emma's eyes fluttered shut as she pulled his head down into the hollow of her neck and kissed his hair.

Her eyes fluttered open a moment later and instantly widened in horror. Samuel lay on his side now and with a small derringer pointed at Tyler's back. In the space of a split second, she screamed as a shot rang out in the clearing and braced herself, thinking Tyler's weight would fall forward. Instead, Samuel Fontaine's body pitched backward to the ground.

Tyler spun to see Cole standing at the edge of the clearing.

His brother lowered a smoking rifle from his shoulder. Never taking his eyes from Samuel's body, Cole trudged forward and stared blankly at the man who had attempted to take so much from them all. Finally, he sank to one knee, pressed steady fingers to the other man's neck and assured himself that Samuel Fontaine was finally dead.

"I had a bead on him before he ever took the gun from his pocket." He rose slowly and turned to meet Emma's eyes. "I wasn't going to let him walk away again, Em. He just made it easier for me to pull the trigger. He tried to kill both of you. For that, he lost his right to be judged in a court of law."

He met Tyler's gaze. The two men came together in a fierce embrace.

"Tyler..."

He turned at the peculiar timbre of Emma's voice, then caught her when she fell against him.

"The baby..." She winced as she doubled over in pain. "Oh, my God...the baby—"

Tyler eased her into the cradle of his arms. "It's okay, honey. We'll get you to the house." He was already heading in that direction, with Cole and Trevor breaking a trail through the thick underbrush.

* * * * *

Tyler burst through the front door with Emma in his arms and hollered for Steven. The doctor sat beside Carrie, who lay on the sofa with a rag pressed to her swollen jaw. Dougan stood a short distance away with Katy and Mamie. He clutched a shotgun in his arms.

"Steve! The baby's coming!"

Tyler's features were ashen with panic beneath the bruises and cuts as Emma gritted her teeth with yet another contraction. He took the steps two at a time.

Steve garnered Katy's attention. "Get some linens and bring them up to the bedroom—I'll be right behind you." The housekeeper hurried to do his bidding as he sank to a knee beside his wife and took her hand gently in his. "Are you going to be all right?"

"I'm fine, Steve. You need to help Emma. Dougan is here with a rifle."

"He won't need it." Cole uttered the words from where he stood in the open doorway with his own gun in his hands. "It's over. I sent one of the men for the sheriff. Samuel Fontaine is dead." He stared at Steven with an unspoken message in his eyes.

Steven nodded his understanding, then squeezed Carrie's hand. "I'll be there as soon as I can." He raced for the steps.

* * * * *

Emma was in the middle of another contraction when the doctor entered the master bedroom. Tyler looked scared to death.

"Breathe, Emma. Don't fight it." Steven said as he crossed to the bed.

"Steven, it's awful…"

"Come on, Em, you can do it. Just remember what I told you." He watched as she took a deep breath, and then released it in a slow, measured exhale. "That's it, try and relax now. You need to rest between contractions."

Rolling up his sleeves, he motioned to Katy when she entered with the linens. They placed them beside Emma. He glanced at Tyler over his shoulder. "All right, Ty, I'm going to leave you in charge of getting her out of that dress and into a nightgown while I sterilize my instruments."

Tyler dragged his eyes from his wife's pale face, then grabbed his friend's arm and hauled him away from the bed. "Is she going to be all right?" he whispered. "Isn't it too early?"

"She's close enough. After the ordeal tonight, I would have been surprised if she hadn't gone into labor."

"You two can quit talking about me..." Emma reprimanded with a half smile that turned into a grimace when an even stronger contraction ripped through her body.

The two men were spurred into action. Steven left to run downstairs. Tyler pulled a dresser drawer open and rummaged through his wife's underclothes until he found a nightgown. Rushing to the bed, he helped her to sit up.

His hands stilled when his gaze met hers. "I thought I was going to lose you tonight."

Emma reached out to gently run her fingers over the cuts and bruises on his cheek. "But you didn't. It really is over, Tyler. He's finally out of our lives—" She clutched his hand with a groan as the pain started again.

They sat through it together and, when the contraction subsided, Tyler helped her remove her dress and put on the nightgown. He gently laid her back against the pillow and covered her with a light blanket. Suddenly, she stiffened.

"The baby's coming..." she panted out and squeezed her eyes shut.

He raced across the room and reached for the doorknob just as Steven entered the suite. "She wants to push already!"

Steven rushed to the bed and pulled the blanket up and over her knees.

Emma grimaced in pain. "I…need to…it's coming!"

Tyler stepped away from the bed.

Emma opened her eyes. "Tyler, don't go… I need you."

Steven was amazed at how fast the labor was progressing. No longer was he the friend. He was a doctor ready to bring a new life into the world—one that was coming fast. "Sit behind Emma, Ty. When I give you the word, help her sit up. Now, Emma, listen to me. You can't push until I tell you. When the time comes though, Tyler will help you sit up, then bear down like we talked about."

"I can't do it, Steven…it hurts too much…" Her eyes were wide with fear.

"Yes, you can." He watched her face tense again with the pain that spread from deep inside her body and culminated across the top of her abdomen. "Don't push yet, Emma."

"I have to…"

"Well, you can't. Breathe deep."

The contraction subsided, and so did another and another. Steven checked her progress. "All right, honey. On the next contraction, I want you to push."

The next pain gripped her almost immediately.

"Okay, Tyler, time to help us out."

Emma felt his hands on her shoulders. He pushed her up and braced her with his chest. "Come on, honey, you can do this!"

Emma took a deep breath, gritted her teeth and bore down.

"That's it, Emma, you're doing great." Steven's hands were busy beneath the blanket. "Keep pushing! Come on, push…push! Don't stop until you feel the contraction slow."

The pain finally diminished. Emma gasped for air as she fell back against Tyler's chest. Beads of perspiration dampened her forehead.

Tyler kissed the top of her head and murmured words of encouragement. "I'm so proud of you, Emma. Rest now, honey.

Breathe, like Steven said." He grabbed her flailing hand and held it firmly as another wave of pain took her again.

"Bear down, Emma! Now! Come on, honey, you're almost done." Steven could feel her straining as he held the baby's head in one hand and guided the emerging shoulder with the other. Suddenly, the child slipped into his hands. Emma fell back against Tyler again.

A lusty cry filled the room as Tyler hugged her from behind. "You did it, Em! Honey, you did it!"

She strained to see the infant and was greeted by the huge smile on Steven's face.

Both husband and wife waited breathlessly as he lifted the child into their line of vision. "Emma, Tyler, I would like you to meet your new son." He gazed at the tiny baby in his hands. "And, Master Wilkins, these two fine people are your parents."

The newborn wailed, his arms and legs as stiff as boards. Steve wrapped the new life gently in a swaddling cloth before handing him to his mother.

Emma fell instantly in love.

She cradled the baby close against her breast, then counted ten perfect fingers. She turned her head to look up at Tyler, her eyes filled with gentle wonder. "Isn't he beautiful?" she whispered softly in awe.

Tyler rested his chin against her shoulder and gazed at his son in amazement. "He sure is, honey. As beautiful as his mother."

"How would you like to introduce your new son to the rest of the family?" Steven asked Tyler. "I'm sure by all the commotion he's created, they know he's here. Emma and I still have a little work to do."

Tyler looked down into the small, wrinkled face as Emma handed the child to him and remembered how he'd felt when he'd held Janie for the first time.

I hope you're looking down, Sara. I hope you can see what I've accomplished. I did it...

The pieces had finally come together to create a whole. He'd found happiness and contentment again, things he'd once thought would forever be out of his reach, and he'd found them in the arms of the precious woman beside him. Tyler knew in his heart that Sara would approve.

The gentle touch of Emma's hand upon his arm brought Tyler's gaze to hers once more. Her green eyes sparkled with unshed tears. She smiled softly. "She knows, Tyler. I can feel it. Sara is happy for you, happy for us."

He was speechless. She understood him only too well, sometimes better than he did himself. She'd never given up on them—for that, he would be eternally grateful. Finally, he found his voice. "I'm sure Janie is waiting none too patiently to see her new brother. As soon as Steven is finished and comes down, I'll bring her back up to see you." His eyes glistened as he kissed her warm lips. "I love you, Mrs. Wilkins. Thank you for my son."

* * * * *

Late into the night, Emma lay in the bed with her son at her breast. Her gentle gaze rested on her husband where he lay stretched out beside her. Light from the fire flickered across his naked muscled shoulders.

Tyler glanced up. A small grin tugged at the corners of his mouth. "You're staring again—what's on your mind?"

A happy sigh left her as she reached for his hand. Bringing it to her lips, she pressed a kiss to his bruised knuckles. Her emerald eyes sparkled in the dim light.

"You've given me so much. I've spent most of my life following a completely different course—one that should never have met with yours. How is it that I was lucky enough to finally have our paths cross and find you standing there waiting for me?"

He reached out to caress the soft shoulder that peeked at him above the covers. She'd called him her shelter in the night, and he'd never forgotten those precious words. Many times he'd wondered if she even realized how her mere presence had healed him and given him hope—that, in effect, she was his refuge.

"I think we were destined to find one another, Em. When I was at the darkest point in my life and just trying to get from one day to the next, you burst through the door of your father's study and my life was changed forever. You dominated my every waking thought. You made me realize that I could have a life after Sara's death, that maybe I could be happy again." He gazed directly into the depths of her green eyes. "Do you know what you've done for Janie and me? Trevor told me once that you brought the sunshine back into this house. He was right. You are my ray of sunshine, Emma, and I'll never stop loving you."

He pulled her close then. With their son nestled between them, they drifted off, never to be lost in the loneliness of the night again.

Epilogue

෨

Emma opened her eyes to greet the new day. She immediately rolled onto her side to gaze at her son where he lay in a small cradle beside the bed.

Tyler peered over her shoulder and chuckled at the sight of the tiny fists that flailed in the air above him. "I think someone's going to start hollerin' real quick if his mama doesn't feed him."

"Isn't he the sweetest thing you ever saw?" Emma's infatuation with the baby was evident in the expression in her eyes and the tone of her voice. "A new little life ready to meet the world," she mused.

Tyler climbed from the bed and tenderly cradled their son before handing him into her care. "I'll get some clean napkins so we can get him changed."

She smiled. Tyler wasn't like most fathers. He was confident in handling his infant son and ready to help at every turn.

Holding her child close, she mused about what life had offered her in such a short space of time. A loving husband, a family she cherished, a beautiful home and now a baby to call her own. A small, contented sigh escaped her lips as she watched Tyler pull on his pants and move about the room. Suddenly, she gasped.

Tyler whirled and rushed to her side. "Em, what is it?"

"I forgot about Bonne! Did she foal last night?"

His mouth sagged open with her words, then he rolled his eyes heavenward, placed a hand over his heart and fell across the end of the bed. "Jeez, you just scared the hell out of me."

She giggled at his antics and nudged him with her toe. "Well, did she?"

Tyler pushed himself up on an elbow and flashed her an incorrigible grin.

Emma's heart quickened as her gaze caressed his handsome face and dark, tousled hair. "You're smiling, Tyler."

"I'm pleased to tell you that Bonne is also the proud mother of a little filly as jet black as her father. When I came back up last night with the news, I forgot all about it once I took a look at the two of you." He rolled onto his knees, straddled her body carefully and, bracing himself with his arms, leaned down to give her a quick peck on the cheek. "Double congratulations to you, Mrs. Wilkins. Your dream of having your own business has finally come true."

"What do you mean, my dream? It was you and your brothers who never gave up and made this whole thing happen."

He lifted his knee over her carefully, rolled off the bed and pulled on a shirt. "Who deserves the credit, my dear, is inconsequential. We're on our way. Last night, we became true horse breeders. In fact, I think I'll run downstairs and check on everything. I'll be back up shortly." He gave both her and the baby a kiss and left the room with a happy whistle as he buttoned up his shirt.

* * * * *

That afternoon, Tyler peeked into the bedroom to find Emma resting against the headboard, reading a book. Their son slept beside her, his tiny mouth opened in slumber. Janie lay beside him, staring at the small person who was her new brother. Tyler chuckled when the baby's little mouth puckered slightly, turned his head and nestled comfortably against Emma's body once more.

Without a word, he crossed the room, carefully scooped Emma into his arms and lifted her from the bed.

"Tyler! What are you doing?"

"I've got something to show you." He carried her to the window. "Look down there," he whispered.

She leaned forward slightly and peered into the yard. Trevor and Cole stood beside Bonne. Seeing her in the window, they grinned and waved. The tears burned behind her eyelids when a small, black foal took one tentative step, and then another, and finally emerged from behind the mare. Her wisp of a tail swung back and forth in the cool air. She leapt to one side, almost lost her balance and repeated the maneuver again with more confidence.

Emma squeezed her husband's arm, but never took her eyes from the group assembled below. "Oh my God, Tyler, she's beautiful…"

"That she is." He leaned forward to gaze out the window himself, then cocked a dark eyebrow in her direction. "You know, we have to decide on two names now. Have you thought of one for the baby?"

She nodded, but her eyes were still glued to the small filly who took a few faltering steps from its mother's side before rushing back in panic. Emma's features softened when she glanced back at her husband. "I thought about it all morning. That tiny foal is part of our future, Tyler. The other part is those two beautiful children across the room. In honor of our *past* though, I would like to name the baby after your father." She raised a playful eyebrow. "Thomas Lakota Wilkins. How does that sound to you?"

Tyler planted a kiss on her lips. His eyes immediately took on a mischievous sparkle. "I think it's perfect, Em."

"Has anyone thought of a name for that little one down there?" She moved her gaze back to the window.

"Yup. Trevor and Cole wanted me to run it by you though, and see what you think."

"Well?"

"How does Spirit of Lakota sound to you?"

Her laughter tinkled across the room. She nodded her head. "As you just said, Tyler, I think it's perfect."

She pressed a kiss to his lips before her gaze moved to the small wooden loon that sat on the sill beside the statue of the Indian. Years later, Emma would still swear that she saw it smile in just the quick blink of an eye.

Her eyes shone with happiness as she watched the little filly prance about the yard with increasing confidence. Neither she nor Tyler noticed the small Indian children who danced among the trees in the distance, flitting in and out of the shadows as they played their childhood games.

A loon sang out to the drumbeat as a young Indian brave with a gray wolf by his side, crossed the field. The frolicking children called out to him and he quickened his pace. Looking heavenward with a smile, he gave thanks. He was home. His long journey was over.

About the Author

ఴ

Picture Ruby with her hair on fire! Yup, that's her every morning when she bounds out of bed and heads for her home office. Ruby thanks her lucky stars that she's a full-time writer and a part-time matchstick. Although, there is a hint of a bulldog somewhere in there, too. Once she sticks her teeth into something, there's no turning back until it works. Her husband says she reminds him of that little mouse who stares up into the sky at a swooping eagle (this would be the mouse with his middle finger up) daring that darn bird, and just about anyone else, to screw up her day when she's got writing on the brain.

Ruby loves to write, plain and simple. So much so that she took a leap of faith in herself and quit her 'professional' job, stuck her butt in front of a computer, and finally discovered what brings her true happiness in the wilds of Minnesota.

Some might think that the life of a writer is glamorous and enviable. This is what Ruby has to say about that: "Glamorous? Think of me in sweats and an old t-shirt just beneath that flaming head of mine, typing with one hand and beating out the fire with the other. Envious? Most times my 'new' job consists of long hours of dedication and damn hard work, cramping leg muscles from sitting too long, and a backside that for some reason is widening by the week. But I wouldn't change my life for the world."

Most people who fantasize about strange people and occurrences are sitting on the sixth floor of some psychiatric hospital. Not Ruby—she gets paid for it!

Ruby welcomes mail from readers. You can write to her c/o Ellora's Cave Publishing at 1056 Home Avenue, Akron, OH 44310-3502.

Why an electronic book?

We live in the Information Age—an exciting time in the history of human civilization, in which technology rules supreme and continues to progress in leaps and bounds every minute of every day. For a multitude of reasons, more and more avid literary fans are opting to purchase e-books instead of paper books. The question from those not yet initiated into the world of electronic reading is simply: *Why?*

1. *Price.* An electronic title at Ellora's Cave Publishing and Cerridwen Press runs anywhere from 40% to 75% less than the cover price of the exact same title in paperback format. Why? Basic mathematics and cost. It is less expensive to publish an e-book (no paper and printing, no warehousing and shipping) than it is to publish a paperback, so the savings are passed along to the consumer.
2. *Space.* Running out of room in your house for your books? That is one worry you will never have with electronic books. For a low one-time c ost, you can purchase a handheld device specifically designed for e-reading. Many e-readers have large, convenient screens for viewing. Better yet, hundreds of titles can be stored within your new library—on a single microchip. There are a variety of e-readers from different manufacturers. You can also read e-books on your PC or laptop computer. (Please note that Ellora's

Cave does not endorse any specific brands. You can check our websites at www.ellorascave.com or www.cerridwenpress.com for information we make available to new consumers.)

3. *Mobility*. Because your new e-library consists of only a microchip within a small, easily transportable e-reader, your entire cache of books can be taken with you wherever you go.

4. ***Personal Viewing Preferences.*** Are the words you are currently reading too small? Too large? Too… ANNOYING? Paperback books cannot be modified according to personal preferences, but e-books can.

5. ***Instant Gratification.*** Is it the middle of the night and all the bookstores near you are closed? Are you tired of waiting days, sometimes weeks, for bookstores to ship the novels you bought? Ellora's Cave Publishing sells instantaneous downloads twenty-four hours a day, seven days a week, every day of the year. Our webstore is never closed. Our e-book delivery system is 100% automated, meaning your order is filled as soon as you pay for it.

Those are a few of the top reasons why electronic books are replacing paperbacks for many avid readers.

As always, Ellora's Cave and Cerridwen Press welcome your questions and comments. We invite you to email us at Comments@ellorascave.com or write to us directly at Ellora's Cave Publishing Inc., 1056 Home Avenue, Akron, OH 44310-3502.

The
☥ ELLORA'S CAVE ☥
Library

Stay up to date with Ellora's Cave Titles in Print with our Quarterly Catalog.

To recieve a catalog,
send an email with your name
and mailing address to:

CATALOG@ELLORASCAVE.COM

or send a letter or postcard
with your mailing address to:

Catalog Request
c/o Ellora's Cave Publishing, Inc.
1056 Home Avenue
Akron, Ohio 44310-3502

Please be advised: Ellora's Cave books as well as our website contain explicit sexual material. You must be 18.

Cerridwen Press

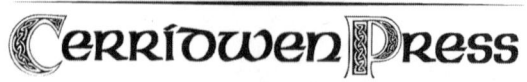

Cerridwen, the Celtic goddess of wisdom, was the muse who brought inspiration to storytellers and those in the creative arts.
Cerridwen Press
encompasses the best and most innovative stories in all genres of today's fiction. Visit our website and discover the newest titles by talented authors who still get inspired—
much like the ancient storytellers did,
once upon a time…

www.cerridwenpress.com